CLOSING SPEED
The Unabridged Edition

TED WEST

E.M. Landsea Publishers

Chicago | New York | Los Angeles

ISBN: 978-1-7326876-0-8

WHAT OTHERS SAY ABOUT *CLOSING SPEED*

"It seems like I've known Ted West forever. He was a dedicated member of the racing press for as long as I can remember, and our paths ran together for many years. He's a very intelligent, honest guy who worked hard to earn the respect he gets. I'm sure the enthusiast world will now enjoy and appreciate his fiction."
Mario Andretti, racing legend

"In this exciting, fast-paced first novel, Ted displays a deep knowledge of racing drivers and cars, plus, of course, the lovely women who follow their chosen sport—and its men."
Brian Redman, factory Porsche 917 driver

"It's a fun read from an eyewitness to one of the greatest sports car racing seasons ever — Porsche 917 versus Ferrari 512 — and here's a chance to relive the season through a story of bravery, ego, high speed and romance."
John Lamm, award-winning motor sports journalist

To the racers, here and beyond.

AUTHOR'S NOTE

Out of the mud grows the lotus. This volume, Closing Speed, The Unabridged Edition, follows the form originally intended for the novel when I first began to write it two decades ago. Differing in theme and content from the edition published in 2010, this story begins in the fictive "present." Its central auto-racing narrative exists as a prolonged flashback reviewing the protagonist's European racing experiences during his twenties. But as may happen in the fullness of life when the spirit is willing, this youthful tale's tension, conflicts, and defeats, seen decades later through the lens of deepening adult experience, offer unexpected rewards. Out of drama and tragedy emerge the hope of mercy, indeed, the glow of vested human wisdom. Life is hard. In times of suffering it wearies, its subtext often obscure. But the great tragedy is to fall away from life before divining the dazzling sweetness underlying all.

Writing this book, I owe sincere gratitude to many good people. First, I owe profound thanks to longtime friend—and "immortal"—the incomparable Mario Andretti, for his kind words about me. Similarly, my dear friend since 1970 when he was a star driver of John Wyer's Gulf Porsche 917s ... the great Brian Redman was endless help in writing this book—and countless other racing stories. My thanks, too, to personal friend, fine writer, and valued associate Jack Nerad, whose support and goodwill seem endless. Working with Jack is like working with myself—only I get along with Jack better.

Another who deserves my richest thank you is John Lamm, peerless photographer and writer, whom I've known even longer—when he was fresh out of Vietnam in 1968 and just getting started. Thanks also to novelist Geoff Loftus and the late fine poet Vincent Byrne; their encouragement was invaluable. Profound thanks as well to fellow professional writers and all-pro readers Steve Thompson and his dear Lannie, Michael Jordan, David Rose, Phil Stern, Stephan Wilkinson, John Tom Cohoe, Rich Taylor and Jean Constantine, Patrick Bedard and Laurie-Ann Devereaux, Amy Markle, Karen Fradera, and "you" (in case you're the one I forgot to mention).

All alone and facing a sentence that won't write, it's a blessing to know, or at least pretend, you're not alone.

Part One

CHAPTER 1

CHRISTMAS EVE, THE NINETIES

NICK THORNE GAZED OUT at the nor'easter. Driving rain drummed its blunt fingers on the windows. Rogue volleys of wind battered the little Cape Cod, infinities of waves on Long Island Sound crumbling over themselves like bulldozed rubble. In other times, other moods, he welcomed a good storm...but on Christmas Eve, this most brittle eve--

The phone rang suddenly.

He made no move, letting it ring again and again--before lunging at it!

He heard the dial tone.

But maybe it *wasn't* his wife. He would call and ask.

He would do no such thing!

A drink would help. He knew what they said, there was nothing in his life a drink couldn't make worse. He had been sober six years, but this cruel Christmas Eve...this was different.

A mighty fist of wind clouted the house, making the window casings clatter.

He crossed the living room, Newton The Cat following him one pace behind. He sat in the big leather chair and Newton jumped up beside him, purring already. When the leather chair first arrived on the Bloomingdale's truck Newton disapproved of its shining burgundy skin. But Thorne never sat anywhere else. Now it was theirs.

Thorne's eye passed over the Sunday Times, fanned out across the rug like a hand of cards. A wild blast struck the house, the impact chilling. He repeated his mantra--she was gone, he was free! But it lacked that certain something. He repeated his other mantra...he didn't have to like the divorce, just accept it. It made no barbarous demands.

His eye came back to the Times, and stopped dead at the Obit page--

"Anthony Devane."

Tony!

He read the notice, his breath stopped. "Anthony Ellery Devane, 55...Lausanne, Switzerland...long illness...Formula One World Driving Champion, nine Grand-Prix victories...World Championship of Makes...brash, irreverent BBC Formula One broadcaster...."

Thorne couldn't recall the last time he'd thought of Devane, insatiable, intemperate Tony. He conjured those long-ago days standing in the pits bantering with a racer about lost nights and found women, and moments later--gone! But the racers freely chose, from time to time they freely lost. It had a ferocious dignity. What brutal imperative compelled them to the mortality of a racing car!

Tony dead.

Yet if Thorne hadn't acted that rain-drenched German afternoon, instinctively and without fear, Devane would have died decades earlier. It stunned him still, the devastation arising from saving a man's life.

He was on dangerous ground, with the divorce, alone on this hellish Holy Eve. Yet he was no more able to stop his thoughts than he could roll back the nor'easter. He saw the fortune-blest creature he had been at twenty-seven, sailing life's high seas for the first time. The racing wars were at their apogee...Ferrari, Porsche, Alfa Romeo, Matra...national pride and personal glory in play on the fields of honor. It was a Golden Time, he was born for this! The drivers were godlike, yet from his close perspective they were more, men of blood and will. They wandered free, divine crusaders sprinting from war to war. Three months among them. It would define him. But ineluctably as his idolatry evolved, it moved in new and difficult directions.

The memories flared in his mind...clowning with Stewart on the starting grid at Jarama, and minutes later Ickx tumbling out of his blazing Ferrari beating his burning driver's suit with flaming gloves! Incomparable Rindt at Monaco, Formula One's only posthumous World Champion, laughing with doomed Piers Courage on a gleaming white yacht, gorgeous Nina beaming at her remarkable husband, lavishly in love.

Tony.

Dead.

Thorne set Newton gently down on the carpet--the big white-and-gray cat gave him a withering glare just the same--and went to the bedroom. He picked out the small black-velvet box of cuff links, shirt studs, tie tacks, bric-a-brac of a more formal time. He drew out the one profoundly unrelated object, a nodule of congealed magnesium. It was pale-gray, the size and form of an apricot pit. He held it in his palm, startled still by its unearthly lightness.

Tony.

He set the nugget on the glass coffee table in the living room...it made a soft, dull sound like balsawood…and mulled his old passion to portray "extraordinary people leading extraordinary lives." The racers defied all risk, all consequence, armed with no more than the nobility of their gift. He traveled thousands of miles, across a continent, an ocean, to plumb their secret. He would write it from the inside! Three months among the world's greatest racers, Brands Hatch and Monza, the Targa Florio and Monaco, Spa-Francorchamps, the Nürburgring, Le Mans…it was beyond dreaming! The bewitched young man he was then bore no resemblance to the stick-figure glinting in the window this stormy night…rush-hour commuter to a toxic job, divorce pending, recovering alcoholic adrift on the chartless seas of therapy. The deepening nor'easter raged.

And Leigh gone.

But she was not its source, it began long before her, the conviction that nothing really came right. Play out your hand, meager as it is, but aim high and you're a fool. That final weekend…Spa…changed everything.

He thought of Devane. Of Angela and Christian and the secrets of Spa. They had the power of life and death.

Ridiculous. Build a fire!

Phone someone…you know what to do!

Impossible. It was Christmas Eve, the Joy-To-The-World-Be-Of-Good-Cheer Reign of Terror. He was on his own.

Since 1970, for decades, he had hidden from Tony and Angela and Christian, relegating their memory to dust and cobwebs, knowing all the while this night must come. He must go back now to its brilliant beginnings, in England. Racing royalty had welcomed him, the young American, into the inner circle. But imperceptibly then it began to close around him. In the end he needed all his strength just to survive!

Now he must resolve it or else fail at his life. Since Spa every serious decision he had made served but one purpose, to close those wounds. None succeeded.

Suddenly Christian Breitemann was as real to him again as if he were standing here in the room. Thorne saw him pulling on the sacramental flameproof white driver's gloves the final Sunday. High noon at Spa. Christian nodded, his smile dimming slightly like thin cloud passing before sun. In his mellifluous Kölnischer accent he stated the matter with chilly clarity: "Wives are different, Nicholas, yes? Especially Grand Prix drivers' wives are different. But in exactly what ways must a Grand Prix driver's wife, this most extraordinary wife, be different?"

Thorne could no more answer on this brutal Holy Eve than he did at Spa half his lifetime ago. He must go back with courage and purpose now, and not look away.

April, 1970, Kent, England

It was the single most intriguing fact he came across four years ago at Berkeley. He was walking with Doc Stephens, his Yeats, Pound & Eliot prof, better known for riding a fast BSA Gold Star motorcycle, when Doc said the triple wipers on a Jaguar XKE could clear its windscreen at 140 miles an hour!

Not bloody likely. Rushing through this Kentish morning deluge at 80, on the ragged edge of control like the Brits all around him, the triple wipers of his XKE Coupe were little more than a metronomic amusement. In their sloshing sweep the green hills of Kent squirmed and warped like things alive.

It sent an icy shiver clattering up his spine. But this tremor was only partly due to the wet and cold, it owed quite as much to the far-fetched fantasy he was living. Of all the devout young motor-racing faithful stalking American racetracks, he had been chosen! His magazine in California had flown him across the Atlantic to the one true Brands Hatch, home of the British Grand Prix, and on this filthy weekend the B.O.A.C. 1000 Kilometers. Proof positive, not only can pigs fly, they can do an outside loop!

The Jaguar intoned its proud twin-cam blare, Thorne visualizing what he would see, starting in minutes! Would it be exotic? Dazzling? Ferocious? Would Porsche or Ferrari--or one of the small, quick three-liter prototypes--establish dominance, rendering matters predictable? Would the Brits and Continentals be charming, xenophobic, difficult...preposterous? Or would the colors be muted, dark? He knew racing's menace. Indianapolis was a harsh mentor. Menace conferred on courage its innermost form.

As he drove deeper into Kent the roads grew narrower and more fiddly. In no time he was puttering between tall hedgerows on a deserted one-lane camel track--this can't be the way to Brands Hatch! Every few moments he met another unmarked Y, neither branch more promising than the other. Despairing, he took a last blind left--

And came toe to toe with the Brands Hatch Press & Participants Gate. Brandishing his letter from the magazine, he was summarily waved through.

After asking once, then once again, he found his way to the press car park. All around under brollies and down-swept brims, waterlogged legions trudged to Eden. Every face wore the Briton's foul-weather cast, a look of cheery disgust.

But he was to meet Trevor Burnleigh half an hour ago! He hadn't a longshoreman's prayer of finding him in these bedraggled masses.

He parked the..."Jag-yew-ah" he was informed when handed its keys in Coventry. White paint is a curse on any car, but on this exquisite XKE Coupe, remarkable. In deference to his magazine the Jaguar Press Bureau loaned him the car for as long as he chose to burden its navy-blue Connolly Leather seats. Two and a half months will do nicely.

In the bitter chill he zipped up his lightweight yellow rainshell, making fists in his pockets in vain. He couldn't feel his toes at all.

Through the murk he made out a massive slant-roofed green structure he knew from photos, Brands Hatch's Start/Finish grandstand. A small distance to the right was a two-story brick bunker he took to be the administration building. In the middle distance were various ranks of rusty rain-dripping wire fencing of uncertain purpose...springtime at Stalag 17.

The inside of the Press Room was a Turkish bath, droplets of moisture tracking down the befogged windows like beads of sweat. The roly-poly gent behind the counter, a Christmasy blend of saggy-pockets green Harris Tweed and red-radish snub nose, beckoned Thorne forward.

He would've preferred the pretty blonde down the counter. She wore frosted lipstick and lick-me-please white leather boots. Did every "bird" in Britain look just like Julie Christie? She shot him a glance, her eyes the cobalt blue of the sea at mid-Atlantic.

Nick identified himself and the smiley gent, fueled by this ayem's medicinal dram, went crimson. "All the way from America--splendid, Mr. Thorne!" he crooned, thumbing through a great shambles of Manila envelopes, his ancient wire spectacles clinging to his radish.

"Haah!" he chuffed drawing out an envelope. Handing over the contents, he beamed like a fresh pint-a, pleased with events.

Thorne took a moment to get gathered up before stepping out into the tempest. He opened the Press Room door at last. Immediately bleak gusts of wind caused the raindrops on his glasses to jitter and dart like translucent bugs.

"Dr. Livingstone, I presume!"

He turned.

And Trevor Burnleigh pumped his hand. "Charming weather we're having..." Trevor enthused, a sweeping gesture taking in his manifold works. Five years Thorne's senior, Burnleigh had a profile fit for a coin. Tall and trim, with the manner of a leading man, his bearing and easy condescension suggested, incorrectly, that he was of the nobility. He had a full sensuous mouth with a certain tightness at the corners, ready to debunk any misinformation vouchsafed his way. His dashing Edwardian muttonchops curled nicely at the tips á la mode, precisely like those of beloved ex-World Champion Graham Hill.

Burnleigh had come to America the previous fall to cover the spectacular Can-Am professional road racing series. On the night of the Road America event during the fourth, fifth and sixth beers, he and Thorne hit it off famously. Following the Can-Am finale at Riverside weeks later, he stayed at Thorne's in L.A. to write his report, and at his leisure plumb the virtues of Phillippe's Original French Dip sandwich and Tommy's inimitable chili-burger stand. Now Burnleigh and his wife would give Nick a bed in South Kensington.

"Well, then, Trevor," Nick said, "still moving to the States?"

Burnleigh squinted through a U-boat periscope. "Of course."

Years before, Fleet St. had dispatched him to Dallas to document the prime beef and sour mash of the three brashest venture capitalists in Texas. By his account they spent money the old-fashioned way, they burned it. Women had been involved, blonde Texan women with long legs and libidos like escaped convicts. Burnleigh formed a deep affection for all things American.

"You're coming, then?" Thorne said, a bit incredulous given the political unrest at home these days. "You're serious?"

"As knickers on the bedpost. My dear fellow, a bit of historical perspective, every country has its little Vietnam. You were ours!"

Pausing not a beat he gave Thorne's lightweight plastic rainshell a filthy scowl. "Here, now, you all right?" He passed the flimsy yellow plastic between his fingers. "We're not in Palm-sodding-Springs, are we."

He tugged Nick back towards the press car park--no arguments. Arriving at an unhappy-looking pale-blue Ford Capri, Burnleigh unlocked the trunk--"boot" it was noted for Thorne's improvement. From the tangle inside he yanked out a huge navy blue-and-gold Goodyear Blue Streak rucksack. It was stuffed with wool scarves, gloves, three stenographer's notebooks, a Nikon F camera with 19-mm fish-eye lens, unpaired socks, tiny motor-racing goggles from the Pleistocene, a bottle of good table Medoc, and at the very bottom a hulking great green mackintosh.

"Put this on 'meejitly."

"Trevor, don't be--"

"Put a sock in it!"

"You'll make a Texan after all."

Burnleigh grinned. But now they heard the siren wail of racing engines. "Come on, guv, they're running!"

Thorne hurried after Burnleigh, buttoning up the big green coat as he went. For the first time since climbing out of the Jag-yew-ah he felt blood-warmth coursing through his limbs. Fine. No, better than fine...this was going to be excellent!.

CHAPTER 2

IN THE FIRST FRIDAY-MORNING practice a winding weaving conga line of brightly painted race cars hurtled into view. Entering Clearways, the fast right-hander before the pits, spray flying from their flanks, they skimmed over its wavy deceptive surface, well known for catching out the unwary.

Roaring past the pits then, they veered hard right and plummeted down the roller-coaster drop of Paddock Bend.

Flew upwards to the tight hairpin of Druid's.

Shot across a small vale behind the pits.

It was road racing as Nick knew it, yet in this rain-drenched English setting it throbbed with the exotic.

Unlike the open-wheelers of Indy and Formula One, these "sports cars" were full-fendered, some with enclosed bodywork, others open to the elements. But they had nothing in common with mundane M.G. and Triumph sports cars. Taking a bewildering variety of forms, they were full-blooded race cars, the fastest of them capable of 250 miles per hour at Le Mans. Low, muscular, ultra-light, their swoopy shapes sculpted for low drag and massive aerodynamic downforce, they were the fastest closed-wheel racing cars on earth.

The grassy banks around the circuit were decked with bannered logos that until now Nick Thorne had only seen in photographs--Lucas, The Daily Mail, Duckhams, Dunlop, Avon Tyres, Ferodo. Despite Brands Hatch's rich Grand Prix history the pits were rude low cinder-block hutches too small for modern racing teams and far too few for today's forty-plus entries. Visible through their open rear doors, sleek nosecones and curvaceous rear bodyshells stood on end, pointed to the sky like launch-ready missiles. Ranks of torpedo-shaped compressed-air cylinders stood at attention. Wet wheels and tires were stacked like outsized poker chips, their fresh new rubber gleaming like black glass.

The scandale du jour, passed among the British racing press like chocolate truffles, concerned as always Ferrari. The three-car team, it was said, arrived from Maranello with only one set of the narrow Campagnolo wheels needed for Goodyear's new rain tire. (Yet again, Goodyear was trying to match Firestone's matchless rain tire.) On his first stroll through the pits, though, Thorne saw two of the three red Ferrari 512S coupes shod with the new Goodyear rain tire, the scandale was mistaken. This diminished its satisfactions not at all. Ferrari excited British contempt for countless reasons, among them that Ferrari's top echelon all spoke passable English but the instant anything went wrong they shamelessly understood not a word.

Along the pit lane Thorne saw Burnleigh with two British reporters gesturing at the big Ferraris and smirking. He was halfway along the pits, familiarizing himself with the European teams that were new to him. Most were lesser G.T. cars--mass-produced Porsche 911s, Alfa Romeo GTVs and Chevrolet Corvettes on hand to race for class victories and give the public plenty to watch.

In the distance now he saw a yellow-and-black Porsche 908 Spyder veer off the track into the pit entrance. A privateer Dutch entry, it was driven by Toine van Pelt and the German, Stefan Heidler. As the saying goes, nothing is older than last year's race car--with a full field of new Porsche 917s and Ferrari 512s, the year-old 908, though it won Porsche a world championship last year, would do well to finish tenth.

Still at high speed in the pit lane, spray boiling out, the 908's four-cam eight-cylinder snarled like a bad dog. Coming closer--

It veered straight at Thorne's ankles!

He jumped out of the way and it swung parallel to the wall, disc brakes squealing. Acrid gray smoke rose from the left front--a bad brake caliper. Race cars constantly suffered potentially lethal failures, profoundly menacing devices.

The rain hadn't let up. Late Friday, having researched the technical changes to the major cars since Sebring in Florida the previous month, Thorne stood behind the inside fence at plummeting Paddock Bend. With minutes left he would watch the final joust.

Far from lacking correct wheels, the three team Ferraris had qualified in the top five. Their Belgian Formula One ace Jean Garand (Porsche's Swabian engineers called him der regenmeister--the rainmaster) had put up the fastest lap and was on the pole, but Porsche was only two-tenths of a second behind. In the closing minutes Porsche lead drivers Christian Breitemann and reigning World Champion Tony Devane would try to snatch the pole from Ferrari. The heat was on.

A steady flow of lesser G.T. cars careened downhill through Paddock Bend. In their midst an occasional big-engined Porsche or Ferrari raged across the slick surface, battling for traction. Gorgeous exhaust notes hammered Nick's eardrums. Dense roostertails boiled upwards. At their passing a fine mist hung on the air, decaying like smoke in the night.

The fastest drivers looked smoothest, but it could be deceiving. In rain the one imperative was to avoid the slippery grass verges.

Along the fence Nick saw a lone petite Mediterranean woman. Dressed in black from head to toe, half her face was concealed behind huge black Audrey Hepburn sunglasses. A black-and-gold Hermès scarf bound her raven-black hair like a surgical bandage, but what struck him was her posture. She stood rigid, bent forward, her black-gloved hands on the fence making tight fists.

He would offer a pleasantry.

He cast about for something to say just as the pole-sitting Ferrari 512 of Jean Garand shot down through Paddock Bend. The helmet in the windshield indicated it was Dante Ruggiero, Garand's co-driver, at the wheel.

The throttle blared.

Slacked.

Blared.

Sliding across the glistening tarmac at horrifying speed, the Ferrari accelerated hard, its V-12 a brain-rattling howl, but it—

Wobbled.

The left-rear tire touched the grass.

Instantly its tail whipped.

Spinning viciously across the grass, skimming free...it seemed to accelerate like an ice cube skittering across a hot griddle. Filth and corruption boiled up...how long could it--

when would it--

It smote the grassy embankment a catastrophic--*Kkk-rrump!*

Debris shot high. The tail climbed up and up, almost to vertical--

Fell back with a trashy rattle.

No movement.

... but no fire.

Safety workers came running in, a pandemonium of shiny full-length black raingear. The sensuous curve of the Ferrari's left-front fender was shattered...in the pits, powerless to resist, Thorne had run his palm over this swollen female form.

Shards of fiberglass lay scattered across the grass like scarlet flecks of eggshell. The mud-caked left-front wheel and suspension were wrenched back across the windshield. A beard of sod hung from the wheel, muck drooping from it as if dredged up from a swamp.

The driver's door flew open and Dante Ruggiero erupted, a high platform diver bursting to the surface. He strutted out and away, never looking back. Ripping off his gloves in operatic hauteur, he strutted off with matador swagger.

The workers reached him but...no, no, no, no, he frowned, he was fine! Stupendo!

The white-green-and-red helmet--Italy's national colors--came up off his head. He punched his gloves into it, still moving away, putting maximum distance between himself and anything so contemptible as a three-wheeled Ferrari!

Nick had flown 8,000 miles to see this, the white-hot flame of European professional racing. At a glance European racers seemed smooth, mannerly, more contained than their American counterparts. It was an illusion. At the wheel fighting for advantage, they were as ruthless as a hard-bitten American dirt-track racer. And just below the Grand Prix elite a volatile pool of battlers clawed ever upwards, defying every demon to scale the last desperate rung to the top. Ruggiero was one, braver than he was gifted, trying too hard. At Daytona and Sebring he impressed Thorne with his knifing through slower cars, yet he had about him a chilly imminence, like a world-class sprinter with an untied shoelace.

Safety workers closed around the wreck.

And the woman in black had fled.

He saw her scuttling away, head down as if ducking under a low bough. It ran counter to experience. At crashes one gleans every atom of information.

Across the track yellow caution flags waved. In response the racers came through in single file at reduced speed. But seeing the wreck was far off the side of the track, with no fire, no need for a racer in fireproofs to pull a driver out, they accelerated away hard...it was nothing, less than nothing.

Friday practice ended before the wreck could be cleared. It was meaningless now anyway, Porsche no longer needed a quicker time to gain the pole. Garand's pole-winning Ferrari had been eliminated. He would be in a different Ferrari tomorrow.

Dante Ruggiero ran across the track towards the pits, eyes darting madly as if searching for something, someone. But no one was missing, nothing misplaced.

He came to the gate at Nick's elbow. His dark glare scorched Nick: "Stupid tires! *Ridicoli!*"

Nick nodded. Jean Garand--the rainmaster--had put the same ridiculous tires on pole.

Ruggiero stormed uphill to the pits hissing expletives at the grass.

Workers picked at the wreck now like buzzards on road-kill.

But Nick could not get the woman in black out of his mind, scuttling away, bent forward, pursued by hellhounds.

CHAPTER 3

JAKE AUSTIN KNEW THE WAY, he swore it. But ten minutes after leaving Brands Hatch, Thorne and he were as Lost-In-Kent as Thorne had been that morning.

Then they saw an Anthracite Black Porsche 911S shriek by in the opposite direction burning a hole in the air. Its driver was Tony Devane, reigning Formula One World Champion. Nick wheeled the Jaguar around and followed his vapor trail. Finding the parked Porsche, they stopped and got out. The 911S's cooling exhaust system was still tink-tink-ing.

Across the road under a toadstool stood the Plough & Anchor, the very model of a Kentish country pub. All conversation in the Plough & Anchor proceeded at maximum volume to be heard above all other conversation proceeding at maximum volume. Loud guffaws bellowed on blue smoky air, fueled by the malty pong of right English bitter. The Plough & Anchor's shoulder-to-shoulder boisterousness anticipated a race on Sunday testing proud reputations, mayhaps disclosing genius.

"You know, Nick..." Austin said, "you worry too much."

Thorne nodded, waiting for the prescribed If-It-Feels-Good-Do-It hippie sermonette. As always Austin's incandescent eyes threatened to set his thick black beard ablaze. Irretrievably into his forties, forever in love or divorce, he was better at drinking on Friday evening than writing on Sunday night. In place of a Tune-In-Turn-On-Drop-Out soliloquy, however, his broad Missouri drawl set forth the Plough & Anchor's storied motor-racing past, its fine Whitbread ales and Cornish pasties like dear old mum's.

The first round of pints arrived and Austin raised his glass: "Lost comrades."

"Thoroughly," Nick nodded with a glint bringing the pint to his lips, when--

Here she was. He'd seen her in pictures, of course, everyone had. You couldn't pick up a magazine or newspaper without coming upon large photos of luscious Angela Devane. Like all British Grand Prix drivers, Tony Devane was a national hero, and like all Grand Prix drivers' wives, Angela's celebrity began with the adulation accorded her husband. But as her husband battled impressively upwards to the peak of Formula One, Angela's notoriety followed its own brilliant and altogether separate trajectory. Neither an actress nor a musician, her sole claims to public attention were her breathtaking beauty and sunny manner. Without effort she became an elite fashion model. And because her winsome demeanor and acute native intelligence were uncannily visible in the beauty of her eyes, rara avis, the finest couturiers in London, Paris and New York fought to have their goods seen on her exquisite shoulders. There had been talk of movies. Without so much as a by your leave, Angela Devane had skyrocketed from pretty-girl-in-Mayfair to the most photographed female commoner in Great Britain, Twiggy included.

But seeing her now in person paces away, Nick was thunderstruck. To say she was beautiful damned her with faint praise--she stopped the heart. Tall and slender, with sublime female proportions and statuesque bearing that made them the more so, she had high cheekbones and violet eyes that on initial contact were almost too exotic. Yet the irresistible warmth of her smile dismissed this momentary severity, in a lesser beauty the price of the exotic. Her cheeks were gently warmed cream with a hint of sun-blest peach. In the Plough & Anchor's friendly glow her shining brunette hair, cut in a stylish "shag," gleamed like Japanese lacquer.

Smiling gloriously at something now, she turned to a man behind her-- and the twist of her body sent a humid tremor through Nick.

When she turned back again their eyes met for an instant. It was an electric shock.

And inevitably Jake Austin was already talking to her! He was without shame--he would hail the Queen for directions to Windsor. But bless him, Thorne was about to be the beneficiary of this impudence...and wasn't this the heart of his mission, to meet the racing elite like Angela Devane?

The answer was plain, no one was "like Angela Devane."

Thorne took a hungry swallow of Whitbread. When the introduction came his smile felt too wide by yards.

"Delighted," she said shaking his hand. "Feeling better...poor drenched thing?"

"Pardon?"

"Your friend here--who bloody insists I call him Jake was telling me heroic tales of you two slogging through the muck."

"Ah, you mean the press room."

Her eyes danced merrily. "Yes, I believe I take your meaning."

Somewhat miraculously he already felt completely at ease. Her smile had the golden glow of late afternoon.

"Mr. Austin--whose *real* name is Jake--says you haven't quite adjusted to our balmy clime."

He admitted as much.

"Nor have I," she said.

"Oh, come on."

"I mean it!" She glimmered. "It asks a certain murky bloody-mindedness to spend one's entire life in this little island...but now you listen to me." Her husky Jackie Kennedy voice had a sleek urgency. "If it's raining tomorrow, and it bloody well is, come to our pits now and again to dry out, will you?"

"Very kind of--"

"No!" she erupted. "I mean *really!* Can't have you dying of the croup ten minutes after touching down."

"Bad form is it?"

"Don't be clever." She engaged his eye, the golden light dropping behind a cloud. "It's miserable enough out there."

She referred to the weather--certainly.

Then, why did he hear some other unspecified complaint.

But her smile rekindled immediately. "And don't you bother about..." she said sotto voce, "The Death Ray." She referred to the famed obsidian glare of legendary team owner Raymond Beacom, one of whose brutally fast Porsche 917s her husband was driving this weekend. The lead driver in the other Beacom Porsche 917 was the brilliant young German, Christian Breitemann. "Pay no attention to Raymond," she nodded in confidence, "he only *looks* slaughterous. Wouldn't swat a mosquito."

"Not a mosquito?"

"Not a swat," she beamed. "Say I invited you."

"I'll say anything you tell me to!"

She gave him a wicked laugh. "You lot do very well over here, you know...Colonial savages."

"Savages!"

She laughed again. "Don't misunderstand--I love Americans."

"Just not right in the house."

Her smile bloomed. She tugged at her husband's arm. "You've met the ball-and-chain, of course."

"Haven't had the pleasure," Nick said.

"Tony, luv, meet Nick Thorne from America. He's a writer, so mind your brutish tongue."

Nick shook the World Champion's hand.

"Well, then..." Devane said, "what brings you to our rude little third-world outpost?"

He had an edge, and what good racer didn't. He'd committed his

14

present and all hope of a future to being incomparable, of the highest order. And he looked the part. His facial features were regular and handsome, backlit with more than a hint of insolence. An inch shorter than Nick, he was compact, intense, with quick predator eyes, a good small-college cornerback. Stylishly dressed in Carnaby Street's best beige gabardine bell-bottoms, he wore a high-collared Edwardian silk shirt of "psychedelic" violet, orange and lime green, with an elegant mahogany leather jacket cut like an African bush coat. His style was unmistakably "hip" in the current Beatles mode, yet he had no trace of drugginess. Alert to every footfall in the forest, at twenty-seven, Tony Devane--with promising Christian Breitemann--heralded a brand-new generation of hardened young racing professionals.

"Where d'you hail from, then?" he said.

"California, actually."

"Ah, yes, idyllic Riverside--not a drop of rain in a decade."

"I don't live in Riverside."

"Don't be silly, nobody lives in Riverside!" Devane beckoned to Nick's empty pint. "Pass it along, mate, you're sucking fumes."

Devane slid Thorne's glass to the ancient crone behind the Plough & Anchor's dark-wood bar. She had a face like a bullfrog but an exceedingly kindly bullfrog. When the pint was drawn she eyed Thorne, arranging her facial pouches in a fetching goblin smile. "'ere, luv. This'll put nutha' log on t' fire."

Nick reached for his pocket but Devane waved him off.

This was rich. In all the pubs in Britain, with all the pints being hoisted this hour, his was bought by the reigning World Champion!

"Cheers," said Devane raising his glass.

Nick drank, awash in heady reflection. Tonight he was well and truly "in it"--at the red-hot center. Surrounded by racers from Porsche and Beacom and Wyer...Alfa Corse and Scuderia Filipinetti and Matra Sport...Martini, Piper and some others he didn't yet know...he counted among their number three World Champions and four comingmen, all of whom would challenge Devane for the 1970 Formula One World Championship.

If they lived.

Entertaining this taboo at arm's length from the reigning World Champion gave him a forbidden quiver. He knew of no more demanding profession. This evening he was among eagles, instinctual, proud, horrifically at risk. In all the world there was no darker discipline, but God help him, he loved it.

He awoke jet-lagged and confused in Burnleigh's pitch-black South Kensington guest bedroom. The clock's glow read four a.m. He did the numbers...eight p.m. in L.A.

If it still existed. He had no proof.

But the covers were warm, all was well.

Then, why did it still play in his head--the chilly moment between Devane and his beautiful wife Angela.

By then, Trevor Burnleigh had joined them at the Plough & Anchor, handing Nick a copy of the official Friday lap times, good bloke. Trevor lifted his first pint, toasting Devane, and did what had to be done. The World Champion's pint, meanwhile, sat on the bar for an hour, three-quarters full. Racing lore had it that in the off-season Devane enjoyed nothing more than getting knee-walking drunk--but he never drank while he was racing. "Our monastic calling," he called it in an interview in Nick's magazine.

"Lovely stuff," Burnleigh smiled setting down his half-empty pint. "And speaking of lovely stuff--"

Angela was just returning from the loo. Burnleigh gave her an amorous embrace, waggling his eyebrows like Groucho behind her back. Nick laughed.

"What are you doing back there!" she said.

"The best I can," beamed Trevor.

"Tony, luv, your friends are right beasts!"

"Just as you like it, I should think."

"You!"

"What d'you think, lads," Devane said, "...a beastie sandwich, Angela in the middle?"

"My own husband and helpmate!"

"Husband, yes, but help with mating you'll not be needing."

Warm and comfy in his South Kensington guest bed now, it caused a chill in Thorne's chest.

And there was the other moment, Angela complaining the track was "miserable enough." She'd only meant the weather, of course. Then, why did he feel as if he had missed something important?

CHAPTER 4

LATE ONE WINTER EVENING after a formal dinner at his Swabian forest estate, Dr. Manfred Fabius, Porsche's Director of Racing, ushered his guests into the salon for cordials and Havanas. Inevitably conversation returned to racing. His guests offered congratulations yet again for achieving Stuttgart's first-ever world championship. It made him visibly impatient.

But this triumph had not been without cost, noted a U.K. journalist.

"Very true," Fabius said. The privateer British driver John Falkes had died at the 24 Hours of Le Mans driving the earliest version of the "long-tail" Porsche 917.

"However, Falkes," Fabius observed, "was unused to such speeds. He should not have been in the car."

"The more experienced team drivers declined to race it," the journalist continued. "It was thought too unstable."

"And so it was," Fabius said. "He made an error."

The silence that followed outlived its welcome.

"Then, tell me, Dr. Fabius," said the U.K. journalist, "it's a point I often ponder. With the enormous expense and risk and all of the rest, why does an automobile manufacturer like yours get into racing?"

Fabius nodded once. "Because there are no wars."

Twenty minutes to the start. The air crackled with tension. Curt sentences and chill clipped words expressed the vernacular of anxiety. Now anything could happen. And Nick felt the lump in his throat. It always came just before the start. Whether it arose from excitement or panic he could not say.

In light rain he, Burnleigh and Jozie Joubert made a last pit walk before the cars were pushed out to the starting grid.

The stroll brought them to the trio of five-liter Ferraris. Strictly speaking these magnificent red cars should not exist. After Ford's huge seven-liter V-8s destroyed all opposition at Le Mans years before, the Federation International de L'Automobile in Paris decided American dominance had lost its charm. For 1970 the World Manufacturer's Championship would be for small-engined (read, European) Group Six prototypes--three-liter cars of about 450 horsepower. But few of these expensive prototypes came forward, and under the rules, starting fields could be filled out with older and less-competitive Group Four and Five cars with five-liter engines. The more cars the bigger the crowds.

Formidable!

All was well until Dr. Fabius of Porsche shocked the racing world, unveiling a completely unsuspected 25-car series (to meet the minimum-production rule) of brand-new five-liter Porsche 917 coupes. Like the Group Six prototypes, the 917s were state-of-the-art racers, but instead of 450-horsepower three-liter engines they had big five-liter engines of 550 horsepower and more. In the blink of an eye, the Group Six cars were obsolete. Outraged by this German effrontery, Paris petitioned Ferrari to build a five-liter Porsche-beater, the Ferrari 512S, and Paris would not enforce the 25-car minimum, which it did not.

Out of the mud grows the lotus. The 1970 war between the five-liter Porsches and Ferraris was the most sensational in decades. It promised the highest speeds ever seen, at some tracks outstripping Formula One. Before Brands Hatch, Porsche had won the 24 Hours of Daytona. Ferrari won the 12 Hours of Sebring. Brands Hatch was the tiebreaker. The racing world stood on tiptoes.

Arriving at the two Beacom Porsche 917s, Thorne, Burnleigh and Joubert gazed. Bright tangerine with navy-blue trim--the livery of sponsor Carnelian Oil--the cars were parked diagonally like fighters on a flight deck. The Porsche 917 struck a nerve Thorne had not felt since as a boy he got a Lionel Santa Fe Super Chief electric train for Christmas. Far too extreme for public roads, the 917's low leading edge met Thorne at the bottom of his ankle. The roof rose barely to mid thigh. The long slanting nose formed a sleek aerodynamic wedge, forcing the tires down at 200-plus miles an hour to produce astonishing cornering speeds. The car went from zero to 60 in 2.8 seconds. On Le Mans' long Mulsanne Straight it reached 248 miles per hour. Standing beside a 917 was an event.

The rain seemed to be lessening. Under his pit enclosure, the Death Ray, Raymond Beacom, stood chatting amiably with his young German star Christian Breitemann. Despite pre-race clamor up and down pit lane, the two smiled and nodded like vestrymen on the parish steps. To Beacom's left stood Peter Whitlaw, "The Mallet." Beacom's team manager, in charge of his eight mechanics, Whitlaw wore an unflinching Battle-of-Britain glare. Piloting a Hawker Hurricane in 1940 he had ushered his full complement of Heinkels downwards to eternity. Everything since was anticlimax.

As the writers approached, Beacom smiled, "Good morning."

In his mid-sixties, with the artificial black hair color to prove it, he was ashen and stoop-shouldered, with cadaverous fallen cheeks. The sole emblems of his inner fires were his coal-black incendiary eyes.

"Enjoying our little coral lagoon, are you?"

"Brisk," said Thorne. "Why the intermediates?"

Moments before the start Beacom's Porsches were on Firestone's shallow-treaded intermediate tire, meant for light precipitation and drying conditions. In anything more than light rain the tire would aquaplane out of control. Contrarily, on a drying track the deep-treaded rain tire would overheat and disintegrate. A wrong choice meant vital time lost in the pits changing tires.

Beacom studied the leaden skies. "We believe it will stop."

"Really?" Jozie Joubert's smirk was skeptical. Beacom's eye twinkled watching Joubert's thoughts. A Parisian educated in England, Joubert was a motoring-press institution. On a first-name basis with everyone worth knowing, he was well respected, in for the long haul. In appearance, however, he fell a trifle short. Blandly dressed, diminutive and homely, with bulging eyes and no chin, he wore Coke-bottle glasses and an unlit black briar clenched between snaggled yellow teeth, bowl down in the morning rain. Burnleigh named him after Phillippe's Los Angeles sandwich, "The French Dip."

Beacom nodded. "Have you met our Christian Breitemann?"

Thorne shook Breitemann's hand. It was surprisingly small. "An honor," he said.

"Oh!" Breitemann laughed. "So old-fashioned! Still it is very nice of you to say."

Breitemann had qualified on pole a scant one-tenth of a second quicker than the Ferrari of Garand and three-tenths quicker than Devane. Wiry and slight, with the light musculature of a marathoner, Breitemann had an expressive face, honest steel-blue eyes and a blond Sundance Kid mustache.

"You are not English, I believe," he said.

"No," Nick grinned. "But I try."

Breitemann laughed. "So, then, you are a Yong-kee?"

Nick's head shook. "Canadian by birth, but they got me out before serious damage was done."

"So you are not truly American."

"To the contrary, all true Americans come from someplace else."

Breitemann's eye sparkled. He liked that.

The machine-gun hammering of impact wrenches rang out all along the pits, teams making their final wager, intermediate tires versus rains.

"Well, I must prepare," Breitemann said turning to the pit enclosure.

His reserved demeanor at Daytona and Sebring had caused Nick to hang back and cede him his privacy. Raised in Cologne near the Nürburgring, racing's Valhalla, Breitemann's career started on motorcycles. After three consecutive German National Championships, he moved seamlessly to cars. But because Germany had produced few world-class drivers since the war, he was not embraced as a talented newcomer from Italy or the Commonwealth would have been. He soldiered on for two difficult seasons in second-rate Grand Prix cars, forcing them far beyond their potential. By 1970 he was a star at Beacom and the lead driver for nonpareil Team Lotus in Grand Prix.

Twice while talking Breitemann had yawned deep and hard, an agonizing groaner. It was the pre-race yawn. In these minutes before a race it had nothing to do with need of sleep.

Thorne held out his palm. The rain had stopped. He looked at The Death Ray.

Inscrutable as ever.

Joubert flashed a yellow-teethed grin. "Two quid says it's raining cats and cows for the start."

Thorne moaned. "I hate gambling!"

"Fine sport you picked, then, Vicar," said Burnleigh with a nod to the track. "Poor buggers racing at full chat on a wet bar of soap."

In the corner of his eye Nick saw it now--Whitlaw's sharp nod into his pit. Immediately crewmen sprang over the pit wall with Firestone rain tires. Whitlaw gave Nick a glint. The intermediate-tire ruse was done...had Ferrari taken the bait?

CHAPTER 5

JOZIE JOUBERT'S TWO QUID were safe, minutes before the start the heavens opened. Torrents clattered onto the out-swung windows of the administration building across from the pits, which Thorne now knew as Grovewood House. Runoff gushed down the grassy banks, surging across the track in sheets. The tempest was so intense it partially obscured race-sponsor B.O.A.C.'s gigantic distant billboard. Visible through curtains of monsoon, the life-sized silhouette of a white-and-navy B.O.A.C. Boeing 747, newest and grandest jetliner in the skies, looked to be making a forced landing in a muddy parking field.

Given the deluge, the racers were permitted an exploratory lap before the start. Only three came to the grid on intermediate tires, a big Lola-Chevrolet coupe, a poorly turned out older Porsche 908 and a mundane G.T.-class Porsche 911S. The Lola, a nasty handful all weekend, was immediately and wisely withdrawn. The 911S tiptoed around, spinning off twice, needing five minutes to return for rain tires. The 908, wholly out of its depth, slid off at Westfield Bend, demolishing its left-front corner, its race over before it began.

Car after car rolled to the grid.

The crews moved back--the fuse lit.

Precisely at noon, the deluge's peak, the start was a spasm of mad aggression, blind ambition and low comedy. Car after car went up in catastrophic wheelspin, fishtailing wildly before making reasonable progress forward. Pandemic veers and near misses were punctuated by the occasionally impressive direct clout.

To Nick's surprise, shared by Joubert, even pole-sitter Breitemann got it wrong. His powerful Porsche crabbed sideways, lost in wheelspin. The Jean Garand Ferrari and Devane's Porsche shot past.

Garand got to Paddock Bend first. With a clear view ahead--and his own spray blinding Devane--the Belgian pulled smartly away.

Breitemann was third, pressing hard already regaining lost ground.

They came past the pits completing the first lap, Garand, Devane, Breitemann, and a weaving and swerving string of spray-blinded factory-team cars. A heartbeat later at the rear of the fastest cars the single remaining Lola coupe spun across Clearways Bend like a helicopter rotor.

It smashed the outside earthen bank.

Debris scattered wide, navy-blue fiberglass flying.

The driver climbed out, unhurt, the crash spectacular but not serious.

Now, however, tire-slashing shards from the wreck littered the track. Yellow caution flags waved wildly--with momentous consequences to come.

Unaware of the crash behind him, Breitemann was now fighting Devane hard for second. Blinded in hurricanes of spray from Devane, he forced himself forward at full racing speed. In Stirling's Bend near the end of the second lap--immediately before Clearways--he braked at the last instant diving to Devane's left and seized the inside line.

The two Porsches streamed through Stirling's side by side in a dead heat. The slightest bobble by either would eliminate both. But now with the better cornering line, Breitemann applied power sooner, shooting forward out of Devane's spray and coming upon--

Wildly waving yellow flags from the Lola crash.

It was blatant, Breitemann had passed in a yellow-flag zone, a fundamental breach of the competition rules.

Given the clouds of spray, Breitemann had no chance to see the flags--but the incident took place in full view of the officials. The issue was never in doubt. Breitemann was shown the black flag. He must make a penalty stop in the pits for "administrative consultation," losing countless racing positions!

He completed one more lap in second place without stopping.

And another...postponing the intolerable.

Howling into the pit lane at last, he braked hard at Start/Finish thirty yards from where Thorne stood.

Gunning the throttle, his steel-blue eyes glared ahead unblinking.

The Clerk of the Course held him.

Twenty seconds passed, Thorne's heartbeat ringing in his ears.

It went on.

At thirty seconds the Porsche twelve-cylinder suddenly shrieked and the tangerine-and-navy racer shot forward!

In a cluster of photographers at the Beacom pits, Thorne saw the missile aimed straight at him. Banshee shrieking filled his chest.

The Porsche shot past inches from his right knee!

Climbing through 100 by the pit exit, it vanished in its own spray,

Thorne's chest banging.

People peered at one another now, chastened. In shocked silence Nick heard a breathy voice in his ear, "Now we'll see."

He turned. Angela Devane was intent. Precisely the point--how will Christian Breitemann negotiate rage? In some it was the end of equilibrium. In others, deliverance.

He'd been wrong, then, Angela was a racer. When she complained of being "miserable" at the track he surmised she hated racing, for a racer's wife hardly impossible. But her curiosity about Breitemann and anger said otherwise. She too studied the violent manipulation of jeopardy.

Then, what "misery" did she mean? He wanted to ask, not because it was his business, not because he could help...because she was so beautiful!

He must be careful. Her complaint Friday had been one of those chill moments when a remark meant to obscure something starkly exposes it.

No. He knew nothing about her, nothing about her marriage.

And he had a lap chart to keep!

The first laps of a rain race are elemental, mere survival. But gradually the racers strung out, each immersed in the preceding car's spray. Jean Garand continued to lead, the only one with a clear view ahead. His magnificent Ferrari V-12 blared fortissimo, the sleek low red coupe skimming over shining tarmac like a speed skater carving brave arcs on glassy ice.

Tony Devane, in second ahead of Corrado Caprese's Ferrari, was content to hold position. Discipline was his hallmark. He gained three of his five Grand Prix victories the previous year patiently trailing cars that were being overdriven. One by one they fell out and he made his way to the front. He did so not for any lack of speed--he was one of the very fastest drivers. But he claimed he could halve the mechanical stress on his car by driving a fraction below the maximum. He conserved "combat-emergency power" until needed--an avid pilot, he used that fighter-jock term. By contrast, Christian Breitemann had but one pace--absolute maximum. He drove for the sheer joy of knowing his car would go no faster. Yet his superlative finishing record was testament to his uncannily smooth technique. It was Raymond Beacom's peculiar talent to cunningly manage these two talents, Devane and Breitemann. Devane's tactics challenged Breitemann to finish well--Breitemann's unrelenting pace pressed Devane to bear down. And Raymond Beacom had disdain for "team orders" requiring one driver to concede position to the other. He took the uncommon view among owners that his drivers were paid to race, even against each other. And Devane and Breitemann would have it no other way.

The resulting rivalry had its uses. At the Daytona 24 Hours Devane won while Breitemann lost hours with mechanical problems. At the 12 Hours of Sebring Breitemann built an embarrassing lead before his car expired. Devane's car expired as well, but he smirked to the press that Breitemann had not finished because he'd "succumbed to a bit of the old impetuous." By Brands Hatch the rivalry burned with a merry wee flame.

Lap after lap Devane maintained his ten-second cushion over third-place Caprese, content to concede the lead to Garand. The Porsche-Austria 917s of Hugh J.K. Breeland and Rudi Stringert were fourth and fifth. Breitemann's disastrous penalty banished him to 27th, deep in the slow G.T. cars.

But watching from the Beacom pits, it was natural for Thorne to keep one eye on Breitemann. His Porsche raged by at enormous speed, the twelve-cylinder intoning a burnished French-horn song. Water gushed from its wheel-wells, vortices at the rear shooting roostertails thirty feet in the air.

Impossible visibility blinkered most, but here and there a few "mudders" surged ahead, and Breitemann was one. He slashed through whole knots of cars, his momentum electrifying. In twenty minutes he was already at the tail end of the factory cars...out-braking a blue Matra into a turn...blasting by a crimson Alfa Romeo onto a straight...surging to a Ferrari's brake lights and vanishing completely in its spray. It was as if he were the lone member of some superior species. Was the Porsche 917 this good, or was it Breitemann? Thorne timed him lap after lap with rising elation. In blinding traffic he was lapping two seconds faster than Garand, the *regenmeister!*

Thirty minutes after his penalty stop Breitemann was already hounding Rudi Stringert's Porsche-Austria 917 for fifth. It was early yet, 1000 kilometers in blinding rain would take hours. Yet already the talk around the Beacom pits turned to legendary drives, Nuvolari at the Nürburgring, Moss in the Mille Miglia, Fangio *everywhere.*

Then the Beacom crew let out a loud *whoop!* In one lap Breitemann passed both Stringert and Breeland! He was bearing down on Caprese for third...something extraordinary was afoot!

The Beacom pit roiled with more and more press, everyone exchanging raised eyebrows and knowing grins. Each time Breitemann raged past, the drama rose. The story pointed to two hair-raising duels, Breitemann vs. the World Champion, followed by Breitemann vs. the rainmaster, when--

All came crashing down.

First, Garand rushed into the pits for an unscheduled stop. Thorne ran to Ferrari. The mechanics were scurrying about like cartoon figures. Garand's indispensable single windscreen wiper was frozen at mid-sweep. It began to sweep.

Jerked sharply.

Stopped dead.

Garand sat in the cockpit impassively, his hard-won 35-second lead over Devane vanishing.

Devane swept past into the lead.

It took Breitemann two hard-fought laps to get around Caprese's Ferrari, the Ferrari blocking every possible way--but he would not be denied.

Devane's pit board read, "Pos 1, +7 Breit." Devane led by seven seconds--but the pit board identified the hated Porsche gaining on him at two seconds per lap. Devane began to bear down.

And two laps later, forcing his way into 180-degree Druid's Bend beside a slower two-liter Chevron coupe, the two brushed each other. With minimal traction on the drenched track, both went dervishing off the verge. The damage to Devane's Porsche was negligible, but the slide deflated his left-rear tire. He had to limp nearly a full lap around to the pits for a new tire and Breitemann shot into the lead.

The unthinkable confrontation...brilliant challenger vs. World Champion...vanished like mist on a pond.

Breitemann's pace never slowed. Nothing like it had been seen.

At the mid-point of three and a half hours, impossibly, his Porsche led by four laps!

The competition rules required each car's co-driver to drive for a stint. Alex Winter, Breitemann's co-driver, was a well-regarded English journeyman, but it was unrealistic to expect him to match Breitemann's pace in the wet. Yet when Winter returned the car to Breitemann after an hour, he had increased its lead.

Elsewhere the race was the usual litany of mishaps and malfunction. Like Garand's car, the other two Ferraris were hobbled with ignition and electrical faults. Ironically the slowest, driven by disgraced Dante Ruggiero, scored the only finishing points for Ferrari. Championship points were scored on the basis of nine, six, four, three, two and one for the top six finishers. Ruggiero's fifth, half a lap behind the reliable year-old Dutch van Pelt/Heidler Porsche 908, in fourth, earned Ferrari a dispiriting two points.

The lone factory Alfa Romeo T33-3 prototype hit the guardrail at Clearways twice, the second impact ending its day. Early on the two intense three-liter French Matras rose promisingly to fourth and fifth, but clutch and fuel-pressure problems dropped them to finishing 12th and 21st.

After getting a new tire, Devane took an hour and twenty minutes to work his way back through the field to second. By then, Breitemann was already three laps in the lead. Then Reine Dinesen, Devane's co-driver, eliminated the car against a guardrail with two hours remaining.

At 6:51 p.m., rain still falling but golden shafts of Turner-esque sun parting violet cathedrals of cloud, Breitemann took the checkered flag. Complementing his masterful performance, Porsche-Austria 917s finished second and third. For the season Porsche had 24 points, Ferrari 15.

At the victory interview mischievous co-driver Alex Winter grinned, as was his wont, saying the secret of the win was his spinning out the 917.

"Ach, no," Christian Breitemann said, "do not seize all credit, Alex, I spun twice!"

"My point precisely," smirked Winter, to thunderous laughter from the British press.

A beaming Raymond Beacom stepped to the microphone to proclaim Breitemann "*der neu regenmeister*"--the new rainmaster. And so he was. He outdistanced the field by six full laps.

But in another way the race betrayed him. His electrifying early rush through the field was blunted by Garand's electrical problems, then Devane's spin and flattened tire. The stark symmetry that elevates a brilliant drive to legend--defeating one's adversaries wheel to wheel--had eluded him.

CHAPTER 6

SOMEBODY KNEW SOMEONE, first cousin of Archie Villiers-St. Someperson, with interests in the West End. An urgent telephone call was placed to St. Someperson's private secretary, and though the Lyceum Dinner Theatre on Shaftesbury Avenue in the heart of London's West End theatre district was packed to the rafters, and though the Brands Hatch contingent of thirty-and-a-few conspired to arrive at the last instant...they were whisked forward to a front-row-center banquet table at arm's length from the footlights. In store was a flashy, fleshy Sunday Evening Dinner Review starring BBC's hottest new comedy duo, "The Two Ronnies."

No less miraculous was Thorne's realization that exquisite Angela Devane, growing more so with each sighting, had gone well out of her way to reserve three spots at the table for Burnleigh, Austin and himself immediately opposite her and Tony Devane!

"American racing reporters..." Burnleigh informed, "are something of a delicacy."

Neither Thorne nor Austin had ever heard of The Two Ronnies. It mattered not a whit. They were clever, bawdy, uproarious. And when the curtain rang down the Brands Hatch contingent carried right on jabbering and haw-haw-ing in the same bawdy spirit. One-liners from The Ronnies were refloated to booming laughter and table thumping that made the silverware tinkle like tiny bells. Nick's Dover sole was better than it had any right to be. St. Emilion and Pouilly-Fuissé flowed hither and yon. Early on Burnleigh raised his glass, pronouncing Saint Emilion the specific for the recent annoyance Hong Kong flu.

Many faces among the party were familiar to Nick from the Plough & Anchor on Friday night, but with the race behind them and all tensions resolved, congeniality and laughter flared like struck matches, naught withheld. Next to Devane sat "Lord Blather"--self-satisfied London motor-racing publisher Alastair Bissent. At Daytona and Sebring he held forth on the insufficiency of German personal hygiene, the catastrophe of American dress and the odiousness of the French in all times and places. Florid, tightly packed, his heavily blooded face gleamed like Andouille sausage. When he spoke, which he persisted in doing, a jewel of spittle clung to the corner of his mouth.

"You watch," Burnleigh muttered to Thorne. "Any more out of him'll dull every knife on the table."

Next to Bissent sat Porsche-Austria's third-place finisher Rudi Stringert with his French girlfriend Nicole. Then came second-place finisher Hugh J.K. Breeland with his wife Mary. Mary Breeland was tall and attractive, with short blonde hair, large cheekbones and anxious eyes. She never let Breeland out of her sight, with cause. Further along sat blow-dried Jiggs Prouty, Carnelian Oil's public-relations man, with his assistant Davida Barrenholtz. Davida was having more than a little to do with the undeniably married Prouty, whose presence at the gathering enjoyed the highest priority. It was his expense account, rivaling the gold of the Incas, that would satisfy the Lyceum's profligate bill.

California photographers Jennifer Whelan and Lester Clark were next along the table. They were "just friends" as only an extremely pretty woman and an immoderately portly man can be. Jennifer had red hair and green eyes that flashed fair warning she intended to be left quite alone by whatever roving swordsmen pulled alongside.

A late arrival, for whom all made place at the very center of the table, was Lionel Ludgate, Carnelian Oil executive vice president. His traveling secretary Vivian Biggs was content to sit at the far end well out of the line of fire. Vivian was six-feet tall and catastrophically bored. Nick had been introduced to her several times but each time, assessing his likely future business dealings with Lionel Ludgate, she discarded his name like a used toothpick.

Gradually--very gradually--the gaiety of the Two Ronnies wound down.

"So then..." Devane said to Thorne at last, "what did you think of our little race today?"

"Hey!" Jake Austin put in. "You might as well ask what we think of orgasms!"

"And what do we think of orgasms?" inquired Angela as if assessing the ripeness of a pear.

Bissent's laugh gushered frothily. "Tony, do pass the gourd."

The St. Emilion came towards him, Thorne taking the opportunity to refill Angela's glass first, then his own.

"Let's get down to it, then," said Devane. "Is Jean Garand the equal of Mario Andretti or isn't he?"

"Certainly he is..." Blather said, "in every way."

"*He's* the American," Devane snapped, "I asked him."

Thorne smiled. "Can't honestly say."

"Thrilling admission, coming from a pressman."

"Have you ever seen Andretti on dirt?"

"Then, that is to be the standard, American dirt?"

"Andretti does things instinctively others take years to learn."

Devane mulled it.

"Does Garand do that?" Thorne said.

"To borrow a phrase, I can't honestly say."

Thorne smiled. "That wasn't so hard was it?"

Burnleigh's laugh boomed. "I'll drink to that!"

"But I wouldn't mind seeing Christian Breitemann on dirt," added Nick.

"You think he's pretty good do you." Devane took something off his grin. "What is it they say, everyone gets his fifteen minutes of fame."

Bissent's head tilted. "He's not half bad--for a squarehead."

Burnleigh groaned elaborately.

"Hush, now, Trevor," grinned Angela meaning quite the opposite.

"So where is Breitemann?" Nick said.

"Is it love, then?" inquired Devane.

"Tony!" Angela protested.

"Beg pardon, luv. You're the one always knows Christian's whereabouts."

"BBC wanted him," she said.

Devane eyed Bissent: "Auditioning for the third Ronnie I expect."

Bissent chortled juicily.

"Tony, Tony..." Angela purred, "mind your jaw."

"Well, we've learned one thing, haven't we," Devane said, his voice like a hacksaw, "... if it's pissing with rain, do make a pass in plain view of waving yellow flags--putting your entire team result at risk while doing so!"

"Hear, hear," said Bissent.

Thorne shot Angela a glance. Everything in her face smiled but her eyes.

Jake Austin chose the moment to ask directions to the men's.

"Follow me," Burnleigh volunteered.

Thorne stood as well.

Angela smirked, "Three schoolgirls off to the loo, is it?"

Burnleigh batted his eyelashes like Ronnie Corbett in drag, which he had been--twice.

In the men's Burnleigh spoke in what he imagined to be American. "Ten o'clock an' we haven't got our cocks sucked yet."

Nick rolled his eyes.

"That's what they say in Manhattan Beach, heard it myself."

"Trevor, what's going on!"

Burnleigh looked mystified.

"With Tony! Is he having his period?"

"Here we go," drawled Austin. "Nick, you shoulda been a shrink."

"And you shoulda been a house-painter."

Burnleigh shrugged, "Tony gets his knickers in an uproar."

Austin studied his hair in the mirror. "He didn't finish the race and he's pissed, is all. Let him have his space!"

"Oh, wwwowww, Jake..." Nick said in California hippie-dippie. "Like, I toad-ully forgot to be rully groovy for a second."

Austin headed for the door with not a word.

Good.

But the instant Austin's back turned, Burnleigh put a finger to his lips and nodded, "La-ter...."

He'd found the sweet spot.

The golden place.

He beckoned the waiter..."Over here, mate--right here!"

The Tanqueray and tonic was set down before him. He nodded to Burnleigh, "Thank God for quinine. Thank God for malaria!"

He nodded cheers! to Jiggs Prouty, Carnelian's deep pocket. Jiggs smiled back. But greetings were needless. It was Prouty's commission to ensure all in life was swell.

The red wine had gone on a mite too long and the quinine's bitter snap was satisfying. This was good. This was superb! He was right where he belonged--all would be fine. A gray-haired quartet, tenor sax and rhythm, had set up onstage for dancing. In frumpy pre-war tuxedos with dandruff they set about making Beatles songs sound like polkas. Angela danced with Devane to "Lady Madonna." It was all the men could do not to drool. She only got more astonishing.

Fine, thought Nick...he'd mastered tonight. Whatever confused him-- simply didn't exist. It was the miracle of gin.

"I don't suppose you'd care to dance."

He realized it too late--Angela was speaking to him!

"Sure, I do..." he fumbled. "Yes."

"Well done..." leered Devane rolling his eyes.

She waited for him to make his way around the long table. It occurred to him that this was a slow dance. He would hold her against him, his hand around her slender waist. He would smell her hair, her skin. Was it insane that--

The other miracle of gin. She was the most exquisite woman he had ever spoken to--the wife of a World Champion! But walking towards her he couldn't deny the midnight surgings. He took her hand. Felt its moist pressure. They were a step from the floor, her hand in his, when--

Bravos erupted near the entrance.

Angela knew immediately. "It's Christian!"

Her hand slipped away, the dance forgotten.

"And The French Dip," Nick said.

"What?"

"Joubert."

"French Dip?"

"A sandwich in the States," he said, giving up all hope.

She smiled beautifully anyway and tugged his hand.

Breitemann's face lit up at her approach. When he smiled--really smiled--the blue of his eyes shot beams of light.

"Angela," he said with a polite hug. "And the Canadian who is the only true American."

"An' doan'choo firgeddit, pil-grum!" Thorne said in a creditable John Wayne.

"Oh, my!" Angela laughed.

Nicole, Rudi Stringert's pretty Parisian girlfriend, put out her hand and Breitemann bent to kiss it. It amazed Nick that a man of Breitemann's youth could pull that off. But he made it indispensable.

Devane arrived now from the loo. "So Christian, you had yourself quite the day."

"Sometimes it all goes just as it should."

"How do you mean?" Nick said immediately.

"You know. You will try to do something—you try and try but never do it. Then suddenly one day you cannot do it wrong!"

"It's a morsel harder than that, I'll warrant," said Burnleigh.

"Of course. Tony can say, always it is hard. But sometimes you are trying just as hard as all the other times, but this time it happens easily exactly as it must."

"It was incredible," Nick said.

"I know..." laughed Breitemann. "I was there!"

His honest enjoyment made Nick laugh too.

Now Angela offered him a drink.

"Gladly," he said. He pronounced it "glet-ly."

At the same time Thorne saw Lionel Ludgate pull Devane's sleeve aside. Dapper to a fault, Ludgate was renowned for his bespoke Savile Row suits, ambassadorial woven-silk ties and four-season Florida suntan. He dispensed Carnelian's millions in large packets in return for very public tête à têtes with his world-famous drivers. He and Devane strolled towards the foyer now--eminentoes on parade.

Nick saw Joubert's eye follow them as well.

Missing not a beat, Joubert toasted Breitemann's drive--the equal, he said, of Stewart's Nürburgring rain race two years ago. Highest praise. It was greeted with hear-hears all around.

"But Christian," said Angela, "I think you'd prefer a sharp stick in the eye to sitting here blushing."

"I am not blushing."

"But you are!" she beamed.

"Yes, well...."

He went helplessly crimson.

Angela laughed affectionately.

He took a sip of Courvoisier.

Nick had thought about it, Breitemann must not be just another Hotspur--he must be The Article. But was it even possible? Could a really gifted racer be "normal?" Breitemann displayed no bluster, no belligerence, no taking offense where none was meant. He was modest and unafraid, moderation itself. Nick could learn from such a driver!

He tipped back his gin and tonic, by his own estimate medium rare. But the butterflies were gone. He was on top of the world. Tonight would go on forever....

He watched Breitemann swirl his Courvoisier in the snifter, coating the inner surface with amber. Breitemann drew gently on his H. Upmann maduro, not overheating the coal, a portrait of composure. With easy humor he recounted co-driver Alex Winter's foolery at the BBC. On the air Winter claimed the only reason he got any time in the car was Breitemann had to use the loo! Then Breitemann described the pretty BBC production assistant giving Winter the dinner tray she'd meant for Breitemann. In its serviette was a slip with her name and number. But when she saw Winter unfolding the note, knowing he was happily married and the father of two...she snatched it away red as a lobster and fled.

Angela beamed. "Poor thing, she fancied you!"

"Very pretty too," Breitemann nodded.

Angela beamed, "I can hardly blame her."

"Oh?" said Breitemann. "Tell me, then, Angela, do you flatter all the men?"

She beamed. "That's for me to know and you to find out. Can't help it, can I, if I like the chaps."

Everyone smiled. No one ventured a word.

CHAPTER 7

A FEW MINUTES PAST MIDNIGHT they stood outside the Lyceum on Shaftesbury Avenue. Not alluding to the obvious--where had her husband gotten to!--Burnleigh asked Angela if he could give her a lift home. She accepted. And not knowing the way back to Burnleigh's, Thorne said he would follow in the Jaguar.

But immediately a glimmer passed between Angela and Burnleigh. "I'd best not," she said, "...you two will get separated and poor Nick here will turn up in Wales a fortnight hence needing a change of linen."

"Nonsense," said Nick, feeling in the way. But repeated protests got him nowhere. Burnleigh hailed a cab and Breitemann opened the door for her.

"Ta," said Angela.

"*Bitte schön.*"

The Austin diesel clattered off into the night. With Angela gone the world was different, different and drab.

"Trevor," said Nick, "does everyone fall in love with her?"

"Now, now..." Breitemann said. "This is a married woman."

"So is Elizabeth Taylor," said Burnleigh, "--for all it matters."

"Give you a lift, Christian?"

"I'm just at the Hilton. I shall walk."

"We'll walk you as far as our garage."

They began, Nick listening to their late-night footsteps on the West End sidewalk. He could suppress it no longer.

"So where is Tony?"

"Ah, Tony. He is, I think, very--" Breitemann paused, hunting a word in English, "... he is complicated."

It hung on the air. They walked on in silence.

"Where are you off to, then?" Burnleigh said at last.

"The hotel," Christian replied curtly. "Just as I said." It made Thorne wonder where else he might be off to.

"I mean, tomorrow," Burnleigh said.

"Testing," Christian said in a business-y tone, "always testing."

"Something secret?" Thorne said.

"*Natürlich*. It is at Ehra-Lessien."

"Where?"

"The Volkswagen high-speed test track on the border with the East."

The next race, two weeks away, was at high-speed Monza. Nick's mind streaked ahead, "The new 4.9?"

Breitemann laughed. "You are not supposed to know about that! But since you do, will you like to come?"

"Would I!"

"Call me in the morning, I shall arrange it--"

"Hey! You lot!"

It was an angry growl from far behind.

"Speak of the devil," muttered Burnleigh.

Devane came rushing after them. Far in the distance Lionel Ludgate stood under the bright lights of the Lyceum marquee.

"Where is my wife?" Devane demanded.

"Home by now, I expect," said Burnleigh. "Where have you been?"

"Fucking hell, when did she leave?"

"Took a taxi not five minutes ago."

"Who with!"

"She might have been with you..." said Breitemann, "if you were here."

"Answer me, goddamn it!"

"She was quite alone," Burnleigh said.

"Well...there was the driver," added Breitemann with an edge.

Devane glared at him.

"Something is wrong, Tony?"

Nick's pulse banged in his ears.

But Breitemann's voice was icy calm. "Your wife went home in a taxi by herself because you had been gone for above an hour."

Devane leveled his index finger. "I'll be needing no counsel from you, mate. After that move you made in Stirling's today, you can sod yourself!"

He stormed back to the Lyceum. Lionel Ludgate waited under the lights. The theatre marquee went black.

At one a.m. the Tiffany lamp fixture on Burnleigh's kitchen table bathed them in a warm glow. Becky Burnleigh was asleep two doors away. Burnleigh poured out two black-and-tans, half Bass, half Guinness, and passed one to Nick. They clinked mugs and drank. Then he swore Nick to absolute secrecy and told him everything...Devane's obsession that Angela was cheating on him, his jealous fantasies, their complete groundlessness.

"If he's so obsessed..." Nick said, "there's something in it."

"Groundless," Burnleigh repeated.

"What makes you so sure?"

"There's something in it, all right, but it's nothing to do with her. Tony's got J.F.K. Syndrome--he's in and out of strange boudoirs like a French maid."

Nick snorted. "And he's obsessing about *her!* That's nuts!"

"Not if you think about it."

Nick took a moment. Granted him the point.

"But how can you be so sure he's wrong?"

"You said it tonight--everyone falls in love with her. She and I have become very close."

The glimmer between Trevor and Angela outside the Lyceum came to mind. Thorne's voice fell now, conscious of Becky sleeping two rooms away. "Trevor, you're not--"

"No, no, mate."

Thorne nodded, reassured, and in a more unsatisfactory way, disappointed.

"When Angela needs to talk, we talk. She says it helps."

"What must that be like?" Nick thought aloud.

"She needed to talk tonight, but there was no opportunity."

"Nonsense. I would've waited."

"For obvious reasons she has to be very careful." Burnleigh stared into the depths of his black-and-tan. "She's the kind of woman who only feels comfortable with men, only trusts men. She's sociable with women--has to be in her modeling--but she doesn't confide in them. Likes the chaps, as she says."

Nick said nothing.

"And she doesn't want something awful to happen to Tony. As you saw, he's a trifle delicate."

The night silence throbbed.

"In the most profound way, she feels responsible."

"Jesus..." Thorne said.

CHAPTER 8

BREITEMANN SMILED.
   "No, no, Jennifer, this time I will try to answer."
   He arranged his thoughts in English.
   "In a racing car, when you enter a corner too slowly, that time is lost forever, yes? And if you enter the corner too fast...."
   His ice-blue eyes left it unsaid.
   "But how do you know!" she asked. "I mean before it's too late!"
   "You know," he said. "When you are too slow it is like the ring of a cracked bell. And when you are right, leaving nothing in reserve, it is the explosion when the tennis ball meets the racket perfectly in the center.
   "Then you put one perfect corner with another and another...explosion, then explosion, then explosion!"
   His elation collapsed like a spent wave.
   "But to corner in this perfect way requires a hard decision. You must commit to an absolute speed at the corner's apex...where it turns sharpest...and you must do it long before you are there. In blind turns, cornering over the brow of a hill or in deep forest like at the Nürburgring, you commit to your maximum before you can see the turn! And everything you are, your best and worst, is visible. Your cornering line is committed. The car is almost beyond control. You cannot go a kilometer per hour faster...yet you must wait to see--"
   His laugh was like shattering glass.
   "If this really is your big one."

Burnleigh's snug little third-floor study in South Kensington overlooked a small garden in the rear. The shelves were lined with books, some leather-bound, a few antique. Under a beige plastic dustcover was Trevor's treasure, a brand-new IBM Corraseable Selectric typewriter.

Nick closed the study door and repeated his writing mantra--remember, have fun. The red shade on the desklamp glowed. He began typing.

Christian Breitemann's extraordinary Brands Hatch race galloped onto the page, as miraculous today as it had been yesterday afternoon. In a field of hardened professionals how had Breitemann conspired to weave such mastery? Was it tires? The Firestone rain tire was better than Goodyear's, but half the field--including the World Champion in an identical Porsche-- was on the same tire. And Christian had no insurmountable horsepower advantage--the post-race teardown proved his engine was fully within the rules. There were three possibilities, it was a fluke, Breitemann was the new rainmaster or he was a wunderkind.

Thorne had a strong inkling. Breitemann elicited awe.

But motor racing creaked with mysteries. Keeping track of these ungovernable people was like reading pulp fiction, everything was bigger than life. To control costs the prior fall Porsche had delivered two new 917s to Raymond Beacom--Carnelian Oil, his American sponsor, would underwrite the expenses of the Porsche entry. But knowing 1970 was a racing season not to be missed, Dr. Fabius secretly prepared two additional 917s in dead of winter and to everyone's shock, not least Raymond Beacom's, the Porsche-Austria team materialized at Daytona in January-- competing against Beacom!

The intrigues were endless. This weekend alone Thorne uncovered two pearls. Confirmed by Breitemann, the 917's twelve-cylinder 4.5-liter would now be replaced by a bigger 4.9, matching the powerful Ferrari 4.9. And with a little reportorial chicanery he unearthed something more outlandish still, a top-secret 5-liter Porsche of sixteen cylinders!

He finished his story and Trevor drove him to Heathrow. He located the crew of the next L.A.-bound TWA flight. The crew's First Officer would mail it locally in Los Angeles--the best way to get a story to the magazine fast. His tight deadlines would test this system to its limit.

On the phone Breitemann told Thorne the secret Porsche test would be on Thursday--and Friday if needed. This left several days to prepare the cars for Monza a week later. A room had been reserved for Thorne in Wolfsburg, the Volkswagen company town near Ehra-Lessien.

But not all was settled. His magazine's meager fee dictated an austere travel budget and when Thorne investigated, the expense of shipping the Jaguar to France by channel ferry was far too high. But Burnleigh proposed an elegant solution. His duties at his paper precluded going to Ehra-Lessien, but he'd been assigned to cover Monza and the Targa Florio. If Nick went to Germany by train, Burnleigh would cross the channel with the Jaguar at the paper's expense. They'd meet in Paris and drive to Italy together.

"Wizard!" gushed Nick like Lord Blather, wiping an imaginary rhinestone of spittle from the corner of his mouth.

Brilliant noonday sun beamed down on Dover. Thorne took his position on the boat-train ferry's windward rail. Lines were cast off and a breathless moment followed. Then the ship lunged to sea, a great quaking in her steel plates bucking beneath his feet. A stiff northerly streamed through his blond hair, pressing it tight against his skull. After the weekend's unending gloom today's snow-white clouds and high blue sky gladdened his soul.

But subtly, ineluctably as the chalk cliffs fell astern, his complacency began to erode. By the time they docked at Calais the metamorphosis was complete, he was *l'étranger*.

The boat train streamed to Paris and out the window the bare April trees bore the stark pen-and-ink severity of winter. But looking close Thorne saw green nubs, the first tumescence of spring aching to burst.

Second Class was deserted. Wonderful. On his first boat train years before as a student in midsummer not a seat in Second Class was vacant-- and First Class was but a rumor. With multitudes he sat on the filthy Second Class corridor floor. Today he had an entire compartment to himself!

After the intensity of Brands Hatch, then the rush to meet his deadline, he was free to ponder his fortune, a secret Porsche test in Germany, guest of the brilliant Christian Breitemann. Then he would go south to Paris, Monza, the Targa Florio in Sicily, Monaco, Spa...he juddered with it! But elation was familiar, life came easily to Thorne. He had gotten A's at Berkeley, while never missing an important late night in the city at the Jazz Workshop or Mike's Pool Hall. And every spring and fall he and his friends trouped to Laguna Seca near Monterey where he absorbed what he could of professional racing. College was a dream--then it got even better.

His senior year he wrote a parody of "After the New Wears Off," his favorite sports car magazine's farthing-by-farthing accounting of what it cost to own, maintain and drive various sports cars. His parody, "After The Paint Wears Off," described the costs, fiscal and spiritual, of driving his bedraggled student 1955 Chevy Delray Coupe to its very last Laguna Seca.

He showed the story to his friend Pam, who established her credentials by bootlegging a sense of humor into his Creative Writing class. She began to read. Snort. Belly laugh. He'd never felt anything like it.

The magazine published his story before he graduated, and the door swung wide open.

The Artois countryside streamed past, an egg-yoke Matisse sun winking through flickering branches, and his mind wandered--

To Angela.

He thought of her endlessly, couldn't stop. Now the rails' glissando was racing him back to her. Ludicrous. She was famously married, infinitely above him, of the very highest caste. But he craved seeing her, talking to her, feeling her hand in his. He had never felt so perfectly undone by his maleness. If his thoughts were sidetracked, they surged to her again like water seeking its level. And every time he thought of her he heard the clashing brass of Tony Devane. Racing was Nick's métier and Devane was World Champion--but he was a gargoyle! Nick had learned more about this demigod in one stormy weekend than he ever wanted to know--

He was doing it again. Right now! Lost in his thoughts of Angela and Devane, his eye struggled to find hidden symmetries in the random scene out the window. The black power lines streaked along, leaping from pole to pole...rising, falling...yet his mind froze them where they were, the pole in the center, the lines sloping symmetrically away to either side. He tried to find in them balance--the telltale of inherent order. If a bird out the window glided between trees, his eye stopped it at the midpoint. If he found himself tapping his fingers while he thought, he began tapping in sets of twos and fours, binary units, every finger tapping as often as all others. He would find the secret equilibrium! The same craving for order had drawn him to racing. He must know how young drivers on the way up could convince themselves there was order, that they alone were immune to the risk. The audaciousness of it made his heart pound. They knew something others didn't...or else were they desperately, disastrously wrong!

It didn't occur to him on the boat train that these were the thoughts of a profoundly romantic young man. Like all romantics, he considered the epithet demeaning. Nor did he imagine a day when these thoughts would seem incomprehensible. His sole misgiving that day took the form of a stark admonition--he spent entirely too much time in his own head.

CHAPTER 9

ARRIVING AT THE TAUBERHOF in Wolfsburg just after ten p.m. Nick confirmed it with Horst Hauser, Porsche's lubricous Swiss p.r. man. The new Porsche 4.9-liter twelve-cylinder had 60 more horsepower than the 4.5--600 in all. It was vastly more than the best three-liter Formula One engine but far shy of the huge bad-dog V-8's in the Can-Am at home.

While gleaning this Nick unearthed less satisfactory intelligence...no fewer than nine other writers were here for the "secret" test. Should the new engine beat Ferrari at Monza, all would ascribe their knowledge to "confidential sources at Porsche." He'd hoped Breitemann's invitation was a personal gesture, but now he saw he'd been invited because he had the minimum requirements, a press credential and a pulse.

While in the lobby he also learned that Hugh J.K. Breeland, the intense Porsche-Austria team driver, had had a big crash at the Nürburgring. Testing his Surtees Formula One car that morning--while Thorne stood enjoying brilliant sun at the channel ferry's windward rail--Breeland came upon a sudden rain squall just before the Nürburgring's Karrusel Curve on "dry" racing slicks. Losing all grip, the car crashed heavily. Breeland was lucky to sustain no more than a concussion, a severe neck strain and a compound fracture of his right forearm. Horst Hauser said he would be out for three months.

Perhaps.

But Thorne knew racers recovered from grievous injury with freakish speed.

Just then Christian Breitemann arrived in the lobby and walked straight to Thorne. "You will be very glad you came. We have prepared two glorious days of North German spring. I hope you brought ski clothing."

Breitemann was brimming over with good spirits and why not? Before him lay a powerful new racing engine and a full day of exploring its tone and temper.

Nick's third-floor room in the Tauberhof was gray and joyless. In bed he studied the alien landscape of German television. The TV western "Big Valley" ("Beek Wally") was on and Barbara Stanwyck was speaking her mind in idiomatic German. Whatever she was saying...she meant. He turned it off.

But as tired as he was from the long train ride, his eyes opened wide at five-thirty the next morning. Despite the hordes of writers on hand, he was excited about a day at the track. He took a hot shower, dressed and was out of the room by six.

Walking the Tauberhof's gloomy third floor he perceived phantom forms out the windows...at first light the external world was only hearsay. His muffled strides on the gray carpet led him to the stairs, the wetness at the back of his hair swaying against his neck. He would have an early Frühstück and--

What *is* that!

He gazed at the pitch black out the window and saw rapid motion--a form running straight up in the air!

Ridiculous. His eyes began to adjust.

The figure bounded up and up in the dark, striding higher...running up a steep outside staircase on the old carriagehouse the Tauberhof used as a parking garage.

The figure ascended. Turned. Sprinted down again--going fast.

Breitemann!

Nick rushed downstairs.

"*Morgen, mein Herr*," said the night clerk.

"*Morgen*," Nick nodded without slowing.

He hurried across the courtyard, the sharp pre-dawn air like a razor on his face. In the dark far above rapid footsteps rang out, running shoes thrumming on wrought iron. Thorne arrived at the foot of the stairs just as Breitemann came bounding down, panting hard.

"*Morgen, mein Herr*," he said like the night clerk.

"*Du!*" said Breitemann. Gasping, he tried to smile. "Why are you here!"

"There's no law against exercise, Christian."

Breitemann made no reply.

"Terribly sorry..." Nick said with annoyance. "I'm intruding."

Breitemann's short laugh acknowledged it. Nick turned.

"No, no, you must stay," Breitemann said, his tone completely changed. "It is fine. I am just not expecting someone here now."

"Don't let me stop you."

"Please, no. Stay. But you must not talk of this."

"Why not? Running up and down stairs in the middle of--"

"You must not," Breitemann said. "I want no one to know."

Already Breitemann's breaths came less rapidly. He was in superb condition.

"It is my secret weapon, Nick."

It was the first time he'd used Thorne's first name. He swiped the sweat from his neck with the forearm of his sweatshirt.

"Pretend you never saw. If I have more endurance, you see--if I feel more stark...you know--strong. It seems foolish to you, I know, but...."

No drivers Nick knew indulged in secret physical workouts. But maybe they were all doing it in secret! Was everyone bounding up and down stairways at pre-dawn...he doubted it.

"It hurts no one--*ja?*" Breitemann said.

"Whatever you say, Christian. I won't breathe a word."

"Not even to Jozie. He would make a huge story of it."

Thorne nodded--Jozie would. And keeping Breitemann's secret struck a nerve. Thorne's mission was to write about everything he learned. But at the same time, keeping Breitemann's secret excited a sleek "insider" sensation.

"*Vielen Dank*, Nick."

Breitemann smiled, his breathing normal again. "I have finished now, anyway."

"Good...you're wearing us both out."

CHAPTER 10

THE RAIN HAD STOPPED. They strolled beneath willows beside a broad pond. Swans glided like clouds.

"You fancy yourself ready for Formula One, then, do you," Lord Boeldieu said, studying the path ahead as if for clues. He held no proper title, but immense wealth and owning a Grand Prix team were quite enough.

"I am ready," Breitemann said.

"And what tells you so?"

Before Breitemann could reply Lord Boeldieu stopped, making Breitemann stop.

Immediately he resumed his pace.

"Do you know how many young men believe they are ready for Formula One, Herr Breitemann? In Great Britain alone, hundreds."

"But you did not invite these hundreds here today."

Boeldieu turned.

"I simply want to impress upon you the seriousness of this step. Do you appreciate the things that can happen?"

"I have known since a boy. My father took me to my first race at Solitude when I was six. A driver died against a tree right in front of us."

"Did this disturb you?"

Now it was Breitemann who halted.

"I shall have this, sir, if not now very soon."

Lord Boeldieu nodded.

Nodded again.

"And we shall be pleased to have you drive for us."

They shook hands.

Breitemann's heart chimed.

And his life was changed forever.

The Volkswagen Proving Ground at Ehra-Lessien was flat, vast, silent. The only sound except the journalists' subdued conversation was a whisper of wind in the field of tall grass beyond the pavement. Set on a broad plateau overlooking a panorama of checkerboard Saxony farmlands--tank country-- the Ehra-Lessien test facility was spartan, raw. It had no formal pit area and only two small concrete bunkers for doing mechanical work out of the weather. Ominously the site was just minutes west of the gun towers, listening posts and anti-personnel mines of the communist East German border. Breitemann said they often heard artillery practice in the East--or was that World War III?

Taking in the scene Joubert grinned to Nick. "Shades of Peenemünde."

In plan view the track had the shape of an enormous hourglass. Billiard table-smooth parallel strips of pavement led to two high circular sections of banking far off at the north and south ends. The banking formed steep bowls, curving gradually around and down onto the long parallel straightaways. An additional serpentine road course with seven turns of varying radii and velocity adjoined the northeast exit of the banking. Today the road course would be combined with the high-speed hourglass, testing the new 4.9 engine's full range of power and flexibility.

In gray morning chill Nick was glad for his warm white fisherman's wool turtleneck, bought in a tough little military-surplus shop Burnleigh showed him off Piccadilly. He nodded to Joubert at the enormous gaggle of writers. "Do you think there are enough of us!"

"You expected a private showing?"

"I believe life should be effortless and ideal, Jozie, don't you?"

Today Raymond Beacom remained in England "on other affairs." More intriguing affairs than this beggared Thorne's imagination.

After what seemed an eternity Peter Whitlaw--The Mallet was running things--gave Breitemann's good-natured and tireless Italian chief mechanic Ermanno the nod. Ermanno climbed down into the low 917's cockpit and the starter motor whined. The cold twelve-cylinder barked, firing sharply...surging and popping in the blustery air. But in moments it settled into a restive fast idle. It would take time coming up to temperature in the morning chill.

Nick stepped closer, savoring its edgy purr, twelve high-compression pistons on feather-light titanium connecting rods, four cams strumming twenty-four valves, the exhaust valves sodium-filled to dissipate heat. The spinning six-blade fan made a scything wheeze, sucking ambient air down over the cylinders' cooling fins. Even at full cry the engine's song was deliciously melodic--it had nothing in common with the massive blare of the water-cooled Ferrari.

Debuting the 4.9 engine at Monza's 230-plus mile per hour speeds served Porsche's ends. If all went well the 4.9 would push Ferrari off center stage at its home track. After decades at the zenith of racing Ferrari's pre-eminence was indisputable. Porsche must play the spoiler.

The twelve-cylinder's brooding idle masked all competing sounds when-

-

RRRaaaaazzzzzzzzzz!

A British Racing Green monoplane came in at them low and fast--

Inverted!

It swooped even lower and Nick crumpled to the ground. An R.A.F. roundel passed by the corner of his eye--

Gone.

Skimming harmlessly eastward mere feet above the main straightaway, the plane rolled right side up on full power and climbed vertically, hanging on the prop. One by one the earthlings regained their feet, brushing off.

The plane had wingtip tanks and a bubble canopy--a doughty little Italian Siai Marchetti SF-260. It was fully aerobatic and then some. It came over the top now in an outside loop, engine roaring, and leveled off.

Joubert laughed... "Idiot!"

"Who the fuck--"

"The World Champion, don't you see!"

Circling downwind the Marchetti executed a crisp "Overhead 360" fighter-plane break and approach. Banking hard left, cutting power and side-slipping steeply, its centrifugal momentum slammed the gear down and locked. Flaring out at the last possible instant it touched down light as a feather.

"Racing drivers," Joubert beamed.

Alex Winter, Breitemann's co-driver, brushed off his driver's suit, mugging to Thorne Crikey! Whether from a split-second assessment of the risk or simple pride, Breitemannn had remained standing.

The deep-green plane taxied to them. In place of an ordinary SF-260's 260-horsepower Lycoming six-cylinder, this plane's elongated cowl and willingness to climb on the prop indicated a 400-horsepower eight-cylinder. It could fly vertical all week.

Precisely at the prop's last revolution and kickback the nose landing gear bowed to a halt. Grinning broadly, cocksure, Devane slid back the canopy and hopped out. He was wearing leather breeches and an oatmeal cable-stitch wool sweater. Angela was still head-down in the cockpit. He turned back for her and immediately his laugh boomed. "When we went inverted her makeup went *evvv-rywhere*, lipsticks and eye-liners buzzing around the canopy like hornets!"

He was a specimen, Nick could concede, confident, brash, ready for anything. But despite the charisma he had about him a singular dissonance. It brought to mind the actor James Dean's intensity arising almost incidentally from his being minutely cross-eyed. Devane's features were handsome and harmonious, but his intensity counselled caution, the momentary chill upon detecting a glass eye.

Peter Whitlaw stepped forward grinning icily. "Are you bloody mad? You can't fly this close to the border, silly git, it's closed air space!"

"Ah, but I've a friend in British Forces, a General friend. He arranged clearance, provided I refrain from provoking a war. Why, old cock, you don't fancy a bit of a thrill?"

"Gormless twit."

Whitlaw pumped Devane's hand cordially nonetheless. Angela was just climbing out. She wore olive tweed slacks with stylish wide bell-bottoms, high-heeled boots and a deep-green woolen pea coat with a fur-lined hood. She smiled beautifully for Whitlaw.

Christian Breitemann stepped forward, arms outstretched, to boost her down off the wing.

"Thank you, Christian," she smiled.

"Always the gentleman," said Whitlaw.

"For all it gets 'im..." said Devane.

CHAPTER 11

NOT A MINUTE LATER AN enormous midnight-blue Mercedes-Benz 600 Grosser limousine rolled noiselessly to a stop at the race-car transporter. Its dark side windows looked very South Florida. All waited to see who emerged.

The right rear door swung out before the uniformed driver could hurry around the enormous car to open it and out stepped Lionel Ludgate, Carnelian Oil executive v.p. He wore a dashing double-breasted trench coat with shoulder and back flaps, belt tightly cinched. Cocked at a jaunty angle above his salt-and-pepper sidewalls was a fine olive Borsalino fedora, a stylish Bavarian brush in the band.

Next, to Thorne's surprise, came Jennifer Whelan, the pretty California photographer. She was followed by her constant companion enormous Lester Clark. They had come up in the world, but Jennifer looked as calculatedly defensive as ever. Medium height, slender and shapely, with red hair, she had the kind of pale porcelain complexion commonly associated with freckles, though she had none. She made men turn for a second look. But her coloring suggested to Thorne some unspecified genetic frailty. She was pretty enough...but somehow he expected more.

She pulled down the legs of her black gabardine slacks, clenched her fists and stretched hard, banishing the fatigue suffered even in stadium-length Mercedes limousines. The contortion of her torso drew attention to her perfectly fitted leather jacket. It looked brand-new. Nick wondered uncharitably how much Lionel Ludgate had had to do with it.

"Stock market closed today, is it, Lionel?" inquired Devane. "Or have you lost it all?"

"Hardly." Ludgate smiled all around. "Have I made a mistake, this is the place?"

Devane eyed the well-tailored Jennifer. "If you've made a mistake, we can't see it from here."

Jennifer smiled at Lester Clark, ignoring Devane. It interested Thorne. But making an entrance moments after Angela flew in upside down inches off the deck, a losing gambit.

Lester Clark unloaded their bulky camera bags, tripods and equipment from the trunk and Jennifer swung her own bags across her shoulder. Accustomed to being admired, she walked straight to the race car.

Ludgate turned to the drivers. "Just beginning? We've missed nothing?" He exercised the prerogative of a rich and powerful man to indulge marginally inane observations.

"Just about to start, Lionel," nodded The Mallet, "as soon as this bloody Jerry racing car will have it." Every syllable of his speech was rendered through clenched teeth. "We're flattered you've come...I say, flattered!"

"Kind of you," said Ludgate with a glimmer, "...I think." He grinned to the others. "Raymond sends his regrets while he remains in England soaking his boils."

Whitlaw emitted a rollicking belly laugh Thorne would have thought beyond his range. The reporter in him still pondered what "affairs" kept Beacom away.

But now Whitlaw shot a glare at Ermanno. The Italian ducked down into the cockpit to check the engine-oil temperature. He returned a thumbs-up. Suddenly Lionel Ludgate, executive vice president, corporate patron, lord of all he surveyed...was mere ornament. Whitlaw fired orders now high and low, awaiting no responses.

"Would you be so kind," he said to Breitemann motioning to the car.

To Devane, still in street clothes, he said, "Kindly get changed, Tony, please."

Thorne didn't know Team Beacom protocol, whether it was significant that Breitemann drove first. In racing everything had a meaning, analyzed from as many viewpoints as there were observers. But from this moment forward the drivers were free to interpret The Mallet's gray unblinking eyes however they pleased, he would offer neither explanation nor consolation.

CHAPTER 12

THE CAR SHAMBLED ALONG the vast front straight on its first warm-up lap. Seeing this intemperately violent object traveling at only 80 miles an hour was strangely disquieting.

The next lap Whitlaw brought the car in to confirm all fittings and connections were tight and dry. He waved it back out.

It made a new sound coming towards them now, gaining mass rapidly. Hurricane winds raged over its skin. It flashed past at 140. Still not at full power, the disturbance was intimidating.

But coming into view in the distance again its engine note dropped. It veered off the track towards them. A gifted test driver can diagnose a car's handling quickly and it would be no surprise to Thorne if Breitemann had that gift.

Still at very high speed, engine off, it rolled towards them clattering loudly, its gummy racing tires scatter-gunning the wheel-wells with pebbles. It came to a halt and Whitlaw and Devane bent down at the forward-swinging door. Nick knew not to be pushy about listening in--but he caught two remarks. The engine was strong in the mid-range...but with more power off the faster corners the rear needed better grip. Breitemann wanted a stiffer front swaybar, possibly stiffer front springs and more rear spoiler.

At the rear Ermanno had the engine cover up--

And there was trouble. He came forward and tapped Whitlaw's elbow.

Tapped again.

"Ermanno...what!"

Ermanno made a throat-slitting signal--a bad oil leak. It was finished.

Whitlaw relayed the news down to Breitemann.

"Scheisse!"

Whitlaw nodded. "A good job we found it now."

Devane, now in his driver's suit, went back for a look. Seated on the side of the car, Whitlaw gazed off into the middle distance, jaw muscles rippling.

At the far side Jennifer Whelan was shooting frame after frame of Breitemann through the steeply raked windscreen. He climbed out now and went to the rear. As he did Devane came to the front with a nettled smile. It would not be the first time a test went up the spout before brunch. His eye settled on Jennifer. He struck a pose next to the up-swung door, grinning, hair handsomely tousled. She shot several frames and nodded thanks. But he wasn't done.

"You'll be from California," he said to her.

He nodded at Nick to watch.

"You already know that," she said.

"Los Angeles?"

"La Jolla."

He winked at Thorne. "I knew by the swarthy complexion."

She had to laugh, her porcelain visage flushing.

"That's more like it. Very on guard with strange men, aren't we?"

"You're not that strange," she said.

It could've gone either way.

Devane's eye was half on Jennifer, half on Thorne, as if demonstrating a parlor trick. Thorne wanted to be somewhere else.

"You know, I fancy a competent woman," Devane said. "They do a special little something for me."

"And pray tell what could that be?"

"You're a competent woman--what do you think?"

"I think I'm going to faint," she said dripping sarcasm.

Devane laughed to Thorne. "Very defensive. Exciting, isn't it?""

Thorne had heard these versicles and responses a thousand times. It was the oldest ceremony on Earth.

But now she began shooting headshots of Devane.

"Truly, Jennifer--" he said.

She shot frame after frame, working hard.

"I'm really harmless."

She continued shooting.

"Utterly."

He picked up three brake pads from the red tool chest next to the car. "Seen this?"

He began juggling the pads like a West-End street busker. She dropped to one knee, shooting up at him. After a few moments he stopped.

"See? I don't bite. Well, maybe just a little."

She looked at Nick. Back at Devane. "Your wife is calling."

He turned without a care. Angela Devane was talking with Joubert and

Ludgate at the transporter. The smile she returned him cost her an effort.

"No, lass, you're wrong, my wife is doing what she does--working the room."

Jennifer looked away, her face a mask. She looked at Thorne, then began walking towards the transporter.

Devane laughed as if to himself. "Must be the California sunshine."

From the back of the car, Breitemann had been watching, Thorne felt it like a presence in the dark--and Devane saw him.

"So what's the prognosis, Christian?"

Breitemann looked at the pool of oil on the pavement without answering.

Devane nodded. "Don't take it so hard, mate. You broke a motor."

He turned to Whitlaw, all smiles. "Bit of a cock-up, what? I don't suppose I shall be blessed with the great privilege of driving today...."

CHAPTER 13

AS IF THEY'D BEEN HOPING FOR nothing else, the mechanics immediately set to work removing the damaged engine and installing a new one. When the gray sky began to drizzle, a huge canvas shelter was extended outwards from the side of the transporter. By European standards the Beacom transporter was enormous, large enough to carry four race cars, two over two. It also had a complete machine shop for producing mechanical parts at the track.

During the delay Joubert talked with Devane in the machine shop. Two pressmen had Beacom chief engineer Ian Swallow cornered in the truck's cab.

But just now Thorne had a taste for the company of women. He walked past Breitemann and Winter, Alastair Bissent sermonizing to them on the nefarious ways of the "froggies." Breitemann shot Nick a glint, both sly and mournful.

At the rear of the shelter Lionel Ludgate was holding court with Jennifer Whelan, Lester Clark and Angela Devane.

Seeing Nick coming Angela smirked, "I'll bet he doesn't!"

"I don't what?"

"Oh, but he does," Jennifer disagreed.

"No," said Nick, in the dark but taking a shot, "...I don't."

"I'm with Jennifer on this," Ludgate decided.

Nick looked to Angela for enlightenment.

She beamed. "Jennifer says we women lose our fairest years just trying to locate a man who doesn't snore."

Nick beamed triumphantly. "And I don't!"

"Oh, they all say that," Angela scoffed.

"Besides," said Jennifer, "you'd be the last to know."

"And who's to say you don't snore?" Nick parried.

"'ere, now," said Angela in her best cockney, "... noyce to the lydies!"

"He has a point," Ludgate nodded. "Only one way to find out."

Nick nodded enthusiastically, knowing a good thing when he heard it.

"Pity..." lamented Angela. "Just another easy Yank."

"This is the Sexual Revolution," Nick said, "ease is required! Too bad Jake Austin isn't here with his Free Love slide show."

Angela giggled. "Oh, I'd like that. Do the men take off their socks?"

Jennifer roared.

But now Lester Clark gave Jennifer a nudge--the crew was uncrating a new 4.9 engine. They grabbed their Nikons. Ludgate followed to admire what his exorbitant budget was financing.

Nick and Angela stayed behind.

"Tell me something," Nick said, "at Brands when Breitemann was blackflagged, you said--"

"Now we'll see," she nodded.

"But what did it mean?"

"You know perfectly well. And we saw, didn't we."

"Did it surprise you?"

"Surprised everyone, I think, even Christian."

They watched the photographers work.

"Christian is something very special," she said. "I think you two would enjoy each other."

"I'm flattered."

"Should be."

He waited a beat.

"How long have you and Tony been married?"

She flashed him an incendiary smile. "Why do you ask?"

"Oh...nosey pressman."

Her eyes turned back to the crowd at the new engine. "Two years. We don't even know where all the buttons are yet. Mind you, I wouldn't say that to just anyone. But some people you trust before it's safe. The first time we spoke, I told you I was fed up and you knew it--I saw you."

He waited, transfixed.

"I was shocked at myself, really. I shouldn't have done it."

"You needn't have worried," he said.

"I wasn't worried--that's just the point. You have to be able to *trust something!* If you can't, it would all be just too ... lethal. Crikey, what's the point?"

She eyed him.

"Is this making you uncomfortable?"

"No," he said. "... but if you make a mistake."

Her laugh was almost threatening. "You *don't!*" She nodded. "It's one of the penalties of having bloody everything."

"I don't think you have bloody everything."

"You're too clever for that. But most people want to think Tony and I have everything—-that we're living the dream! They need to think it, but it's a prison."

"I wouldn't know."

"Good. Keep it that way!"

Devane emerged from the transporter's cavernous interior, leaving Joubert behind. He jumped down to mutter something in Jennifer's ear. She made a show of not responding.

Then he came to Thorne and Angela.

"Well, here they are, Simon and Garfunkel. Every time I turn around, you two are murmuring itsy-bitsies to one another."

"A singularly blockheaded remark," said Angela.

"Here's what I think, luv, our Mr. Thorne here fancies you. I know I would."

Moth wings beat in Nick's chest.

"And you fancy him--when you're not fancying Christian."

She said nothing.

"Come, luv. Christian is well thought of hereabouts, is he not?"

She turned away from the others, her breath ragged. "You are just a bit unbelievable, Tony. What have you been doing all morning long right in front of my face!"

She glared at Nick: "You must excuse us."

Devane pulled her out into the drizzle. They stalked around to the front of the transporter, bent over in anger, heading to Devane's second Porsche 911S. Unlike the black one in England, this Signal Red car was provided to him whenever he was on the Continent.

Joubert came to Nick immediately. "What happened?"

Nick's head shook.

"Tell me!"

"A disagreement."

"I see that!"

Nick was silent.

Joubert nodded. "Then, it's happening."

"What is?"

"It's happening."

The oil-dripping engine came out of the car and a fresh 4.9 was bolted in. Thorne watched without seeing. When Angela called Breitemann "something very special," it was obviously at Devane's expense. How bad had things gotten between them? Jozie knew, too. Yet Angela was bright, brimming over with character. If things were so bad, why didn't she just put him on the bus?

But Thorne had answered that just an hour before--Devane was "a specimen." She was trapped in her own tar pit.

Devane came back in out of the drizzle--and no Angela. He hopped up into the truck, all bounce and high energy. Immediately Alastair Bissent lumbered up after him. Devane looked distracted, but the minute he turned to Bissent he beamed with charisma.

Nick had to satisfy his curiosity. He stepped out into the drizzle and walked to the front of the truck. The Signal Red Porsche was gone. Angela had taken the "geographic cure."

When he returned to the shelter Devane saw him and stepped away from Bissent. "Just a blip on the radar between us, mate," he said. "You won't mention it, of course...for Angela's sake."

"Where is she?"

"She'll be back. We've got coffee and the squarehead equivalent of scones on the way."

"Thank you."

Devane turned to Bissent. "You were asking about the Targa Florio."

"I was indeed. How does one memorize all those hundreds of turns?"

Devane laughed. "One doesn't, don't you see? One just keeps in mind how filthy it would be spending all summer in hospital."

Elated, Bissent scribbled it down. "Capital!" he gushed, spattering his notebook.

CHAPTER 14

THE RAIN STOPPED AT ELEVEN, but by one, with the new engine in the car and running, the sky was darkening again. As Breitemann requested, stiffer front springs had been fitted. Devane still had not driven.

Breitemann did six fast laps, confirming the changes were good. He brought the car in and now Devane put on his helmet. But the minute he did raindrops the size of June bugs spattered the pavement. He gave Whitlaw a filthy glare.

"Old boy," said The Mallet, "if you must look at people that way, wear a full-face helmet."

Devane smirked.

Gave him the fisted forearm.

Climbing up out of the cockpit Breitemann removed his helmet and slipped off the fire-retardant Nomex balaclava. Worn over the head, it covered everything but the eyes. After conferring confidentially with Whitlaw and Devane, Breitemann drew a crowd.

And once again Thorne marveled. If he himself had just pushed this violent car to its limits, his breath would be coming in adrenalized gasps. Breitemann, by contrast, was sunny, placid, calmly analytical.

"So how is it?" said Joubert.

"How do the Americans say," Breitemann replied, "... there is no substitute for cubic inches?"

"But Christian," Thorne said, "we were talking about sex."

Breitemann laughed.

Joubert persisted. "Do you feel a difference?"

"I should be unconscious if I did not! It has wonderful torque at the middle revs...excellent!"

They strolled towards the shelter of the transporter. In no time,

Manchester pressman Christopher Garrett, all thick glasses and pimples--
"Garrett The Ferret" Joubert had dubbed him--insinuated himself between
Breitemann and the world.

"Christian, will it be quicker than Ferrari?"

Joubert's laugh was sly. "That's just Christopher's way of reminding you
that speaking to the press isn't all fun."

Breitemann smiled. "I will tell you exactly, Christopher. If Ferrari is
making no big improvements, we will be very competitive, gut?"

Garrett looked pleased.

"But in return you must telephone to Ferrari to ask if they are making
big improvements--they do not take my calls."

After an initial barrage of oversized droplets, the rain settled in--not
heavy but steady. The crew began putting on rain tires and disconnecting
the car's front and rear swaybars to suit the wet track. Devane stood waiting
under an oversized Firestone umbrella. A damp driver's suit introduces
moisture into the cockpit, risking fogging the windscreen.

Jennifer Whelan, in a slicker now and broad-brimmed rain hat, knelt at
a low angle with her Nikon shooting the crew at work. Far from being
inconvenienced by rain, she was energized by it. Nick had admired a moody
black-and-white series of Formula One cars in the rain she shot at Watkins
Glen. She was very good.

He walked towards her.

Devane watched her as well. "You really needn't be that way, you
know," he said.

There was an aggressive familiarity in his tone--or was it just race-driver
effrontery?

She continued shooting.

"I'm talking to you, Jennifer."

A rain tire slid onto the car's left rear. The impact wrench jack-
hammered it tight. The motordrive of Jennifer's Nikon whirred.

"You've been mistreated by men, I think." Devane grinned. "Shockers,
I should say by the look of it."

She stood and looked in the direction of the transporter. Angela was
talking with Breitemann, but her eye was on Devane.

"Listen," Jennifer said, "I'm here taking pictures for Carnelian--that's *all*.
Kindly bugger off, Tony."

"All in fun, as I think you know."

"I know very well what I think I know."

She headed to the transporter. For the second time Breitemann's eye
was on Devane, and this time Devane returned it.

"Christian," he said.

Breitemann didn't respond.

"A word with you."

Breitemann came forward. Instinctively Nick moved to the far side of the car, conceding them privacy. But Devane's volume remained fully audible.

"Something on your mind, Christian?"

"Something?"

"You were looking at me as if you have something you needed to say."

Breitemann was silent.

"You don't approve of me, perhaps."

"You do not make the choices I would make."

"Ahh...."

Devane mulled it. "But we're agreed on one choice."

"And this is?"

"*My wife!*"

The German's head shook sharply, his English deserting him. "Your wife makes everything she can to be loyal with you, Tony, but you make this impossible!"

"That is how you see things? Then, you must be delighted!" His laugh was scathing. "You're no different to me, mate, not a bit. I do nothing you aren't doing this bloody minute. I've seen you talking to her, it's all over your face!"

"This is foolish, Tony."

"I know that look, mate--I invented it! Where do you come off being so bleeding sanctimonious?"

"I do not know this word."

"Holier than thou!" Devane snapped.

"Tony, here is what I think--"

"You must have me confused with someone who gives a shit what you think!"

Breitemann turned away--but Devane grabbed his arm.

He spun back and the umbrella dropped from Devane's hand.

They were toe to toe.

"Bloody hell!" Whitlaw roared, arriving in a rush. He shoved himself bodily between them.

"Step back--both of you."

Neither moved.

"Now!"

They did.

"Christian...go to the truck."

Whitlaw turned to Devane. Breitemann had not moved.

"Go!"

Breitemann turned.

Whitlaw spat out his words like carpet tacks. "Tony, are you bloody mad?"

"Not a bit of it, guv. I feel ducky!"

"Mad as a tick! You're not driving until you calm down, mate...until you calm right down!"

Devane's eye followed Breitemann now, his voice rising. "I invented that look!"

"Keep moving," Whitlaw ordered. Breitemann was almost to the transporter.

Devane nodded. "What was his time, Peter?"

"That was in the dry...bloody fool."

"Do you think I don't know that! What was his time?"

"3:02.8."

"Well, well...fastest ever."

Everything at the transporter had stopped.

Devane looked at his wife. "Did you hear, darling? Christian is faster than I am!"

Her face was blank.

"Tony," Whitlaw growled, "this is not a race!"

"No, no, Peter, this is celebrity billiards!"

Devane pulled his helmet on angrily, climbing down into the cockpit. Ermanno knelt on the pavement by the 917's door, ready to help with the safety harness. But Whitlaw waved him off. "Give it a few minutes, Ermanno, there's a good lad."

Ermanno nodded and set off towards the transporter.

Whitlaw looked down at Devane. "My suggestion to you is, sit there a while and imagine yourself on a lovely sandy beach in warm sunshine--will you do that for me? Just let's cool down."

Devane looked up from the cockpit. Whitlaw nodded with finality and stalked off towards the transporter.

In the same moment Devane started arranging his safety harness by himself. He closed and tightened the five-point quick-release at his belly. Tugged the shoulder-strap tabs, pulling them down hard, first the left, then the right. Thorne wanted to alert Whitlaw--but it was not his place.

The cockpit door slammed down.

The engine blasted to life.

The car shot away, Whitlaw shouted down by six-hundred raging horsepower.

CHAPTER 15

IN THREE LAPS DEVANE'S LAP time came down to 3:37.0--for Ehra-Lessien in the rain, said Whitlaw, extraordinary. Devane stopped after six laps. Climbing out of the car, he met Whitlaw's eye. Neither spoke. He was World Champion.

Alex Winter, Breitemann's co-driver, was next.

Jennifer Whelan and Lester Clark wanted to go out to the north end of the circuit and shoot pictures up in the banking. Thorne and Joubert would go too--and Lionel Ludgate determined they should go in style. All climbed into the Mercedes 600 limousine, beaming at their extravagance.

The windshield wipers clak-clak-ing, the enormous Mercedes followed the outside of the circuit northwards, traveling against the flow. Twice Alex Winter streaked past, the 4.9 bellowing a fortissimo French-horn song. The scene seemed anything but photogenic to Nick--a paved moonscape animated for brief instants by the bright-orange comet. But Jennifer and Lester, the interested parties, looked pleased.

Seeing the Porsche streaking along high up in the banking brought to mind the Daytona 24 Hours in January. At two a.m. Nick and two friends had stood on the roof of the Daytona press room above the main grandstands in freezing cold. Far in the distance Porsche and Ferrari headlights streaked along the pitch-black back straight and flew into the banking, climbing and veering at 225--spears of light impaling the void. Moving at this unearthly rate in the night they could only be fighter aircraft skimming along at full chat--feet above the deck!

The Mercedes continued around the outside of the circuit to where the road course climbed into the banking. Winter roared onto the banking, slanted at a mad angle. In moments he was racing south again at over 230, a minuscule sliver of orange above the guardrail.

Jennifer got out to look. It would do.

They all got out and the limousine returned to the pits.

Meanwhile Winter finished his laps. Breitemann was next.

Except for the whisper of rain, in the lapse between practice runs all was silence. Nick and Joubert waited at the side of the course, not a breath of wind disturbing the calm.

They heard it then--Breitemann coming. He was behind the low ridge on the road course.

The twelve-cylinder howled.

Backed off.

Howled--

Bursting over the ridge.

Thorne brought up his stopwatch, Breitemann veering left, setting up at 150 for the fast left-hand sweeper immediately in front of them. Thorne clicked the watch. The Porsche climbed into the banking, its song rising.

Thorne felt an electric jolt. It was a command performance--Olivier and Gielgud!

Beyond the guardrail the car raced south, an orange glint in the spray.

Behind them Jennifer and Lester stood high atop the rim of the banking. The car would rush into their lenses, careening through a madly tilted world.

Breitemann reappeared. Thorne clicked the watch. 3:36.4.

More than half a second faster. Joubert grinned--Breitemann confirmed. In two more laps Breitemann was down to a 3:35.8.

The track was silent again.

Thorne mentally thanked Burnleigh again for the warm green mackintosh keeping out the rain.

The car reappeared, Alex Winter driving. After six laps he did an excellent 3:36.3--a fast co-driver.

But Devane was coming. Thorne saw the famous helmet through the windshield, a gleaming Union Jack in red, white and gold. The 917's single wiper blade swept the steeply raked windscreen. Devane completed his first flying lap and Joubert looked to Thorne.

"3:35.6."

"Faster than Breitemann!" Jozie enthused.

Thorne grinned, "What did Tony say about not touching off a war?"

"He is World Champion..." said Joubert, "allowances must be made."

As always, Joubert took the long view. Thorne considered what it might blind him to....

But Devane was at his brilliant best. In three laps he got down to 3:35.4.

The low orange Porsche coupe burst into view again at the ridge, spray boiling up. Devane streaked into the fast left-hander before them and Nick clicked his chronometer. Cornering hard at 150, engine on full song, it banshee-ed ahead with desperate speed, bearing left, when--

It swung hard right.

Hooked!

Spun backwards...typhoon winds rushing beneath it--the tail rising.

The car lunged upwards violently, teetering on empty air, the sky black with it.

The nose swung under

windmilling massively.

Its trajectory collapsed, slamming into the top of the guardrail tail first. A black wheel shot free, booming across the rain like a cannonshot. Body shards scatter-gunned, a chaos of tangerine fiberglass.

The car jack-knifed back up high and over, pinwheeling out beyond the guardrail, raging in the air like a fighting black marlin--

now diving straight down

smashed on the pavement

stopped dead.

Before it was over Thorne was running.

Flames leapt in the distance beyond the guardrail.

He ran flat out--it was taking forever!

Jumping the guardrail, his heart stopped. He saw three unidentifiable objects. The farthest burned furiously--he could not decide what it was.

Nearer was a metallic boulder...the engine and powertrain. It lay sideways like an uprooted tree stump, one crushed wheel pointed skyward.

Broken fuel pipes and spear tips of torn aluminum chassis tubing jutted out.

In the middle distance, he saw the remainder of the front end, the steering rack, foot box, controls, windscreen, the shattered right-front fender.

But Devane--

Where!

He remembered hearing...in a testing crash the 917 snapped in two at the cockpit. He translated it. The right-side fuel tank--at Devane's hip--was the cube of flame forty yards ahead.

Now he saw it at the engine--

Movement!

He ran to its far side.

The seat was mounted on the side of the rollover structure, still in place--Devane strapped to it. He was slumped on his side in the harness, legs limp. Lethal claws of torn chassis tubing pincered his torso.

"Tony!"

"*Unngghhhh.*"

It smelled sickly sweet

...gasoline!

"*Can you move!*"

Devane stared out with mannequin eyes.

The broken fuel line behind him dripped on the pavement--*tik-tik-tik-tik*. The stained driver's suit was black with it...raw gasoline! The pavement had an evil blue sheen--

and broiling engine heat gusted at Thorne.

NO CHOICE!

He yanked at Devane's safety harness quick-release. Devane collapsed heavily to the pavement, the jagged chassis tubes tearing his driving suit, gouging his ribs--

"*Unnnnhhhh!*"

Joubert arrived now--too spent to help. "Petrol!" he barked reflexively.

Nick grabbed Devane under the shoulders, pulling him back and away.

"*Aaaawwwwwwwnngggg!*"

Devane's fuel-soaked driver's suit left an iridescent blue trail.

Nick stopped.

Got a better grip.

Dragged Devane farther back--

Almost to the guardrail.

FFFoooofffff!

Blast-furnace heat struck Thorne's face.

Leaping flame engulfed the engine.

He lugged Devane back farther away, Devane struggling weakly.

"Tony--*stop!*"

There.

Safe now.

He propped Devane against the guardrail, battling for his breath.

Joubert knelt before the World Champion.

"Don't touch the helmet," Thorne said, "... his neck."

"I want to see how he is!"

"Sore," croaked Devane half to himself.

"It's a miracle..." breathed Joubert.

Thorne wanted to hear emergency vehicles.

Cars.

Trucks.

Anything except the flames' hoarse breath. The magnesium right-rear wheel atop the engine had already begun to burn, a festering malignant yellow-white flame...he thought, they'll play hell putting that out!

... it was the first voluntary thought he'd indulged since seeing the car start its spin.

"Cozy blaze," Joubert said.

"From 'ere..." croaked Devane.

Joubert's head shook: "A bloody miracle!"

Violent flames clawed higher, black smoke swirling round and round in the overcast.

"Anything broken?" Joubert said.

"Who cares," Devane breathed.

He touched the side of his ribcage.

Hissed.

"Something amiss there."

His head fell back against the guardrail.

"Who cares...."

Devane's eye dimmed. Went behind cloud.

It scared Thorne.

And he didn't like the way Devane's helmet lolled to and fro, weaving like a snake-charmer's cobra. Devane repeated the same mantra again and again..."glad you blokes" then "on fire, on fire."

Suddenly Nick realized--raw gasoline in the driver's suit was eating Devane's flesh.

Nick came to his feet. "We've got to get you out of that."

Devane was light-years away.

Nick took off the macintosh.

"Jozie, we'll put him in this."

Half-conscious, Devane fumbled haplessly with the driver's suit. Still in Nomex driving gloves, his hands worked like lobster claws.

Nick unzipped the suit and they worked it off his shoulders. They lifted him gently and Joubert slid the fuel-soaked suit and Nomex underwear away. His flesh was cherry-red.

Thorne wrapped him in the warm macintosh.

Joubert folded his own coat around Devane's legs.

They sat in silence then...where was Whitlaw!

On the horizon a small white Mercedes 220 ambulance appeared. It was followed by a Mercedes sedan, and farther back, a red VW Combi with fire equipment.

The ambulance driver came to a halt well short of the flames. He and his aide hurried to them with blankets and a field stretcher. With hand gestures Thorne warned them about Devane's ribs.

Whitlaw, Breitemann and chief engineer Ian Swallow climbed out of the Mercedes sedan. The medics eased Devane's red-white-and gold Union Jack helmet off.

Lifted him onto the stretcher.

Setting him down, he hissed like a tomcat.

Blankets snugly around him at last, Thorne pulled his macintosh back on. It stunk of gasoline.

The medics carried the World Champion to the ambulance just as a fourth vehicle arrived at speed--the Signal Red 911S. It slid to a halt and Angela stormed out.

Whitlaw glared at her. "Angela, I asked you not to--"

"You go to hell--where is my husband!"

"Angela--"

"Damn you!"

Breitemann nodded soothingly. "Angela, Angela...Tony is well. Be calm."

"He's well?"

She glared at the blazing wreckage.

"In that!"

"Come…" Breitemann said softly, "you will see. He was very lucky."

"Lucky--yes, I'll say!"

Tears of fury streamed down her cheeks.

"Bloody madness!"

Breitemann took her arm. "Angela, you cannot help this way."

She trembled catastrophically, in an ecstasy of rage.

"Angela."

Breitemann put his arms around her.

"He is well. Come and see."

Her shoulders collapsed at last and she began sobbing.

"We will go to him," Breitemann said guiding her to the ambulance. The others followed a pace behind. But when she saw him wrapped in blankets behind the ambulance she fell to her knees.

"Oh, Tony...my dear, dear Tony."

She covered his face with kisses. Nick cautioned her about his ribs, but Devane smiled wearily, "No, no...it's fine."

His voice had begun to heal.

"My baby is here," he said, "and it's fine."

Her tears on his face mingled with the raindrops in rivulets of relief.

"My dear," she whispered, kissing his forehead. "I was afraid you had gone."

"Never."

He was lifted into the ambulance. She climbed in and the door closed. The ambulance moved away.

Whitlaw's glare came to Thorne. "You saw it?"

"Something broke in the rear."

"Oh?" he said accusatively. "You know that?"

Thorne had never been more conscious of the gulf between him, a pressman, and this hardened professional roiling with contempt for those who had not suffered his bitter losses.

"It wasn't Tony," Thorne said. "It happened all at once--a broken hub carrier or suspension arm. Possibly a tire."

Without a word Whitlaw approached the wreck seeking his own answers.

Remembering suddenly, Thorne pulled out his stopwatch.

"Peter."

Whitlaw turned.

"His last lap was his fastest, 3:35.2."

Jaw clenched, Whitlaw nodded. It could mean anything--thank you or fuck you.

The men from the VW Combi billowed white fire-retardant foam on the burning wreckage. The magnesium wheel burned with a sparking stubborn white flame, refusing to be extinguished.

Nick turned.

Joubert watched the ambulance lights recede. "Further proof that nobody really knows anybody."

That morning Thorne would've argued.

He simply nodded.

The ambulance lights grew small.

Smaller.

Gone.

Part Two

1000 Kilometers of Monza

CHAPTER 16

CHRISTMAS EVE, THE NINETIES

Newton The Cat brushed Thorne's shin heavily, putting his shoulder into it. Perfectly right. Christmas Eve or Armageddon, it's dinnertime.

The nor'easter moaned outside, the night coal black. Thorne put the teakettle on and opened a can of festal Christmas tuna. Newton paced to and fro, to and fro, crowing. In no time he was gnashing and grinding, salvo after salvo of premium bluefin finding the mark.

Thorne pondered his own dinner. But he had no appetite.

When the kettle whistled he rinsed the blue ironstone teapot with boiling water, emptied and refilled it just as he had been taught by Becky and Trevor ages ago in their little kitchen in South Kensington. He opened the large dark-green Fortnum & Mason tin from Maison Glass in the city.

The blend was called Celebration Tea. Unsettling.

But the resulting bronze brew was sturdy consolation. He went to the living room--their living room. It was their favorite room.

...he must stop thinking in the collective.

Setting the teacup on the side table under the lamp he watched its vapors coil upwards, spinning a genie spell.

Years ago, to please his wife, he concluded a brittle truce with his employer. As Senior Editor at Sporting Life (away from the office, "Pond Life") he would sweat out every word choice, every pull-quote, every deck and caption...he would write the obligatory drool about pickup trucks and bass boats and jackass plaid hunting caps...just do it! He was into his fifties now, time to come to terms. He had turned away every job feeler. They could've moved to Los Angeles, to Detroit--he could've had copy-writing jobs he loved. But his wife's job at Bergdorf's was too important and no wonder! Her sense of entitlement was the match for her limousine-trash clientele!

What was she doing right now? He needed to know.

But if her father answered....

Why was the prospect of speaking to Chester Langfield Higbee, the Duke of Saddle River, so daunting--yet it was.

Making a mistake that could easily be avoided, he dialed the phone.

After three rings she said, "Hello?"

"How are you?"

"Fine," she said.

"That's good."

"How are you?"

"Fantastic. This Christmas is everything I hoped for."

"I'm sorry," she said coolly.

"How's Crosby?"

They agreed that Crosby, their other cat, would go with her.

"Fine. And Newton?"

"Fine," he said. "I'll tell him you asked."

Time for another avoidable mistake. "Have you done any thinking?"

"Yes," she said.

"And?"

"For us everything is a struggle. We don't live like other people."

"Don't compare our insides to other peoples' outsides."

"Oh, please."

"You think everyone else lives this charmed existence," he said, "no problems, no disagreements."

"And you wake up in the morning hunting disagreements!"

"I don't have far to hunt."

His heart was banging already. He must stop.

"I'm sorry," he said mechanically.

"You asked if I'd done any thinking. Well, I have--"

"And surprise, surprise," he said, "...the problems in our uniquely difficult marriage, the only difficult marriage in the history of the Judeo-Christian peoples, are all my fault! I'm so glad we've made this breakthrough, Leigh. On the phone Thursday the only personal thing you said in the entire conversation was, did I miss you--did I miss you! Nothing about whether you missed me--that isn't even a subject!"

She said nothing.

"And I said I missed you because...I don't know--I miss my marriage. I hate being alone--"

"This is getting us nowhere."

"But no, I don't miss you, Leigh!"

"Then, you must feel wonderful."

"I feel terrible!" His laugh was a growl. "And all you care about is who's winning on points!"

He heard a click.

The dial tone.

"Shit!"

He slammed down the phone.

He wouldn't get so damn mad if she didn't make him so damn mad!

It was settled, then. He would date Sheila Stafford at Pond Life. She was obviously interested. Nice body. They'd have dinners in the Village. See shows, movies--

They would not.

Leigh was his wife.

Until she was not his wife he did not do that.

But what difference did it make...the marriage was dead!

He knew what difference it made--he had known since Spa. And he was never able to hear his wife's complaints against him without counter-attacking furiously. Like her, he thought nothing of withholding the truth or distorting it to win an argument. But on this ferocious Christmas Eve, alone with his thoughts, he would not cheat with Sheila. Two wrongs don't make a right...he would go for three wrongs!

The black nor'easter boomed.

Uneasy but knowing he must, he reviewed the phone call. He had told her he didn't miss her, but the instant he did...it was true! To her, of course, it was only rhetoric. A debate point. She would accept a new Mercedes and a house on the shore as reparations, all part of the game. They'd stopped communicating years ago. It was as much his fault as hers. For thirteen years of sparring they communicated in code, denying the blood-and-sinew wounds beneath. "To keep the peace," as he put it to himself, he chose to ignore the times when she was hiding a bad motive beneath a good one ... the times when she did the opposite of what she promised ... but what's so unusual about that?

Absolutely everything. It was a disaster! Her self-absorption had grown and grown while he said nothing, "keeping the peace." By now her world was so narrow, so engorged with dishonesty, it only had room for one liar-- her. Some people's disorders mainly damage themselves. Hers damaged everyone around her. His ex-wife--he would use the term--was a catastrophe. He should be grateful she set him free!

And still he felt tortured. He loved her--and deplored her! For him, separating from a woman never came easily. He loved women. His truest pleasure arose from sharing a woman's company. Even in this liberating divorce, the loss ran deep....

His eye settled again on Tony's magnesium nugget. It was the only physical evidence that Spa ever happened. Yet it defined his life for all the decades since. Breitemann's conundrum about Angela came back again:

"Wives are different, Nicholas, yes? Especially Grand Prix drivers' wives are different. But in exactly what ways must a Grand Prix driver's wife, this most extraordinary wife, arrange to be different."

Get on with it!

He closed his eyes. He would ask for help.

But as he did, his thoughts rebelled ... not everything that 1970 spring was so bleak, so awfully desperate. In many ways his prospects had never looked brighter! And even as the world around him began to darken he clung to the conviction that every enigma has its resolution, every riddle its key.

1970, Wolfsburg, West Germany

In one rotation of the earth Thorne became a notable. The European papers were filled with the Ehra-Lessien crash, made irresistible on a slow news day because it was accompanied by excellent photos shot from the high banking by Jennifer Whelan and Lester Clark. In moody black and white they documented the car's slide, its horrifying flight and crash, the rescue of Devane from the holocaust. The tabloids ran huge photos on page one and Thorne was the epicenter. He'd saved the World Champion's life. It confirmed, said Lord Blather, Americans' unhealthy appetite for the spotlight.

The firestorm of publicity the crash generated dictated a Porsche press conference in the Wolfsburg hospital the next day. Porsche's Swiss p.r. chief Horst Hauser asked Joubert and Nick to be present. An unruly mob of press assembled in the hospital lounge. At the appointed time Hauser announced there would be a slight delay--Devane was with his doctors. Nick detected in this the oily hand of the p.r. professional orchestrating the drama. Meanwhile, Hauser introduced Thorne and Joubert. Camera shutters clattered, flashes flared, the press lavishing upon them the thunderstruck fascination reserved for any unworldly public display of good intent.

An English writer asked Thorne his thoughts running to the wreck.

"Didn't have any."

"Come, now."

"I couldn't find him. It looked like a head-on crash between garbage trucks, I didn't know where to start."

"How did you find him?" asked another.

"He was the only thing that moved."

"Your feelings at that moment."

Thorne's head shook. "Didn't have any. I just hoped it wouldn't all go up!"

"You thought that?" asked another.

"I have no idea! It's automatic. You go as fast as you can, there's no time for thinking. Wouldn't you say, Jozie?"

Joubert nodded for Thorne to go on.

"And if it exploded!" the writer persisted.

"It didn't."

"But if it did!"

"You have to try. He was strapped to the thing! Wouldn't you try?"

"I'd like to think I would."

"I'd like to think you would, too!"

It was a loud, declarative British voice at the rear. Devane made his entrance in a wheelchair, pushed by his gorgeous wife. Loud applause erupted.

Thorne shot a glance at Horst Hauser, who looked well pleased.

"If you don't try," Devane added, "I'm Beef Wellington."

A round of eerie laughter.

"Please, please," Devane said, "I was only the bun in the oven." He gestured to Joubert and Nick. "These are the master bakers!"

A second round of applause arose, more polite than the first. Devane shifted his weight uncomfortably in the wheelchair, wincing as he did.

"In place of Beef Wellington, I'm a sort of race-driver tartare."

Lurid images hovered on the air.

The questioning began in earnest, Devane downplaying his injuries.

"Preposterously minor," he smiled. Apart from painful gasoline burns, he had suffered two cracked ribs and the inevitable severe bruising. That he was well enough to meet "you lot," he said, was proof of his singular good fortune. "I'll soon be right as rain."

He smiled at Nick and Joubert.

"And all prior evidence to the contrary, these two ink-stained veterans suggest your tawdry trade has its uses."

It brought a blend of hear-hears and jeers from the British.

After five minutes Horst Hauser, gauging his audience keenly, cut the interview short, "... doctor's orders."

Being pushed from the room Devane took a last question from a French writer about the cause of the crash.

"Honestly don't know, Yves," Devane said. "I have no clear recollection of any of it and our Mr. Whitlaw says there wasn't enough left of the car to determine a cause."

The press conference had an unexpected effect. At the crash, Thorne had simply obeyed the imperatives, yet now his actions were being dissected as though to determine their merit. Stripped of their inherent simplicity, they felt gaudy and suspect. It was his first time on the other side of the typewriter. He didn't like it.

After the conference he and Joubert were invited up to Devane's room. Lunch would be brought in.

They rode the hospital elevator to the third floor, Thorne feeling thoroughly drained. When they entered the room, Devane stood very slowly, Angela steadying him at every stage. He straightened his back by slow degrees like opening a rusty pocketknife. Twice he hissed in pain.

"So..." said Joubert, "how do you really feel?"

"To feel at all is to feel splendid."

"And you'll really be out a month?"

Devane laughed--but stopped with a wince.

"Please, Jozie, no low comedy." He turned to Angela. "Speaking of which, we need a pill, luv. Call Nurse Mengele."

Thorne laughed.

"Angela's name for her."

Devane beamed at his wife.

Then his eye turned to the empty pill container on the side table. "The heartbreak of addiction. They're quite marvelous, really."

"You deserve all the pills you can chew," Thorne said.

"Seriously," Joubert said,"... you'll give Monza a miss?"

"I've already said, Jozie, making me laugh is heartless and cruel. I'll be at Monza, rain or shine, if they have to rivet me to the car! Can't let a little cracked rib stop the match."

"Two cracked ribs," Nick specified, "and very nicely cracked. Can you drive like this?"

"Bloody well try. What do you think, luv?"

"Do you want my opinion?" she said. "Or my answer?"

Devane grinned.

"Your answer...I think."

"You'll drive."

He nodded at Joubert: "Knows me better than I know myself."

She smiled into the middle distance.

"High time I find out what I'm made of." His eye engaged Thorne. "By the by, Whitlaw says the right-rear hub carrier broke. Thought you'd like to know."

"Thank you."

A portly nurse strode in like a Clydesdale. Fiftyish with gray eyes and huge down-sloped breasts like rocket nosecones, she ignored the others. Devane *ding-a-ling-ed* the empty pill bottle to her.

"Gut," she said and left.

"Sultry Nurse Mengele..." mused Devane. "Give her stirrups and a whip, she'd ride you down to a bloody stump."

He was in remarkable spirits. And judging by Angela's warm smile, the crash had been salutary for them both.

Devane walked to the bed now, moving like a stick figure.

"Bloody tedious, this."

He turned. Thorne knew what was coming. He didn't want to hear it.

"I owe you lot considerably more than a bad hospital lunch."

Neither replied.

"If you will be our guests at Monza, we should be most grateful."

Angela's million-dollar smile commanded acceptance.

"It's hardly necessary," Thorne said.

"I think it is."

"Do," said Angela.

"Delighted," agreed Joubert.

Devane looked to Thorne, who made no sign.

"Then, it's settled."

"There is a complication," Thorne said. "I'm traveling with Trevor Burnleigh."

"Suspiciously loyal of you--are you sure you're in the press?"

Joubert laughed.

"Trevor will be most welcome," Devane granted magnanimously.

"That's quite enough, now, dear," said Angela. "Mustn't be too nauseatingly gracious."

The nurse marched in and placed two pills in Devane's palm. After watching him drink down a full glass of water with them, she left, preceded by her twin artillery shells.

"A bit suspicious, really," Angela grinned. "Before Nurse Mengele came on duty, nothing was wrong with Tony's ribs."

CHAPTER 17

BREITEMANN SMILED. "No, I do not race to become a hero--that would be very strange, I think."

The writer from the New York women's magazine scribbled furiously getting it all down.

But gently, Breitemann put his hand on hers.

"No, no, stop writing and listen a moment."

She did.

"Do you write for your magazine to be a hero? No, of course not. It is your profession, your way to earn food. It is not heroic. You do it because you must."

"Yes." She smiled uncomfortably. "But if what you do is not heroic, what do you do about the fear?"

"Which fear--the good fear or the bad fear?"

"That something serious will happen."

"In a racing car something serious is always happening."

"Then, you don't consider what you do heroic?"

"A hero does impossible things. I do what I do every day as a workman, just as you do."

"But surely, there are heroes."

"Ja, natürlich, many and great heroes--but none of them drive racing cars."

They were seated in the back row at Aux Deus Magots under the trees on Boulevard St. Germain. Trevor Burnleigh raised his golden glass of cold Stella Artois: "To the hero of the hour and the free Monza lodgings that go with it. Good of you to include me, mate."

"Yes, it was," said Thorne.

Burnleigh laughed and they drank.

The beer was sharp and "mousie," as he remembered it. A dappled gray Parisian sky was brightening after morning rain. In the first shafts of sunlight slivers of water in the ancient cracked sidewalks of St. Germain glinted like splinters of glass. Piping-hot croques monsieur were on the way. April in Paris, it was all they said.

"But I'll have you know I'm no hero," Thorne stipulated, "Lord Blather is sure of it. He said it all smacked of being a bit showy."

"May his bowels stop, and judging by his breath they have. Did the papers get it right?"

"No idea," Thorne said. "All the papers I saw were in German. But they got the pictures right."

"Stunning. Who took them?"

"Remember Jennifer Whelan?"

Trevor's brow rose. "Nice bit o'lunch, that."

"And Lester Clark."

"Ah, well."

"They had a hell of a payday."

"And you?"

"Me?"

"Are you having a hell of a payday?"

Thorne frowned. "I had my fill of publicity in the first five minutes."

"Nickie, old cock, this happens but once in a lifetime. Think carefully."

Nick watched the darting traffic on St. Germain. "It's not why I'm here."

Frumpy little French sedans, sputtering motorscooters, corrugated-steel vans peeped and squawked like Gershwin. Under a shy spring sun they ate hungrily, splashing the croques down with Stella Artois. Burnleigh left a handful of Francs on the tablecloth and led the way to the parking garage.

Thorne was impatient to see the beautiful Jaguar again. He needed to drive a long way very fast. There had been aftershocks since Ehra-Lessien, grisly images and dark dreams he awoke believing. Driving fast and long would clear his mind. He would fix his energy upon driving the Jaguar, letting speed dictate his thoughts.

They collected his bag from Joubert's flat in Marais, shoehorning it into the sleek coupe's hatchback. In minutes they were veering off the *Peripherique* headed towards Italy, guests of the suddenly transformed World Champion and his adoring wife.

Passing on the left in a car with the Jaguar's right-hand drive was proving a thrill. Burnleigh, in the left-side passenger seat, thought it hilarious to give

Thorne the go-ahead to pass just as a huge international transport truck was bearing down in the oncoming lane. Either Trevor was crazily brave, or bravery didn't enter into it.

They raced south along tree-lined two-lane routes nationales. Joyous sun warmed the fields. Breezes combed new green leaves on the trees. Passing slower traffic (everything was slower) Nick used the Jaguar gearbox with careful vigor. Early E-Type shifting forks were famously fragile, though by 1970 they had improved. Still when driving British sports cars hard, scrupulosity was rewarded.

The route veered southeast to Dijon. Nick lamented not continuing straight south to Beaune and Mâcon, the heart of the Burgundy country, but Burnleight said not to worry, they would stop in Dijon for a plate of mustard.

At dusk they were in the high Juras. The road twisted and whipped, lunging upwards. The overhead-cam six made its handsome baritone. This Jaguar's handling was no match for Thorne's Porsche 1600 Super Convertible D at home, but the big 4.2-liter climbed beautifully.

Burnleigh proposed dinner at Le Cheval Noir near Nyon and Lac Leman, a "must" for racers, he said. Its proprietors were the parents of Jean-Louis Montigny, a journeyman Swiss driver killed at Monza two years before.

In a high valley of the Juras, Thorne took the left fork for Nyon. No longer battling gravity the Jaguar coupe streamed downwards through the dark, braking, cornering hard, on full throttle. Joy filled Thorne's heart. He knew again why humans race automobiles.

After a long descent the road leveled. In the distance loomed the black void of Lac Leman. Five minutes later the Jaguar's Dunlop "dog-bone" treads were grumbling and popping over the coarse crushed-stone car park of Cheval Noir, a rambling great Swiss farmhouse. In the lights Thorne made out a stream and a small working waterwheel.

They climbed out, the evening air sweet.

They were ravenous.

The moment they walked in Madame Montigny came rushing to Burnleigh. In her sixties, short and plump, her figure reflected well upon her husband's kitchen.

"Monsieur Burnlcigh...such a surprise! Bienvenue!"

Burnleigh gave her a big hug and introduced Thorne. She smiled happily. Her face was round, flushed, comfy as a down pillow.

"*Enchanté*," Thorne said.

More than half the tables were full this midweek evening, a good sign.

"You have the *cervelles au beurre noir*, Madame?" Burnleigh asked. He had raved about the house specialty--calf's brains in drawn butter.

"*Mais oui...toujours.*"

"I was hoping you might enlighten my ignorant American friend."

Thorne's smile at Burnleigh noted an off odor.

"But if this is not to your liking, Monsieur Nick," Madame Montigny allowed, "... perhaps you will prefer *Fondue Gruyères*."

"No, no, Madame. After Trevor's description of your cervelles, expressed with signature British pomposity...I must have them!"

Madame laughed, understanding all. "*Formidable,*" she said and took Nick's arm. "I like your friend, Monsieur Burnleigh."

They were seated at a window table. Moments later Madame arrived with complimentary cordials. They raised their glasses to her. Immediately Nick recognized the elegant lilt of Lillet.

Despite knowing what he was to order, he studied the menu with interest. But looking up after a moment--

He froze.

"What," Burnleigh demanded.

"Her!"

Nick nodded to the entrance.

It was the woman in black--the petite Mediterranean in the rain at Brands Hatch, fists clenched on the fence against some unspecified horror when Ruggiero crashed his Ferrari. She talked in low tones to Madame near the entrance. Still dressed in black, her head wrapped like a bandage in the black-and-gold Hermès scarf...she was unmistakable.

Even in Le Cheval Noir's glimmering farmhouse light she wore enormous Audrey Hepburn dark glasses.

Burnleigh chuckled, "Oh...her."

"You know her?"

"Everybody does. That's Luciana."

"Luciana?"

"Don't know her last name...Montigny's old girlfriend. You know the story."

Thorne didn't.

"She's with Dante Ruggiero now, but years ago she was to marry Jean-Louis. The arrangements were all made, the guests in the church, the organ playing as she came up the aisle, tears streaming down her face. When she got to Montigny, suddenly she shrieked, '*No!*'...turned and ran out, leaving him standing there! Deliciously Italian. Made all the papers."

Nick allowed it to sink in.

"She's terribly sweet, they say, but not very tightly wrapped."

"And now she's with Ruggiero...no wonder!"

Thorne described her scuttling away from the crash, chased by wolves. "Montigny's crash was in the rain, too, wasn't it?"

"Rain and fog," Trevor said. "Horrific. But nobody's holding a gun to her head with Ruggiero, are they."

Nick's head tilted as if he hadn't quite heard.

"Well...are they?"

Nick nodded. "I hope you show Becky a bit more compassion than that."

Burnleigh laughed. "Becky isn't hanging around with Dante Ruggiero is she...or do you know something I don't?"

"Perhaps," Thorne said, having a very different point in mind.

"Come, Nick. You play with tigers, et cetera, et cetera."

Thorne watched the woman with Madame.

"Is she pretty? You can't tell a thing with the goggles."

"Quite."

"And you know her?"

Burnleigh snorted. "You want a date?"

"Do you know her?"

"I know quite enough wobblies already, thank you."

"But what is she doing here?"

"Lives here--ever since Montigny took the cruise. Madame took her in."

"And she travels with Ruggiero?"

"What's wrong with that?"

"Nothing, I guess."

The waiter arrived. They ordered cervelles, salade verte, and Nuits St. Georges. When the waiter left Thorne turned. Luciana was gone.

Burnleigh frowned. "Who knows what goes on in women's heads...."

After the recent startling rapprochement between Devane and his wife, Thorne had nothing useful to contribute. And the cervelles were spectacular. He was happy to add this to the list of favorites he would have whenever available. After profiteroles and espresso Burnleigh inquired if Madame could recommend a place for the night. She nodded wait right here. A minute later she returned. A room awaited them in a pension at the lake.

At the door of Le Cheval Noir, they were joined by Madame's husband. He had a pencil-thin William Powell mustache and he was the antithesis of his wife--rail-thin, trim, delicate as a leaf. Nick mentioned he'd seen the woman in black--Luciana--in England.

Monsieur Montigny smiled. "Yes, yes. And now she is gone to another race in Italy."

"Monza" was discretely left unspoken.

"We're going there ourselves," Burnleigh said.

"*Evidemment*," nodded Montigny. "We all travel such grand distances only hoping to arrive at ourselves. *Au revoir, messieurs.*"

CHAPTER 18

FOLLOWING THE CUSTOM IN EUROPEAN hotels, breakfast conversation in L'Auberge du Lac's small dining room was hushed, every utterance delivered like a family secret. Coffee cups clucked on saucers. Out the open window breezes raked ultramarine Lake Geneva. To the south and west the French Alps' sharp gray teeth gnawed high blue sky.

The pretty Swiss girl with sunlight in her auburn hair brought them meusli, fresh baguettes, sweet butter and cheese. Her cheeks blushed rosy pink whenever she spoke, commanding devoted attention.

Minutes later they strolled to the Jaguar. In direct sun its chrome gleamed blindingly. By eight they were on the road to Lausanne, Montreux and the high Simplon Pass. It continued to confound Nick...he was being paid for this!

Burnleigh drove the first stint through rolling lakeshore country. In Lausanne, however, Nick could resist no longer. On the flight from Los Angeles he had vowed not to, it would only be upsetting...but he hopped out at a kiosk and bought the *International Herald-Tribune*, and at Burnleigh's insistence two Mars bars.

The headline was predictable.

"Nixon To Pull Out 150,000 Troops In A Year." It meant Nixon would not pull out 150,000 troops--at least, *not* in a year.

The Vietnam shitstorm was unending. He had resolved to ignore the waking nightmare but it was impossible--he needed to know about home. Story after story covered what Jake Austin liked to call the Power-To-The-People Show. Next to the lead story was an account of the previous day's coast-to-coast anti-war demonstrations protesting new B-52 bombing strikes in Cambodia. Another story, citing an "unconfirmed source," said

81

U.S. ground forces had now entered Cambodia--denied by Nixon, thus true. Student strikes were expected today at Berkeley, San Francisco State, Stanford, Montana, Ohio, Princeton, Yale, Wellesley, Columbia and a score of others. The National Guard had been called out at San Francisco State, Ohio State and the University of Georgia...Georgia! The soul-sickness had no boundaries.

"What now..." Burnleigh said, reading Thorne's expression.

"They keep putting National Guardsmen with live ammunition in front of rock-throwing students day after day——it can't go on."

"Here we go...."

"Trevor, what the fuck do you know! Move to Belfast for a week!"

Burnleigh glimmered. "...hit a nerve, did we."

Thorne went back to the paper. A new item leapt out at him--the aborted Apollo 13 mission.

"Jesus, Trevor, did you know about this?"

"A very near thing," Burnleigh nodded. "Could've lost them all."

On Apollo 13's way to the moon, an oxygen tank explosion destroyed the main life-support systems. The three astronauts had to retreat to the tiny lunar module and return to earth, very nearly freezing to death on the way. Now, days later, they were safe in Houston. The photo showed them shaking hands with Nixon.

Thorne looked out the window. "If there was nuclear war, racing wouldn't know about it until after the season."

He looked through the paper...more of the Vietnam meat-grinder. He was opposed--it seemed obligatory. Yet he had heard it more than once——a man who isn't liberal at twenty has no heart and a man who isn't conservative at forty has no brain. It reduced conviction to the lowest banality, yet it had a certain ring.

The Jaguar continued east around Lac Leman. At Montreux they stopped at Château de Chillon.

Water lapped at the foundations of Byron's dour lakeside fortress. Morning sun warmed its biscuit-hued stone.

"Enough winge-ing about politics..." Burnleigh said climbing out. "It's time you do something nice for yourself."

The Mars bars were off the scale, immeasurably superior to the eponymous candy at home. Some decades America got nothing right.

Burnleigh proposed that Nick drive--the Jaguar, after all, was his. It was Trevor's finest hour.

The route veered east through the deep Vee of the Rhône Valley. In late morning the tiny villages were still hidden from direct sun. At Brig the road suddenly leaped skyward. In moments they were in blinding light.

Above the treeline the sun bleached white in the way it does in the high country. Berets of snow capped boulders along the road. Rugged granite vaulted into cobalt blue, the snow on the cascading talus slopes making them squint. Through the open window freezing mountain air flowed onto Thorne's skin like a lotion, the severity of this life-threatening terrain touching a forbidden elation.

The Jaguar labored into ever-thinner air, its SU carburetors starving for oxygen. The engine ran thick and sooty and Thorne empathized with its struggle. It was early in the season yet and the Simplon summit was deserted. Thorne pulled over and switched off.

"My sentiments precisely," said Burnleigh.

They brushed snow off two flat stones at the brink and sat. The Italian Alps marched off to the south and east, too steep and spikey for snow to gain purchase. The road below them plummeted into Italy, a sidewinder of tight curves and steep pitches. In the wind's melancholy sigh the sky was vast, the prospect perfection.

After a time, unspoken, both stood and walked to the car. Thorne asked again if Burnleigh cared to drive, and rejoiced again when he declined.

Heart thumping like the first ski run of the season, Thorne pointed the Jaguar down.

Approaching the initial switchback he tested the Jaguar's disc brakes. They were good. He bent the car through the turn and fed in power, the tires at their limit.

He added power and the tail stepped out.

Accelerating to the next switchback he left his braking later, carrying speed into the turn. The ball of his right foot rolled smoothly off the brake to the throttle. The Dunlops gripped the pavement turn to turn. He used more power--and more...upshifting...heel-and-toe braking...double-clutch downshifting. The Jaguar's swaying attack was elegant.

Sque-eeeze the brakes

Roll on power

Sque-eeeze the brakes

Heel-and-toe.

The Jaguar whirled and rushed, saved from catastrophe millimeters at a time. His skills were on full emergency power--nothing was like this. All-consuming, mortally serious, he had no idea how long he drove, how many turns or minutes.

... dab the clutch

breathe the brakes

... power on--

down and down.

And at the brink, oblivion. He drove for all he was worth, making his highest claim to personal grace.

The road leveled momentarily at a ridgeline, the car climbing through 80 over the brow...falling steeply away, when in the corner of his eye--

Red!

In the tiny rearview, a red Lancia--

insanely sideways!

It surged up to him

not tucking in...

coming right past!

Tail out, in perfect balance, the little four-cylinder streaked by--

"Jeee-zus!"

Burnleigh was whooping!

"Did you see--Sandro himself."

"Sandro?"

"Sandro Munari. His Fulvia HF rally car! You just got passed by the greatest rally driver of all time!"

Very gradually, Thorne came to a halt. Heart bamming, he let out a whoop! and got out to walk it off.

"I know when to quit," he laughed, feeling intensely alive.

"Not to worry, mate," Burnleigh said. "Not five drivers in the world will stay with Sandro."

"And I'm not one."

"He's the best!"

Thorne nodded happily, "You drive now. And make a note, 'racing driver' comes off my résumé."

Burnleigh blared downstream towards Stresa grinning like a pirate. It occurred to Thorne to wonder if there is motor racing in heaven.

Not a chance.

CHAPTER 19

LAGO MAGGIORE WAS AS HE remembered--exquisite. He wanted to stop.

"All in good time, mate..." Burnleigh said cryptically.

A few kilometers beyond Stresa Trevor stopped the Jaguar by the sapphire-green lake. At Nick's door a dilapidated low plaster wall led out to a sun-blasted abandoned boatdock. Warm air danced in the sun. On a mission for God...Burnleigh opened the Jaguar's sleek hatchback and pulled out his suitcase. "I've a small surprise."

Despite his curiosity Thorne couldn't resist gazing out across the water. In the foreground, a small island, its shores lined with elegantly concise Lombardy poplars, housed a magnificent Romanesque villa, its ramparts crowned with sun-baked red tile.

Burnleigh opened the suitcase and Thorne heard a muffled clink. Trevor had his full attention.

Out came a bottle of Lambrusco. Purchased from Madame last night at Le Cheval Noir while Nick was in the loo, it was crisply chilled by the high Simplon air.

"Saving this for just such an emergency," said Burnleigh, producing a corkscrew and two proper wine glasses.

"It's genius!" Thorne exclaimed.

In triumph Burnleigh poured, the ruby liquid frothing giddily. He passed Nick his with a, "*Cin-cin.*"

"Mud in your *occhio*..." Thorne beamed back.

The wine was fresh, full, bright as ripe strawberries. They strolled onto the dock and sat, the bottle between them, gazing at the lake's gleam.

"Rah-*ther*..." said Burnleigh with a gap-toothed Terry-Thomas leer.

Time streamed by, no need of talk. There would be other days like this...a few.

When the time came, Burnleigh refilled the glasses.

Thorne's eye was on the farthest horizon. "I have a question."

"By all means," Burnleigh said, sipping Lambrusco.

"You know what I told you at dinner about Tony and Angela suddenly making everything right after the crash?" He had detailed not only the crash but the Devanes' earlier bitter infighting. "Can we believe it?"

"What, that they love each other? Certainly they do."

"No, no--the rapprochement? Is it real?"

"Well, I don't know," Trevor said. "Getting a glimpse of the end can change things."

"So you believe it is."

"You don't?"

"No idea," Thorne said. "I thought I was beginning to understand them, but I'm back to wondering if they're the crazy ones or is it me?"

Trevor nodded. "Reading the surface you'll never know, they're too good at the game. If you watch Becky and me, you stand a fair chance of seeing how things really stand--we're just people. But with Angela and Tony and the way they live, constantly in the limelight, what you see is definitely not what you get."

Nick nodded, his eye on the horizon. The World Champion was an alpha male—-and Angela was the compendium of female power. Beyond her beauty she had something more, an irresistible mind...or had he lost all perspective?

Yes, he had.

But one thing he knew--her presence transformed men. They didn't merely defer to her, they were compelled to win her.

It exhausted him thinking about them. They were the most commanding figures he had ever known and he meant to understand them. They made choices that were forever beyond others. They lived with risks and penalties few could endure...they were too exotic by half. The wise course was to stand well back--but his infatuation with Angela made it impossible.

Out of nowhere, Burnleigh said it: "She's making a movie, you know."

Thorne looked at him. "So?"

"It's still a secret."

"It's great!"

"It's not great," Burnleigh said. "It's terrible."

"Why!"

"It would be great to anyone else. Not Tony. It's out of the question."

"Which is why it's a secret."

Burnleigh gazed across the water. "If she gets entangled with 'that movie crowd,' he says, their marriage is over and done."

"He doesn't trust her."

"We already know that. He doesn't trust her for the most compelling of reasons--the weakness we dread in others is the one out of control in ourselves. He believes she wants to cheat because he keeps cheating on her."

The lake lapped at the pilings.

"But there's no changing Tony...."

Burnleigh finished his Lambrusco with a flourish as if applying the final brushstroke to a masterpiece.

"I ask again," said Thorne, "...is the reconciliation real?"

"It's irrelevant. They love each other. The only question is, do they love each other more than they love making war?"

CHAPTER 20

THE JAGUAR DROVE THROUGH the front entrance, its tires popping on the raked white pea gravel of legendary Villa d'Este. Two doormen in livery rushed forward in greeting.

"*Benvenuti, signori, alla Villa d'Este,*" beamed the more senior of them.

This dream of Thorne's showed no sign of fading....

At Berkeley he had read and reread the great Henry N. Manney's reports of European racing weekends like this one. Once or twice during the long season, for reasons of convenience, tradition and sheer indulgence, all the teams chose to stay at the same hotel. It fascinated Thorne to ponder how these rare creatures would behave among each other. Were there jealousies? Grudges? Unexpected friendships? Could they set aside self-interest long enough to admire the elegance of each other's plumage? He would see.

The teams convened in this hallowed spot for the best of reasons--Villa d'Este was nonpareil. A High Renaissance palazzo built in the 16th century by a cardinal, it had been home to an endless succession of royals, dukes, marquis, baronets, Napoleons, Garbos and Rockefellers. On Como's western shore in Cernobbio, it was set amid lavish formal gardens. Its long winding walkways led past fine statuary. Its splendor and exclusivity were matched only by its agreeable proximity to Autodromo Monza, a distance south.

Burnleigh released the Jaguar's rear hatchdoor and Nick reached for his bag--but the doorman swooped in.

"*Permesso, signore.* I can?"

"Thank you."

At the front desk Thorne identified himself, prepared to explain they were guests of Mr. Devane. Before he began, two room keys were produced and the desk bell rung.

"We are pleased to have you with us, *signori*," said the well-clipped man behind the desk. "You will find your luggage waiting in your rooms."

"*Grazie*," Thorne said.

They hadn't even been asked for their passports. Across Europe passports were always held the first night--not at Villa d'Este.

Another man in livery stepped forward to take their room keys from the concierge.

"Please to follow me, sirs."

They passed through a towering frescoed main salon, their guide's heels clicking smartly on gleaming marble. They were ushered into an ornate elevator..."lift" in the patois. Adorned with intricate inlaid hardwoods of countless hues, its filigreed extravagance put Thorne in mind of a meticulously made Oriental jewel box on a monumental scale. The door closed with suitable creaking. They ascended ensconced in Italianate elegance with but one motive, to amuse and delight.

Their rooms, next to one another, faced east. Thorne crossed immediately to his floor-to-ceiling balcony window and opened the doors. A dazzling view of Como and the far shore in late-afternoon light met his eye. Morning sun would warm and cheer the room. Now it was in deep shade. Perfection.

He ducked his head out, gripping the wrought-iron railing, his senses engorged. In the same moment the doors to his left swung open and Burnleigh's head popped out. Thorne's brows waggled energetically. Burnleigh laughed.

There were no true secrets in motor racing, only faster and slower branches of the grapevine. But nearly every rumor bore some relation to the truth. Thorne was not surprised, therefore, at the first substantive remark out of Jake Austin's mouth.

Burnleigh and he were sipping Cinzanos by the pool overlooking the lake when Austin appeared. Mentioning his surprise at bumping into "these two bottom-feeders," Austin said the new Porsche's 4.9 had oil-seal problems.

"Nice to see you, too, Jake," smiled Burnleigh expansively.

"Then, you're really staying here?" said Austin. "Amazing how far a little cheap notoriety goes...all the way to the Villa."

"Two first-class rooms, old man," Burnleigh stipulated. "With a right view of the lake." He pointed to the third-floor balconies. "Mine's the one with the hanging laundry."

"Is it true about the oil leaks?" Austin persisted.

"Was a week ago," Thorne said. "We're going to the track for our credentials. You coming?"

"Why not?"

Burnleigh frowned. "You'll ride on the roof, then, we've only two seats."

Austin groaned. "You brought the Jaguar."

Burnleigh smiled.

"Fiat loaned me a shitbox 128," Austin said. "Wanna race?"

"It goes without saying."

They climbed four flights of concrete steps to the very top at the rear of the main Art Deco Monza grandstand. The landing was windswept, scraps of paper and dust swirling on vortices. At the far end they saw a knot of jostling people all gesturing and barking like commodities traders in a crashing market. At the center, protected only by a flimsy folding card table, his back literally against the wall, stood a very small, very dark man with round smoke-tinted glasses. He shook his head back and forth, back and forth, in animated conversation with himself.

Thorne's eye slid to Burnleigh. In Britain an orderly queue would form waiting for the gallows.

"Buck up, mate," Trevor beamed. "You're always saying you're going to make good things happen--now's our chance."

Burnleigh strode straight into the melee one step behind Jake Austin.

And there was hope. Hardly daring to look up, the short dark man behind the card table took a letter from someone. Glanced at it without looking. Issued a pit pass. One letter at a time, a glance without looking, the Fellini-esque sacrament was repeated.

And looking on the bright side, Thorne decided the shouting and shoving served to pass the time. He let himself be ingested by the scrum. Gradually peristalsis inched them forward. Austin broke the tape first and handed the little man a letter from his magazine. Immediately he signaled to Burnleigh and Thorne to pass their letters forward, laying them on the table. He lifted three fingers--and regretted it. Some fundamental rubric of moral rectitude had been breached. The little man erupted suddenly at Austin in a white fury of hand gestures and grand opera indignation. Austin tried to explain and multilingual miscommunication blossomed, neither man understanding the other. Burnleigh waded in to clarify the broth--soon yelling at operatic volume himself. Each failed exchange added heat and fuel, when--

Jozie Joubert appeared.

In arpeggios of fluent Italian, Jozie nodded first to Austin, then to Burnleigh, last to Thorne. Thorne caught two references--to Ehra-Lessien and Tony Devane. The crowd went reverently still. Finishing his summation, Joubert presented Thorne with a long narrow Manila envelope. It was pliable and judging by its thickness and weight, it contained a good deal more than paper.

Thorne opened it and withdrew the gleaming red-leather armband of IRPA--the International Racing Press Association. It was the universal European racing credential.

Ahhhhhhs rose all around.

"We thought you should like to have this," Joubert smiled to Thorne, replacing his pipe between his yellow teeth with a *click*.

Beaming extravagantly now, the press officer bowed--an important luminary participating in this historic moment. Ceremoniously he bestowed upon Thorne his personal Monza Press/Photo credential--now completely redundant given Thorne's red-leather armband.

Bowing effusively just the same, he now bestowed upon Burnleigh and Austin their own Monza Press/Photo credentials. With that the seas parted. Those nearest Thorne clapped him on the back with a heartfelt *bravissimo!*

"*Grazie tanto*," he smiled all around like a victorious politican.

Joubert led them to the stairs with his sturdiest salamander grin. "Let this be a lesson...when saving a life--make it a World Champion."

CHAPTER 21

HE LEANED ON THE BALCONY railing gazing out at late afternoon. Deep violet painted the shore, earth's shadow leaning across the lake to the eastern shore, aquamarine melding to black glass. At the pool deck below the window a huge green-and-yellow-striped canopy, open on all sides, had been erected. Waiters in formal uniforms with double rows of brass buttons were spreading linen tablecloths upon five large circular dining tables. Elaborate floral arrangements wer set at their centers.

"Trevor--" said Thorne just loud enough to be heard through Burnleigh's open balcony door. Burnleigh's head popped out. Thorne nodded to the green-and-yellow canopy.

"I smell Jiggs Prouty."

Then his phone rang. He ducked in to answer.

"Welcome to La Bella Italia." It was Angela's smoky voice. "Are you and Trevor in and safe?"

"My God, what a place!"

"Rather splendid, no?"

"How's Tony?"

"Fearfully well. He wanted to be sure you knew about dinner."

"We just saw out the window...you're spoiling us."

"We hope so. Everybody will be there, Ferrari people and some from Alfa Romeo. A little before eight."

"Super."

She rang off and he felt the lightness of talking to her--mawkish twit.

He returned to the window. "You know about dinner?"

Burnleigh nodded to the tent, "This is us?"

"With bells. That was Angela."

Burnleigh's smile diminished minutely.

Thorne moved on as if not noticing.

"I say we go downstairs and locate something with a lime in it."

They ducked back into their rooms.

Nick opened his ornately painted antique armoire and drew out a Burberry's summer-tweed jacket and tan slacks, the best he had. Motor racing was scrupulously informal. He hoped he had enough nice clothes for this desperately nice weekend.

Minutes later he tapped Burnleigh's front door. Trevor wore a double-breasted blue blazer and regimental-stripe tie, a not-bad page out of Esquire.

"Can I peek?" Thorne said stepping into Burnleigh's room. "Good grief, is every room different!"

"That's how the Eye-ties do things...can't organize a queue to save their life, but their style'll knock your eye out."

They strolled along the high-ceilinged hallway towards the lift. Its inlaid wooden door opened, creaking like a comfy old rocking chair.

They descended, eager for what evening might offer.

"When bigger tabs are rung up," said Jiggs Prouty of the brightly striped tent, "I'll do the ringing."

"Utterly fab!" Angela beamed, satisfying the conventions. "And just you wait until Monaco!"

"Ja," Breitemann grinned. "Jiggs has leased the Mediterranean."

The fifty at the five tables laughed.

Prouty raised his glass. "To a safe race."

"Hear, hear," said Burnleigh.

In glowing candlelight all glasses tipped.

Formalities dispensed with, pent-up conversation gushed. The primo *piatto* was a superb *risotto alla marinara*. Dinner proceeded seamlessly, the last trace of twilight lingering. By *zuppa inglese*--custard with spongecake soaked in liqueur--the last-quarter moon cast a bluish glow on the water, the lake lapping pleasingly at the villa's ancient stone bulwarks.

Joubert treated the table to a hilarious rendering of *le tre imbecilli inglesi*, Nick, Burnleigh and Austin, debating the meaning of life with *Autodromo Monza's* famously out-of-his-depth press chief Dottore Imanuelle Montefino. The good doctor did not fare well.

Hugh J.K. Breeland, neck in a brace and arm in a massive cast after his crash at the Nürburgring, cackled so painfully he begged Joubert to stop, his recovery would be set back a month. Representative of the breed, he found it impossible to stay away from racing even one weekend. Throughout dinner Mary Breeland contentedly sliced his dinner to bite-size pieces.

93

Next to Mary Breeland was Ferrari's Grand Prix star Jean Garand with his beautiful, and by the look of it teenage, Belgian amour, Ghislaine. Garand himself was a very "young" twenty-three, peering out at the world with youthful mischief. He and Ghislaine looked well together.

Dante Ruggiero and the diminutive Luciana (Nick had learned her surname was Podesta) sat beside Garand. And Burnleigh was right, without the big sunglasses she was a stunner.

Nick was curious to see how Devane and Breitemann would interact. Breitemann could easily have sat at a different table, but that was not the racer's way. He sat directly across from Devane. They were scrupulously civil and why not? Devane seemed a changed man. In constant pain, he moved stiffly, limiting all movement that threatened to disturb his ribcage. But his demeanor was genial, relaxed, in enormous and some indefinable way relieved. He even looked different--younger and more gallant. The storms within had ceased and the skies cleared. His conversation, while always intense, located the pleasure in whatever was said.

Watching Devane and his wife tonight, she more glamorous than ever, it seemed they exemplified exactly what Angela had spoken of so despairingly at Ehra-Lessien--they had "everything."

The fact that two of the four Porsche lead drivers, Breeland and Devane, had suffered life-threatening crashes within a week and a half came in for discussion. And Breeland noted superstitiously that bad things came in threes.

"Then, I am next?" said Breitemann.

"Don't you say that!" Angela snapped hotly.

There was an awkward moment. The previous spring a driver was killed on the same weekend of the month four months' running. On the fourth month Nick waited for the Monday paper to learn who had died, and was promptly informed.

Breeland's Nürburgring test session had been going well, he said, and he was pushing his Surtees hard on the 17-mile, 187-turn German circuit to get a fast lap in before the rain. But arriving at a blind corner on dry-weather slicks the heavens opened. The car aquaplaned and he flew up the bank at a tree.

"A good job my arm hit the tree and not my head. But then the bloody *Boche*--" He glanced at Breitemann. "Sorry, old man, but they really were unforgivable...didn't get to me for above ten minutes. I was pinned in the car, the fuel filler neck cracked and raw petrol running down over my shoulder into the cockpit--Blimey."

Garand listened, his boyish eyes luminous.

"Rain diluting the petrol was all that saved me, otherwise g'night, all."

Mary Breeland stared at her plate.

"We must start a club, Hugh," Devane proposed, "The Medium-Rare

Boys. Yours happened a day before mine, so you're president."

"Ghoulish notion," Angela said.

Devane smiled.

"Imagine what racing would be like without fire," Thorne said.

"Wouldn't be racing," Joubert said.

"I'd take it," said Devane.

After dessert cigars and liqueur were served. Garand and his beautiful Ghislaine wandered off for a moonlit lovers' stroll by the lake. Devane excused himself as well. He had no taste for cigars or liqueur, he said, he craved a soft pillow.

"That's where I come in," said Angela.

"No, no, luv, you stay here and enjoy yourself. I'll be fine."

"Certainly not."

His head shook. "Stay--I mean it. Without you these sods will get into a pub brawl and tomorrow's a track day."

His steady eye confirmed it.

Burnleigh smiled at Angela. "We need your civilizing influence."

Angela bowed graciously.

Devane bent stiffly at the knees, gave his wife a peck on the cheek and walked off to the palazzo. The table was quiet.

"Can he do it?" said Joubert.

"Drive?" Angela said. "Says he can. And if he says it, he bloody will."

"No confusing this with badminton," Thorne observed. It gave him an inadmissible pleasure. He was glad this was not some stick-and-ball game...he *had* to be here.

The conversation turned to who shopped where and bought what. Breitemann meanwhile drew peacefully on his cigar. "So tell me about America, Nick."

"Come and see for yourself."

"I hope to do this."

"Do I hear a Can-Am driving deal in the making?" Joubert inquired.

"Oh, no, no," Breitemann laughed, "...you must not get me in problems with Chubby." It was racing's whispered nickname for the gently broadening Colin Chapman, founding genius at Lotus, Breitemann's team in Formula One.

"But I can say," he said, "I would not mind seeing what an 800-horsepower Can-Am car feels like."

Thorne gave him a knowing nod.

"*Ja?*"

Thorne grinned. "Definitely *ja!*"

Breitemann's eye moved then to Angela, Luciana, and Mary Breeland. "But surely we are able to talk of something other than racing."

"Can't be done," said Angela.

"*Ma certo,*" Luciana said, "there is very much more to talk about--the beauty of the night, the pleasure of talking to fine people, so much more. Have you ever noticed there are no children at racing?"

"Very true," Burnleigh said.

"Never children at racing..." she repeated in her lavish Turinese accent. "Why not?"

"Many racers have children and families--" Angela began.

"*Si,* but they are never brought to the racing! It is something bad...they must be kept away."

Ruggiero, with limited English, had spoken to Luciana exclusively during the meal. Now he put up his hand, quelling her.

"No, no, Dante," Breitemann said, "Luciana is right. The children do not come. I came to racing when I was very young, but my father was not a driver--it is different."

"Why different?" Luciana retorted. Her tone indicated a strong opinion.

Breitemann laughed softly. "It is not very nice to say."

"Tell us, Christian," Angela said.

"If I am raising up a child," he said, "I should not want him spending his time in the company of people like me. I should not like my child learning how to live from people who must always force themselves ahead of all the others. Raising up a child is too serious for that."

"Rubbish," Breeland said.

"I should not want my child to believe success must come at the expense of all the other children."

"Everyone lives that way," Breeland scoffed, "...it's natural!"

"But few do it as a profession."

"You believe that?" Thorne said.

"I love to race," Christian said. "As you see, it is my life. But I easily can see there are other ways to live, perhaps better ways."

Nick wanted to explore his meaning--but Angela's beatific smile as Breitemann spoke stopped him cold. He was jealous.

"It is as if--" Breitemann stopped. "What is it when a horse runs at top speed?"

"Gallop," Angela said.

He nodded. "Racing is like a galloping horse. Everyone would like to ride it a little while--but few want to spend all of life galloping, that is too extreme."

Suddenly, Luciana buried her face in her hands, turning away.

"Luciana, dear," Angela said immediately, "are you all right?"

Ruggiero put his hand on her arm, but she pushed him away.

Angela got up and came to her. "It's all right, Dante, let me."

He looked away and she bent forward, whispering to Luciana too quietly to be overheard.

Luciana nodded. Angela said something more. She straightened then and smiled.

"We're going for a walk. I expect you lot can entertain yourselves."

Luciana came to her feet. Arm in arm she and Angela walked slowly towards the lakeside. Their footsteps on the gravel faded in the night.

Heartened in her marriage and prospects, and recognizing in Luciana a woman who could claim neither, Angela initiated a friendship that Villa d'Este night that against all odds broadened and deepened. One of them from Porsche, the other from Ferrari, neither was inclined towards close friendships with women. Yet this seeming impediment only tempered and toughened their alliance.

CHAPTER 22

RAW FLAME LIKE SUN-FIRED DIAMONDS blinded him.
Warping and leaping, its heat sudden and complete, he heard screeching
    far away...
    in a dream.
    Mustn't move--don't breathe.
    Arms against sides, legs together
    safe!
    The stubby Formula One windscreen sagged
    buckled.
    Don't move... dreaming calm--
    but a sharp fang tore his neck
    GetOutGetOutGetOutGetOut!
    He struggled hard, pinned in--
    the belts!
    He punched the quick-release, legs running in place, going
    ...nowhere.
    Squirming in eyeless glare, back and up and back,
    the hip-tight cockpit clutching him--
    Jesus-Jesus...not breathe!
    he burst free--
    neck and wrist shrieking.
    He rolled out and out and down away. They closed on him like wolves,
whipped foam slathering over his scorched-rag stench.
    Breathe!
    He gasped in, the air too huge to take, when--
    catastrophically

he experienced
pristine perfect
pain--

In high broiling Milanese sun Raymond Beacom looked more cadaverous than ever. He ducked into the shadows behind the Monza pits before practice, conversing darkly with Peter Whitlaw and chief engineer Ian Swallow. In spite of suspect oil seals, one of his Porsches, for Breitemann and Alex Winter, would use the new 4.9-liter engine. Covering his bets, the Devane/Dinesen car would rely on the trusty 4.5-liter.

Porsche-Austria had split its assets as well. Rudi Stringert would have a 4.9, the second car the 4.5. The latter would be driven by short-fused New Zealander Owen Piggot, replacing the injured Breeland. Piggot was fawned over by the British press despite the fact that at the previous year's Monaco Grand Prix he was so busy shaking a fist at a driver ahead, he crashed at Ste. Devote. Such intemperance in a Frenchman or Italian would have earned scalding censure.

By early afternoon the Porsche engine strategy went up the spout. Breitemann's 4.9 set fastest lap and promptly joined Stringert's 4.9 in the paddock, both engines with oil leaks. Beacom ordered Breitemann's engine replaced by a 4.5. Under the fierce glare of Dr. Manfred Fabius Porsche-Austria would labor all night to repair and modify its 4.9. Of the four Porsche 917s only Stringert's had the big engine, a profound advantage at Monza's 230-mile per hour speeds.

Technological drama aside, Team Beacom was a portrait of tranquility. In some strange way Devane's injuries suited him. When not in the cockpit he smiled sunnily, talking to anyone with anything germane to say. When the time came he struggled down into the cockpit, enduring terrible pain with stoic calm. And he was in top form. His lap times with the 4.5 were within four-tenths of a second of Breitemann's time with the 4.9. Only Breitemann and the 4.9-liter Garand Ferrari outqualified him. Stringert's 4.9 Porsche was a disappointing five-tenths behind Devane, who looked every inch the Champion.

Thorne had seen little of Angela at the track. Then Friday noon he came upon her and Luciana behind the Ferrari transporters. He realized only too late that he was intruding. Luciana smiled brightly nonetheless. Despite direct sun she wore no big sunglasses now. The beauty of her smile transformed her face...but standing next to Angela she was a rose beside an orchid.

"What are you two cooking up?" he said

"Wouldn't you love to know," said Angela.

"I think I would."

Luciana's smile was unshakeable. "He is harmless, I think."

"Tante grazie," he bowed.

What he wouldn't give to learn the hard-won confidences passing between these women.

"Haven't you got someplace to be?" Angela said with a smirk.

He smiled hugely, covering his retreat.

"I daresay we've offended him," she said.

He winked heading towards Matra. It was a relief to be back in the manageable masculine world of camshafts and pistons and internal combustion.

Autodromo Monza made no pretense of presenting twisting hill-and-dale "road" racing. In the 1920s its designers had one object--sustained top speed. Like Montlhéry near Paris and the old Avusring in Berlin, the track combined a ground-level course with high-speed curved banking. But Monza went a step farther. On each lap the cars raced around the lambshank-shaped ground-level course past the grandstands and spiraled up into the banking to pass the grandstands a second time, doubling spectator enjoyment each lap.

But the risks of sustained top-speed racing were severe. In 1933 three greats, Campari, Borzacchini and Czaykowski, died in one afternoon. By 1970, after decades of weathering, the banking was far too rough for modern racing speeds, but the ground-level circuit remained smooth, wide and blindingly fast. It had just seven turns, three of them extremely fast doglegs. Only Curva Grande, the pair of ninety-degree Lesmo Curves and the 180-degree South Curve interrupted the track's top-gear progress. At maximum velocity the cars "slipstreamed" each other like American stock cars, gathering speed in the shadow of the car ahead, then slingshotting past--to become vulnerable to the same overtaking strategy themselves. Cars passed and repassed at top speed constantly until one or two broke free.

Thorne lay in his canopied Villa d'Este bed in the dark before the race trying to visualize how it would be. Excitement and something darker swirled in his head. Butterflies in the stomach the night before a race were not new, but he'd never felt so personally invested. Long ago he had fantasized being personally involved in racing, but this was no fantasy. He was inextricably "inside." His palm ran over the mahogany Villa d'Este bedstead, back and forth, back and forth as if polishing the surface. Sleep was impossible. He must endure the expectation of...what? His pulse drummed in his ears. Tonight would be long.

And tomorrow would be resolved at 235 miles per hour in flashes of Ferrari red, brooding Alfa Romeo maroon, French Matra blue...with

Beacom's brilliant orange and Porsche-Austria's white and blue.

He tried to picture it and couldn't. Defeating a rival at 235 miles an hour, by inches--it was more than judgment or skill...it was destiny.

CHAPTER 23

AN HOUR BEFORE THE START THORNE was talking to Passini, Ferrari's team manager. Heat waves shimmered on the cars' red fiberglass, fragile as eggshell, capable of prodigal violence. Bespectacled and professorial, Passini listened, nodding. He had nerves like a tuning fork, his eye darting to and fro, with cause. At this quintessentially Italian race Ferrari must win. *Il Commendatore* (Enzo Ferrari preferred the title *Ingegnere*, Engineer) had hired two brilliant past-Ferrari Grand Prix stars, Chris Amon from New Zealand and British World Champion on both motorcycles and in F1 John Surtees. And there was cause for optimism. Three months before at Daytona the five-liter Ferrari 512S had serious aerodynamic lift at speed and enough drag to neutralize its 4.9 engine's power advantage over the 4.5-liter Porsche. Immediately the Ferraris began sprouting chin spoilers and aerodynamic tabs to reduce lift. Now they had a new anti-lift nose and vastly less drag. They were ready.

Speaking to Passini Thorne kept an eye on Jennifer Whelan. She was shooting the Ferrari pits--but then she turned and began shooting him with Passini. He was flattered. No one took pictures of writers.

Passini was taking his *domani, domani* time disclosing Ferrari's improved aerodynamics--when Dante Ruggiero suddenly arrived. In rapid-fire Italian he asked something about Luciana--Thorne couldn't make it out.

Passini replied with an Italianate shrug--who knows!

But Thorne took a stab.

"Luciana was in the paddock ten minutes ago."

"Paddock?" Ruggiero said.

"Ten minutes ago. Back there."

Thorne pointed to the Ferrari transporter.

"Ah. *La Signora* Devane."

Thorne shook his head: "Alone."

Seeing this interruption as his cue, Passini turned quickly and began barking orders to his crew--interview over. The Ferrari mechanics nodded tiredly. It had been another all-nighter.

Jennifer Whelan smiled at Thorne. Her Nikon rewinding a roll of film made a precision mechanical whine. In bright sun her red hair glinted like spun glass.

"So..." she said, "learn anything?"

He grinned.

"No?"

"What are you doing in the pits?" he said. "I thought you'd be out along the course for the start."

"I'm shooting the pits for once," she said. "Angela is looking for you."

"Probably needs career advice."

Jennifer giggled. "She does cast a spell."

She lost him with that.

"Now and then," she said, "she should give the rest of us a chance."

"I doubt you need it. And where is Mr. Ludgate this weekend?"

She laughed caustically. "Is that what you think?"

Again she lost him.

"But naïve is okay," she concluded.

"I have no idea what you mean."

She busied herself loading another roll of film. "You're probably right, with a bit of luck I'll find a lover just like Lionel, well-dressed, powerful, rich, homosexual."

She spun on her heel beaming over her shoulder.

"We must do this again."

He struggled with his thoughts. Ludgate? No wonder...all the high-profile *tête à têtes* with drivers. In London he even wandered off with Devane!

No, that was ridiculous. And Ludgate's relationship with Jennifer is the bane of every self-respecting heterosexual. He was the escort society women hire to show them off--"a walker."

In the next pit Jennifer zigzagged through the four sleek Alfa Romeo T33-3 prototypes, shooting as she went. Thorne followed the line of her tight-fitting black gabardines. It had been a while. And Jeff, his friend at home, always said he was blind to women who showed an interest. He hadn't seen a better pair of gabardines in a long time.

The cars were being pushed to the starting grid under a broiling sun. Thorne wore the new Blue Streak baseball cap Charlie at Goodyear gave him. He met Angela's eye. "You called?"

"Not me." She gestured to her husband, behind her.

Thorne nodded. "How are the prime ribs today?"

"They're there," Devane said drawing him aside. "I want you to do something for me."

Angela drifted off and Devane reached into the breast pocket of his driver's suit. He drew out a globule of metal the size of an apricot pit and handed it to Thorne. "Keep this, will you?"

Nick manipulated the metal. It was light as balsawood.

"Peter gave it to me," Devane said. "It's melted magnesium from a wheel at Ehra-Lessien."

"I don't understand."

The World Champion shook his head. "You don't have to."

Angela gazed off along the pits intently--waiting for a bus.

"Give it back to me after," Devane said. "Between us. Just give it back at the finish."

Nick studied the precious object in his palm, speechless.

CHAPTER 24

AT THE BLAZE OF HIGH NOON the green flag fell and three dozen race cars raged along the mile-long front straight. Legions of Ferrari *tifosi* in the grandstands across from the pits bawled their pagan wrath. The weaving roaring centipede vanished in the distance....

In a minute and a half they streamed into view again on the front straight. The hazards of racing wheel-to-wheel at peak speed appalled Thorne. Every swerve invited chain-reaction catastrophe. It took an act of will to hold his eye on them, but when he did, he'd never seen anything so exciting.

Breitemann led from the pole, Garand's Ferrari tucked in behind. The remaining six big Porsche 917s and Ferrari 512s were a swarm dueling furiously for third. Then came the three-liter Alfa Romeos, Matras and private Porsche 908s running three and four abreast.

Finally an endless stream of G.T. cars spred out over half a mile.

On the second lap Garand's 50-horsepower advantage pulled him ahead of Breitemann's 4.5--and his slipstream pulled Devane ahead with him.

On lap three the order was Devane, Breitemann, Garand, Surtees, Piggot and Amon...and a lap later, Breitemann, Garand, Amon, Devane, Stringert, Surtees...the order meaningless. It reshuffled randomly every lap. In ten laps no driver led two laps in a row. The first seven cars were covered by just three seconds.

At lap 14 Stringert's big-engined Porsche retook the lead from Breitemann. Garand, Devane and Amon fought three-wide for third--but now it changed. Stringert's 4.9 began to pull away and Breitemann tucked in an arm's length behind. The two cut a long sleek tunnel in the wind. On the strength of Stringert's 600 horsepower they began inching away. In two laps they separated from the pack.

At horrific closing speeds Stringert and Breitemann knifed through complex knots of slow G.T. cars--mundane Ford Mustangs, Porsche 911Ss, Alfa Romeo GTVs. To the lead cars they were 160-mph hazards.

And inevitably, coming out of Lesmo Curve, hot-tempered Owen Piggot's Porsche-Austria Porsche 917 was cut off by a slow Porsche 911S. They touched. Spun off at ferocious speed. Piggot clouted the guardrail, dust and corruption boiling up. His right-rear wheel jutted off at a zany angle, his race over. He had to be restrained, just as inevitably, from punching the 911S driver.

Moments later Surtees' Ferrari blew a tire and fell out of the lead group.

Breitemann slipstreamed Stringert brilliantly all the while a car-length back. Garand, Amon and Devane were twenty lengths behind.

Breitemann applied constant pressure to the bigger-engined Porsche as though they were equal. On lap 24, running nose to tail, they put up a lap time in 1:24.8--average speed, 151.68 miles per hour. It was the fastest lap of the race and Monza's all-time record. It would remain so--five miles per hour above the fastest Formula One time put up in that September's Italian Grand Prix.

But the very next lap, harried tirelessly by Breitemann, Stringert overshot his shutoff point entering the fast Curva Parabolica. Carrying too much speed, he veered wide. Before he could regain his line Breitemann shot ahead. With more horsepower Stringert could regain lost ground on the straights, but Breitemann's mastery in the blindingly fast turns was fully a match for the power deficit. By tiny increments--impossibly--Breitemann pulled away.

Eleven seconds behind, the battle for third was bitter, each car doing everything it could to frustrate all others. This infighting slowed the entire group. Thorne needed to remain impartial--but Breitemann's brilliance was measurable on the chronometer...and he could measure it as surely in his breathless chest.

At the first round of pit stops Breitemann waved off co-driver Alex Winter. Stringert waved off his co-driver also, determined to regain the lead. The Beacom crew got Breitemann out of the pits five seconds ahead of Stringert.

Devane pitted two laps later in fourth. Conscious of the nugget of magnesium in his pocket, Thorne tried to imagine the pain in Devane's cracked ribs. The moment he did he forced it out of his mind.

Ferrari was due in the pits. Thorne hurried there--and it was madhouse. All three Ferraris came in at once, crewmen squeezing between the stopped cars. They bumped into each other lugging full fuel cans. The cars had been fast and consistent, running third, fifth and sixth, but in this melee Devane roared by on the front straight, overtaking the stopped Garand for third.

On the track again it took Garand sixteen laps to catch and re-pass the gallant Devane for third. The order was Breitemann and Stringert...then Garand and Devane...finally the Ferraris of Amon and Surtees.

Stringert's 4.9 continued to attack Breitemann, but whenever he came close, he would misstep and fall back. Breitemann never put a wheel wrong. For an hour the race settled into three well-spaced groups--before Stringert's left-rear tire blew in Curva Grande. He rode it out at 180 miles an hour without hitting anything, but on the way around to the pits the disintegrating tire battered his engine oil catch-tank to pieces. He was out. Breitemann led alone.

At Breitemann's next pit stop Alex Winter took over. Breitemann's frustration at surrendering the car spoke volumes, but the rules dictated it. And during the tire change the crew had trouble with the right-rear hub nut. Ermanno leapt over the wall for a new one. The car lost forty seconds. Breitemann's lead on Garand became a nine-second deficit.

Winter blasted out of the pits and fought to keep the Ferrari in sight on the long straightaways, but he could not shorten the gap. War cries rose from the grandstand, yellow-and-red banners with Ferrari's black prancing horse waving in the Italian sun...*Forza Ferrari!*

Breitemann wiped his face with a towel.

"I think I make more sweating when I am out of the car!"

He took a swallow of San Pellegrino.

"There is nothing really to say," he said. "The car is good, the handling is very good--and Ferrari leads. Life is not perfect."

"What about the lack of power?" Austin said.

"You can see! Stringert catches me on the straight and coming off the turns--nothing I could do. The one chance is to stay in his slipstream when I am behind or get very far ahead. It will be the same now with the Ferrari."

"But you stayed ahead!" Thorne said.

"Our car stops better," Breitemann said, "and corners better for the same reason--it is light. An interesting competition, I think, their engine against our chassis. But I hate this waiting!"

He wiped his face.

"And how I would love a 4.9!"

"You're not tired?" Burnleigh said.

"I am never tired in a race car. Well, maybe at Le Mans after 24 hours."

The Ferrari passed, its loud V-12 holding Winter at bay.

Breitemann eyed Peter Whitlaw.

"Still nine seconds," the unsmiling team manager said. "Identical."

"Alex is extraordinary," Breitemann smiled.

Whitlaw frowned. "Not extraordinary enough."

Winter pitted at the third hour. Trying everything to gain on the Ferrari he had overheated his tires, degrading his handling. He lost seven more seconds. Struggling up out of the cockpit he yanked off his helmet, red-faced and weary.

"Hot 'nuff?" said Austin in his Missouri twang. Winter's eyes rolled.

"No substitute for cubic inches," Thorne said, sympathizing with Winter.

Winter gulped water as Breitemann roared away.

And Ferrari was about to pit again. Nick walked in their direction.

After a short driving stint co-driver Luiseño Pasarell brought Garand's car in solidly in the lead. Four tires went on. Fuel cans were lugged to the refueling necks at the sides of the windshield. Garand climbed in. But in the haste of refueling gasoline had spilt underneath the car. When Garand started the V-12 sheets of flame engulfed the car's right side.

Garand shut off and sprang out. Two crewmen lunged for an extinguisher and knocked each other down. A third grabbed it and rushed to the car. Garand himself leaped over the wall for another extinguisher. Thick white foam gushed over the gorgeous red body. In seconds the blaze was out, but now the car had to be cleared of foam and the windshield cleaned. Garand got back in, his youthful face grim.

He blared onto the track just as Breitemann streamed past--a full lap ahead. It took fifteen minutes of maximum effort for Garand to pull his Ferrari up to the rear of the Porsche. But Breitemann was determined to keep his full one-lap advantage. He veered and weaved down the straightaways denying Garand his slipstream. On this wide track it was impossible to block, yet Breitemann kept the red car at bay for over an hour.

With five laps remaining, conserving his engine to ensure he finished, Breitemann let Garand by at last. Even then he tucked in close behind the Ferrari. The red-and-yellow flags in the stands waved doggedly, hoping Garand could miraculously unlap himself. Breitemann surrendered not an inch. He took the checkered flag, Garand second, exactly one lap behind.

In a 4.5-liter Porsche at Monza's ferocious speeds, no other driver could have controlled Jean Garand's 4.9-liter Ferrari. The Ferraris had been fast and reliable--they should have won. Instead they swept second through fourth. Devane was heroically fifth, after his co-driver spun at mid-race. Porsche had 33 championship points, Ferrari 21.

Angela cautioned Nick to stay close after the finish. It seemed a friendly gesture. It was far more.

Suddenly at the finish she yelled, "Come on!" and pulled him towards the Beacom garage. Cars continued around the track on the cool-off lap, but hordes of young Italians flooded out of the grandstand onto the track, running full speed to the pits. The Carabinieri made a half-hearted attempt to wave them back and were summarily overrun.

For protection, the cars were impounded behind the pits. The last ones had to swerve menacingly from side to side getting through the mob.

Thorne followed Angela into the windowless Beacom pit garage. All along the pits garage doors came crashing down. The Beacom door slammed shut and was bolted securely from the inside, but this only enfuriated the mob. Fists beat the stout wooden door like summer thunder. *La Ferrari* was beaten...and Porsche's villains cowered in their bunker!

Angela gave Nick a can-you-believe-it glint. Everyone had made it in, Beacom, Alex Winter, Austin, Burnleigh, most of the crew. Whitlaw and three crew were at the impound getting the cars safely in.

After several minutes the back door from the impound opened and in walked Devane, steadying himself on Whitlaw's arm. All cheered and applauded. He was ashen, his flameproofs black with perspiration. Looking at him sent a shock through Thorne.

Angela gave him a gentle kiss, her smile bleak with his pain.

He nodded to Beacom.

"Lads, give him a seat," Whitlaw ordered.

But Devane shook his head. "I don't think I've ever in my life so thoroughly enjoyed standing up!"

The warm laughter was compromised with concern.

Graham Tully, Devane's crew chief, brought a folding chair and San Pellegrino.

"That's the stuff," Devane enthused. "*Jeee-zus!*"

He looked at Angela, all breath escaping his lungs. "It's just as you say-- I should've been an accountant."

Another round of concerned laughter.

Raymond Beacom took charge. "Come along, old man, sit you down-- you're all in."

By painful degrees Devane lowered himself onto the chair.

"The hero of the day!" Beacom proclaimed to loud applause. "No doubt of it...."

"Fifth place," Devane said weakly, "...some hero."

"Hero of the day," Beacom repeated to vehement applause all around.

Devane smiled disconsolately.

The back door opened again and Breitemann came in--to another round of applause and cheers. Breitemann walked straight to Devane.

"Tony, how have you done it?"

"Finish fifth? I got beaten by four others!"

"Aww," Breitemann grinned hugely. "No, no, you are the Champion!"

"But you won."

Devane swallowed San Pellegrino.

Breitemann's head shook. "I could not have done it like you, there is no possibility."

Devane nodded dismissively. "Is there more water?"

"Tony needs water," Breitemann said.

Lord Blather, red-faced from the Monza sun, brought Devane and Breitemann San Pellegrino. Angela stood over Devane, her hand resting on his neck. His face was dark with fatigue and pain and something more. The others shook Breitemann's hand.

In the commotion around Breitemann, Devane beckoned Thorne.

"You have it, then?"

Nick reached into his pocket for the magnesium nugget.

"Good bloke."

"Absolutely remarkable," Thorne said.

Devane nodded.

"Absolutely fifth place."

CHAPTER 25

THORNE WAS IN HEAVEN. Elegant surroundings, perfect weather, European racers everywhere. At Sebring and Daytona he had seen them in the pits, but they seemed exotic and unapproachable. At Villa d'Este, as "the American," he was now the exotic bird.

During breakfast Breitemann organized a tennis foursome for doubles, himself, Thorne, Burnleigh and Dante Ruggiero. The hotel furnished the court, rackets and balls. Minutes later Thorne and Burnleigh came down dressed in khaki tropical shorts and tee-shirts. They would never pass as serious tennis players, but this was not serious tennis--until Dante Ruggiero appeared in blinding whites carrying his own brand-new Wilson.

Burnleigh gave Thorne a look. This was going to be funny.

The luck of the draw teamed Thorne with Ruggiero, a good thing. Ruggiero won two games before either Breitemann or Burnleigh returned a serve. Most players would sportingly lower their game to make it a contest-- but Ruggiero was a racer.

Still they and the gallery, Jennifer, Angela, Luciana Podesta and a half dozen more, enjoyed themselves at all costs. With each new service ace from Ruggiero, Breitemann and Burnleigh volleyed taunts about their opponents' lack of grace, doubtful hygiene and intimacies in the animal kingdom.

"Quiet, please," said Thorne. "Mr. Laurel serving to Mr. Hardy."

After an hour they were running low on insults. Ruggiero smiled thinly throughout as if somehow the joke were on him. He ensured it was. The combatants were drenched and panting. Over Ruggiero's protests the match was declared a draw. "Now," said Angela, "they would take consolation in a bit of lunch."

Showered and refreshed, Burnleigh and Thorne returned to the pool deck. The group awaiting them had broadened dramatically. At a dozen tables sat every notable in the World Championship of Makes. Raymond Beacom, Peter Whitlaw and Alex Winter were with Ferrari's Jean Garand and his dark-eyed Ghislaine. Thorne envied the couple their devotion to one another.

At the next table Ferrari drivers Pasarell and Fariano sat with Rudi Stringert and the injured Hugh J.K. Breeland. Not surprisingly Ruggiero joined this table. Luciana sat separately with Angela and Jennifer looking slightly ruffled. Had they had words about taking tennis too seriously?

One table was occupied entirely by drivers' wives--Thorne would've loved to listen in there. And the British press formed its own table, Christopher Garrett, wan and cringing, and Alastair Bissent--Lord Blather--manifesting unintentional self-satire.

Even Carnelian's executive vice president Lionel Ludgate, recently identified by Jennifer as "light in his loafers," turned up. The previous afternoon he arrived in the paddock at the race's midpoint, fashionably en retard. Now he sat with Jennifer, Angela, Breitemann and his mordant traveling secretary, the six-foot Vivian Biggs. She looked as if she'd swallowed a fly.

Angela waved Thorne and Burnleigh to two seats she'd saved for them.

"Mr. Ludgate!" Thorne said. "We thought we'd lost you this weekend."

"No, no. I wanted to see if the team could find their way to the front without me. They can."

Thorne sat between Angela and Jennifer. Burnleigh sat beyond Angela.

Ludgate turned to Jennifer now. "So you decided to give Paradise a chance."

She smiled.

"I told you to stay at the lake. Downtown Milan is all very well, but heaven is heaven, admit it."

She smiled. Nodded.

"Wait..." Burnleigh said, "I thought you said--"

"Trevor!" Nick barked. He smiled then, pointing to the bottle in front of Burnleigh. "Pass the wine, will you."

Trevor reached for the bottle, Angela's eye on Jennifer a moment too long.

Jennifer raised her wineglass. "Delicious, isn't it?"

"Usually is," Thorne said, not having tasted it yet. He poured his glass and refilled hers.

Angela picked up her bread, tore off a piece, set it on her plate without looking. Her eye was on the tablecloth, singleminded, transfixed, as if watching a tarantula.

Thorne and Jennifer ordered Insalata Nizza, served with a superb extra-virgin olive oil-rich vinaigrette, and Lionel Ludgate insisted on selecting for them an elegant white Orvieto.

Conversation returned again and again to the tennis travesty, enjoyed by all said Angela, except "*il Signore Napoleone.*" Thorne's eye slid to Ruggiero two tables away. Given Angela's closeness to Luciana, his lover, Thorne could only guess at the epithet's subtext.

The meal was almost finished when Devane reappeared. He had spent the morning lying down. He looked no better for his rest. Breitemann brought him a chair and everyone shifted their chairs noisily making room.

"You are in pain, Tony?" Breitemann inquired.

"I am fine."

Angela looked at Burnleigh without seeing him.

"I have pain-killers in my room," Breitemann said. "If you--"

"I've all the pills in the world, thank you. Is this our waiter? *Cameriere!*"

Angela shook her head and beckoned a different waiter.

Devane ordered a *caffelatte.*

"Congratulations on a truly noble drive, Tony," Ludgate said. "A prodigy of determination."

Devane nodded and asked what they had been doing.

Immediately Thorne, Burnleigh and Angela were stepping on each other's lines describing the tennis.

"A world first..." said Trevor, "a doubles match with one winner and three losers."

"Well, he's good at something..." Devane said.

"Be gracious, dear," Angela said.

Luciana Podesta's expression hid behind the big black sunglasses.

Ludgate smiled hugely at Angela now. "So tell me, my beauty, what are these rumors of a movie? Smashing idea!"

She smiled looking down at her plate. "Nothing, really."

"That's not what I've heard."

"Where on earth did you hear that?"

"It isn't true?"

"A wonderful idea!" Breitemann said immediately.

Her smile was hooded. "Nothing will come of it, trust me."

"But you must!" Breitemann enthused. "What kind of movie? What is the story?"

Thorne glanced at Devane. His expression was thunderous.

"A spy thriller," she said. "Set in Berlin--the usual tripe. I'd be terrible."

"You could not fail!" Breitemann looked around the table for agreement. "Would she not be excellent? You must do it!"

"She won't," said Devane.

"Why not?"

"She won't."

Breitemann turned to Thorne to understand.

"I want a stroll, Angela," Devane said.

"But your *caffelatte*...."

Devane rose. "Coming?"

Breitemann's smile died a slow death.

To hell with it, Thorne decided. Tony and his damn magnesium lump! In this ego-besotted profession some were thugs--he'd seen ample proof at home in the person of the All-American "hero" A.J. Pratt. But to date, Devane was his closest brush with the dark side. He meant to get to the heart of the sport, but from now on he would keep Devane at arm's length. In his anger, three words at the next table caught his ear: "Apollo 13 hoax."

It was Lord Blather. Thorne turned.

"Yes, yes, well, all of that is as it may be," nodded Alastair Bissent in his frothy nobody's-fool chortle. "But I shall tell you what I think--we're never going to know if a single bit of this twaddle is true. I mean, there's never been one scintilla of proof they even got to the moon, has there? For all we know, they could be playing out this entire charade on some bleeding Hollywood soundstage!"

"Come now, Alastair," someone objected.

"No-no-no-no, you listen...consider the source! I wouldn't put it past the Americans, not for an instant. The gap between what they say and what they do, is, well...look at Vietnam! You can't prove to me they've been anywhere near the moon! We see a noisy blast-off but how do we know what is really onboard! Days later this nasty great black thing is dangling from a parachute over the Pacific Ocean...or is it Santa Monica Bay?"

He chuckled.

"Could've dropped it from one of their bloody B-52's, we'd never know. You ask me, it was shot on a soundstage next to "Laugh-In" just to make the filthy Russkies look even more pathetic and unwashed than they already are." He laughed. "I'm not taken in, not for a minute."

Thorne's mood coalesced to something colder. "Alastair..." he said.

"What's that?"

"There is a bad odor at your table. I think you've stepped in something, or is it your mouth?"

"Well, I say..." Bissent said.

"You've already said, Alastair." Thorne stood. "Jennifer, let's have a walk before I need to insult someone."

She pushed her chair back.

Burnleigh gave Thorne a wink. It didn't matter whether its referent was Jennifer or Alastair Bissent, he was grateful.

Jiggs Prouty caught Thorne's elbow as they left. A private late-afternoon cruise had been arranged aboard *Geppeto*, Como's oldest and largest cruise boat. They were invited.

Thorne nodded thanks. Jennifer beamed.

They strolled the gardens for awhile getting to know each other, discussing available topics, racing, her photography, Ehra-Lessien. In one of Villa d'Este's two restaurants, La Veranda, they had *caffelatte* and delicious chocolate-mousse cannoli. On the lake, flying in the face of reason (Thorne had put a finger in the freezing water), Breitemann and Jean Garand were water-skiing. Jennifer and Thorne sipped coffee watching them skim along behind two exquisite hardwood runabouts. Garand performed expertly on one ski. Christian needed two skis to get up but in no time dropped a ski and was slaloming as well as Garand. Then in a tantrum of knees and elbows, he crashed. Thorne and Jennifer giggled in horror imagining the icy water.

An hour later they boarded Geppeto, a long, slim 1900s lake boat of 90 feet. Casting off, it made for the eastern shoreline to take advantage of the late-afternoon sun. But soon, with quiet melancholy, the sun sank behind the ridge. In falling light the air on the lake was fragrant, sweet as new-mown grass. Alone, Nick and Jennifer sat in cushioned rattan chairs at the bow.

And no sign of the Devanes. Good.

They sipped Jiggs Prouty's chilled champagne, the breeze of Geppeto's gentle progress lulling.

"So is there anything I should know about you," Thorne said, "besides that you're beautiful and smart?"

Jennifer wrinkled her nose, "Nope, that's it."

He laughed.

"And who are you?" she said. "Besides a patriot in an unpatriotic time?"

He peered through his champagne, "Your worst nightmare."

"You enjoy overstating things. Are you so unsure of yourself?"

He shrugged.

"You don't mind me saying you're unsure of yourself?"

"Not if you're wrong."

She laughed back.

"Listen, I have to ask," he said. "Why didn't you stay at the lake? If you had we could've started exploring my insecurities a day or two sooner."

"You really believe I should tell you?"

"I do."

She brooded a moment, then met his eye. "Between us?"

"Strictly."

"Tony."

"Tony?"

"He's scary, or hadn't you noticed?"

He grinned a nod.

"When he trains his mind on something," she said, "there's no saying no. If I asked him how his ribs were, merely to wish him well, he would rush off in some far too personal direction and never look back. I'm not going to get caught up in a jackpot between him and Angela, she's too nice."

"That's all that's stopping you?"

She gave him a cool glance. "All right, then--I told you."

"Doing great."

"He's not my type. Remember the bad-boy in high school?"

"He's hardly that."

"He is smart and clean-cut and incredibly successful, but way behind the smile, back where you can't see unless you look hard, he's the guy with greasy hair and a leather jacket standing next to a chopped-and-channeled '49 Mercury."

Nick admired the knowledge in the image.

"Has he done anything to you?"

"Do I have to wait until he does? He's not my type."

"And what is your type?"

Her laugh was caustic. "Professional wrestlers, can't you tell?"

His hands came up defending himself.

"I like people who know their limits," she said. "In just about every way that's a poor description of Tony Devane."

"But he excites you--a little."

"Oh, please."

"He does!"

"Do I sound excited to you?"

"Women love bad-boys. Look at Angela."

"Some women love some bad-boys--like some men love some sheep."

He laughed.

"And you're showing your hand."

"What do you mean?"

"You're jealous of him," she said.

"Because of Angela?"

"Everyone is," she said. "That's what she does, she can't help it."

"And you're telling me it isn't just a little flattering having a World Champion hit on you?"

"How little men know."

"But we can keep sheep happy."

She smiled watching the water slip past. Somewhere in the last minute he had stopped enjoying this. "And what are men supposed to know about being hit on anyway?"

"Another thing you know nothing about, Nick."

He signaled the waiter for more champagne without replying.

"You have a hair trigger, don't you?"

"Sexual politics is bullshit," he said.

She gazed across the water, the evening light failing.

CHAPTER 27

THE CHILL ON THE FOREDECK drove them inside. Thorne was just sliding the salon door shut when he saw Christian Breitemann coming in from the stern. Christian smiled to him, nodding at various others through the smoky salon. Table after table of drivers and crew sat smoking, drinking, telling insulting stories on each other. Now and again scathing laughter erupted.

After his water-skiing Breitemann had toweled off and dressed hastily, making it to the boat just in time. His hair was tousled and going in all directions. On him it looked great. He gestured to an empty table midway in the salon and Thorne nodded. Arriving first, Christian pulled out Jennifer's chair. She told him they had seen his spectacular crash on the lake.

"Ah, but it was far worse than you think, Jennifer. My bathing suit came around my knees. Two millimeters more and--" He snapped his fingers with a twinkle.

"Fascinating!" she beamed and her smiling tone sold it.

"An excellent opportunity for a telephoto lens, I think," Breitemann nodded.

"Or a macro," she said.

Thorne's booming laugh startled Breitemann.

"I do not understand."

"It's a lens," Thorne said, "that makes very large pictures of very small objects."

Breitemann laughed hard.

"You must understand, Jennifer, this water is very cold!"

Her belly laugh topped them all.

The waiter arrived and Dom Perignon was poured. Jennifer raised her glass. "To warm waters and all they promise."

"You are a beast," Christian grinned.

They touched glasses and drank. Nick fought the deflation he had felt on the foredeck. He was bad at disguising his feelings, in his profession a cardinal failing.

His eye slid to Garand and Ghislaine. They sat two tables away...the last two creatures on earth.

"Very nice to see, isn't it?" Christian agreed.

Jennifer frowned. "Too healthy."

Christian's nod turned to a laugh.

"But don't look so sad, Nick," Jennifer said, "all is not lost."

Breitemann watched her with amusement. Then his knuckles rapped hard on the table. "So! Herr Thorne, why are you really here?"

"The free champagne."

"*Nein, nein, nein,* why are you in racing?"

"To see who wins."

"No, I don't think so. I can see there is very much more."

"Of course."

"What, then?"

Thorne looked to Jennifer.

"Come--you must say!" Breitemann winked at Jennifer. "A very serious person, our Nick."

She nodded, verdict confirmed.

"You're just as serious," Thorne said. "And nobody cares what I think, they only care about you."

"You should be a politician answering like that." Breitemann's eye twinkled. "And unless I win, no one cares about me. But I believe you think there is some sort of secret in racing, something hidden."

"Why do you say that?"

"But it is not so," Breitemann said going straight on. "Racers know as little as they dare. The technical things we know, of course, but I think you expect to learn more. You want to know why!"

Thorne grinned. "Why would you say that unless you'd thought about it yourself?"

"You would have made a fine racing driver, Nicholas, you fight hard. Tell me about yourself."

"Nothing to tell."

"We'll stop you if it is boring, yes, Jennifer?"

She nodded with a grin.

"Growing up, what interested you? How did you get involved with racing? I think you cared about it always, am I right?"

"Always. But the rest is predictable. I grew up in a forgettable house on a forgettable street in a forgettable time."

"Hah!" Breitemann's eyes glowed. "And you must find something that is not forgettable, yes, I see!"

Nick looked at Jennifer. "Predictable. Like I said."

"Not at all, " Breitemann said. "You and I have lived the same life, my friend."

"Hardly."

"Oh, yes, you would be surprised."

"And you claim you haven't thought about--"

Breitemann leaned far forward.

"I think about why I am a racer all the time! My heroes were all racing drivers. I love everything about it--the feeling of driving a great car at ten-tenths. How it looks when others do it. The style and the noise and bright color--but most of all, the speed! I believed there must be something very important about it or people would not risk dying to do it. But the longer I am in racing the less I know what it means. We are not all such wonderful people, you know, I have been particularly naïve about that. I have wanted to believe that being a very great racing driver means you must be a very great human--that being your best when the danger is greatest makes you better in all things. I wish it was so, but the more I learn about it, racing has no logic."

"And still you do it."

"Of course. I love it!"

"Like an addiction."

"Addiction--what is this?"

"Heroin."

"*Ach...süchtig.* No, not at all! I love to race, I am forced to race, but racing is not a thing that makes life smaller as heroin does."

"Hippies say drugs make life bigger," Jennifer said.

"They are wrong. If I take heroin I must continue taking it whether it makes me less or more. I have complete freedom not to drive as Van Gogh had complete freedom not to paint. But stopping would be too ugly, like stopping breathing."

"Yet you have no idea where it leads!" Nick said. "That isn't freedom."

"It is the one freedom! None of us knows what happens in ten more minutes--nuclear war perhaps. A sudden flash and we are gone. To have no idea what happens next and still love life, I am sure that is freedom. To have no idea what happens next and to live well in spite of it, that is the only happiness."

Thorne's head shook. He needed more, wanted Breitemann to give more.

He sipped his Dom Perignon.

"We are so much alike, Nicholas. *Ser Romantischer.* Like me, you want to know unknowable things. That is a valuable hunger, but the answers are not where you are looking. Racing is not more...I don't know the word...wise? Intelligent?"

"Enlightened," Jennifer said.

"Yes!" He patted her hand affectionately. "Racing is not more enlightened--and not truly more dangerous--than other things. Everything is dangerous, really...all of life. No matter what people say, no matter how hard they argue, life is the cause of death. To live in blind fear of death, to have fear that stops you from using your life--this is the worst tragedy."

Driving Jennifer Whelan to her hotel in central Milan at midnight he followed the navy blue-and-white Centro directional signs. It had been a good day. They had had friction and gotten through it, no small feat on a first date. But there was a problem. Thorne loved the company of women and he knew he must learn from them--but with Jennifer something was wrong. He didn't know what it was, but it got in the way. She was bright and pretty, but--

Ridiculous. The woman next to him had a body like a five-alarm fire and this was the Sexual Revolution!

But that was what he so admired in women--they had such a keen view of whom to take as a partner. A man could possess all the necessary enticements, he could be handsome, smart, rich, the World Champion...yet not be "right."

"Christian is amazing," she said suddenly.

"I know no driver like him. It's more than just driving talent. Angela thinks he's very special."

"So is she," Jennifer said.

"So you said tonight more than once."

They arrived at the Grand Hotel Duomo on Via San Raffaele. At the end of the street the lacy grandeur of the Duomo glowed in the spotlights.

"This looks wonderful," he said.

She smiled. "But now I wish I'd stayed at the lake."

"I like the sound of that."

She was flying to London in the morning. She would miss the Targa Florio next weekend, but she would be at Spa in three weeks--and he hated this confusion he felt about her. What was it about?

The hotel doorman opened her door. She nodded thanks but didn't get out.

"I wish you were staying," he said feeling predictable.

"But you have to write..." she said, doing the same, "then drive to Sicily."

"You'll be at Spa?"

"With bells."

She turned to him and they kissed long and warmly, her softness pressed against him. When they stopped the doorman was gone.

"I wish I was staying," she said.

"I just said that."

"But I do."

"Can you?"

So predictable.

"No." She gave him a wet kiss. Touched his cheek. "Think about me."

He laughed.

"It'll be good for you," she smirked.

He waited for the invitation to come up to her room. When it didn't come he was crestfallen.

She blew him a kiss and he watched her walk into the hotel.

CHAPTER 28

LATE SUNDAY NIGHT WAS NO TIME to be lost in Milan. The streets were empty. Even the whores were gone.

After driving blind for what seemed an eternity he found a directional sign for Como. From then on he drove in the Italian manner, going like the clappers. When he pulled into Villa d'Este it was one o'clock. He switched off the Jaguar, the hot exhaust system cooling...*tink*...*tink-tink*.

His phone was ringing when he got to his door.

(She was an animal.)

"Hello?" he said.

"Nick?"

"I know that gorgeous voice."

"Well, don't you sound a bit of all right!" Angela said.

"And so I should. This is my first midnight phone call from a movie star."

"Please."

A moment passed.

"Are you all right?" he said.

"Fine."

"What's the matter--tell me."

A moment passed: "Is Tony there?"

"No," he said.

She didn't respond.

"Have you tried downstairs?"

"He's not there," she said.

"Or Trevor's room? I can try his door."

"He wouldn't be there. It's all right."

"It takes just a moment," he said.

"I already phoned--no answer."

He tried to think what to propose.

"Never mind, luv," she said, "he'll turn up. Sorry to bother you."

"Not to worry."

"Listen to you...not to worry. You're sounding more Brit every second. And you have smashing taste in the ladies!"

"A bit self-congratulatory of you."

"I mean Jennifer, silly!"

"She'll do?"

"A diamond. Listen, I need to ask you something."

He waited.

"Did Jennifer say anything about Tony?"

"No," he lied.

"All right. But it would help terribly for me to know. This is all very awkward, but, well, you know--you were at Ehra-Lessien."

"Yes."

Again there was silence.

"If you need anything..." he said.

"You're a friend."

He wasn't so sure. He felt bad lying to her about Jennifer.

He heard the dial tone and hung up.

Out the open balcony door he heard a Fiat Cinquecento horn in the distance across the lake, a forlorn squawk. Then silence.

Three stories below, the lake licked at the shore. Who before him had stood at this balcony late at night gazing out across black water, thoughts teeming? In the centuries since the wealthy prince of the church ordered this mansion built, how many Tony Devanes and Christian Breitemanns, how many Angelas and Lucianas and Jennifers, how many wily Beacoms and battle-hardened Whitlaws had stood gazing out, thinking troubled thoughts, rehearsing inconsolable dreads? How many before him had struggled to wrest a modicum of peace from their storm-tossed, infinitely privileged lives?

Monday afternoon Thorne met Jiggs Prouty, Carnelian's tireless public-relations vassal, in the Villa d'Este lobby with his Monza story. Jiggs was flying out that evening and would get it onto a Los Angeles flight in London. Of all people, Jiggs understood its urgency.

Back in his room Nick sat drinking grappa and wondering why, putrid fluid. The more he drank the more vile. He kept drinking. He wanted to be drunk. He hated ambiguity--most of all about Jennifer. Pretty, smart, well-grounded, something about her upset him, and he was going to drink grappa until he got to the bottom of it or the bottom of the bottle.

The notables had left--the usual Monday morning auto-racing diaspora. Devane and Angela went to London, Christian to Germany, Garand and Ghiselaine to Belgium. Tomorrow Christian would test the incontinent 4.9 to see if it could be made to hold its oil.

Thorne pondered Christian. He knew his interest was more than journalistic. Christian was becoming a friend. He should feel honored. Yet drinking his grappa he felt unease. After Ehra-Lessien he had been recruited by Devane, not as a friend but some kind of priest. Breitemann was different. Having a driver as a friend in this mortal profession was not to be taken lightly.

Thorne worked his way through the grappa. He would not think of Devane. That was better.

But the spring was underway. Where would it lead in a week? A month? It was obviously the beginning of something--but what?

Breitemann's Monza drive had been brilliant. In its very different way, so was Devane's. Devane was injured, direct comparison between the two was unfair, but Nick felt the conviction that Devane was no match for Christian. No one was. Christian was a "master." Every era had one or two--Nuvolari, Fangio, Moss, Clark, Stewart, Andretti. The superiority was inborn. Devane, though a World Champion, was a journeyman professional. Nick sensed this assessment spreading across racing. It was the secret everyone knew, including Devane.

He felt no concern for Devane, only for Angela.

He poured grappa.

Tomorrow he and Burnleigh would drive the Jaguar down the Italian boot. They would follow the Sicilian coast to the Targa Florio. It saddened him to leave Villa d'Este. In some way he knew he would never return.

But the Targa was the oldest road race in the world. He'd read the crazed accounts of its 44 miles of narrow, twisting mountain road, its hundreds upon hundreds of turns, each a new threat. Six grueling hours. Nearly 500 miles. Sicilian madness.

He poured grappa, content to despise it.

Part Three

Targa Florio

CHAPTER 29

CALTAVUTURO, SICILY

The men stood on the ridge and it was coming.

Thorne and Burnleigh were high in the mountains above Cerda, past the fork to Agrigento, above the turn for Sclafani, at the very top in the cool razor-sharp winds of Caltavuturo, and it was coming.

Thorne stopped the Jaguar and they got out. They looked down the long deep valley and saw nothing.

But the sun-hardened Caltavuturo men stood silent, waiting. In mauve late-afternoon mountain light they gazed down the gash in the land leading twenty miles to the sea. It was there.

Thorne moved the car off the road. Above them was a narrow lane of scarred pavement daubed with ugly lumps of farm-tractor mud, the mud imprinted with the tracks of men and cattle. It rose steeply to the hard little hamlet above.

A gust of mountain wind combed the field grass, so like the golden mountain grass Thorne knew at home. He and Burnleigh shielded their eyes to see. They saw nothing, but it was there. They saw it in the men's eyes.

There!

A glint--

It vanished behind a ridge.

Silence....

Screeeeeaaaw!

Thorne looked up. At the crown of the 800-foot granite crag towering above the hamlet an eagle glided, wings spread wide.

It tilted. Wobbled. Wheeled, working the updrafts.

Miles below, the point of light appeared, raging nearer. Its report in the distance arrived with authority...engine full-on.

Full-off.

Blasts caromed off the mountains--drawing nearer.

With homicidal insistence, the point of light became twin lights.

Headlights.

They could not see it clearly but the men were nodding, their mountain eyes knew.

With dignity they wagered among themselves, Ignazio Giunti or beloved "Nino"...Sicily's national hero, the Targa Florio master Nino Vaccarella.

A new blare--

Darting behind a headland.

Quiet.

Raging into view a kilometer below.

Blasting over a brow, exhaust note juddering over corduroy asphalt...shutting off...roaring...tail slewing...it skittered sideways on the pavement, menacing.

Each volley echoed, repeated like cannon fire.

It was blood red.

A red Ferrari Spider.

A white helmet.

Three turns below Thorne saw driver hands

black gloves--

snap the shifter

whirl the wheel.

A white open-face helmet

the green-and-red stripe--

Il Maestro

Nino!

The sound grew to skull-rattling hysteria.

Before they could prepare, it rounded a curve immediately below! They turned, the Ferrari rounding the climbing curve. It shot past shin high--

... into the valley beyond.

Silence.

Eerie calm.

They'd seen the face swaddled in flameproof Nomex.

Goggles full of eyes.

A puff of wind combed the grass.

Screeeeeeaaaww!

Nick looked up.

Back down the violet valley, putting it all together.

The men of Caltavuturo didn't crowd down to the pavement when he passed as the foolhardy young Palermitanos would on race day. In good weather, they said, there would be perhaps 300,000.

The men of Caltavuturo nodded. Those who bet Nino collected *cinquecento Lire.*

Contented then like livestock headed to the barn, they climbed the steep mud-daubed lane to supper.

Vaccarella in the Targa Florio mountains. Definitive.

For weeks, on no schedule, practice for the Targa proceeded, drivers pre-running the course again and again trying to learn its countless cues and menace. It was insanity to drive a racing car at full racing speed on open public roads, a tiny Fiat or pottering three-wheeler full of chickens around the next bend! But since 1906 it was the Sicilian way. Long before young Enzo Ferrari drove in his first Targa Florio the year after World War I, it had been to Sicily the litmus test of courage. If bad things happened it was Fate. One accepts. What has been must ever be.

As diligently as the drivers practiced, no one "knew" the Targa, there were only varying degrees of not knowing. A professional rally driver's photographic memory was a precious advantage. Porsche's Rudi Stringert and Frenchman Gerrard Larrousse, veteran rally drivers, made a sort of sense of it. But Palermitano schoolmaster Nino Vaccarella alone could claim Targa Florio mastery--he grew up in these mountains.

In view of the race's supreme difficulty, for years Porsche had tried painting hieroglyphs on roadside boulders and tree trunks at key points warning Porsche drivers of hazards. But local *Ferraristi* and *Alfisti*, having no fondness for Germans, went around the course the night before the race defacing each symbol beyond recognition. Sicily would countenance no "easy" way in The Great Race.

After rainy Brands Hatch, then Monza's chilling velocity, the Targa Florio was a fascinating new test for Breitemann. Given its complexity Christian must rely on reflex, instinct, fortune.

Thorne and Burnleigh stood along the road at Caltavuturo a few minutes. But the mountain men knew--there would be no more racers in this evening indigo.

Nick started the Jaguar. The men had given it an admiring "*bella macchina*"...but it was no Ferrari.

As evening declined to a honeyed glow they continued their lap around the long mountain circuit, descending through Collesano and Campofelice to the coast road. Nick ignored the Palermo autostrada in favor of the older two-lane road. Arriving at the first town, Termini Imerese, they picked their way through suspicious pools of standing water. The air had an off odor.

Anxious-looking dogs wandered aimlessly looking vaguely hunted. They would try the next town.

Santa Flavia sat on a low bluff above the sea. It was compact, plain, innocent of charm. But it was a short drive from the Targa Florio pits in Cerda. They'd been warned that race-day traffic could take hours to move a few miles.

The proprietor of Albergo La Stella, unshaven, dressed in a sweat-stained pot-belly undershirt, smiled, "*Perche no?*" A room was theirs.

They lugged their bags in, the stairs lit by a single bare bulb.

"Not the Villa d'Este..." Burnleigh noted.

"Is it?" he said.

Nick flounced down on his squeaky bed, bone-tired and famished. In Como they had been at the center of the universe. Tonight they were on the outskirts of Mars.

"Is it..." Burnleigh repeated.

They both laughed.

The desperate little enterprise across the road, Ristorante Umberto, served them delicious calamari fritti. They drank more wine than required, left a bigger tip than appropriate, strolled back across the road laughing louder than seemly. It was that kind of night. Entering the albergo, Burnleigh imitated frothy Lord Blather explaining exactly how the Americans had lost the Revolutionary War.

Nick made notes on Vaccarella in the mountains while Burnleigh investigated Albergo La Stella's supply of hot water, a vital element of his evening shower. There was none. Hot water would resume next morning.

Bene....

Nick turned out the light. Trying to visualize Jennifer's green eyes he caught not a glimpse.

CHAPTER 30

AT SIX IN THE MORNING Nick was up and outside for a walk. Early mornings were hardly his custom, but curiosity about this rude Sicilian outpost of Santa Flavia tingled in him.

Heavy coastal dew coated the Jaguar's windows in front of Albergo La Stella. The chill gray overcast was bracing.

He walked along the town's main road in the direction of the sea. The pavement was patched and potholed, whole sections of it regressing to gravel washboard. He passed scarred little domiciles and stunted small businesses sealed tight against the world behind heavy steel shutters. Something sharp and foul tinged the air. Abandoned up ahead he saw a rusty cement-encrusted wheelbarrow standing in the middle of the road.

A tiny Fiat Seicento fizzled past, and not much later a chugging Lambretta three-wheeler. Both swerved elaborately around the wheelbarrow like stray dogs avoiding a man with a staff. Dust and trash swirled in their wake. Both veered right at a side road up ahead. He would investigate.

But first the Anglo-Saxon in him must be served. He walked into the road and moved the wheelbarrow to the far side.

With a destination in mind now, his pace picked up, his senses sharpened. From Naples south the swarthy faces out the Jaguar window had made an impression. After Como's Baroque splendor the hard-bitten visages along the Southern Italian roadside were unmistakable--heralds of North Africa.

He came to the turning. Through gray mists an enormous blood-orange sun loomed low above the Straits of Messina. The side road led steeply down to a flat seaside promontory of hard-packed yellow dirt. Dust-covered three-wheelers, motorscooters and miniscule Fiat trucks were parked at random. Two fishing boats and a dozen skiffs bobbed offshore at their buoys. In the foreground two fishermen in a skiff were heading out to their boat. The oarsman faced doggedly seaward, knees braced, never looking back. Far out to sea were various tiny specks, the fleet on its fishing grounds. In the middle distance two other boats moved seaward on a gentle swell, white froth gurgling astern. Their motors made a distant, staccato *pup-pup-pup-pup*.

He reached the edge of the promontory. The anchorage was anything but idyllic. The land dropped steeply away, its seaward face composed of the detritus from decades of building demolition. Cinderblock and shattered stucco, granulated plaster, fractured chunks of pebble-studded concrete jutted out at all angles. The spot had been chosen for the most expedient of reasons--it offered parking near the water.

Nick made his way carefully down the steep rubble, slab to block to slab. In the absence of a beach oily swells surged lazily up the shattered concrete slabs, sloshing and receding. Wood and half-submerged fiberboard bobbed in the water, the telltale of workboats in the vicinity. He put a hand in the water. It was freezing. He stepped back with new appreciation for the morning's gathering warmth.

He sat now watching the oarsman. The skiff reached its fishing boat, a small van Gogh splash of brightly painted panels, orange and light green, lavender and Chinese red. It was a proud little craft of no more than twenty feet. The skiff bumped against the boat's rough timber--*mmmm-mummpp*. The oarsman shipped his oars with a clatter. His mate held the skiff to the boat while the oarsman stepped aboard. The skipper, no mistaking him, walked the skiff forward now, its painter in hand, and tied it off on the buoy. After much scuffling about and the loud opening and closing of wooden hatches the boat's motor cranked over.

Cranked over again.

Sulkily it fired, barking black soot. It began warming its oil.

Nick could sit for hours under this enormous emerging sun. Watching people do what they do well satisfied him in a way that his own doings never could. Skill looked better on other people.

The mate untied the bowline and the little one-lunger pushed out to sea, the captain's eye on the horizon.

In minutes they were beyond earshot.

Nick stood at last and climbed step by handhold up the jumble of rubble. The air was warming nicely. The afternoon would be hot. He looked at his watch. Five to seven. The little boat was tiny, blending with the green glittering vastness.

The sound of another engine turned his head--a motorscooter. It was not a diminutive Vespa like most but a big Lambretta. It stopped absolutely as far away from him on the plateau as possible, but its rider, scowling indiscriminately, interested Nick. In his twenties with thick blond hair and a crimson complexion, the signature of fair skin deployed to too much sun, the rider looked out at the boats. He looked at Nick--and immediately away. He was not Sicilian, Nick decided. He looked German. Perhaps he had come all this way south to see Porsche win their fifth-straight Targa Florio. Nick had an impulse to say hello...*Wie geht es?* Why not, two foreigners in a foreign land? Maybe he too fantasized the virtuous life of a fisherman.

The Lambretta restarted with a clatter, its rider still scowling. He met Nick's eye a second time and Nick nodded, getting less than no response.

The Lambretta raged up the road in a plume of yellow dust and two-stroke oil. But Thorne recognized the ritual. On late nights in Los Angeles when he felt lonely, he would drive out along the cliffs at Portuguese Bend to stop a few minutes and gaze up at the moon, listening to the collapsing waves hundreds of feet below...maybe their cosmic freedom would transmigrate into him. It never did.

He walked back up the road towards Albergo La Stella.

CHAPTER 31

TO TREVOR BURNLEIGH'S HORROR the Carabinieri made Thorne park the Jaguar at roadside, not a blade of grass shielding it from racing cars hurtling past at 160 miles an hour!

But not a tick later then Trevor shrugged with an elaborate Chico Marx "Eeets-a gonna be jooost-a fine!" Burnleigh had been acting mildly inebriated all morning--and he wasn't. The source of his intoxication was all around. Warm, golden sun painted the mountains, sea and cloudless sky in smiling Cezanne hues of terra cotta, green, gold and tremulous deep blue. The prospects for pleasure on the Targa Florio's official Qualifying Day were limitless. This was the only day before the race that the entire circuit would be cleared of civilian traffic. Now the world would see which drivers came closest to knowing this unknowable circuit. And if that weren't enough to explain Burnleigh's inebriation, he had begun to reexamine, as do the English traveling south, the possibility that gentle climate and leisurely pace are not, in themselves, the brink of moral collapse.

Nick's new red-leather I.R.P.A. armband received a crisp wave through the pit gate from the Carabinieri. The pit area, on a high bluff above the sea, was an unadorned strip of curving pavement rising steeply away from the two-lane coast road. Beneath the bluff a broad flat coastal plain stretched a kilometer away to the Mediterranean, covered with orchards and long rows of plantings. It was too early in the season to guess their crops, but they were bright green and extravagantly healthy.

Only a single-rail wood fence separated the pit enclosure from the circuit itself. This circuit was already ancient when George Patton's Sherman tanks raced along the coast road in 1943 chasing the Germans to Messina. In place of modern guardrails, the edges of the track were lined with fine yellow dust, tough scrub and the sort of low prickly plants that love constant cruel sun.

Across from the Start/Finish line stood the Targa Florio's single rickety grandstand, seating perhaps a hundred. The seats were free, if you came early and never left. The covered Tribune next to the grandstand was reserved for scorers, officials and the demimonde of locals referred to as "dignitaries." It resembled a Dustbowl-era farm produce stand. It was the only shade for miles.

A gargantuan field of 78 cars would race. Professional team drivers from Ferrari, Alfa Romeo and Porsche would mix with racers named "Apache," "Poker," "Gimmi," "Zorba," "Black and White" and more. *Noms de guerre* were a don't-tell-Mamma tradition stretching back to the dawn of Italian motor sport. The main pits accommodated only the most important teams, all of which also had emergency fuel and tire depots up in the mountains. Porsche's refueling strategy for the race would include a "splash" fuel stop in the mountains every two and half laps, allowing them to run three full laps before making a formal refueling stop here in Cerda. The other factory cars all needed to make a refueling stop every two laps, costing them far more time in the pits during the race's eleven laps.

Lesser teams set up their pits wherever they could in town side streets, roadside turnouts, farm entrances. It was an honor for one's farm entrance to be part of The Great Race.

Strolling up the curving rise of the pits the first time--Thorne and Burnleigh stopped dead. The Porsche paint schemes were familiar, but the cars were a complete shock. In place of big Porsche 917s, they saw four instances of Raymond Beacom's "blunt instrument." The stubby Porsche 908-3 was built expressly for the writhing Targa Florio--and equally writhing Nürburgring 1000 Kilometers a month later. The car was tiny, quick, violently fast, a formidable weapon for this race's countless short bursts of acceleration.

The three maroon Alfa Romeo T33-3s further along were elegant, earnest, and alas, out of their depth. Presided over by pumpkin-shaped ex-Ferrari chief engineer Carlo Chiti, seated on his folding tripod stool in the middle of their pit, the Alfas desperately needed a change of fortune. Possibly the Targa Florio would oblige.

Beyond Alfa was the single factory Ferrari. Enzo Ferrari withheld the full three-car team from the Targa Florio, which he disliked, sending one Ferrari 512S to uphold the honor of Sicilian idol Nino Vaccarella. And next to the Vaccarella car was a non-factory Ferrari 512S entered by the Swiss Scuderia Filipinetti. The big Ferraris, like the absent Porsche 917s, were too bulky by half for the Targa's tight curves, but Vaccarella and Giunti would give it their all.

One after another the cars went onto the course to qualify--and immediately came word that American veteran Masten Gregory's Alfa T33-

3 had blocked Vaccarella's progress for ten minutes until the Sicilian sent Gregory flying up a bank and flipping over before the village of Collesano. Legendary Gregory, survivor of some of the most violent crashes ever seen, was unhurt and livid. The spare Alfa came off the truck, confirming qualifying was well and truly underway.

But even-handed Justice waited only fifteen minutes. In the village of Scillato, Vaccarella slid his Ferrari into a wall hard. The spare Ferrari too came off the truck.

Countless reports of hair-raising events filtered down to the pits--a Lancia Fulvia front wheel coming off in Cerda, three racing tires stolen from an M.G. pit in Collesano, an Alfa Romeo GTV catching fire in the mountains.

In the end Breitemann's Porsche was fastest by an enormous margin, setting a lap record of 34 minutes and 10 seconds. Ex-rallyist and race lap-record holder Rudi Stringert's 908-3 was next, a long 27 seconds behind. Vaccarella, in the big back-up Ferrari 512S, was third.

The Carabinieri opened the course at three p.m. so families in the mountains could go to market--the circuit was the only road to town.

Burnleigh beamed at Breitemann. "Then, you did learn the course!"

"*Nein, nein.*" Breitemann's head shook. "Rudi is the rally driver."

"The clock says you are."

Breitemann only glimmered.

Thorne had seen it before at Monza, Christian's quiet self-assessment that he was not without brilliance.

In chill night air the square in front of Hotel Santa Lucia in Cefalú was a-buzz. Portable generators groaned. Klieg lights glared blue-white. The four little Porsche 908-3s were scattered about in no particular pattern. Under harsh light the German mechanics cast outsized shadows on the surrounding walls, their forms gliding and swooping like goblins in an old black-and-white horror movie.

Hotel Santa Lucia was Porsche headquarters. The young men of Cefalú stood on the peripheries smoking and talking animatedly, as if their presence added gravitas to the doings. The mechanics worked in silence, removing practice engines and replacing them with new race engines.

Until the Targa there had been two distinct Porsche camps--Team Beacom's two Carnelian Oil cars versus Dr. Fabius' two Porsche-Austria 917s. With the new 908-3s, however, Porsche itself assumed control. For this race, Beacom would supervise his Carnelian drivers, but Fabius, representing Porsche, assumed tactical command. And instead of only two Porsches wearing Carnelian Oil bright-orange, for this race three of the four wore Carnelian livery, each with its own readily identifiable navy-blue design motif.

"Well, well..." Joubert barked from behind Nick.

"Jozie!" Burnleigh boomed. "Where've you been?"

"God's country--Caltavuturo."

"We went up yesterday," Thorne said. "Delicious."

"Providing an Alfa GTV doesn't roll off the hill on fire."

"You saw it?"

"Someone named 'Sancho,'" Joubert said, "from the Jolly Club. He was unhurt but he made a right mess of the hillside. The locals trudged right in to get him, though--the fire never had a chance." Joubert nodded to an ominous threesome--Beacom, Whitlaw and the hard-eyed Dr. Fabius. "If Beacom is The Death Ray and Whitlaw The Mallet...what do we call him?"

Dr. Fabius was the driving force behind Porsche's racing. Even in polite conversation his eye was impatient to get on with it. Not having to compete against him, Nick indulged the luxury of enjoying his company. Fabius had all the salient aspects of a really good battlefield commander.

They made their way closer and Beacom nodded, "Gentlemen."

"Porsche seems to have things very much to itself," Thorne offered.

"Hah! You think?" Fabius shook his head. "Fighting that big powerful car as he did, Vaccarella is a devil. Impossible what he did today!"

Joubert's eye twinkled. "The devil as a Sicilian schoolmaster, nice concept."

It was both Vaccarella's profession and demeanor. When not in a race car, he spoke in a modest schoolmasterly hush.

"The Alfas too look ready to fight," Fabius said. "Fourth fastest is not slow. Far too many surprises will happen before this is finished."

"Then, you expect to lose," said Thorne blandly.

There it was, the shark grin. "I will not say that--never! If I believed we would lose, we should go home!"

Nick smiled. "How is Tony?"

"Speaking of a devil," said Fabius. "Half a minute behind Vaccarella with two broken ribs--fantastic!"

"A shame he doesn't appreciate himself," Beacom mused.

"Few are born to be champions," said Fabius. "Tony has his demons."

In harsh light and black shadow Whitlaw's jaw clenched and released, clenched and released. "We shall be fine," he said, "...provided no one puts water in our fuel."

The Sicilians were notorious for trying to sabotage Porsche.

"Speak of the devil..." said Joubert, "literally."

Devane and Angela strolled out of the hotel. In the evening chill Devane wore a beige cashmere over his tightly wrapped ribcage. Angela had on crimson pants with wide bell-bottoms and a white sweater, dangerously beautiful. At her elbow was Luciana Podesta. It startled Thorne. Ruggiero had not come to the Targa, so why Luciana?

"We were just talking about you," Thorne said. "Another astonishing drive. How do you feel?"

"Fine," Devane said.

Whitlaw grunted. "A needle in the eye would feel as fine."

"No one else could have done it," Joubert nodded.

"You don't know that," Devane said.

"If you don't stop being nasty to yourself..." Angela said. "I mean it!"

"She means it," smiled Beacom. "Have you seen Alex?"

"He was looking a mite green," Angela said. "He's in his room."

For this race only Alex Winter was paired with Devane. Devane's usual teammate Reine Dinesen was in Monte Carlo preparing for next week's Monaco Grand Prix. For the Targa, rally driver Bengt Bjornson would team with Breitemann.

"I'll look in on him," Beacom said. "Dr. Fabius?"

Fabius nodded and the two strode to the Santa Lucia conversing in low tones. Whitlaw waded in amongst the cars.

"Green?" Joubert inquired regarding Winter.

"Intestinal bejeezus," Devane said.

"Speaking of which," said Angela, "have we eaten?"

"Revolting segué," Thorne beamed. "And no, we haven't."

"Carnelian's buying," she nodded.

Burnleigh laughed. "Such a *nice* evil oil company!"

"Where is she?" were Breitemann's first words at the dinner table. "I expected to see her with you."

Thorne smiled. "The marriage is off."

Angela watched with interest.

"When you are willing to let a woman make you angry, Nick, as she did on the boat," said Breitemann, "I think it is serious."

"What's this?" Angela said. "Angry?"

"Nothing," Thorne said.

"Definitely something," said Breitemann.

Thorne felt blood-warmth in his face.

"Yes, I see!" Angela laughed.

"I wish she was here," Thorne said. "There, Christian--is that better?"

"With that..." Angela smiled, "we eat."

The wine and antipasti were served.

"And you, Christian?" Nick said. "Why are you always alone? Race drivers have no trouble finding women--they're all over you like ants."

"But finding a woman of worth, that is not so simple."

"Worth?" Angela said. "Like...how much a pound?"

Breitemann refused to be distracted.

"Racing drivers meet all the wrong women."

"The heart bleeds for you," sniffed Burnleigh.

"I prefer to find someone very special."

"Amen, Brother Breitemann," said Joubert, raising his glass. "To the Christian life, and we know which Christian!"

Beaming, they all touched Breitemann's glass and drank.

"Tony, you're feeling better, I can tell," Burnleigh said. "A laugh like that two weeks ago would've put you in intensive care."

"I'm setting the lap record for mending."

"Hear, hear," said Burnleigh. He brought their glasses up again. Devane only sipped from his.

Dinner was family-style, delicious fresh fish, rosemary roasted new potatoes and garlic-and-oil fava beans. Luciana told them stories about going to school in Modena in the Fifties and seeing all the great Ferrari drivers in local restaurants and cafés. It was all people talked about, she said, Ferrari, Maserati, Lancia...the latest news about Formula One and the Mille Miglia. She had seen Alphonse de Portago on the street in 1957 the week before the great thousand-mile race. He signed his nickname on an envelope for her, "Fon," and five days later he, a crowd of spectators and the Mille Miglia itself were all dead.

"A bitter sport," Joubert said.

"But if you are close to it, really in it," Luciana said, "what can you do? Will you suddenly stop and open a shoe store? It is a life--an entire life."

Driving back to Santa Flavia the night's coolness cleared Thorne's head. They had had too much wine, followed by too much scotch with Beacom and Fabius. Devane retired early, again suggesting Angela remain downstairs to entertain herself, at which he said she was expert.

Breitemann spoke of going to his room as well, but then he decided to stay. Thorne pondered its meaning. Over-sensitized by fatigue, he was nettled that Breitemann now took it upon himself to escort Angela.

At eleven o'clock they went outside to check on the cars, the Devane/Winter car in particular. On his last lap of practice Winter hit a roadside boulder above Collesano, damaging the right-front suspension and steering rack. In klieg-light glare Whitlaw oversaw its repair, not missing a turn.

Jozie Joubert was staying in Cefalù's other main hotel. From his description it was something like Albergo La Stella. He announced he was turning in. Thorne and Burnleigh followed suit.

"Love your car," Angela said with a flirtatious smile.

She and Breitemann stood arm in arm under the dim-yellow streetlamp.

Their image in the tiny Jaguar rearview as Thorne drove away stopped his thoughts. Arms entwined, gorgeous, they were the two most compelling people he had ever met. The image of them together in the Sicilian night achieved something very near perfection.

CHAPTER 32

"THESE THREE BENDS...very fast.

"A bridge.

"Then turn in early here--sharp curbstones...can cut the tires."

Nick watched the malign curbstones blur past, Stringert accelerating hard.

"Long smooth right--

"Zigzags--two.

"Rough pavement...stay to the inside."

The Alfa Romeo Berlina sedan leaned left, right, left, on full throttle.

"Dab the brakes at the apex--stay to the middle over the bumps."

The car wobbled crossing them.

"Next five turns close together--olive tree in the last. Slippery."

On the fifth zag, a left-hander, the Alfa Berlina sedan passed under an olive tree, the pavement stained black with fallen fruit. Stringert corrected and the Alfa obligingly slipped sideways.

Thorne glanced back at Burnleigh and Joubert, their eyes backlit.

"Farmer's field here--mud sometimes...but clean after first lap."

The sedan swung wide, veered in, hairpin to sweeper to esses. Each turn demanded a unique attack yet the motions of the car were dreamlike, pitching and gliding in perfect harmony with the road surface. Again and again Stringert turned in too soon, the Alfa careening madly sideways...but a deft flick of the wheel sent it straight to the apex, clipping it like a Giant Slalom ski racer clipping the gate at speed.

Systematically, impossibly, Stringert described each coming set of bends in careful order...in a foreign language! His glass-smooth gear changes were detectable only by ear. His hands on the wheel moved sleepily, in slow motion, far ahead of the car's needs. The Alfa required no apparent attention, sliding and pitching in ceaseless crisis.

At last they were coming down through Campofelice to the coast. Stringert turned west towards the pits at Bivio Cerda and floored the Alfa.

"Here we rest," he said veering in and out of traffic at 200 kilometers per hour on the long straightaway.

When he stopped at Cerda they thanked him, amazed.

But in minutes Thorne was overcome with torpor...too much adrenalin for far too long.

Driving back to Cefalù Burnleigh enthused about Stringert. And Thorne marveled that Breitemann, driving on blind reflex, was even faster.

Stringert passed them in the oncoming lane and waved. Thorne honked.

They parked on the square at the Santa Lucia. Joubert pulled his Fiat in behind. Alex Winter and Rudi Stringert were surrounded by throngs of young Sicilians. Winter signed autograph after autograph, smiling, enjoying himself at all costs.

"Where have you lot been, then?" he boomed looking up from his autographs.

"We were teaching Rudi the course," Burnleigh said.

"I think not," said Stringert gruffly. "If so, you must race against me tomorrow!"

Nick made a note to omit irony when kidding Swabians.

But with a conspiratorial grin that was outright fiendish, Winter beckoned to Burnleigh. "A moment, Trevor?"

He nodded to Stringert to come as well, muttering something under his breath Thorne and Joubert couldn't hear. Without another word, Winter, Burnleigh and Stringert entered the hotel.

CHAPTER 33

THORNE GAVE JOUBERT A LOOK. He got the same quizzical look in return. "Search me..." Joubert shrugged.

They walked into the hotel. Winter, Burnleigh and Stringert were nowhere to be seen. With nothing more creative to do, they ordered two gin and tonics and went back outdoors. There they saw Breitemann surrounded by an even larger crowd than Winter's and why not, he was fastest qualifier.

"Rudi took you around, did he?" he said.

"Unearthly!" Joubert glowed.

Nick nodded enthusiastically. "He knows every bird-dropping."

"He is excellent," Breitemann nodded.

Now Winter, Stringert and Burnleigh reappeared at the hotel entrance grinning like minks.

"What is it, you three?" Breitemann said immediately.

"Not a thing..." beamed Winter but his tone said quite the opposite.

"Nothing at all--eh, Rudi?" said Burnleigh.

"No, no," said Stringert innocently.

Breitemann's grin narrowed. "Come, on, Rudi...what!"

"We just think you should save your strength," Winter offered with a frown.

"My strength?"

"For tomorrow," Stringert said. "You should not waste yourself, Mr. Beacom will not be pleased."

"What are you talking about?"

Winter looked to Burnleigh.

"Your date, Christian..." Burnleigh said. "Didn't think you had it in you?"

Breitemann waited in vain.

"Dicey," Burnleigh nodded, "fraternizing with the locals."

"She has a very sweet way about her, though," Winter offered.

Breitemann looked at Thorne. He could be of no help.

"Prettiest bird in Cefalù," Winter said. "Well..." he smirked, "not quite a bird."

Stringert's grin looked as if it would break his face.

"But must you keep her locked in your room like this..." said Burnleigh.

Immediately Breitemann marched into the hotel. Burnleigh waved to Thorne and Joubert to follow.

Breitemann crossed the lobby. Climbed the stairs. Strode along the hall to his door and--

Leapt back with a start.

The hall reaked of lanolin. What they heard next was unmistakable:

"*Mmm-a-a-a-a-a-a-a.*"

"*Mein Gott!*"

Winter fell to the floor, in tears. Thorne and Joubert shoved forward.

"*Mmm-a-a-a-a-a-a.*"

Tethered to Breitemann's closet door, a full-grown ewe gazed up at Breitemann with trusting expectant eyes. On the bed was a pair of olive-drab hip boots.

"Bastards!" Breitemann growled, laughing deep in his chest.

Word spread through the lobby. In no time a crowd rushed up the stairs.

On cue Breitemann went straight to the boots. "I must see that they fit."

He began pulling them on.

"Excuse me, my darling," he said to the sheep.

Stringert joined Winter on the floor, bawling.

Angela and Luciana arrived--

And shrieked in horror! Their keening laughter brought more people upstairs.

"*Mmm-a-a-a-a-a-a!*"

Breitemann--deadpan--held the hip boots up at his waist like beltless trousers.

"Christian...stop!" Angela wailed. "They'll throw you in jail!"

Breitemann paid no heed, *kuh-loppp-kuh-loppp-ing* along the hall to the top of the stairs in the rubber hip boots. He beckoned to a waiter, "Send up grappa and clover, we wish to be alone."

Back along the road the blue-white glare of Klieg lights in front of the cars cast barbarous shadows on the hotel walls. Two mechanics were finishing the repairs to the Devane/Winter Porsche.

"Sheep again..." Thorne grinned to Breitemann.

"Again?"

"On the cruise at Como, Jennifer and I had an exchange about men and the care and bedding of sheep."

Breitemann grinned. "I think she is very modern!"

Nick laughed.

The little roadside bar they had found just down the main road from the hotel had three outdoor tables. The large Cinzano umbrellas were wrapped tight around their poles for the night. Nick sipped his vino rosso. Breitemann drank acqua minerale.

"A very pretty woman," Breitemann said. "Is she as interesting as she looks?"

"If I say yes, I'm encouraging you to move in."

Breitemann's smile clouded. "No, no, my interest is not there."

"Then, you have an interest somewhere?"

"Everyone has, *nicht war?* Even we bashful ones."

"I'd hardly call you bashful."

"Oh, yes, my friend," Breitemann said. "There are many kinds of bashfulness, some very useful."

"Well, I certainly can't agree with that!" Thorne was letting the wine from dinner do the talking. "Bashfulness keeps you from getting the things you want."

"Oh? You are so sure?"

Nick nodded promptly. "As they say--if it feels good, do it."

"And if doing it causes only pain?"

The conversation was proceeding in code, a topic debated without being identified. It stung Thorne--he wanted to know what "it" was.

"But if you never go after what you want," he said, "you never get it!"

"I don't agree," Breitemann smiled. "Some things, important things, you get only when they are given to you. Other things you never get at all and should not."

"That's just defeatist."

Breitemann nodded. "It is not American, no. But some things we want, we must not have."

Nick hated this. Breitemann's fame granted him virtually anything he wanted!

"If you were in my profession, Nick, you would know. Too often you see a thing you must have...a fastest lap, a place in the fastest team, someone you must have in your personal life...and you try for all you are worth, forcing it."

"But you have all those things!"

"Not all. And for many years I had none of them. Those years taught me well. The good things come to you only when you stop needing them too much." He watched Nick's frustration. "Learning to live is very hard, Nick, yes? Even for racing drivers--especially for racing drivers. No matter how much you have, always you must have more. It can be fatal."

The word chilled Nick.

"But the most important thing is to see the value of waiting," Breitemann said, "and to prepare for the possibility of not getting what you are waiting for! It happens even to people with the very greatest luck."

"Strange coming from you. You're saying, if you want something, give up!"

Breitemann's head shook. "The secret is to want what you have. That is very, very hard for racing drivers."

Thorne listened, confused and tantalized. It was like some fatuous Zen paradox the only cunning of which was in its self-contradiction and word trickery. Why did this driver, blessed with vast intelligence and talent, limit himself so sternly? Nothing in Thorne's experience prepared him for it. He believed if he worked very hard he would get what he wanted! If in his darker moments that seemed to mock him--and it did--he could point to proof in his own experience. The funny letters he wrote home from this trip were not the letters of a person denying himself things he wanted. He reread each letter before mailing it, dazzled by the fantasy he was describing. He had more than he could ever have asked!

"I don't understand, Christian."

"You will."

"Don't be patronizing."

"You must understand, Nick, I love my life. I have had more good fortune than any man deserves. But life is not so easy as I thought. I say this only because you and I are so much alike. You refuse to live in blindness-- like me, you are a searcher."

Thorne said nothing.

"Everyone wants more, even those who have everything, but it is a trap. Look at Tony." But something behind his eyes collapsed. "I must not..." he said.

"What about Tony!" Thorne said. "Because he is World Champion?"

Breitemann said nothing for a moment, then nodded as if complying. But instead he moved in a completely new direction. "It is natural to decide what things you must have, Nick, the most natural thing in the world, but you must never believe you are owed them, that is too painful."

"What are your disappointments, Christian--tell me!"

"Like everyone's."

Thorne's curiosity burned to know. "Come on, really. We're only as sick as our secrets," he said and immediately felt cheap saying it.

"I like that." Breitemann smiled. "Very American."

The moment passed. Thorne knew it was his doing.

"Don't worry, Nick. It will make sense when it must, not before. Racing has taught me something very important--the inevitable has already begun."

Thorne shook his head. "I don't understand."

"No," Breitemnn nodded. "The time is not now."

The Jaguar blared west along the coast road, Burnleigh recounting how Alex Winter procured the ewe, committing to the Santa Lucia's owner that he would make good any indiscretions committed by her. But she had been a perfect lady.

Thorne nodded, his thoughts universes away. The job of a racing driver was to control events--it was everything. Yet Breitemann said happiness rested on passively accepting whatever life in its shambling way offered. Given the dangers in Breitemann's life how could he live with such blind risk? How could he approach the abyss again and again without believing, mistakenly or not, he could dictate the outcome?

Thorne told Breitemann he didn't understand, but it was a lie--he understood and was horrified.

CHAPTER 34

THEY LEFT ALBREGO LA STELLA in a steady drizzle at four a.m. It was pitch-black yet the autostrada was already at a standstill. And Whitlaw had said the Carabinieri would seal off the course at five--they would never get up into the mountains as they'd planned.

The Jaguar inched ahead. The autostrada, normally two lanes, had swollen to four door-to-door, bumper-to-fender columns, every driver trying to sneak ahead of every other driver. In no time Thorne was juking and thrusting with the rest.

"Filthy buggers," Burnleigh muttered for Queen and Country.

It dragged on.

At first light the drizzle thinned to a dense mist. The four lines merged impossibly to three for the one-lane exit at Bivio Cerda. The twenty-minute commute had taken three hours. The first parking Thorne found along the coast straightaway was far past the entrance to the pits. They began the long hike back. At 7:30 they were waved into the pits. The first race car was scheduled to depart in half an hour.

When they arrived at Ferrari Passini rolled his eyes. Both his drivers, Giunti and Vaccarella, had the flu. Driving the big 512S was already difficult, but in rain, with the flu, impossibile!

"And you have heard?" he said. "At Caltavuturo is making the snow!"

"What!" Burnleigh said.

"Si, si, in this moment! E pazzo. Madness!"

With a wounded glimmer Passini stalked to his race car. Further along they saw Breitemann, and a few paces beyond, Angela and her husband. She smiled at the low wet clouds. "A touch of home, this."

"Blimey..." said Burnleigh.

Devane, looking ashen, beckoned to Thorne and pulled him aside. Reaching into his fluorescent-green Porsche team jacket he drew out the magnesium nugget.

Nick had no recourse but to take it. "How are you?" he said.

"Alex is to drive first," Angela answered for her husband. "Like everyone else, Tony has the flu."

Devane, ever the warrior, confessed no weaknesses.

"A nightmare," Thorne said.

"No..." said Breitemann, joining their circle.

"You like a race when it's impossible to learn the course?"

"I love it! It is like jazz--Miles Davis and Bill Evans."

"Bill Evans?" Thorne said lighting up. "You know Bill Evans?"

"We are not deaf in Germany--everybody digs Bill Evans."

Nick laughed...it was the title of Evans' first big album.

"You like him too?" Breitemann asked.

"It goes beyond like."

Angela gave Thorne a triumphant smile. Just as she'd said--he and Breitemann were alike. He smiled back happily. In some elemental way she saw him clearly, read him inside and out.

The stupendous race-morning traffic jam, in its delicious *Siciliano* way, was heaven sent. At eight, the appointed hour for the start, Targa Florio officials, race drivers and the entire Sicilian timing and scoring team with all its equipment were marooned in traffic somewhere between Palermo and Cerda. By necessity the start was postponed to 8:30, then 9:15. All the while the skies were clearing and a warm sun emerged. When the first race car finally departed an hour and eighteen minutes late, the circuit was drying rapidly and the last traces of snow in the mountains had vanished.

By rule the cars departed in qualifying order, fastest cars first...but the two fastest cars were German and this was Sicily. More especially, the race organizers hoped Enzo Ferrari would favor them with more than one race car next year. To that end, the two big Ferraris were accorded the honor of leaving at the head--first, the private Swiss entry for driver Herbie Müller, followed fifteen seconds later by Vaccarella's factory Ferrari. Then every fifteen seconds another car was launched and its starting time recorded. In twenty minutes all 78 cars were racing.

The Targa Florio was like the Battle of Waterloo. On 44 miles of writhing road an infinity of individual combats raged, oblivious to everything else ahead and behind. From the loftiest perspective every tiny victory pointed in its miniscule way to the ultimate triumph--but on the ground each combat was no less than mortal bloody survival. In Cerda and Caltavuturo, in Campofelice and along hundreds of curves between, countless individual wars raged, some witnessed, the majority forever unrecorded. The most spectacular events were passed on by word of mouth, and in the exuberant Palermitan excitement distorted beyond recognition. Sicilian bravado, Italian pride, British grit, Gallic condescension and Teutonic cold obduracy ensured no account could be taken at face value. Even the official bulletins were suspect. Many hours from the start a bona fide winner must emerge...but until that golden time objectivity had no place. Thorne loved it.

Yet would he ever make sense of this ungovernable cataclysm! How could he relate these chaotic events, one to another? At the thought butterflies fluttered in his chest. All the while the race circulated, unfolding irresistibly in a narrow corridor of time, distance and combat. Fanciful tales and full-blown folklore bloomed like weeds in spring rain.

The significant decision to allow the two big Ferraris to start first had rich Sicilian irony. Heavy rain the prior evening had washed wide deltas of silt down across the pavement at many curves and each new car's passing would serve to scrub the racing surface clean. In practical fact, however, the first starters, the honored big Ferraris, far from receiving an advantage, got the very worst of the mucky going. And early in the first lap leader Herbie Müller's Ferrari slid wide on the mud in a curve and struck a curb. His right-rear tire began slowly deflating. As he went slower and slower for countless twisting miles, the first phalanx of cars bunched up in an angry knot behind him, unable to pass. In consequence everyone's windscreen, goggles or faceshield was sandblasted with wet silt from the balked car immediately ahead.

And not two miles above Cerda early in the first lap Porsche-Austria driver Vic Elford, a former winner highly touted among the favorites, veered wide trying to pass the car ahead, hit a rock and destroyed his Porsche 908-3's front suspension. In almost the same moment farther back the Alfa T33-3 of Umberto Maglioli, another former winner running his 21st Targa Florio, crashed terminally...in minutes two masters gone.

At the pits the long wait for the leaders dragged on.

Breitemann was first to complete lap one, already well ahead of Vaccarella. (Müller had stopped at his emergency pit in the mountains for a new tire, dropping him far behind.) Breitemannn led on the road, but the surprise leader on elapsed time was the year-old Porsche 908-2 of French rallyist Gerrard Larrousse. He had started back in the field, but while the cars at the front fought miserably, balked by Müller's deflating tire and scrubbing muck off the pavement, Larrousse had a reasonably clear run.

As the track was progressively scrubbed clean the pace quickened. On lap three Larrousse still led on elapsed time, but the Porsches of Breitemann and Alex Winter, starting the race for flu-weakened Devane, were flying. At lap four, two hours into the race, Winter, showing tremendous speed, took everyone by surprise, setting a new lap record and seizing the lead. Breitemann, meanwhile, had been held back in a tangle of infighting G.T. cars in the mountains.

Now all eyes turned to Vaccarella. Despite being weakened with flu, in three laps he raged forward from seventh to third. The Start/Finish grandstand came to its feet each time the big difficult Ferrari blared past. On lap five Vaccarella was second...and a lap later, to public apoplexy, he took the lead!

But the big car was a punishing exercise. The gloved palms of both Vaccarella and co-driver Giunti were bloodied from fighting the Ferrari gearshift. On lap six Breitemann replaced co-driver Bjornson and simultaneously Winter replaced the ailing Devane. With cool inevitability both agile little Porsches overtook the big Ferrari, Breitemann leading Winter by a handful of seconds--

When everything in the pits stopped.

Thorne looked for a source--he knew this menacing paralysis.

In the distance Burnleigh listened to Fabius. He waved Thorne over.

At Cerda, Winter had crashed.

His Porsche shot over the curb and hit a utility pole. Its right-side fuel tank shattered, engulfing Winter in flame. He struggled free, on fire, but rolled out and down across the pavement extinguishing the flames.

He was alive.

Conscious.

But it was very bad.

The team had no way to get to him, said Fabius, they must wait.

And Thorne saw it in Luciana's eyes.

A veil descended over Angela.

They knew without being told.

Fabius demanded a Med-Evac helicopter...no, no, no, snapped the Targa official, the driver was alive and conscious, no helicopter was needed.

Suddenly, without explanation, the helicopter was ordered.

Very bad....

The crisis descended like a bank of smoke, muffling the passing race.

Fabius came back from the officials nodding catastrophically. He was alive, Fabius nodded...nodded...as if nodding itself were beneficial--

But he cannot see.

Fabius said it again.

His eyes are burned.

He cannot see.

Angela and Luciana clung to each other.

The helicopter was on the way, the official said. All was

arranged...everything in order. The driver would go to Termini Imerese. Every shred of information was breathless, relayed in shorthand. The balding Italian in horn-rimmed glasses behaved with extravagant firmness, a schoolmaster governing rebellious children. Nothing about him inspired confidence. Thorne's fists clenched tight.

"They have a burn specialist?" Beacom demanded.

"A good hospital. The nearest."

"He needs a burn specialist!"

"The nearest hospital. The best that can be done."

"No! He must have a--"

"He goes in Termini! Doctors are there, many and good doctors. All is satisfied."

He repeated it: "No helicopter come here. *Impossibile!*"

It was clear Ferrari would not win--the road to Palermo would be jammed with partisans leaving early. A helicopter was the only expeditious way to Termini....

It welled up in Nick, the cruelest possible image. He saw Alex Winter and the ewe last night...tears of laughter streaming from his charred sightless eyes.

CHAPTER 35

"*PILOTO INGLESE.* ALEX WINTER. *Un piloto corso della Targa Florio,*" Fabius barked into the Polizia Stradale microphone, his brittle Italian suspended in hard Deutsche inflections, a butterfly in amber.

"*Sì, sì. Winnn-terrr. Piloto inglese della Porsche!*"

A half hour of trying to locate Winter...rushing back and forth between race officials and the *Polizia Stradale*...arguing, pleading, threatening...came to nothing. Finally the police agreed to contact military Air-Evac in Palermo--they would try to patch Fabius through.

Impossibile....

And Dr. Steigler, Fabius' personal Stuttgart-Zuffenhausen physician, in Sicily for the week to combine a vacation with watching the race, left no doubt: "Do not keep him here. You must get him away from Sicily!"

Angela tugged Thorne's arm. "Where is your car?"

He told her.

"We'll go to the hotel for his things--he is not staying here!"

"But how to get there, luv?" said Burnleigh.

"By autostrada with a police escort--surely they'll do that much! They have to!"

"The Jaguar is too small," Thorne said. "What are you driving?"

"Right," she said. "Trevor, you're responsible for the Jaguar. Nick and I will take our Mercedes, the crew can get Tony back to the hotel."

"We still need an escort," Thorne said.

"Don't you worry."

She went straight to Beacom. He had already settled upon flying Winter home to England on the Carnelian Oil executive plane. Angela told him she would find Winter.

"Good." Beacom turned to Fabius. "We must arrange police escort to the hotel, then to hospital. Can you do that?"

Fabius reached for the race official. He spoke in rapid-fire Schwäbischer Italian. The man abandoned his officious manner, powerless to object. Fabius glared at Angela.

"They will come. What car have you?"

She pointed to a light-blue Mercedes 280SEL 4.5 sedan behind the pits. Good, Thorne thought, a V-8. They'll need it.

Fabius held the official's shoulder pointing at the Mercedes. The official, under orders, headed off in the direction of the police command center.

"*Viel Glück*," Fabius said to Angela and Thorne, lightning in his eyes. "Good luck. Herr Beacom and I will be along as soon as we are able. When he is found, you must prepare him to leave."

Angela handed Thorne the key. He started the Mercedes. The V-8 made a satisfying thrum. Angela hurried in the opposite direction to tell her husband where she was going.

In minutes a *Polizia Stradale* Alfa Berlina sedan arrived at the Porsche pits. Klaxon squawking, red light flashing, it led them out of the pits.

For the moment they were in luck. Heading eastbound to the hotel in Cefalù traffic was moving well. But the opposite direction westbound to Termini and Palermo was stopped and honking like Mardi Gras. Getting to Termini would be an ordeal.

At the hotel the desk clerk handed Angela the key to Winter's room. They threw his things into his suitcase and black Bell Helmet bag. In ten minutes they drove west behind the *Polizia Stradale's* flashing light and grating klaxon...but even if traffic chose to make way there was no room. The klaxon parted the waters with agonizing slowness, inching ahead.

Angela's face was grim.

"Don't worry, we'll make it...doing fine," she said--to herself as much as to Thorne.

They had left Cefalù at 2:45. Four o'clock came and passed.

Just before 4:30 they turned off the autostrada for Termini. The police car rushed through the raw little town to a rudimentary one-story plaster building. It looked like a disused army barracks. The awning over the entrance hung at an angle, its anchors pulled out on one end.

"Bloody hell!" Angela growled.

"Wait and see," Nick nodded, "...wait and see."

They hurried in and Thorne stepped forward to the nurse. "*Vogliamo trovere uno piloto corso inglese. Si chiama Winter.*"

Angela was shocked. "No speaking in tongues--you. You're American, you know."

The receptionist's head shook. "*Non e qui.*" She spoke in a torrent of Sicilian far too fast for him to grasp. It ended with "Palermo."

"*Il va a Palermo?*" he said.

She spoke in very slow English. "This piloto no here." She shrugged enormously. "He can *ospedale Palermo, non lo so.*"

Angela groaned.

The policeman came inside to check on their progress. He was young, very dark, with a gently simpatico manner. He wore an ill-fitting gray twill uniform that was shiny where it met the Alfa Romeo's seat. His uniform shoes were cracked and scuffed. The nurse named a Palermo hospital.

"*Bene, molte grazie,*" he nodded sharply. "*Andiamo,*" he said ushering them to the door.

They struggled on through the jammed traffic like salmon battling up a waterfall. Again and again Angela clicked her tongue, no longer using words, replaying some inner horror. He offered comforting sentiments. She listened as if to a train schedule.

An eternity passed. They were nearing the city.

At last the traffic began to disperse. Free to maneuver they hurried across Sunday evening Palermo, following the Alfa Berlina away from the seafront on a wide city boulevard. It turned into a smaller one-way street. They drove blocks and blocks, the klaxon blaring, traffic skittering out of the way like cockroaches.

They passed through an ornate wrought-iron gate. The hospital ahead was massive and forbidding...early Mausoleum. Its nineteenth-century stonework and brick was blackened by decades of soot and neglect. Extravagant detail swirled and scalloped this way and that in massive granite scrolls longing to roll closed. False cupolas and battlements protruded. Its tall ground-floor windows gaped out, black, impenetrable, its sheer mass threatening to crash through the earth's crust.

The low sun hovered just above the mountains, a half slice of orange. Thorne held the hospital door open for Angela. The policeman insisted politely that Thorne precede him. Inside, he stepped forward to the desk. Nick tried to understand what was being said. The thrust was plain, Winter was not here.

"*Ma dov'e?*" Nick asked.

The woman at the counter protested innocence.

"We must find him!" Angela raged, her tone communicating what words did not.

The woman shrugged.

"Help us!" Angela demanded.

At this the woman put up her hands, "*Momentino, signora.*" She picked up the phone and spoke into it quietly. Hung up.

"What!"

"*Calma, calma.*"

The policeman gave Nick a gentling nod--the Head Nurse was coming.

Angela paced to the door and back. Time passed...roaring in their ears.

A very short older nurse appeared. She had glasses on a chain around her neck and a salt-and-pepper mustache. The policeman explained their mission and she nodded, her eye on Thorne and Angela. "Bene," she said. There was another rapid-fire exchange. Thorne picked out "clinica locale"-- a local clinic. She listed three in the vicinity of Cerda. The first, Termini Imerese, they had eliminated. Second was Cefalù, to the east beyond the course. Between was San Nicola Marina.

"*Non possiamo telefonare?*" Nick asked.

"*Momento,*" the nurse said.

She went to an inner office. A minute passed. When she returned, her head was shaking...the telephone *non funziona*. Italy had not changed since his first trip seven years earlier. The best hope was San Nicola Marina. Failing that, they would go to Cefalù. Thorne thanked the Head Nurse. She nodded with a frown of sincere concern. Angela was out the door already.

Nick started the Mercedes and they followed the flashing red light through gathering dusk. The sky was deepening from brass to lavender. At the seafront they raced east on the empty autostrada, the Alfa leading the way at 180 kilometers per hour, klaxon squawking.

Exits ticked past. A sign announced Termini. Three exits later came San Nicola Marina.

They turned down a steep winding road. The violet dusk in the Mercedes rearview was the color of Angela's eyes.

Passing through San Nicola Marina three days before, Thorne and Burnleigh had not been tempted to stay. It was no more inviting now. They passed the rude dusty town square, a tangle of motorscooters and Fiats parked in any pattern that fit.

Since Palermo Angela had made not a sound. He looked at her.

"How are you doing?"

"Let's just get there!"

The Alfa Romeo turned into a dirt lot, dust swirling up in the Mercedes headlights. Beyond the building was the garish green and yellow of an AGIP gas station, then a small shop. Its grafitti-covered steel shutter was shut and locked.

The clinic was pale stucco. It reminded Nick of the shabby single-story row buildings in Los Angeles housing small businesses destined to grow smaller. The entrance was lit by a single bulb over the open door. No sign was needed, everyone knew what it was.

The policeman led to the door. Two unshaven men, smoking defeatedly, eyed him.

Walking inside, Nick felt the grime of decades under his soles. Mashed-out cigarettes lay where they'd been dropped on the dull green linoleum. Unlike the sharp tang of disinfectant in the Palermo hospital, the *clinica* had the dead breath of a warehouse. Near the entrance a makeshift front desk stood in the middle of the floor like an abandoned altar, loose papers scattered over it. The greenish tint of fluorescent lights overhead *bzzz*-ed like yellowjackets. Each wall housed a row of beds, all but two occupied, none by Alex Winter.

Women milled about tending people in the beds and barking rebukes at children in the universal tongue of mothers stretched thin.

A barefoot little girl with two front teeth and dirty arms chased after an even littler boy. Without seeing, she crashed into Angela. Angela caught her arms and she looked up. She shrank back as if from the Virgin.

Of the twenty or so in the room Thorne saw only one who might be staff. A stocky middle-aged man in a stained white smock bent over one of the beds. He looked in their direction--and looked promptly away.

A woman in a faded print housedress, seeing the policeman, straightened up from feeding an old man broth. She came to them carrying the spoon like a baton and spoke to the policeman.

Nick shot a glance at Angela. She was horrified.

Nick heard the woman say *Inglese*. Englishman. The policeman nodded to Angela. The woman gestured to a closed door at the far end.

"*Grazie, signora*," said the policeman. Angela was halfway to the door, but the man in the stained smock rushed forward to block her way. He wagged his finger in her face, fully at ease being prohibitive. Shortish, built like a fireplug, he had wire glasses and a faintly greenish hue under the lights. On the side of his chin was a purple mole, one black whisker curling from it.

The policeman introduced them, the doctor glowering like a priest with a parking ticket. He confirmed there was an English racing driver but immediately shook his head.

"We're going in," said Angela.

His head shook fiercely.

The policeman nodded appeasingly to both, speaking calmly. The doctor's head still shook. He was told they were from Porsche, the driver's team.

He nodded coldly: "Dottore Santarelli."

The policeman continued his ministrations. Grudgingly the doctor gave them "*cinque minuti.*" Five minutes.

Angela pushed past him, Nick a step behind.

The room was a vacuum. Winter lay motionless, wrapped in white gauze--a mummy's head. It had holes for nostrils and mouth, but ominously none for eyes. The hands were heavily bandaged, the right arm wrapped to the elbow. The sleeve of his flameproof driver's suit must have torn struggling out of the burning car.

The swollen mass of the face beneath the bandages terrified Thorne. Angela stepped closer. "Alex?"

"Who is there? Is--"

"Angela, luv. And Nick Thorne. We found you."

He made no sound. Then it welled up in him: "Angela...."

He took a sudden sharp breath.

"It's all right, dear, we're here."

His breath caught again. His chest heaved massively.

"Easy, mate," Nick said. "Going to be all right."

"Done it this time, I 'ave."

"Nobody knows anything yet," Nick said, wondering where the gentle voice in him was coming from. "We're getting you to good doctors, don't you worry."

"Don't know a thing yet," Angela said, "... never you mind."

It sounded like he was choking. Angela looked at Thorne with alarm.

But it stopped. He lay still.

The policeman stood in the door next to the doctor. Seeing Angela's pain, he offered a sympathetic nod.

"We're getting you home," Nick said. "Tonight!"

His bandages rustled, the beginnings of a nod. The thought of his scorched flesh flexing gave Thorne shimmers.

The doctor took a step forward, but when Nick made a placating gesture he stopped.

"Don't move, Alex. Stay still. We've found you and it's going to be all right."

"Where is this?"

"San Nicola Marina. A clinic," Angela said, her voice chilled, "...if you can call it that. Do you need anything?"

"A doctor...speaks bloody English!"

"You will have it," Thorne said. "The best in London."

"Thank God you've come."

His breath caught again. He was wracked with terrible stifled gasping.

The doctor took another step forward. As if unknowingly, Angela stepped in his path. Tears welled in her eyes but her voice remained clear. "Not to worry, dear," she said.

She sat on the creaky wood-and-cane chair by his bed, a hand on his pillow, and bent down. The quiet things she murmured gentled the air.

The doctor left at last.

She looked where he had stood with hatred.

This inner room was no cleaner than the big front room, but at least Alex was away from the clamor of defiant children. The room was bare, windowless, with only the one bed. Next to Angela was a new, incongruously shiny metal-and-enamel side table, gleaming white with black trim.

Angela told Nick to ask if there was a telephone. The policeman frowned he doubted it, but he would ask, and left.

"Don't tell her," Winter said, reading Angela's mind.

"I'll tell her you had a crash," Angela said. "And some burns on your hands."

He made the slightest nod. "No more. It will be bad enough when she sees."

A moment passed.

"I feel much better," he said. "You've no idea how much!"

Angela smiled. "Good."

The policeman returned--the telephone was only for official business.

"Outrageous!" Angela fumed.

The policeman smiled apologetically, it was beyond his control.

"I'm going to find a phone." She stood. "The others must be told where we are." Her eyes referred to the policeman. "You may as well thank him and tell him to go."

Nick debated keeping him. He might be useful if the doctor came unstrung. On the other hand, he might feel obliged to take the Sicilian side.

Nick beckoned him to the door now. In schoolboy Italian--it would have to do--he said, "*Ora tutto va bene qui, signore. Grazie per tutto.*"

The policeman said he was quite willing to stay, but Nick smiled with the faintest shake of the head, it wasn't necessary. "*Tanto simpatico,*" he said, "*... moltissime grazie.*"

The policeman made a polite bow and salute. "*In bocca al lupo.*"

It stopped Thorne. In the wolf's mouth? He didn't know what it meant.

"*In inglese,*' said the policeman, "*... gooot lawck!*"

"Ah," Thorne nodded, "good luck."

"*Ecco!*" The policeman beamed. "*Addio,*" he said with a bow to Angela and left.

"What was all that?"

"Nice guy," Thorne said.

She turned, no longer interested.

"Alex, I must find a phone."

"I'm not going anywhere," he said.

For the first time in hours she smiled. Beneath the bandages and charred flesh...the same whimsical Alex.

"Back soon," she said.

The door closed after her.

"Still there?"

"You've had quite the day," Nick said.

"Cor'...I was like a load of turnips going to market. Bloody ambulance driver should've been in the race!"

"I thought they used a helicopter!"

"They did, but then they couldn't land here. They put down wherever they could, loaded me into the nearest farm wagon and off we went. No idea how far--bloody far enough!"

"What happened up there, or don't you--"

"Bloody steering rack. I turned into the corner and the fronts just snapped sideways. Smashed the tank. Petrol went up, me bathing in it."

The image took a moment to subside.

"I was onto the ground and trying to get the fire out, eyes closed, 'oldin' me breath, as you must. I reckoned I couldn't see, because the fire burned me goggles. But then I reached up--no goggles."

His voice went breathy.

"Ohhh...what will I do!"

"Far too early to know anything yet, mate. Wait till you're in London." Again Nick couldn't place the gentling voice in his chest. "Let's get you home, now."

"Before the start old Fabius tells me, if you absolutely *muzzt krrresh*, he says, do not hit zee rrright side where is zee fuel tank. Exactly where I hit...."

It trailed off to infinity.

"But nothing else is broken?" Thorne said.

"I think not. Just burns."

"How's the pain?"

"He gave me something wonderful, makes me feel like a crouton in Brown Windsor soup, luvly business. When it gets bad, they toss me back in t'soup."

It was far worse, but it would not be spoken of.

"Angela?" Winter said into the air.

The storm was building again.

"Getting bad, Angela."

"Yes," Thorne said.

"Bad. Tell Angela."

"I will."

"Where is she? Need her."

He said it again. "Need Angela."

"She'll be here, Alex."

"Tell them, Andrew--really bad."

He had no idea who Andrew was--someone in Alex's family, his past. Thorne hurried out to the front room, but the doctor was nowhere to be found. A squat woman with thick ankles and dark tragedy-laced Maria-

Callas eyes looked up from beside the nearest bed. It was impossible to know if she worked here or was tending a relative.

"*Signore?*" she said.

"His pain," Nick said. "*Ritorna piu grave il male.*"

She nodded.

"*Il dottore, dov'e?*" he said.

"Ehhh!" she grunted...wouldn't we all like to know!

"No-no-no," Nick said gesturing to the closed door. "*Il male...e piu grave.* Getting worse!"

"*Si, si,*" she nodded, "*ho capito.*"

"*E serio. Molto urgente!*"

She shrugged--it was out of her hands.

"Where in the fuck is he!" he said to the world.

He stormed to the front door just as Angela was coming in.

"There you are!" he said. "Have you seen the doctor?"

The woman in the print housedress who helped them when they arrived followed Angela through the door.

"Dottore?" Angela said.

"*Si, si!*"

He told her the racing driver was in great pain.

She nodded, the doctor was eating his dinner. When Thorne asked how long he would be, she frowned, "*Il viene.*" He's coming.

"*Ma subito!*" Nick insisted--immediately!

"*Presto,*" she said. Soon.

He led Angela to the room in the rear. She was trembling with frustration. Fabius was nowhere to be found, she said, and Beacom and Whitlaw had left hours earlier, trying to find them. She left word for Beacom and Whitlaw at the Santa Lucia.

They were on their own.

CHAPTER 36

THE PAIN GUSHED LIKE LAVA. Winter was in a trance. His head weaved side to side seeking a way out. Primitive gurgles rose in his chest, ancient guttural rumblings pre-dating language. Nick could do nothing--and he could not look at Angela.

"Where the fuck--" he said suddenly and stormed out the door.

The doctor was near the front arguing with the woman in the housedress.

"*Per favore, dottore!*" he yelled.

The doctor looked at him with smoldering impatience.

"*E molto grave il male, dottore. Molto grave!*"

"*Momentino, signore--*"

"*Momentino*, my ass. Now!"

"*Stranieri*," the doctor said...foreigners.

He crossed the room and stopped at a locked steel cabinet. Unlocking it he withdrew a vial. Nick stood over his shoulder. He turned, intending to say something, but seeing Thorne's eye he thought better of it.

"Anna!" he barked.

The woman in the housedress followed him with disinfectant and cotton swabs. He opened the door, bowed to Angela without politeness, "*Signora.*"

The woman in the housedress, Anna, prepared Winter's forearm. The doctor inverted the vial and filled the hypodermic. Fluid spurted from it. His technique was balletic, a performance with flourishes and follow-through.

But the shot hit the mark. Winter melted.

Good.

Nick nodded to Angela.

The doctor left and Angela closed the door behind him. Her voice wobbled, "We are getting him out of here!"

Winter was adrift in Brown Windsor soup. They must wait.

Angela told him to get some air. Without reply he walked out into the night, forbidding his thoughts. He checked his watch--twenty to midnight. The AGIP station was dark. Lit by one dim lamp the street was murky. In night quiet he listened to the beating of his heart. He was aware of every pebble beneath the soles of his shoes. Nothing in his surroundings held the slightest interest--but seeing and registering every sensation, the mean little buildings, the scarred doorways and ugly steel shutters, the trashy disorder served to consume more of this day's bottomless perpetuity.

In the distance the Mediterranean stretched off into the void, all-consuming, a pool of tar...should he be doing something more? Was there anything he had not thought of?

No.

... and no.

This bitter day, in its enormity, took no account of him, no account of Angela. It cared nothing for their doings and intentions. It rendered him--with Angela and Beacom and Fabius and them all--sublimely irrelevant. The future of a life, of a family of four, had stopped, all for love of "sport." Alex Winter was a journeyman who drove race cars. He did it to support himself and his family and because it was his identity. But it would never make him rich. He would never be famous. He performed his workday as do other workers, routinely, mindfully, with diligence and detail. But he would never be World Champion, never be a Christian Breitemann shooting across the firmament. He was a journeyman race driver. Who was blind.

Nick walked back into the clinic. In the room at the rear Angela sat next to Winter, hands motionless in her lap. She turned to Thorne. Turned back again without seeing. Nothing was new. She had sat in too many hospitals late at night. But in Nick's eye she had never looked more captivating. The irritation on her face was the emblem of the spirit inside her. Once he had said to a bright woman friend that the secret of Ingrid Bergman's stunning beauty was the intelligence in her eyes. You can't see intelligence, the friend scoffed! Of course you can, he said, it's just like seeing stupidity--but the opposite.

Tonight it was so, except Angela evinced more than intelligence. Her humanity was visible. She was livid that a person should be blinded, could die and that she was implicated.

"Is there anything I can get you?" he said.

"No."

"Anything?"

"I'm fine." Her eyes did not move. "A million miles away."

"What?"

"A million miles away he is..." she said.

"Where...ARE...they!" she raged suddenly.

Nick walked around behind her chair. Gently, with gradually increasing pressure, he kneaded her shoulders. Her neck muscles were tight as bands of steel.

"It's going to be all right," he said with determination. "You'll see."

She bent her neck forward letting his hands work.

"You are going to be all right," he said.

"I know that!" she snapped.

"You are."

"This isn't about me!"

"Of course it is."

"It's about Alex and his wife!"

"It's about all of us."

"You think that makes it easier!"

"Keep your distance."

He felt anger rippling through her like a molten current.

They were quiet then for minutes, his hands gently working.

"You have your rough edges," she said at last. "You know that."

He did.

"But they're the good kind."

"It isn't Tony, Angela. Remember, keep your distance."

She snorted. "That's all I ever do!"

But the tantrum in her neck was beginning to release.

His hands slowed.

Stopped.

She smiled--that beautiful smile. "You don't know how much that helped."

"Yes I do."

He was on the very brink. Teetering.

He refused to acknowledge it--any of it.

An hour passed yet the individual minutes refused to move. Alex Winter made no sound. The door burst open suddenly and Nick and Angela jumped.

Peter Whitlaw strode in with Race Engineer Ian Swallow.

Raymond Beacom followed looking mortally pale.

The doctor stood in the doorway eyeing the new arrivals. They had had words. He turned then. Whitlaw nodded good riddance and closed the door.

Beacom walked to Angela and kissed her forehead. "Bloody aborigines...sent us to Termini Imerese, then Palermo, hot on your trail all the way from all I gather. We've the best burns man in England waiting. Worked on several drivers in the past--R.A.F. specialist from the war. He knows the music. The Carnelian plane is waiting."

Angela's eye sparkled with hope.

"But this will take some doing," Whitlaw warned. "That bugger won't part with him without a fight."

"You think?" Thorne said.

"Mr. Whitlaw knows whereof he speaks," Beacom said.

Thorne envisioned it, Whitlaw and the doctor toe to toe.

"We have given him an address to send the bill," Beacom said, "but money doesn't seem to be the issue. He wants to keep his trophy fish. No matter. Dr. Steigler, Fabius' man, will accompany Alex straight on to England just to be safe, they're at the airport now."

Whitlaw went to the bed.

"Alex?" Getting no reaction, he looked to Angela.

"He slips in and out," she said.

"He was clear as a bell three hours ago," Thorne said, "but then he was in pain and needed a shot. Since that he's nowhere to be found, just as well."

"He is all right otherwise?" Whitlaw said. "Apart from the burns?"

"He says so," Thorne said.

"Well, let's hope. We'll get some clothing onto him. You have his passport and everything?"

Thorne said his papers and clothes were in the Mercedes.

"Get the clothes, please." Whitlaw's voice lowered. "And we must cause a minimum of commotion until we're ready to leave."

Thorne nodded.

"Angela should go to the car, I believe," Beacom said. "The *dottore* will be goners for her."

She grinned. "We're already a bit beyond that, Raymond."

"Oh, really," he smiled. "Well...good."

Thorne said he would go and Beacom nodded.

"And Angela," Beacom said, ever the strategist, "might you stage some sort of ruckus as we're taking him out? You know--a diversion of some kind?"

She beamed. "I'm quite good at that--ask Tony."

For the first time in hours the flame burned bright in her again.

"Well, Mr. Thorne, shall we?" said Beacom.

Released at last from the tyranny of waiting, Thorne hurried out. And he was in luck. In the front room only two dim nightlights burned. *Dottore*

Santarelli had vanished again. Thorne went out to the Mercedes and returned with Winter's suitcase. Still no *dottore.*

And Thorne saw a wheelchair abandoned along the far wall. He went to the back room to drop off Winter's bag and left again for the wheelchair.

"Quietly, now," Beacom admonished as he left.

The ancient wood-and-cane wheelchair squeaked sharply with each rotation of its big right-rear wheel. Tilting it onto its left side to reduce the disturbance, he rolled it into the back room. The door closed behind him.

They slid Winter out of his cotton smock, lifting him this way and that to pull his pants up around his waist. With great care they brought his torso gently to vertical and slipped him into a shirt.

"Good lad, Alex..." said Whitlaw as if to a cooperating child. Winter was mumbling softly somewhere off in Tibet. "Have we anything warm for his shoulders?"

Nick passed Whitlaw the orange-and-navy Carnelian Team Beacom parka.

"That's got it."

"By the way," Thorne said, "who won?"

"Ever the journalist..." nodded Beacom. "Christian did and by a whacking great margin! His last lap was 33 minutes, 36 seconds under the all-time record!"

Whitlaw grinned. Thorne returned it. Whitlaw nodded to the wheelchair now and Thorne rolled it forward, the bad wheel chirping.

But suddenly the woman Anna burst in.

"*Lei!*" she barked at Thorne. "*La sedia a rotelle!*"

Whitlaw shook his head, understanding not a syllable. Angela looked to Thorne, who understood no more.

"*La se-di-a a ro-tel-le!*" She pointed to the wheelchair in a fury.

"That tears it!" Whitlaw snapped. "Get a move on, now, lads, no time to waste. Help me quickly!"

"*No!*" Anna raged.

"Come on!" Whitlaw growled to Swallow, lifting Winter under the shoulders.

"*Incredibile! Assasini!*"

She ran out shrieking at the top of her lungs. All the lights in the big room came on with a bedlam of commotion and shouting.

Thorne guided the wheelchair under Winter and Whitlaw motioned him to get a move on. He pushed the wheelchair forward to the door--

When the *dottore* appeared.

Hurling threats and invective, he blocked the door, arms crossed on his chest with pouting Mussolini bravado. Knowing they would not endanger the sagging Winter, he dared Nick to come closer. Brandishing his forefinger like a dagger, he made fiery reference to *la polizia* and *la legge*--the law.

"Here, now," said Beacom, stepping forward, "*Dottore*, you must--"

In a rage, the doctor stiff-armed the frail Beacom backwards, Ian Swallow just catching him before he fell.

Instantly Angela lunged at the doctor. "You pissing coward!"

She reached back with all her might and slapped his face--

Krakkkk!

He held his cheek, frozen with pain and shock.

But Peter Whitlaw gave him no time to react.

"Buh-leeeeding, nasty git...*clear bloody off!*"

Whitlaw took a violent step towards him, but the doctor lunged backwards into the main room. Whitlaw waved Thorne on, clearing the way. Thorne pushed Winter out going fast, the wheelchair screeching. Patients were upright in their beds yowling and pointing.

In the commotion Winter began to come around. "Where is this?"

"Alex, it's Raymond," Beacom said calmly. "We're going home."

"Home...." Winter's voice cuddled the word like a kitten.

Swallow rushed ahead to the Mercedes to open the rear door.

The doctor followed at a distance, invoking *la legge* and *la polizia* with every halting step...but it seemed now he was inclined to let officialdom perform the enforcement.

Thorne and Whitlaw got Winter into the back seat. The dottore stepped back into the clinic, lunged for the telephone and began dialing.

"Ian!" Beacom barked at Swallow, pointing to the doctor. But Angela was already there. She yanked the telephone receiver from the doctor's hand and slammed it down. He didn't move.

"What's the matter, *dottore*? Am I not *old* enough to hit!"

He backed away.

She marched to the door, trembling with rage.

Whitlaw steadied Winter in the Mercedes back seat and climbed in next to him. Beacom sat in the right-front seat. Swallow and Angela would follow in Whitlaw's Alfa Romeo.

Starting the big Mercedes V-8 Thorne glanced at his watch, 3:15 a.m. Would this day never end!

He rushed the Mercedes through the scruffy little town piazza. The Vespas and Lambrettas and Fiats parked there when they arrived were gone. Climbing the winding road up the escarpment to the autostrada the Mercedes accelerated powerfully. In the distance they heard a police klaxon squawking. It grew fainter, rushing in the opposite direction towards the clinic.

"All right back there?" Nick said.

"Fine," said Whitlaw.

"Home..." crooned Winter, in a dream he'd so richly earned.

CHAPTER 37

THE NEXT DAY AT LUNCH in Cefalù Beacom told Breitemann the entire desperate tale of Alex Winter. Thorne could not have written it with half the aplomb. Winter had flown out with Dr. Steigler on the Carnelian plane at four a.m. The main English burn center, East Grinsted in London, was closed due to an infection. Winter went to a hospital in Manchester. Beacom added grimly what Dr. Steigler said, with burns there is no rush, what's done is done.

Thorne felt sick and hungover though he'd not drunk a drop the previous day. He described chasing the Polizia Stradale Alfa all over Sicily in search of Winter. Whitlaw listened, moody as a German Shepherd. Breitemann nodded and nodded, hearing the fate of his driving partner. Nick hated the story, it made Christian subject to the same grisly fate.

When Nick finished Breitemann described the crash site.

"I came to it on the cool-off lap. I saw nothing but a deep hole melted in the pavement with a crankshaft in it. You couldn't tell it had been a racing car. Whoever was driving, I thought, was surely dead."

"Not our Alex," said Beacom with an overcast smile. "At last report he was making bright remarks about feeling like grilled Black Angus."

Breitemann shook his head with a glare. "I wish he could have won by ten laps!"

Breitemann's own victory--and his miraculous final lap 36 seconds below the all-time record--never came up.

When Thorne and Burnleigh returned to Albergo La Stella Monday afternoon Nick was exhausted. He went up to the room and flopped onto his bed. But in minutes he was up again. He couldn't lie still. Hearing a filthy electric *bzzzzz* in his head he walked across the street to Ristorante Umberto. Trevor was indulging in a double espresso, mostly because he adored pronouncing the Italian word for double...*doppio*. He delivered it with a florid Italianate gesture, vastly amused every time.

Burnleigh looked up from his book, *Slaughterhouse Five*. It was needless to ask how Nick was feeling. "You best get some rest, mate," he said. "You don't want to sleep through the whole voyage tomorrow."

The next morning they and all the racers would begin the journey north on the big Palermo-Naples ferry. Burnleigh said his paper would be pleased, yes, honored, to underwrite the Jaguar's passage. Jiggs Prouty had added their names to the ship's manifest.

Thorne ordered a *caffelatte*--it didn't have quite the loopie high spirits of a doppio--and Burnleigh filled him in on what he'd missed of the race during his search for Winter. Perfect. Nick would write on the ferry. Feeling the same unpleasant deviousness he felt prodding Breitemann two nights before about disclosing his "disappointments"...but being a writer is being a writer...Nick knew Christian would probably be more inclined to talk about his extraordinary last Targa Florio lap when another day had passed since Winter's crash.

After Burnleigh finished his account of the last few laps, he said he was expected in Cefalù for drinks. Thorne declined.

"You look bloody awful," Burnleigh said.

He was fine, he said, but Burnleigh's eye narrowed.

"Trevor, I'm fine. Go on--get wall-eyed drunk, do it for me!"

"That's what 'feeling fine' sounds like is it...."

Brandishing the Jaguar keys, Burnleigh crossed the road and drove off.

But Thorne needed a walk alone. He set off to the fishing boats...when in doubt, go to the sea.

The afternoon sky was leaden. Today had none of Como's day-after-the-race Sunday brilliance. He retraced his steps past the potholes and broken pavement, paying them no heed. His sensibilities had begun to suit the Sicilian realities. It was the end of the fishing day and three-wheelers, Fiat Cinquecentos and Seicentos rushed towards him, horns squawking at each other like troops of monkeys. The snaggle-toothed old wheelbarrow was back in the middle of the road where it belonged. Every vehicle swerved grandly avoiding it.

In minutes he was back on the hard-packed yellow-dirt apron above the water. A dozen fishing boats, their brightly painted clipper bows bobbing on a light chop, pointed to sea at their moorings. Fifty yards out a skiff was being rowed ashore. From the bottom of the landing, fishboxes were passed from hand to hand up the landfill seawall. Rough shouts from below met hoarse croaks above, gruff, impatient, routinely annoyed. Watching the men, some old, some in their prime, others too young to merit courtesy, they were like a different species. He had nothing in common with them, yet their industry and sturdy self-sufficiency satisfied him. If the world beyond the horizon ceased to exist they would go right on day after day just as now.

From time to time one of them glanced at him, but he was invisible, a weed. His life was beyond meaningless, it grew out of no necessity.

Yet he believed in life lived as art, a life like Breitemann's...and Alex Winter's. He loved what Breitemann did, the beauty of the cars, their elegance and rarity and menace. He loved seeing mortal force tamed. Racing was all things to him--terrible, beautiful, unforgiveable. It validated the investment of being alive.

Standing amid these hoarse fishermen's shouts and the clatter of fishboxes he heard the other engine again, the young German on his big Lambretta. He came to a halt at a distance to watch them work, scowling implacably. In today's overcast his scowl could not be attributed to bright sun. Handsome, well proportioned, his hair a crown of blond in this swarthy land, he had the conscious arrogance of classic statuary. Yet it was his pained, watchful eye that was intriguing. Thorne had provided him with a story...he was the lovechild of a Wehrmacht grenadier in the war. His blondness would in other places be his identity, but in this dark land it was the emblem of his alienation.

Nonsense, there were blond Sicilians.

But this story pleased Thorne. In a way, they were alike. The gulf between him and the fishermen could not be bridged, just as the gulf between Thorne and battle-scarred Peter Whitlaw could not be bridged. Beacom's hard-bitten crew chief represented the elders of racing, eternally suspicious of those who had not lost enough. By profession Nick was a voyeur. No matter what barbarity befell Alex Winter, Thorne's only role was to bear witness, and Whitlaw's to despise him for it.

CHAPTER 38

UNDER BRIGHT SUN AND BLUE SKY, the Mediterranean was vast and still. Wind eddies spread gooseflesh across its placid surface. The forward rush of the big Palermo-Naples ferry had a handsome urgency...but Thorne was in no humor. The day was beautiful and he knew it too well-- nothing is more hurtful than feeling low amidst beautiful surroundings. Everything is pain, the sun's warmth, the lacy hiss of the ship's wake, the way people swan about on deck, mindless and without a care. Despicable.

Monday night he lay in bed for hours, too worn down to sleep. It felt as if he hadn't slept at all, though he couldn't say for sure--but he had no memory of his dreams. This morning he quivered with ill-digested angst...for poor Alex. After lying awake much of the night he decided the best thing to do today was write.

And of course it was impossible. The universal black spite he felt-- blanket contempt for his surroundings--unnerved him. He sat alone on the leeward deck struggling to work. Trevor had supplied him with all the race facts he missed, what was stopping him? But arriving as they had secondhand from Trevor, the facts were empty. Dead. He would rather describe Trevor relating the facts over his fucking *doppio*. That at least was alive.

He'd begun the story over and over, but with each new start he could make only half-hearted revisions. They carried him farther and farther in the wrong direction. The wadded sheets of paper at his feet, four attempts, stirred listlessly in the breeze. Maybe after talking with Christian...maybe that would be real!

He put down his pen. Perhaps this bewilderment had a purpose.

He got up and walked into the sun to port. It was blinding. Devane shaded his eyes, sitting with Whitlaw, Ermanno and some Beacom crew. A group of Porsche-Austria people sat in a larger circle farther aft. Beyond them Burnleigh and Angela sat by themselves. Devane looked measurably better today--and Angela measurelessly worse.

He stopped at Devane's chair. "You're looking chipper today." Devane nodded dismissively. "Had quite enough of feeling ill, mate." His smile contained none of the relieved grace Nick had seen in the hospital in Wolfsburg. But then, maybe a World Champion needs discontent. It was all just too bloody exhausting! Boarding the *Bartolomeo* this morning he saw Devane for the first time since the morning of the race. He returned the magnesium slug and Devane said not a word. Perhaps he would not be favored again with the damn thing.

He continued aft to Angela and Burnleigh. Her smile met him at half strength.

"Am I interrupting?" he said.

"Not a bit," she replied.

Thorne pulled a chair alongside. Whatever she and Trevor were talking about, they ceased.

"You look a mite grim," he said.

"It's going around," she said with a penetrating nod. Even in low spirits, her most attractive organ was her brain.

"What we all need," he said, "is a really good gavotte."

"That's it," Angela said, not smiling.

"I've just spent all morning writing myself into a corner."

"Things have consequences," she said. "Things take their toll, even when you don't know it. When Mike Spence was killed last year I lost eight pounds in a week. I thought I was doing splendidly, taking it all in stride, but I'd wake up in the morning feeling hungover without drinking a drop. I feel like I've had five minutes' rest since Sunday morning." She shaded her eyes. "And you are sufficiently generous of spirit to show how you're feeling as well."

"Not an asset in my business."

Her head shook. "If you were like some, you'd never show a trace. You're lucky." ٰ

"Lucky." He rolled it around on his tongue.

"It's an expensive gift," she said. "I can count on my thumbs the men I know who can afford it. Use it for good things." Her smile brightened, modulating to the major. "Speaking of which, Christian is asking for you. I told him you were working. He looked disappointed in you."

"Can't have that! Where is he?"

"The stern, 'e was," said Burnleigh.

"But don't go streaking away just yet," Angela said.

"Have to talk to him, luv. I'll be back."

He met her eye. "But thank you."

She nodded. "Just another episode in life's rich pageantry."

"I feel much better."
"And well you should."
She smiled with not a trace of irony.

CHAPTER 39

THORNE PONDERED AGAIN THE MYSTERIES of the master bedroom. Publicly criticizing the faults of one's spouse in a still-negotiable marriage...imprudent at the very least. Which Angela was not. Her disgust with Devane paralleled his own.

He came to the stern--and no Breitemann.

He continued around to starboard and heard the comical arpeggio laugh. Breitemann was surrounded by a group that included his co-driver and fellow victor Bengt Bjornsen and the suddenly radiant Luciana Podesta.

"There!" Breitemann boomed to him. "Take your head out of your books, schoolmaster!"

"My head's been in far worse places."

Luciana gave him a kiss on the lips. "You must play, Nick, not work all day!"

"Kiss me again and I'll retire."

She laughed.

He scanned the ship, the sky, the sea. "We're calling this 'work?'"

"We are lucky people, the very luckiest" she said, her smile shining. "Don't you think, Cristiano?"

Thorne saw the other Luciana, the woman in black, still visible around the edges. But she was less visible this morning.

"Christian," he said, "I was told you took a shortcut on the last lap."

"A shortcut? What is that?"

"You eliminated several kilometers of the track."

"Show me this short road and I will use it!"

"There is no way you could have gone that fast using the entire track."

"I simply drove very, very fast, Nick. You cannot imagine that?"

"So tell me how it was."

Breitemann nodded happily, collecting his thoughts.

"Well, Alex was really flying, you see," he began, "and I was completely determined to be ahead of him at the end. I wish someday you could have such a feeling as I had, Nicholas, it's something you would never forget. What happened was, I began to know that I understood the track and--no, no, this is not right, I did not understand the track any better than before. But I knew suddenly the track could not fool me, do you see? It wasn't that I knew the track as you know a closed circuit like Brands Hatch. I became certain that I was driving so well, the track could not trick me, could not force me into a big mistake! I could react so fast and so correctly if I began a mistake--and I did many times--there was no danger at all...I could get myself free before any damage! And as soon as I knew that, I became in a rage! It made me so angry with myself that I had been afraid to push hard, when now I knew I could react faster than anything could go wrong. I could force the car completely beyond the limit and still bring it back! I was out of control constantly, rescuing myself every second--it was so wonderful!"

Nick listened spellbound.

"I was surprised when I saw the lap time was only 33 minutes, but it felt to me like ten minutes or two hours--it made no difference! I remembered nothing afterwards. Maybe a plaster wall here...a broken pavement there. The car was going side to side, almost out of time with the road...yet always heading where it must. It was like a wonderful dream! All I remember from it is the smell of hot brakes and," he laughed, "... the pain in my hand from the *verdammt* shifter! It was a moving picture and I was just watching!"

But suddenly, his laugh growled.

"Then you come to the end and come out of it, and you think, *what!* Am I completely mad! The answer is, yes, of course I am."

Nick had his Targa story.

"Do you ski, Nick?"

"I love to ski."

"You know the feeling when you have pointed your skis straight downhill, and you are making long fast turns at maximum speed, nothing holding you upright except the force of your speed against the skis cutting the snow? When you are skiing that way, where you are is unimportant--it matters only where in the next second you will be! That is how it was in the car--pure instinct."

"But Cristiano," Luciana said, "surely it is not as good as sex."

Breitemann laughed. "It is different, but it is as good."

"Awww," she frowned looking at him, then the others. It was hilariously obvious they had been together last night.

"You cannot know what I am talking about," Breitemann said, "until you feel it yourself. The terrible thing is, so few people ever have the chance! But driving really well, life moves at light-speed, without thought--just look at Alex. He was doing it himself!"

It stunned Nick that Breitemann mentioned Alex so soon after the crash. But it was the racer's way, straight no chaser. A crash happened. The next crash will happen. The reality of ideal driving is what matters.

"We must ski together sometime, Nicholas," he beamed.

"I may not be fast enough."

"I think you are. And you do not have to win the Olympics to have this feeling--you only need to ski at your maximum and feel the joy. We shall find out who is fast enough, Nick."

"In Colorado next winter," Thorne agreed. "I'll show you the tails of my skis."

Breitemann was delighted. And even if he were no skier at all--though surely he was--one way or another Christian would get to the bottom first.

In the ferry galley, they had a leisurely lunch of artichoke hearts in oil and rich delicious tagliatelle al burro. Afterwards they rooted around for something of interest in the gift shop, without success. Thorne bought an *International Herald-Tribune*. He'd been a week without news. Had the hard-hats burned down Columbia? Had Nixon gotten a closer shave?

But the headline stopped him cold. At Kent State in Ohio anti-war students took over the campus. That afternoon in a parking lot the National Guard shot four dead.

"What's the matter?" Burnleigh said.

Thorne explained.

Burnleigh nodded. No wisecracks this time.

Thorne sat in a deckchair to study the story.

Part Four

Grand Prix of Monaco

CHAPTER 40

CHRISTMAS, THE NINETIES

It was 12:20 a.m. Christmas morning. He knew all about being alone on this day, you do it one minute at a time. You plan your moves carefully and never ask, what will be fun to do next?

The nor'easter battered the little Cape Cod. Thorne had felt a crisis-driven elation as the storm was building, but now it blasted on and on, his unease rising. As each new wave of violence declined, he thought, *good*, it's over--only to hear the violence gathering anew.

Tonight he'd arranged a small celebration, his secret. He would have Christmas champagne, it was in the refrigerator right now.

Yesterday for the first time in six sober years, he went to Shoreside Liquor, the self-consciously cozy little cottage in the village. Geoff Binchy, the owner, greeted him with long-time-no-see holiday joviality...how's he been...what's new in his life...on and on. But both of them heard the unasked question. He was glad to be out on the street again. He held the heavy plastic bag tucked tight under his arm like a football.

He wondered how it would be--

A drink.

But if ever there was a night....

He knew all the A.A. preventives. He could drink tomorrow--all he wanted, just not today. Cheap trick. Tomorrow is never, but today he can't.

Easy does it.

This too shall pass.

Blah-dee-blah-dee-blah.

Every breath he drew was electric. A drink was not the point, this black Christmas could kill him.

He tasted it on his tongue, the numb metallic tang of defeat.

Scrabblescrabblescrabble....

thp-thp-thp-thp-thp-thp!

Newton The Cat raced down the hall! Streaked past Thorne's feet, claws clutching the carpet for traction.

Newton wheeled sharply--tail high.

Stood stalk still, back arched! He glared at Thorne, his green eyes like limes. He hadn't put on a Young Newton display like this in years!

The whites of his eyes flared--

And Thorne clapped!

Newton was off like a cheetah, clawing down the hall, spinning a "Brodie" on the bathroom tile...careening back--

On Christmas Day!

Pathetic. Newton didn't know it was Christmas, didn't know about drinking or not drinking.

Thorne walked to the refrigerator. He grabbed the thick champagne bottle by the neck, savoring its heft--after six years so familiar. Removing the mushroom-cap of foil he inspected the crosshatched safety wires securing its cork. Systematically he reviewed the skills. He would grip the cork just so. Jigger it out carefully, thumb and forefinger assertive, deliberate.

Why was it so complicated!

Why not? He'd bought premium Piper-Heidsieck, did he expect a bottle cap?

Precisely the point--what did he expect.

Would champagne help?

Would it be a dream adrift on tropical seas, lavishly at peace?

Or would he dog-paddle, struggling for breath, loose in the four a.m. horror that had no dawn....

Fuck it! He loosened the crosshatched wires, his fingers twisting...twisting. The wire claw relaxed. On Christmas *to feel this terrible!*

He lifted the wire claw up and away. The bottle was armed. A grenade, the pin pulled. The cork would blast out like a .44 Magnum. He heard his boss at Pond Life, lobster-faced Mayburn the Great: "Loosen up, Thornie! Drop o'champers...teach you wutcha need to know!"

He knew what he was doing.

The very point...he *knew* what he was doing.

The four a.m. horror that had no dawn.

They said A.A. ruins your drinking.

He was in free-fall...plummeting.

Slowly--then feverishly--he settled the wire claw back over the cork. Centered it, his fingers moving fiercely. He twisted the wires down, cinching it tight.

But--was he insane? A bottle of champagne *on this night of horrors!*

He set the bottle down in the kitchen sink and in a fury released the wires again. He forced the cork out--

Foooommmmp!

A gurgitation of golden froth foamed out over his hands, the suds sliding down the sides of the bottle. He turned it upside down into the sink, shaking it out angrily, the bottle gagging. The blast from the cold-water tap gushed out, diluting and diffusing the sickly

sweet

exquisite

... Piper-Heidsieck.

He knew its play on his tongue

the needling sizzle....

It was pumping out now as fast as it would go, both water taps blasting. He imagined just one taste

... *dreamed it*

the pastel nectar

perfect

so elegant

innocent....

It confirmed who he was and was no more.

In all its tumult, this Christmas was eternal peace compared to his last few years of drinking. They came decades later, but he knew Spa was their headwaters. The downward slide from Spa was glacial, imperceptible, facilitated with smooth sleek denial. When he hit bottom six years ago

it almost killed him....

Last Tuesday he and Gail Loring from *Vogue* had their annual holiday lunch--blinys and red caviar. It was an annual observance from years before at the old Russian Tea Room...and for the record, Gail noted, Blinys celebrated Russian Easter, not Christmas.

But this was not Russia and they were American skeptics.

After exchanging near-term aspirations and far-term goals, the common currency of the season, Thorne regaled her with the ongoing narcissism and barnyard halitosis of Mayburn the Great, Media Heavyweight. Mayburn O. Mitcher "of the Sulphur Springs Mitchers" was elephantine in all the ordinate ways, obese, bombastic, vain, toxic. In Manhattan's publishing demimonde he had parlayed to legend his autocratic tenure as Editor-Publisher-Hood Ornament of *Sporting Life*--but that was the old news. Now at a quarter past sixty, Mayburn O. Mitcher discovered Hemingway. The affliction raged out of control....

"He let slip," Thorne said, "that the pals at the shooting club had taken to calling him 'Papa.'"

Gail Loring laughed.

"He says things like 'the business of the shooting.'"

"Oh, come on."

"He announced that last Sunday he 'shot cleanly and well.'"

She was appalled.

"He's the poster child for ego blastoma, but show me one publishing pro in this flyblown cowtown with the..." he drew out the Castilian guttural, "*co...jjjjo-nes* to say so. This isn't Pig Sump, Kentucky, it's New York!"

Gail Loring's smoky Lauren Bacall baritone purred it ever so softly: "Nickie, darling, you should know by now...there is no big time."

Thorne had never heard it put so neatly. All his life he had believed in the big time as an acolyte believes in priests. In his twenties he was at its red-hot center. Drifting away in his thirties he felt the chill. He punished himself in his forties because once upon a time in his twenties he'd been "in it." He groused that the big time was over-rated, misshapen, but never once had he challenged its fundamental legitimacy.

Yet it was not a complete fraud. Christian Breitemann was not a fraud. He knew when not to believe.

But even Christian denied his mortality.

Didn't he? Thorne had no idea. Christian welcomed life with open grace, showing no hint of self-pity. Thorne remembered his own unease as they began to be friends...what a miniature he proved to be! Coexisting with mortality defined Christian, yet Thorne was completely unprepared for it. And every decision Thorne had made since those failed days was a "strategic withdrawal"...he could risk no more losses. He took jobs because they presented no real challenge. He chose his wife because she offered no resistance. She represented values he abhorred, but no matter. For years his marriage was the ugly armoire in the bedroom that must be removed--but not today.

Today was here. Losing his marriage and examining that distant European spring were unrelated and inseparable.

He rinsed out the empty champagne bottle, all trace of its life-threatening soft bouquet erased. He took it out to the garbage, jammed it down between two bags, sealed the lid tight.

He'd gotten as far as Monaco. He must go on.

1970, MENTON, THE MIDI

It was the golden hour. Burnleigh and Thorne sat in an outdoor restaurant on the quay in early evening eating crusty bread and *soupe de poisson*. The Kronenbourg was cold. The yacht masts bobbed and swayed, halyards slatting and klink-ing in a soft breeze. Time passed gently. Why was this so familiar...Thorne had never been here before. During his European summer in college they didn't stop on the Riviera--they took the train straight through, Barcelona to Marseilles to Rome, thirteen hours with no seats and no rest, it was etched into memory like a burn scar.

Yet he knew this scene...sunset beside the Mediterranean, eating contentedly, white-sand beach arc-ing into the distance below purple bluffs. Checkerboard red-tile roofs cascading gently to the sea, interspersed by green palmettos and black-green pine, honey-dripping sun melting into the blue horizon. The first chill of evening made the hairs on his bare arms stand and--

Santa Barbara. The summer after graduation. They found an outdoor restaurant across from the yachts that year, he and Gina, beautiful Gina. They dipped lobster in drawn butter and watched the sun decline. With evening's first chill he leaned forward to hug her for warmth and for many reasons.

How had they failed? How had he allowed it! In these days, plagued by Angela's presence, Gina seemed perfection.

Crossing into France that afternoon Thorne and Burnleigh had been lucky to find rooms in Roquebrune-Cap-Martin down the coast from Monte Carlo. On the Naples ferry Angela suggested a modest hotel in Menton, but they were not surprised to find it booked for the Grand Prix weekend. The ostrich-woman at the desk, eyes bulging as if she were being throttled, phoned two hotels for them. The second, in Roquebrune, had the last two vacancies before the Italian border. They thanked her and she nodded, pecking her feed.

The vertical nature of racing society required that drivers and team principals reside in the deluxe hotels of the principality, to be close to the circuit, but just as surely, to confirm only they, Greek shipping magnates and English petty nobility could command such lodgings. For years Nick had read about the Monaco Grand Prix, a mock coronation, throngs of commoners straining to glimpse motor-racing royalty, which repaid the adulation by ignoring them completely.

What a pissy mood he was in...they had driven hard all day. Beyond commenting on the delicious *soupe de poisson* they were too tired to talk. Fine. Being over-tired was punishment in advance for offenses yet to be committed. He repeated his writing mantra--Remember, have fun.

But this European spring was wearing. First, there was Alex Winter. They had heard nothing, it meant nothing good. Then there was Devane and his wife. In the past week Nick's enthusiasm for Angela had changed. He remained smitten, if that was the word, but the ordeal in Sicily had cost him. The carillon peals of exhilaration he felt driving to Brands Hatch in the rain...only four weeks ago...had gone silent. European racing was everything he expected, heady and unforgiving, but flying so close to the flame proved demanding. The racers' struggles were not his struggles, yet at such close proximity it was only half true. He couldn't talk to Burnleigh about any of it, certainly not about Angela. He couldn't describe her pondering the eyeless Alex Winter, Thorne's hands kneading her outraged neck and shoulders...then nearly, so very nearly--

Remember, have fun.

In trumped-up gaudy Monaco.

Burnleigh had undergone a sea change too. He dismissed the Devanes now as "tawdry," his face a mask. Could it be, as Trevor claimed, their conflicts were nothing more than the friction needed to keep the flame lit?

Trevor was too facile by half. It was a problem.

The apparition came to Thorne again...Angela and Breitemann arm in arm in the Jaguar rearview in Cefalù. Perfection. Despite her marriage covenants--because of them--she was unmistakably in play.

Burnleigh eyed Thorne with a grin as if awaiting a reply.

"Wot..." said Thorne.

"Wot indeed," nodded Burnleigh.

He knew what Burnleigh wanted. He would not discuss it. He beckoned to the waiter, they paid and left.

For the first practice Friday morning the racing line through the principality's public streets was coated with grime from twelve months of incontinent Renaults, Peugeots and Citroën vans. For much of the day the racers' own tires would scrub the track clean. Only then did lap times become material.

Thorne hadn't seen the open-wheeled Formula One cars since last fall's U.S. Grand Prix at Watkins Glen. The narrow cylindrical single-seaters were small, light, fiercely goal-oriented--quite different from the larger nominally two-seater enclosed sports cars of the World Manufacturer's Championship. And instead of 1000-kilometer-and-longer endurance races, Grands Prix were desperate jousts of about two hours, one driver per car. The driver with the most points in thirteen Grands Prix won racing's highest honor, the World Driver's Championship. It was not uncommon for the best Grand Prix drivers, Garand, Breitemann and Devane among them, to contest both championships.

Several new Formula One designs had appeared since Watkins Glen. Four boxy March 701s would be driven by Tony Devane and three others. Jack Brabham continued with his brilliant aquamarine-and-yellow Brabham BT33. And to the displeasure of "Chubby"--Colin Chapman of Lotus-- Christian Breitemann refused to race the brand-new untested Lotus 72, a sleek wedge-shaped racer designed to generate maximum downforce. Until the new car had been properly sorted out he insisted on the old Lotus 49. It won the World Championship two years before, in Grand Prix time a millennium.

Gradually lap times began to pare down. By the end of Friday, in spite of his cracked ribs, Devane's 1:24.1 in his March 701 was impressively fastest by a full half second. Nick pondered its marital repercussions.

Jack Brabham wrestled with brake-balance problems throughout the day, as did Jean-Pierre Beltoise in the lead French Matra. For his part, Breitemann seemed quite off form. He was capable of no better than sixth fastest of sixteen cars. Then his Ford-Cosworth V-8 exploded in gray smoke right in front of the pits. Minutes later his offhand shrug dismissed Thorne's concern, "It is early yet, Nicholas. You will see."

"What does Chubby say?"

Breitemann beamed. "Frustration is good for him. Nick, you must not look so troubled! You will never find a beautiful woman wearing that expression...and here comes one now!"

Thorne turned. Jennifer Whelan walked towards them smiling under the pit area row of pine trees.

"Jennifer!" Thorne said. "I thought you weren't--"

"Changed my mind, a woman's prerogative. Must I go back to Paris?"

"Oh, I think not," Breitemann boomed. "Nick, you must say something!"

She smiled. "I can stay?"

Thorne gave her a big hug, inventorying in humid detail the forms, convex and concave, crushed against him. Two syllables came to mind...oh-oh.

CHAPTER 41

IT WAS VITAL TO THORNE to understand the drivers. When one didn't behave according to form it annoyed him, annoyance being more satisfactory than confusion. Annoyance at a racer like Tony Devane was effortless, but to be annoyed with Christian Breitemann...hurt.

Yet there could be no debate, Christian was being absurd. After practice they had gathered in Christian's suite at the Hotel de Paris for an aperitif, Jennifer Whelan, Jozie Joubert, Christian, Burnleigh and Thorne. The high-ceilinged drawing room around them was grandiose, antique white, just the least bit shopworn--a set for a 1930s MGM black-and-white about the travails of the rich. Every line of the room's paneling was stated and restated in scrolled plaster moldings that gathered and flowed and fluted around the room's corners like artificial drapery. The double main doors of the salon were ten feet high, with door handles at the center of the door rather than at the closure. Covered in gold-and-gray striped fabric, the interior surfaces bore the fine patina of decades of impromptu soirees precisely like this one. The drapes, swept back dramatically, revealed great floor-to-ceiling windows opened outwards. The afternoon was gray and humorless, but down steep Casino hill the tourmaline Mediterranean was studded with enormous white ketches and yawls and great clipper-bowed motor yachts, arranged like jewels on a brooch. Moored to massive cut-stone seawalls and finger piers these nonpareil craft had arrived at yachting's Olympus, the Monaco Inner Harbor at Grand Prix Week. Everything about the scene proclaimed shameless grandiosity--yet Christian Breitemann was objecting to the price of a haircut!

Every year during Grand Prix Week the drivers were welcomed to a private reception and dinner at the palace, guests of Prince Rainier and the elegantly fading Princess Grace. And being streng Deutsche, Christian was determined to observe the proprieties. In Thorne's opinion, Christian didn't really need a haircut--his blond hair hung just below his ears, neither long nor short by the fashions of the day. But being received by the Prince and Princess of Monaco, Breitemann insisted he must prepare and know it.

When he learned of the Hotel de Paris barbershop's rates, however, he was scandalized. Winning his first German National Championship on motorcycles, he said, he spent less money for a month's food. Two hundred and forty Marks...out of the question!

He read the annoyance in Thorne's eyes, but his head shook adamantly. "Jackie Stewart has far more money than I, I will say, and never will he pay so much for a haircut!"

"But my dear man," Burnleigh said, "Jackie is Scottish!"

Breitemann waited, the distinction lost on him.

"No, Jackie isn't Scottish," Thorne grinned, "he is German."

The booming Gallic belly laugh from Jozie Joubert was too hearty by half for the circumstances.

Breitemann smiled at Jennifer, gradually inferring the lore of Scottish parsimony. Still he nodded firmly. "You think I am a fool, but to pay 240 Marks, it is a shame."

Jennifer stepped into the fray. "Tell you what, Christian--I'll cut your hair."

"You!" Burnleigh erupted.

"I used to cut my brother's hair all the time. I'm very good."

Breitemann's eye twinkled. "And how many hundred Marks do you charge?"

"C'mon," she said turning to the door, "it'll be fun. I have scissors in my room."

"She's serious...'' Thorne said.

Jennifer turned in the open doorway. "Come! I can't cut hair with my fingernails!"

"You're staying in the Hotel de Paris?" Thorne said awestruck.

"Dah-ling," she Tallulah-ed, "everyone who's anyone stays at Hotel de Paris. Play your cards right and you will too!"

Whatever annoyance Thorne suffered over Breitemann vanished in the drubbing Christian took getting his haircut. He sat on an upright chair in the center of Jennifer's white-tiled bathroom, everyone grimacing at every second snip lamenting the botched job in progress.

Christian smiled sportingly throughout...240 Marks to trim his thatch--intolerable!

From time to time, Jennifer too clicked her tongue, looking concerned.

But at Christian's searching smile she belly laughed--all was well.
"There we are," she said at last. "What do we think?"
He turned and looked in the mirror. "*Phantastisch*, Jennifer!" He looked
around at the gallery. "Wonderful, is she not?"
"It's a good job you can't see the back," Burnleigh said.
"No, no, it is perfect I am sure. And if it is not, Princess Grace will
discover I am a gypsy only as I am leaving."
He eyed Nick meaningfully. "*Phantastisch.*"
"I hope that means good," she glimmered.
The beauty of her smile stunned Nick.
Then as if to prove his objection to local tonsorial rates was principle,
not parsimony, Breitemann hosted an extravagant Hotel de Paris dinner.
Accompanying it were numerous bottles of the coveted Burgundy Thorne
and Burnleigh had foresworn veering east from the Côte de Beaune
towards Switzerland.
Wading into his Grand Marnier dessert soufflé Thorne had no
recollection of being annoyed, not by Christian, not by anything.

He had drunk more than he should, but when you're having a perfect time
you're required to drink more than you should! His eye kept meeting
Jennifer's. Breitemann was his customary measured self. Nick watched him
take two glasses of Burgundy--just two. He marveled at how Christian first
tasted the wine when opened, pronounced it excellent, then left it almost
untouched. When Nick enjoyed a taste he must have more.
At ten-thirty Breitemann went up to his suite alone. He refused to
indulge the excesses of legendary racing drivers, too peaceful by half. Apart
from objecting to Monegasque barbers, he was fully and graciously at ease.
Whatever he lacked in life--at dinner he said his great priority was to marry
happily--he was confident all would come to him in good time.
Ten minutes later Christian's unruffled ease only served to nettle Nick.
He was walking Jennifer downhill to the harbor under the principality's
wrought-iron Belle Epoque streetlamps, his arm around her tiny waist. She
was so slender and responsive to his touch he felt he could move her any
way he wished...spin her with a twist of the wrist. The wine had been
wondrous--he knew it by the attention he paid to the animal clench of her
hips in his palm with each step. Yet Christian! He had no woman and no
hint of one anytime soon. Luciana had been a night's dalliance for them
both, but how could he contrive to be so content, at peace! Whence came
this unshakable confidence that everything he needed would come his way!
It was not racerly, not manly, never mind that when Nick looked at how
successful he was at "making things happen," he fell short. The nicest
happenings in his life had not been his plan, they simply unfolded. But he

was young yet, his skills would improve. And Christian was brilliant and famous. How could he abdicate responsibility for his life? He was wrong!

"You're awfully quiet," Jennifer said. "What are you grinning about?"

"I'm not grinning."

"All right, frowning."

"Not frowning, either," he nodded. "Thinking."

"What about?"

"Everything."

"That much?"

"Your waist. How good it feels."

"No, no, what are you thinking about?"

"Christian. Do you agree with him? Should we all just sit back and let things wash over us like he says?"

"I don't think that's what he was saying."

"Okay, what was he saying--I want to understand. It sounded to me like, you can't make good things happen--just be passive and what happens is fine. I don't believe that, do you?"

"It pisses you off."

"It's weakness!"

He waited for her to say something.

She matched her steps carefully to his.

"Is that how you want to live, Jennifer, just waiting for a good thing to happen, and if bad things happen, do nothing to resist?"

"It's a little easier for a woman."

"What's that supposed to mean?"

"Well, women are supposed to wait passively, or pretend to, until a man invites them to walk down to the Monaco harbor after a wonderful dinner."

"That makes it a virtue?"

"Not a virtue--a rule."

"I don't believe that. You have goals for yourself, don't you? You have ambitions and plans and a vision of what will make you happy?"

"Of course."

"Well? Here you are in Monaco having dinner with one of the greatest grand-prix drivers in the world. Are you asking me to believe it's mere accident? You did a lot of things with your photography that made getting here inevitable--you made it happen. Or was some housewife from Winnetka supposed to be here instead?"

"You're right, I don't want to be a housewife from Winnetka."

He laughed in spite of himself.

"Christian feels strongly about patience," she said. "And it's true, he could be out having a bigger time. He's handsome, smart, successful. Women would rip off their clothes just saying hello."

"So why not?"

"Like you, you mean?" She grinned. "He doesn't want to. I don't think that makes him wrong."

"Maybe it does."

"It's the same reason he doesn't want to pay 240 Marks for a haircut--because he's Christian. That's okay, isn't it?"

"I guess." He shrugged, unsatisfied.

She smiled up at him.

"It's okay with me. How would you like me to give you a haircut?"

"Do I need one?"

"I'll give you a haircut you'll never forget."

"I think I'd like that."

"Me too," she said.

He pulled her to him, her mouth pressed wetly to his. The kiss they shared held no secrets. His hand slid to the firmness of her bottom. She locked her thigh tight against him, her tongue probing, pressing, caressing.

Their lips parted and she held her face against his chest, his breathing gone ragged. He laughed quietly.

"What?"

"We don't need to see the harbor, we've seen the harbor."

They turned back up the hill. Glancing downwards under the streetlights, she smiled.

"I see you have something in mind."

"If I can get through the lobby without being arrested."

"This is France. They'd elect you president."

They crossed the lobby. The elevator door slid shut.

He held her hips in his hands, and they had no time--he could not think of any other thing than now or have any other thoughts. He saw it in her eyes, felt it in her hands...vanishing into one another, light into shade, gone far beyond...he felt its force and knew without knowing exactly how it would be.

He swung the door of her room closed. She left the light on.

They rushed each other's clothes off, moving on each other's bodies, circling and twisting and straining like Greco-Roman wrestlers.

They lay back panting, their voices raw.

Minutes passed. The air was musky.

Only gradually they returned to where they were.

"Right back..." she said after another minute. She hopped off the bed.

He marveled again at the gulf between men and women. After sex she was energized, ready to dig a hole in the parquet floor. He could barely move.

She came back. The warm damp hand towel she brought stroked him.

"Better?"

He nodded happily. "You are the greatest of rarities."

"Sounds promising."

"You look better with your clothes off."

"You like?"

She turned in profile and cupped her breasts for him.

"Yes," she said. "I see you do."

She came down on all fours over him. Slowly she dragged the fleshy pink nubs of her nipples across his lips. They budded on his tongue.

"Mmm..." she breathed.

He held her still, her legs spread wide around him. Holding her with his hands, not letting her move, he moved down the bed beneath her. The reddish-gold tangle of ringlets was above his lips, her flesh crimson. Dew-covered. Provoked.

He pulled her down and met her with his lips. She gasped in elegant despair.

"Nothing's like the first time," he said.

She disagreed.

"Nope," he said. "A shame but nope."

"The second time was just as good."

He laughed. "That's not what I mean--they were both the 'first time.'"

"The second time was best of all!" she teased, giving him a funny grin. "Or were you faking?"

He nuzzled her breasts. "No wonder you wear clothes. Men would be mounting you in the fish market. You'd have to join a convent."

"And do without this?"

Gently, she raised him in her hand.

"I don't suppose you'd...."

"Go for the record?"

She smiled. "Not if you don't want to."

She brought his hand up to her breast, but he guided her fingertip to her nipple, bewitched at her response to her own touch.

She rolled onto her back and his tongue parted her soft inner creases. She sprawled back, treasuring her nipples like twin diamonds.

He pressed her down hard, rushing into her.

CHAPTER 42

"I WAS GOOD FROM THE START--I always was good."
The directness of Breitemann's eye dismissed irony.
"My first race was on a small 125-c.c. Puch motorcycle. I crashed badly
on the very first lap--I was trying too hard. I did not know yet such a thing
was possible. So I got up and restarted, and by ten laps I had re-passed all
but one motorcycle--and I beat him by half a lap in the following race. I was
good, so as things go, I must continue until I found someone who is better. I
could not. I switched to cars and still I moved upwards. It was exciting.
Others had better cars but still I did not find the one I could not defeat.
"After awhile I was no longer testing myself against others, I was testing
against myself. It was different. I became like an artist--I must constantly
improve my technique, my way of thinking and seeing. That was even more
exciting. But without knowing it, now I was trapped--I must only go on.
And the nearer I came to the top the narrower the road became.
"It sounds like madness to be trapped by pleasure--like some low story
about love. But if you have a talent it happens quite easily. I will never be
free, always I will be trapped...or I will be afraid of what I might have done
if I had tried just a small degree harder."

"Well, now, mate, you look a bit of all right this morning!"

Thorne didn't respond. Burnleigh was taking a bit too much pleasure in this.

"Slept well, did you?"

Thorne pondered the light rain. "Are we back at Brands Hatch?"

In truth, the wet and chill suited him...and last night was none of

Burnleigh's business.

They stood under the line of pines running down the center of the Monaco pit area. The narrow strand of open-air working spaces was about twenty yards wide, separating the harbor-front straight from the Start-Finish straight. Each team area was loosely defined by stacks of wheels and tires, and when they weren't on the track, the race cars themselves.

The morning rain was no surprise. For half a century this tiny intensely mercantile principality had staged a May grand prix. Spring on the Monegasque Riviera could be wet and cool. A motor race ensured an early start to the tourism season.

Saturday-morning practice began at 7:50, but a severe thunderstorm made the session a washout. A few cars tested the slippery track and one, Graham Hill's older Lotus 49, had its fuel-injection play up at Gasometre Curve, then abruptly come on full force. The sudden burst of power on the wet pavement sent him crashing into the curb, destroying the car's right-rear cross member. Repairs would take all morning.

The rain stopped. Time passed. It looked as if the track would dry out. But before it could, a second cloudburst hit. Morning practice was a write-off.

Immediately smiling ex-World Champion Jack Brabham, well-loved "Blackie," did a slow lap at the height of the deluge, a big red umbrella hand-held above his open-face helmet. Fizzling along at 40 miles an hour wearing a huge Aussie no-worries grin, he drew lusty cheers all around--none of which he heard. Sitting ahead of a shrieking Formula One engine for more than a decade had cost him the greatest part of his hearing.

The rain stopped at last. Thorne would speak to Ron Tauranac at Brabham. Black Jack was just pulling off his unique white racing helmet. It had domes of sound-deadening insulation over each ear to conserve what little hearing remained to him.

But to reach Tauranac, Nick must cross the Trimmer pit. Devane's navy-blue March 701 lurked there beneath a rain-dripping tarpaulin. The World Champion was nowhere to be seen, but Angela saw Thorne. Her eyes lit immediately.

"Nickie, dear, did you hear the murder?"

"What?"

"An axe murder. In the Hotel de Paris about one o'clock last night."

"Axe murder!"

She nodded. "Jennifer's floor. Some poor thing was being hacked to bits one bloody morsel at a time--or so it sounded." She engaged his eye. "Of course now and then some of us rather enjoy a right hacking."

He nodded: "Another precinct heard from."

"Here, now, luv, it's the Sexual Revolution...you said so yourself. She's positively glowing!"

He felt a confusion of emotions, pleasure, embarrassment and something more conflicted. "Angela, you enjoy making people squirm! Has this been discussed before the entire Grand Prix Driver's Association or must it wait until after practice?"

"You're one of us, Nick! If it had been Christian, wouldn't we all be gaping and gossiping?"

"The editorial 'we,'" he nodded. "Is that you and your tapeworm?"

Her belly laugh thundered. She reached out and touched his cheek with her fingertips. "Why am I not surprised, not even a bit."

She turned on her heel. Showing her very best side, she walked towards her husband's navy-blue race car. At her approach team-owner Nigel Trimmer smiled graciously. Wealthy distinctly horse-faced Trimmer was a Yorkshire construction baron. His prowess as a judge of young driving talent discovered the current World Champion three years before, supplied the car, coaching and confidence, guiding Devane to the world title.

Powerless to avert his eye from the perfection of Angela's bottom, Thorne pondered the things she'd said. It was not "if" she fancied him but "how much." He even heard a hint of jealousy. Yet if matters were reversed and Angela took a lover, wouldn't he too feel a clang? But on one point he had no doubt--having just finished screwing himself hoarse with one woman, now all he could think of was throwing another down in the gorse. No mystery that the brain and the genitals are located at opposite ends.

Intermittent rain kept things off balance all day. Then high tide and strong winds began whipping the harbor water up over the seawall onto the track in the Chicane.

After two weeks' healing, Devane's physical condition was much improved. But now more than ever the scalpel agility of a grand-prix car suited him. Despite widespread doubt about the March 701, confirmed in mediocre times by its other three entrants, Devane maintained an impressive half-second advantage over everyone. Judging him by any other standard than F1 was a mistake. He would start the race from the pole. Since passing was legendarily difficult at Monaco, it was a massive advantage.

Farther back Breitemann hovered around sixth fastest in the old Lotus 49. Trying to improve his time he'd twice gotten caught in a downpour without getting a clear run. Colin Chapman began murmuring Christian was under the weather. When Nick asked Christian about it he was greeted with a grin. "Chubby fears they will say his car is no good. It was the greatest Formula One car of all time two years ago, but that was a different century."

"You're fine?"

"Yes."

In truth, Christian looked to have lost all interest.

Only one description suited François Courtault--gorgeous. He had the intense sort of male beauty that is off-putting to men and makes women look at each other and titter. Gleaming black hair broke across his brow like a curling wave. His large beautiful teeth flashed bright white when he smiled—which he did constantly. His sensuous full features were, like Clark Gable's, so pronounced they bordered on caricature. Tall and athletically proportioned, he had luminous blue eyes set deep in heavy black brows, taking in all with beaming alertness.

Courtault stood with Angela at the entrance of *Aurore*'s main salon. It was the same 155-foot motor yacht used by Bogart in the 40s for infamous all-night parties while shooting Beat The Devil. Courtault's arm was snug around Angela's slim waist. The two of them together conjured a Hollywood commissary in the Golden Age, Gable, Rita Hayworth, Heddi Lamarr and Gary Cooper all eating chicken salad, beggaring human pulchritude.

"My God!" Jennifer breathed to Thorne seeing Courtault.

"Looks a bit like me," Thorne said.

She giggled. "He's perfect!"

Angela beckoned to Jennifer, Thorne and Burnleigh, fanning the air with hurry-hurry urgency. She smiled gloriously. "You all know François."

"I don't," Jennifer said offering her hand. Courtault took it, closing his hand around hers with a squeeze.

She responded with her incendiary smile, the one given Breitemann finishing his haircut. It was exclusively for drivers...wearers of the Nomex.

The fashion in high-end p.r. functions this season was evening yacht cruises. Lake Como had been one of several, but tonight Jiggs Prouty outdid himself. *Aurore* was a huge steel ocean-going yacht lavishly encrusted with hand-carved mahogany, forests of teak, brightwork gleaming like Orrefors. Her diesels came up now as she nudged away from the dock, backing down in a tight wheel on her port screw. Her rakish clipper bows headed to the narrow gap in the granite seawall. She sailed seaward, Prouty welcoming all. He conceded that of the countless yachts present *Aurore* was only third largest. "The largest and second largest," he beamed, "belong to Onassis and God, in that order."

Tonight's cruise, he said, celebrated two occasions, tomorrow's grand prix, and François Courtault's brilliant victory in the rain in today's Formula Three race. Formula Three was a desperately competitive junior open-wheel series formed to identify future Formula One stars. Winning in Formula Three was almost as hard as winning in Formula One.

Cheers greeted Courtault, who bowed all around with joy.

As for the inclement weather, said Prouty, "We urgently requested clear skies and a beautiful sunset, but God was out and Onassis could not be disturbed."

The hundred or so aboard cheered and applauded, prepared to make do.

Jennifer wore a slinky black sheath that was chic, shapely, crushably erotic. What was it Nick thought at Ehra-Lessien...pale and unhealthy? She was the match tonight for supermodel movie star Suzy Parker, the recommended look in ivory-skinned redheads.

But still she troubled him. The relaxed, playful Jennifer snipping Breitemann's hair, fetching up short as if making a blunder, was inside this little black sheath--but where? It pleased him that she was beautiful, but she stirred something more, raw sexual envy. He remembered the haunted hush when word spred that dark-eyed Marnie McEvoy, the prettiest girl at Palo Alto High, was dating a Stanford student. Nick and his fellow Seniors felt undone--no Stanford coeds wanted *them!* They were dorks, but Marnie was a woman. Girls blossomed explosively but becoming a man was taking forever.

"Has anyone ever told you you're beautiful?" Jennifer said.

"Yes," Courtault said with a twinkle. "But I just deny it."

Angela swung her arm around his neck and pulled his cheek down to her lips. "Isn't this the most sinful man!"

He laughed again. "What am I to do, with World Champions' wives kissing me! The only answer is to drive very fast and see who else will kiss me!" He turned suddenly to Thorne. "Don't you think?"

Thorne laughed. He was a writer and a fan and Courtault had been matchless in the rain today. This joyous young Parisian, a comet in the racing skies, cast a spell over them all. Thorne wondered if Christian had ever been so carefree, so wildly enthusiastic--but he had, Thorne saw its traces. And Courtault was only a baby. Christian had struggled through difficult years in Formula One. He'd seen more and lost more. But it pleased Nick that Courtault, at twenty-two, was brimming over with enjoyment. He and Christian were different in ways, but they shared that. Angela's devotion to Courtault was obvious--she deferred to him openly. The youngest Formula Three Champion ever, he was on his way. His closeness to Angela was interpreted in England as a telltale that Nigel Trimmer, her husband's entrant, would sign him. Meanwhile, Courtault was to drive a brand-new Belgian Ferrari 512S the next weekend at brutally fast Spa.

Aurore moved out to open sea, the guests paying no attention. Consumed in conversation, drink and their own nonpareil company, the party was in full swing.

"You're not at the palace, Angela." Thorne said, getting it out of the way.

"Nick!" Jennifer glared. At this hour Formula One was dining with the Grimaldis.

But with not a flinch Angela said, "I thought Tony might have a go at Princess Grace."

Nick gave her a quiet smile, good for her.

"So let's eat and drink," she said, "...and drink and drink."

Courtault led them to a window table and drew out a chair for Angela.

"Ta," she said, her smile behind a cloud. But better to have it said, Thorne believed.

He pulled out a chair for Jennifer. The rain made a pleasant murmur on the windows, Aurore's diesels rumbling distantly. The ship bumped and swayed through a confused swell.

"You don't get seasick, do you?" Nick said to Jennifer.

She shook her head.

"Good," he said, "you can clean up after me."

"You're so romantic," Angela said, back to her party face.

"Don't be prissy," he said. "You're every bit as gross as I am!"

"Impossible."

The deep-gray dusk out the windows was darkening, the setting sun but an inference. The massive Corniche towering above Monte Carlo dimmed to a Ryder-esque black smudge, the lights of the principality in the distance blinking on. In the salon golden candlelight glowed warmly.

To Nick's and Burnleigh's congratulations, Courtault nodded. "It was not a victory, really," he said modestly, "it was luck."

He had won despite losing third gear in the last corner of the last lap. One more corner and he would have lost.

"No, no, François," Angela objected sharply, "victory is not negotiable, you must learn that. There are worlds of drivers who are fast, but only a few who know how to win. Often the winner is not fastest. Pileggi was fastest for 20 laps today but he crashed--he always crashes. And you always win."

"Not always."

"More than the rest," she said.

Courtault frowned. "But Angela, luck is not a skill."

Her laugh was fierce. "It is the very greatest skill! Without it you are only part of the queue, there to give the skilled one competitors to beat. Make no mistake, you made a name not because you are fast, which you are, but because you know how to win. Tony is the same, even though some are faster."

"Not this weekend," Jennifer objected.

It made Nick look at her.

"He has done well," Angela agreed, "but he has a good car. I take it

199

back, the March is not a good car but Trimmer made it good. And Tony is World Champion--he should be good."

Nick could not deny the ruthlessness in it.

Seeing his thought Angela's head shook, "No, Nick, racing has no good intentions. I hope Tony does well tomorrow--I hope he wins--but hope counts for nothing. Points aren't awarded for sincerity. At the end of the day there is one winner and fifteen losers. Knowing how to win is done moment to moment, every inch of the way. The winner is the fastest driver with that skill. Tony has it or did last year, it comes and it goes. New drivers learn it, but few keep it. You, François, and one or two others, have as much of it right now as anyone. You must ride it for all it's worth!"

"You said one or two others..." Burnleigh said.

"You know perfectly well."

"I don't."

"Come now, Trevor--*Christian!* He is in the wrong car this weekend, nothing to be done about it. But he has what Tony and François both have." Her eye turned to François. "And you must find out how deep it runs--it can be very cruel. Often when you should win, you don't...and when you shouldn't, you win. The hard ones to watch are all the rest. They lose patience, then hope. They press on year after year praying for a change...until something happens."

There was silence.

She smiled joylessly. "They are no more than scenery."

"And how does one continue being a winner?" Courtault said.

"Francois...if I knew! The very smartest ones, even Trimmer, don't know! The best they can do is recognize when it's gone. Right now, I'd say--
"

She stopped.

"What?" Nick said, knowing what must follow.

She shook her head.

"What, Angela!"

"You already know."

"But you need to say it!"

Jennifer clasped his forearm to stop. The moment passed, but Courtault's smile was gone. He knew too.

"Winning is cruel," Angela said again.

Courtault sipped his scotch gazing beyond the curvature of the earth. "I would like to be driving tomorrow, that is all I know. I would give anything. It is my greatest dream since a small boy--to drive in a grand prix. After Spa perhaps."

But then, as if measuring something measureless, he leaned far forward speaking under his breath.

"Mr. Trimmer and I talked today. I am telling all of you in the strictest secrecy...please. I begin with the French Grand Prix!"

Angela was thunderstruck.

"Tony will continue, of course," he said. "There was never a doubt of that. But a second car will be run."

The cold algebra of winning and losing crossed before Angela.

Courtault smiled quietly. "I am telling you because you are all serious racing people." Then his laugh bubbled. "And because I cannot bear not to!" He beamed at Angela. "You, mon ange, you are right--winning today was very important."

Burnleigh raised his glass jubilantly: "To today!"

But Courtault's hand came up, quelling him. In this salon full of racing people he must attract no undue attention.

With a very quiet toast, they drank, smiling as if their faces would explode. He nodded thanks softly. The rain pattered on the windows. Aurore nudged through bumpy seas.

Perhaps it was the rain and the dark, but in spite of Courtault's news Nick felt subdued. Angela's smile, though genuinely happy, took other counsel as well. Beautiful women too face blind apexes at maximum speed, risking all.

"Angela," he said, "no one understands racing like you--no one."

"Oye'd 'ave ter, woutn't oye," she said in stage cockney. "It's me mum-in-law these many years...."

Jennifer went to the loo. Courtault was circulating among the tables "working the room." Two tables away Burnleigh had found a short blonde with a gap in her teeth. Nick and Angela were alone.

"There's been a change," she said.

"Change?"

"*The Spy's Wife.*"

"The movie? You never mentioned the title."

"They want me in London to discuss it."

"Fabulous!"

"Not everyone agrees," she said.

"But you are not one of them."

"I'm not."

"Good. You not going to the palace...what can he be thinking?"

"Don't be predictable."

But her eye signaled it, Jennifer was returning.

"If I can help..." he offered under his breath.

He stood to slide the chair beneath Jennifer.

"So what's the hot gossip?" she said. "I haven't heard anything juicy since leaving Paris."

"I should think if anyone would know...."

Angela left it there, her eye chilly. She and Jennifer behaved for all the world like friends, but now and then came a cold current. Women's ways. Thorne stood in awe.

He looked out the window. He hadn't been paying attention--*Aurore* was passing through the breakwater again already, returning to harbor. This ostentatious evening, fitting preamble to the most ostentatious of grands prix, was ending. The ship maneuvered skillfully in the cramped Inner Harbor. Arriving at her mooring with a minimum of disturbance, the gangplank was lowered and guests made their chattering, foot-dragging way, moving by twos and threes onto the quay in the rain. Nick held his umbrella over Jennifer and Angela. Burnleigh intended to get lucky with the gap-toothed blonde, but by the look of it luck wasn't required.

A clamshell Citroên ID19 taxi drove Jennifer, Angela and Thorne up steep Casino hill to Hotel de Paris. They climbed out. After taking a kiss on the cheek from Thorne, Angela went in alone.

Thorne smiled at Jennifer. "All play and no work makes Jack a dull writer. I need some sleep tonight." He grinned, "For a change."

The smile he got back fell well short of the mark.

"But can we have dinner tomorrow?"

"Love to," she said too politely. The goodnight peck she gave him came nowhere near.

CHAPTER 43

RACE-DAY MORNING A GRAY RAIN slanted across the Midi like pencil-drawn shade. But by eleven it stopped and the sky brightened. Thorne saw a first shadow cast by a stack of racing tires at the back of the Rob Walker pits. In no time bright sun blazed down on Monaco, the Med a riot of rough-cut diamonds. It reminded him of another brilliant day--the summer-vacation Como Sunday.

Amid last-minute preparations for this most celebrated of grands prix, Nick moved from pit to pit putting faces and forms to the Monaco pit photos he had studied since he was a boy. A novice in holy orders, he wandered among the College of Cardinals.

But thirty minutes before the start he was suddenly informed by a pit marshal he must leave the pits. He pointed to his brand-new red-leather International Racing Press Association armband, surely, he could stay. The pit marshal's head shook. And strictly speaking, he was not writing a grand-prix story. But banished from Nirvana moments before the start--he couldn't bear it!

"*Mais non!*" he insisted pointing at his armband.

"*Non, non.*" The marshal wagged his finger, pointing to the outside of the track.

"*Ça suffit pour rester ici,*" he insisted. "*Ça suffit!*"

The marshal took him by the arm, but he yanked himself free. "*Laissez-moi!*"

"*Il faut aller!*"

He refused to budge.

The marshal put his whistle to his mouth and blew sharply. Across the track a gendarme turned. The marshal beckoned. Thorne was beside himself--he could not leave!

But the gendarme commanded him to cross the track. With no option, he began towards the far side, the marshal at his elbow. He yelled back desperately to Angela. When she saw him, she came running. He refused to move until she arrived.

"This bastard says my armband is no good!"

She gave the marshal a glare--she would make it right. She turned on her heel. He saw Jennifer watching from the Trimmer pit. She had no pass either, but she had the ultimate credential.

Angela stalked to Devane and Nigel Trimmer while Thorne was escorted to the outside guardrail. Now Nigel Trimmer himself hurried across the track, "Follow me, young man."

They pushed through the back of the crowd and into a spiraling driveway auguring down beneath the towering high-rise across from the Trimmer pits. It was no coincidence--Trimmer resided here.

Eyes adjusting to subterranean darkness they arrived in a cavernous parking garage. Trimmer strode to a magnificent white Rolls-Royce Corniche and unlocked the trunk. Producing a blue-leather briefcase--the same medium blue as his Formula One car--he handed Thorne an Entrant/Worker credential. Stunned by this kindness moments before the start, Thorne apologized for pulling Trimmer away from the track.

"Not to worry, lad," he said. "If we aren't ready to race by now, we never shall be. Let's go, then. Mustn't miss the punch-up." Trimmer led the way. "Let's see the bastards stop you now!"

The marshals waved them across the track to the pits--not a blink from the gendarme. The other marshal was scuttling away along the pit lane. Thorne arrived next to Angela, Devane's car being pushed to the starting grid. She leaned against him. "Here." She handed him the magnesium nugget. He put it in his pocket.

"About Trimmer," he said, "... thank you! Unbelievable!"

She looked to the grid. "Nonsense--you're one of us."

The drivers were pulling the flameproof balaclavas over their heads, then their helmets and gloves. One by one, they climbed in and tightened down their five-point harnesses...minutes to go.

Half to demonstrate his Entrant/Worker pass, half because he could not fail to do otherwise, Thorne walked amongst the crewmen on the grid. Starting at the back, he stepped between the fat-tired, shin-high single-seaters, their brilliant colors ablaze in direct sun. They lined up two cars per row. For safety--such as it was--the rows were staggered in a checkerboard pattern. It was his first Monaco grid but he had made this walk at countless starting grids. Row by row he took them in: Graham Hill and Pedro Rodriguez, Garand and Peterson, Siffert and McLaren, Courage and

Rindt...farther to the front, Pescarolo and Beltoise, Breitemann and Ickx, Brabham and Hulme...and at the spear's tip, Devane and Stewart.

In two hours, one may be gone.

It took his breath away.

Nothing went according to logic--in the greatest races it never does.

Devane's Ford-Cosworth V-8 scorched immediately off the grid into the lead. An advantage established, he pulled away from Stewart at nearly a second per lap. By lap 10 of 80, his navy-blue March led Stewart by 7.5 seconds, Hulme's cantaloupe-orange McLaren in third and attacking Stewart.

But after 15 laps, Hulme was losing a step here and there, fading. Brabham held position in fourth, watching the battle just ahead. Beltoise's Matra came fifth, followed by Breitemann's old Lotus in sixth.

By lap 20, pushing hard, Devane had crafted a brilliant 12-second lead over Stewart. He looked untouchable. After a long struggle, Brabham nipped past Hulme for third, Beltoise fifth, barely a car-length ahead of Breitemann.

Beltoise fell out with a broken ring-and-pinion, but holding out little hope, Thorne kept an eye on Christian's red-white-and-gold Lotus, now fifth.

Devane stretched his lead to 15 seconds--but suddenly came past the pits sounding like Chinese New Year. His engine was backfiring madly. He pitted for a new ignition, losing two full laps. He re-entered but five laps later, the wounded engine failed, ending his day.

Until this point, the race had followed the dictum of comparative speed, but now things changed. Stewart led Brabham, Hulme third and Breitemann fourth, Christian forcing impossible speed out of the old Lotus.

Stewart and Brabham fought bitterly for the lead, the interval never greater than half a second. Then Hulme lost top gear, and Breitemann shot past the orange McLaren into third.

Stewart, leading, gradually built a 2.5-second lead over Brabham...until his left-rear A-arm snapped. Stewart too was out.

Fourteen laps remained, Brabham leading, with Breitemann second, an insurmountable 15 seconds behind. Howling, arms waving, Lotus boss Colin Chapman ran right onto the track to encourage Breitemann every time he passed the pits. And Christian had the bit in his teeth. He cut into Brabham's lead steadily. With eight laps to go, he was 10 seconds back. He cut it to seven seconds. In the three-year old car, he was gaining on the cutting-edge Brabham BT-33 by two seconds per lap!

And feeling the pressure from his pit signals, Brabham began to bear down.

At the same time, in sixth place and about to be lapped by Brabham, Josef Siffert's engine began to suffer fuel starvation. With only four laps left, Siffert's engine was banging and popping for lack of fuel climbing the long Casino hill. Trying to slosh fuel into his starved fuel pickups, Siffert weaved and swerved upwards...just as Brabham arrived at full racing speed!

With no option, Brabham almost stopped to avoid Siffert. He got past-- but now Breitemann was just three seconds behind.

Chapman's arms flailed madly as Breitemann passed the pits, but Christian needed no urging. Broad-sliding through the corners on full throttle at opposite lock, he broke the Monaco lap record lap after lap. With just one circuit to go, he was 1.5 seconds behind and gaining.

The two roared up the long hill, past the Casino, down Mirabeau into the tunnel, the gap unchanged. They reemerged from the tunnel, shrieking along the waterfront. A lapped BRM balked Brabham's entry into the Chicane--and Breitemann was right on his tailpipes!

Accelerating out of the lefthander at Tabac nose to tail, they had only the severe Gasometre righthand hairpin before the checkered flag.

But just ahead of the final turn was one of the slow Marches. Its driver, seeing the leaders nose to tail, drove down the center of the track, conceding to both the maximum room to pass.

Brabham shot right.

Breitemann veered left.

Both braked hard for the hairpin, Breitemann a car length behind.

But Brabham, to the right, was off the racing line. His braking tires "on the marbles" with no traction, his wheels locked instantly, tire smoke broiling up.

Brabham's car, no longer turnable, slid straight forward!

He nosed softly into the outside hay bales--

While Breitemann crossed behind him, raging into the hairpin.

Rounding Gasometre in a brazen four-wheel drift, tail out all the way...Breitemann hurtled ahead to the checkered flag and into Monaco history.

Chapman was apoplectic.

Even Princess Grace leapt to her feet in the royal box waving wildly-- Christian the winner!

... and here came runner-up Brabham at last, motoring slowly to the flag, his hand waving sportingly to the crowd.

The other cars still raced hard for finishing position...but no one cared.

When the last car crossed the line the crowd surged down onto the track, swarming Breitemann and the Lotus. It was the most dramatic finish in Monaco history! In an outdated car that had been raced hard for two solid hours, Breitemann lowered the lap record repeatedly. His final lap bettered the record by a full two miles an hour.

The crowd chanted, "Chris-tian-Chris-tian-Chris-tian," clapping in unison in the European fashion.

Nick scanned the multitudes. He saw neither Angela nor Jennifer. Then he saw Angela's shining brunette hair in the very middle hugging Christian.

Reflexively he glanced at the Trimmer pits.

No Devane.

A sharp tap on the shoulder startled him. He turned.

Devane gestured at the sky. In ten minutes of delirious celebration...the sun had vanished. Thunderous black clouds boiled above the Corniche. He gave Devane the magnesium just as a fat first raindrop struck his forehead.

Instantaneously deluges clattered down. They soaked through his shirt to his skin. Women ran in all directions, screaming. The crowd veered and darted like panicked shoals of fish. Princess Grace was rushed into the back of the royal box shielding her face. A man held an umbrella in front of her, the rain volleying in sideways.

Thorne backed away towards Team Trimmer, avoiding being knocked down. A young woman dressed in suddenly intimately disclosing yellow cotton slacks, her transparent white blouse and sheer brassiere revealing chilled breasts, fell to her knees in front of him. He grabbed her arm to help her up, almost knocked down himself.

He pulled her back from the crowd, all rushing to the shelter of the hotels.

"*Laisse-moi,*" she raged at him, "... *salôt!*"

She was carried away in the stampede.

Along the pines he saw Nigel Trimmer sitting on a stack of tires. His umbrella protected only his head, the torrent drenching his shirt and slacks. He smiled as Thorne approached--the deluge beginning to moderate.

"Not a great day for you," Thorne smiled.

"Can't all be. But you'll never in your life see a better drive."

"I'm not alone, then..." Thorne said, "Christian is special."

"You're not alone, lad."

Trimmer smiled over Thorne's shoulder. Breitemann stood amid the hordes holding a Gold Leaf Team Lotus rainproof over Angela's head hurrying towards the hotels.

Trimmer nodded. "Not at all alone, I should think."

The downpour wound down to a steady rain. Then in twenty minutes it stopped completely. Jennifer had vanished. Nick searched for Burnleigh or Joubert...and found Jake Austin instead.

"Thornie! How's that for an ending!"

"Astounding. Have you seen Trevor?"

"Not a feather. I need alcohol."

Nick couldn't naysay it.

The crowds under the hotel awnings dispersed only gradually. Austin led Thorne to the nearest. They all looked the same, a row of cigarette cartons standing on end. But far below this hotel was Nigel Trimmer's elegant white Rolls-Royce Corniche.

The bar inside was five deep. Without hesitation Austin nosed in. "Gin and tonic," Thorne said passing him some Francs. In moments, drinks in hand, they turned from the bar and--

Nick froze.

Among groups of celebrants Jennifer sat at a corner table. Bent over her, their faces touching, was Devane. Nick watched, trying to interpret Devane's posture. Jennifer nodded conceding something. Then Devane cupped the back of her head. He gave her a long deep kiss. She accepted hungrily.

Austin was facing the opposite direction.

"Salud," Nick said and they drank, he trying to keep Austin's back to Devane and Jennifer. It worked in movies.

Then Austin turned. "Jesus Christ, isn't that--"

"Yes."

Austin was already on his way. Nick grabbed his elbow to tug him back, but the sharp movement made Devane look. He smiled, all but his eyes. "Bloody crawling with Yanks, this. You two look a positive wreck."

Thorne would not look at Jennifer. If ever he needed to be tough...if ever he needed to walk straight up grinning cold like Bogart....

But Christian was wrong, he would never make a racer.

"Sit down," Jennifer said.

"Can't." His eye passed over her, seeing the wall. "I'm meeting Trevor at Hotel de Paris," he lied.

"We'll go with you."

"No."

He put down his drink, hardly touched, and hurried out.

Climbing the hill to Hotel de Paris was taking forever. He could feel eyes on him...watching him...everyone thinking, how is he taking it?

The chill exchange between Jennifer and Angela last night aboard Aurore came to him.

Forget it...it's the past. There was brilliant Christian to consider.

Epic drive.

The greatest!

All the way up the hill, eyes on him...watching. He couldn't hold his mind still.

Jennifer drawing strength from Devane's kiss.

He hurried up the hill, his mind blaring.

He must hurry and hurry but never arrive.

In Casino Square Angela called to him. He didn't want to see her.

"Nick! Damn it!"

Seeing her hurt. He looked at the sidewalk.

"Nick--please!"

"What's the matter?" he said knowing too well.

"Nick."

She clung to him, hanging on for dear life.

"It's been coming for months..." she said.

He waited.

"They were together all winter."

"How the fuck would I know!"

"You wouldn't. You wouldn't. And there were others. His Dinky Toys. But she was the one."

"Why didn't somebody tell me!"

"You're angry and you should be. Nobody knew except me. I think they were together last night after you left. I never told Trevor who--I was too humiliated. He just knew Tony was seeing someone."

"And Angela, where do you stand?"

"No bleeding idea. Carrying on." She clung to him. "You're sweet. It's the weak ones need to have it their own way."

He felt a swoon of emptiness. Ever since arriving in Europe he'd fantasized holding her--but never like this. He couldn't think. He couldn't feel. It was a bloodbath.

Part Five

1,000 Kilometers of Spa

CHAPTER 44

CHRISTMAS, THE NINETIES

It was the end, only Spa remained. And it was impossible. He looked at the clock--four a.m. Christmas morning. Where was Newton?

On the bed asleep, nothing personal.

Thorne looked out the windows. The nor'easter was spent, the night sullen and silent. He studied the black void.

Play the hand you drew. Deal with it!

He had studied his divorce from every angle trying to ameliorate it. At least it hadn't come down to some tawdry infidelity. It was plain enough...a structural collapse. He was afraid to consider what he would become now, formally alone, the reflection of a shadow of an echo. He had no vision of himself. He could point to nothing in his life he trusted, no reward he deeply deserved.

Except music and Newton. He deserved music and he deserved Newton because he loved them. He was the sum of the things he loved. His writing no longer rewarded him, Pond Life had seen to that. Yet he'd had no choice. Leigh had her expectations. She wanted a goddamn Mercedes, a goddamn house on the goddamn shore...and clothes, clothes! He chased paychecks down every dark alley in Manhattan being a good husband. He'd given up being strong--it took all his energy to be weak.

No. It was Christmas morning--tell the truth, it was not her fault. He made those choices knowing they were wrong. But decades ago that Sunday evening in Monaco, Angela, in her neediness, clung to him for strength. When she told him Jennifer and Devane had been together for months he thought only of his disgust, not of why she clung to him. She clung to him because he was a man of character--she demanded it! That moment was inside him all these decades. Yet tonight when he needed it most, when he needed strength for himself and his own well-being, he felt nothing.

Easy does it, they said.

Keep it simple.

Stopping drinking six years ago had been his greatest test. It took everything he had. Yet in another way it was given to him freely, he did nothing to deserve it...it was a blinding miracle. Would he have the character now, tonight, without drinking, without flying apart, to put his marriage behind him?

Tony Devane dead.

It was official now at least.

Tony's all-night binges before BBC grand-prix telecasts were, in their wrong-minded Brit way, a sort of national treasure. But they were more, in his alcoholism he knew all about them. Tony had never stopped hiding-- behind mortal risk, raw aggression, cold contempt, sexual plunder, in the end small beer. Thorne had once thought Tony's willfulness to be the price of his pitiless profession but it was wrong. In identical circumstances Christian was compliant, honest, generous. Christian faced all the same harsh realities with goodhearted grace.

Thorne heard paws in the hall. Newton wanted to know why he hadn't come to bed yet. He met Newton with a smile and picked him up.

Music and Newton. He deserved them because he loved them.

To feel love is the greatest gift. He would indulge it.

Putting his cat down gently, he went to the front door and stepped outside, Newton hanging back...there were monsters.

The night was still, moonless, cold. The air had a stern wintry density. He walked the driveway towards the water, the cold a lotion on his skin...like that glorious morning with Trevor in the Jaguar on the high Simplon.

Far above him, a gust of wind stirred the pines. They *sssseeewwww*-ed...a distant choir. He loved the sound and scent of pines. They conjured summer cabins and outboard ski boats and a cold beer with Dottie's father years before he was of age.

Beer.

Of course.

But that was his life. It had been dangerous and costly, but he'd survived. They said only one in thirty-two alcoholics gets sober...him!

Beneath the soles of his shoes rain-saturated gravel on the driveway gurgled softly. He stepped past "her" Mercedes. It was older now and showed it, like her. How ever would she conceal that? He feared for her, she had a lot of dissembling still to do.

His eyes bid him halt at the seaward end of the drive. He'd lost more than a marriage this year, he'd lost part of his eyesight. Ischemic optical neuropathy--dithery title. It left a velvety void in the vision of his right eye.

But he had rolled with that punch, he'd shown character. Angela would approve.

Long Island Sound clattered against the rocks below the drive, the waves annoyance still stirred after the storm. He turned. The little Cape Cod looked inviting and why not. Newton lived there.

He didn't know if he could go on to Spa....

Stop! He was wasting time.

In the warmth of the house again he picked up Newton and held him close, Newton's motor running. He set him down then and went to his record albums. Four a.m. Christmas. If ever there was a right time. The jazz station didn't play Bill Evans anymore. He was white and dead more than a decade. "Uncool." Bill Evans no more needed to be "cool" than Maurice Ravel.

"New Conversations" was the last Evans record Thorne bought before switching over to compact discs. He drew out the album, cleaned the record and set the needle on Ellington's haunting "Reflections in D." The orchestral Evans piano led off, rich, forceful, as impassioned as Rachmaninoff...to Spa and the end of everything.

1970, THE ARDENNES

Burnleigh was not taking it well. All the way north from Monaco he spoke in monosyllables. After a point Thorne did the same. The long drive became an exercise in anger deferred. If matters were reversed and he, not Trevor, fell from favor with Angela, he would not take it well either.

After a satisfying run up the German autobahn at 140 and crossing into Belgium, the moment came.

"Trevor, I don't blame you."

"Blame me?"

"She confides in me."

"I don't know what you're talking about."

"I've done nothing. It's not my fault."

"Never is, is it."

"This time it isn't."

"As you say."

Thorne did not say the next two things that came to mind. He squeezed the pedal down and the Jaguar surged. One thing about the open road--it didn't sulk.

On his Michelin map he had found the 8.3-mile triangle of Belgian route nationale constituting the Spa-Francorchamps circuit. Spa's murderously fast straightaways were long enough to show up on a roadmap. Le Mans, also on the map, was more famous and traversing Le

Mans' three-and-half-mile Mulsanne Straight at full throttle through rain and night fog was chilly enterprise. But Spa was worse. Le Mans' lap average was 145 miles an hour, yet even with the dead-slow 40 mile per hour La Source hairpin, Spa's record average was four miles per hour faster. This season the five-liter Ferraris and Porsches would demolish those averages.

In steady rain the Jaguar passed through St. Vith to Malmédy. They were on the track itself. Images flared...shrieking down this surface at 235, setting up for the next wet blind bend, no clue how fast it could be taken. Horrifying.

After a few minutes the Jaguar stopped in front of dour three-story Hotel de La Gare. It was Spa's cheapest pension. More to the point, it had the only vacancies for miles. At home it would be a "commercial" hotel for footage salesmen with scuffed shoes and bad breath.

Across the street under a low black-and-white World War II Belgian sky stood the gloomy Spa train station. Wrought-iron bars imprisoned its lightless windows, sooty voids in a bloodclot of dark red brick.

The moment the wipers stopped, rain warped the Jaguar windshield.

"Nasty prospect," Thorne said.

Angela was right, he sounded like a Brit.

Burnleigh made no reply.

He pulled his jacket over his head and rushed to the hotel.

Au Chat Fou--Crazy Cat's--was the prototypical bar-across-from-the-*gare*. Occupying one side of Hotel de La Gare's ground floor, it was long, narrow, its air thick with blue smoke. Workmen in blue twill coveralls took their first breakfast vin rouge here and on rainy nights like this nursed Calvados and pondered rampant injustice.

Burnleigh was upstairs in his room, the good man wronged. It was how he wanted it. Thorne looked at his glass of dark Belgian porter. There were worse places to be. The barman's name was César. On this filthy night Thorne's inner monologue dubbed him Filthy César. After his second porter, it stuck. Filthy César was unsmiling and roly-poly in a perspiring, high-blood-pressured, tight-collared way. He had a pencil-thin mustache across his upper lip and his skullcap of oiled jet-black hair gleamed like a plastic toy. Thorne paid him and he made no acknowledgement at all. But with each new porter served, César, a marketing genius, included a small cube of cheddar sprinkled with celery salt. For the cheddar's protein, Thorne ordered a third porter. He savored the rain and gloom. Au Chat Fou's steamed windows and the nippy cheddar kindled a humid stay-put satisfaction. He didn't care where the racers were--Devane, Angela (if she even came), Christian, Joubert, Austin.

Jennifer....

He should not think. It was raining, be amused by the rain. Too little rain in California--except when it rained too much. Let it pour. After three porters rain was *magnifique*.

He left a handful of aluminum coins on the bar, refusing to gawk at their unfamiliar denominations like a dumb American. He achieved the front door without being cursed by Filthy César...it had been adequate.

He headed down the incline towards the center of town, flying drizzle coating his flesh like a cold sweat. In twenty paces his glasses were opaque, the headlights in the road starbursts. In the chill he needed more cheddar. Three porters hardly lit the boiler.

Careful. He felt fragile tonight.

The street was lined with ugly masonry storefronts like funerary vaults, but far ahead along the sidewalk he saw a bright yellow glow. What could it be, a merry-go-round? Taxi dancers in ostrich feathers? He thought of Jennifer. It was one thing to have reservations about a woman, another when she had reservations about you.

Nearing the glow he smelled cooking oil. Bacon? Fish and chips? He looked through the bright steam-clouded window. *Pommes frites!* He walked in, tantalized. In schoolboy Français rendered fearless by Filthy César's cheddar, he placed an order. If they'd served porter with cheddar in class at Berkeley his French would've been fluent.

The Belgian--not French--fries were golden, crusty, too hot to touch. But eaten with a swipe of Belgian mayonnaise...ambrosia. Belgium may be Europe's Delaware, but they had a way with a fryer.

Munching contentedly he went outside. In no time he was walking back up the rise to the hotel. In the attacking mist his timing was sweet. With the last golden *frite* he stepped into Au Chat Fou.

Filthy César sat behind the bar mulling grim decades still to be endured. Thorne nodded, no response. But Filthy César reached for the cheddar. The celery salt. Already, a regular. Nice.

CHAPTER 45

"IT WAS AT BADEN-WURTEMBERG--my first time racing a car. For the first practice, I went out onto the track in the middle of many others."

Breitemann grinned at himself noting lessons learned.

"We made it through the first three turns nose to tail because the car at the front was very slow. Then in the fourth turn, a very fast uphill right-hander, the maroon Opel ahead of me spun off. It flew up the side of the track on the dirt, flipping over and over. The bonnet flew off and a door...it was very violent. But I thought just one thing--"

His finger snapped!

"...it is not me. I was like the hunter in the forest--nothing mattered except my hunt. Never before had I felt so definitively alone. I was hunting the car ahead--it was the only object. Still today, I have that feeling in a racing car.

"People ask, is it like sex? It is, I suppose--but when you are in it, it is forever.

"The driver who crashed had a broken arm. Not serious. But in a good hunt, the hunter must have risk. For a racing driver sometimes to be hurt is as natural as seeing a bird in the cat's teeth...."

The day before Spa practice Thorne awoke heavy lidded. He looked out the window--Seattle in December. He rolled over and went back to sleep.

Two hours later he sat in Au Chat Fou, which doubled as Hotel de La Gare's breakfast room. Filthy César glowered cordially behind the bar. Eggs and bacon were being served. Nick had not had a proper breakfast since Villa d'Este.

Burnleigh walked in and Nick said, "Look. Eggs!"

Burnleigh smiled. A night's sleep hadn't hurt.

After breakfast they drove to the circuit. Nick parked the Jaguar and they strolled down a short paved path through the trees. On the way they came across two college girls from the University of Michigan. Bubbly, enthusiastic, they were spending their spring semester visiting every European racetrack they could get to. Burnleigh announced why he and Nick were there and they grinned, yeah, sure.

At the bottom of the path Nick stepped over the steel crash barrier onto the Pit Straight. Immediately he felt the energy through his legs...the juice. He had felt it before the first time he set foot on the track surface at Indianapolis. He was in direct contact with the enigma. What was it about this pagan pastime, why did it bring college girls halfway around the world chasing it? It was no civilized undertaking. It had no needful result. Yet it encapsulated everything he knew about fortune, destiny.

His eye followed the black macadam, rushing steeply downslope past the line of pits on the right, a deep ledge in the forest.

At the bottom it flared, rising violently into the blindingly fast linked "S" curves called Eau Rouge. Christian said they were the most demanding in racing, but done well, the most satisfying. There it was. Severe risk brought the deepest satisfaction. Without it racing was only stunt-driving.

Thorne turned and looked up in the other direction. At the top of the straight was the famed hairpin of La Source. Even with this extremely slow right-hander Spa's average speed was faster than Indianapolis! He felt cold awe. Lap after lap at 230 miles per hour, they raced on tree-lined public roads, nothing preventing them flying off and bashing a tree or stone farmhouse, the car exploding like an artillery shell!

He felt fear for the drivers--and a fiercely forbidden joy.

He looked down again at Eau Rouge. He had waited all his life for this.

Burnleigh wanted a drink up at Auberge de La Source, but first, Thorne needed to see more. They walked down the pit lane.

Spa's pit enclosures were terraced along the steeply sloping pit lane. Walking the Start/Finish straight Nick visualized accelerating down this fast chute to Eau Rouge, going all out. Streaming to the bottom, accelerating hard at 170, the world closing around him, he would force himself to hold the throttle down--launching violently into Eau Rouge, veering left, then climbing right, his body weighing tons, the spindly suspension arms strained to the snapping point...then flying out harmlessly over the mountain's brow into forest darkness. He had had dreams.

Up and down the pits, crews were unloading race-car transporters, preamble to another fatiguing cycle of twenty-hour workdays. The tirelessness of racing mechanics was legend. They seemed without temperament--or they found other work.

In the unglamorous labor of offloading the transporters and setting up the hardware of racing, team managers and drivers were nowhere to be found, with one excited exception. Down at the very bottom they saw electrified François Courtault. He stood among a group of men Nick didn't recognize...Ecurie Bresson, the Belgian racing team whose brand-new Ferrari 512S he would pilot. Privateer Stephane Bresson's team was well respected in European racing. Short of a factory-team Ferrari, Courtault couldn't have done better.

The exquisite bright-yellow Ferrari was just rolling off the transporter as Nick and Burnleigh arrived. Yellow was Belgium's national racing color, as green was Britain's, blue France's and red Italy's. But with sponsorship liveries becoming dominant as racing costs escalated, Team Beacom's Carnelian colors a prime example, the old traditions were breaking down.

Courtault beamed at Nick, "Look what I have found!"

"Gorgeous," Burnleigh enthused.

"Yes?" Courtault laughed hugely. "You think? It would be a shame for such a beauty to be covered with others' spray and muck, so I have decided to run it up at the very front, no one ahead!"

Nick beamed. "Excellent plan! Where is everyone?"

Courtault pointed up the hill. "We are at Auberge de La Source. Most of the others are at Le Pavillon."

"Where?"

"In the town."

"Yours sounds more convenient," Burnleigh said.

"Yes, but it is the desert. We shall go to Le Pavillon simply to be among civilization. Where are you?"

"Hell's Half Acre," Nick said. "Hotel de La Gare."

"Ah." It was a complete sentence.

"You wouldn't like a spot of something liquid?" Burnleigh inquired. "Nick's buying."

Nick smiled. "Come on, François. We will explain to you how to run at the front."

"Thank you, but no, I must stay to be fitted to the car. *À plus tard.*"

They nodded and began the long walk up to Auberge de La Source at the hairpin.

The Auberge was a gloomy, rambling brown-shingled inn set in the trees. It was large for a roadside inn without being in any way imposing. On the front porch under the roof were fifteen or so tables with cane-and-rattan chairs. Sitting in them they wheezed asthmatically. When no waiter came out to serve, Thorne went inside to order.

The waitress arrived with bottles and glasses and a cube of cheddar for

Nick's porter.

"You should try this," he said.

"Wog beer."

They drank, Thorne taking a bite of cheddar. A moment passed.

"Trevor, hear me out," he said. "Angela talks and I listen. You would do no less. The things afoot in her life are a good deal more pressing than a bit of wounded pride."

Burnleigh considered his pils.

"If I've done something wrong tell me what it is."

"Perish the thought," Burnleigh said.

Thorne waited.

Burnleigh nodded into the distance. "As you say, only a bit of wounded pride."

"Come on, Trevor, I didn't mean it that way!"

"How did you mean it?"

Nick said nothing.

"Wounded pride suits me."

"And so it does."

They drove back to the hotel. Nick took a porter upstairs to his room and tried not to think. But the moment his door closed, Jennifer flooded his mind. Shit. He sat on the bed, moving not a muscle for a very long time.

CHAPTER 46

IN PITCH-BLACK HE FUMBLED for the lamp. Three-thirty in the morning. Too many beers two nights in a row.

No matter. A bump in the road. He must keep his poise. He got up and took three aspirins.

He'd wanted to go to Le Pavillon and find people he knew. Christian. Maybe Angela. But maybe Devane. Maybe Jennifer. Since Monaco, some things were off limits. Instead of going out, he stayed in his room listening to jazz cassettes on his battered faithful Panasonic cassette player...Bill Evans and Miles Davis, just as Christian had mentioned. When the music didn't work he knew how bad he was.

He tried going downstairs to watch Au Chat Fou's television, but that was worse. He struggled to follow the idiomatic French of a poorly lit black-and-white movie peopled with sharp-featured unattractive women, hair piled on top of their heads, and round-faced men with puffy cheeks and 1940s mustaches, one Oliver Hardy after another.

He went back up to his room after an hour and said it aloud: "Oh, God."

Friday morning the pits were transformed. In every enclosure universes of tools and spares were arrayed in perfect order as if for military inspection. Transporter machine shops were whirring and grinding. The rest of the haulers were parked side by side behind the pits like cordwood.

The skies remained leaden but the drizzle had stopped. The pit straight was dry though it meant nothing. Like the Nürburgring, Spa was infamous for sudden cloudbursts anywhere along the circuit. The low steel-wool clouds offered no odds.

Thorne walked through the narrow companionway from the paddock to the pits and there they all were, Christian, Angela, Devane, Beacom, Whitlaw, Joubert...Jennifer. They crowded around smiling François Courtault. Obligingly he cavorted and played the fool for them like in a home movie. But the terrain of this playfulness struck Thorne--did every tidepool of smirking celebrities have as many deadly undercurrents as this? He walked straight into their midst, and as if by chance Jennifer drifted off to the peripheries, caught in a separate eddy. She could go to hell.

Angela held out her arms and Thorne gave her a big hug, savoring her elegant frame. He hoped Jennifer would turn and see. She did not.

He released Angela but her leg remained pressed against his...she too had people to wound. In a movie it might have been low comedy.

Thorne glanced at Devane and quickly away. He was the sum of his attributes, gifted, handsome, malign.

But François' thick black brows waggled to Thorne a semaphore hello.

"So are you all blind?" said Thorne joining the game. "Can't you see he's driving a Ferrari?"

Breitemann smiled. "And we wish him the best possible result for a Ferrari...third."

Courtault laughed. "This is the best? Not second? Not even first?"

"You've a rich fantasy life," Devane said.

"And you?" François beamed. "You will be first--or will you be second?" His eye slid to Breitemann. "Come, now, who will it be?"

Raymond Beacom stepped in with an adamantine grin. "You may make a racing driver yet, young man. Now, leave my senior citizens alone."

Amidst general laughter, Angela cupped Courtault's face in her palms. "Pay no attention to the big bad wolf, he is all snarl."

"I believe you."

Beacom nodded, "At your peril."

Courtault winked to Breitemann. "Take care the bad wolf doesn't bite you!"

And with a huge laugh he was off down the slope to his magnificent new yellow Ferrari. Angela's eye followed his departure. "Glorious sight."

Devane made an elaborate show of ignoring her.

"You are a beast, Angela," said Breitemann.

"I rather am."

Being in his twenties, Nick could not fathom what women found attractive about men, sweaty, hairy, shapeless, flatulent...but Angela's admiring smile was a pleasant moment.

The morning weather held, but the threat of rain overhung everything like a bad conscience. Controlling dry-weather slicks at 230 in a sudden downpour...Thorne would not even think of it. At the Nürburgring, at least, the speeds were lower.

But after an uneventful two hours of practice, reflexively, he downgraded the risk--they were getting away with this. Spa wasn't so horrific after all. He remembered the same ingenuous shift during his first day at deadly Indianapolis.

Almost finished recording the technical changes this weekend to the most important cars, Thorne saw Breitemann's Porsche coming slowly into the pits, its left-front tire in shreds. Ian Hayford, the replacement for poor Alex Winter, was driving. With each revolution the tattered tire made a slatternly blappa-blappa against the wheelwell, battering its fragile fiberglass to pieces.

It stopped and Hayford climbed out, pale as a corpse.

"I was flat out--Masta to Stavelot." He spoke to no one in particular, talking compulsively. The Masta Straight was one of Spa's fastest sections.

"Bloody tire just...*blammm!* Am I still here?"

The car's nose came up on the manual lift. A clattering impact wrench loosened the wheel. It stank of burnt rubber.

"How does he do it..." Hayford said now.

"Do what?" Thorne said.

"He's a demon. It happened to Breitemann an hour ago!"

"Christian?"

"Flat out just after the Masta Kink." Hayford's expression struggled to come to grips. "245, toppers, and he climbs out bloody smiling!"

Hayford wandered off, having no idea where.

It was an all too common anomaly--Breitemann's car suffered two tire failures in quick succession, yet Devane in a sister car with the same wheels and tires...no difficulty.

Breitemann appeared now.

He went straight to Ian Hayford. "You are all right?"

"I felt something just after the Kink." His head shook. "And...powww!"

Breitemann went to the front of the car.

"You think it's the wheels?" Joubert said.

"They're twelves," Hayford said of the 12-inch front wheels. "Just like Tony's...everything the same."

Breitemann came back.

"See anything?" Joubert said.

Breitemann's eye was luminous: "The face of God."

He looked at the sky. "I wish it will rain and be done with it."

Nick had forgotten the weather. It seemed no more menacing than anything else in this profoundly threatening place.

Devane howled past now on full song. He veered left into Eau Rouge. Snaked madly upwards and right, blasting out across the ridge, the twelve-cylinder wail caroming through the forest in cannonades.

Okay.

Good.

After Hayford's pallor--and Christian's dour tone--Thorne needed to see a Beacom Porsche 917 driven with absolute abandon, running straight and true.

CHAPTER 47

MAY SUNSHINE DANCED ON THE fast-rolling Seine. Brooding Notre Dame loomed.

He'd bought an International Herald-Tribune for his morning stroll. He would save the brilliant humor on the back page until he sat down with a coffee to savor it.

Browsing the front page he--

froze.

Bruce.

Goodhearted Bruce

testing at Goodwood

dead.

An elite few, Brabham, Hulme, Stewart, Donohue, would survive, but before them all, gifted, circumspect Bruce McLaren would survive!

And he was in peak form. Two weeks ago in Spain he finished second....

The rear body of his new Can-Am car had flown off at 160.

He spun

hit an earthen bunker

dead.

One day as a boy Nick was racing Ronnie Booth on bicycles in the park, pedaling blindly on the cracked concrete sidewalk. His tire caught a rut and his chest hammered full force into the ground.

The light blackened.

His lungs jammed

like a heart attack.

He felt that now
Bruce
dead.
Everything was changed.
No one was safe.
Grief was obsolete.

He stood up the hill atop the righthand bend of Eau Rouge. It rose full bore past the ridge. It was the first corner in racing with a raised painted inner curb--the white-and-black-striped curb prevented "cheating" an inside front wheel onto the dirt to straighten the curve.

A dense thicket of photographers were gathered several paces back, the six-inch curb all that stood between them and cars raging past at 175. Now and then a photographer stepped forward and shot down into a car.

In the windscreen, glaring eyes.

He would experience this legend for himself, the fiercest pair of esses in racing.

The Garand Ferrari raged by.

Then Stringert's Porsche-Austria 917.

The Ferrari of Dante Ruggiero....

François Courtault's bright-yellow Ecurie Bresson Ferrari came hurtling uphill, a purgatory of conflicting physics. Its furious four-cam V-12 raged. Fat racing tires clawed tarmac. The yellow fiberglass skin quavered, in agony.

When it passed...a closed fist of blare.

It was primitive. Elemental.

Only photographers, corner workers--and him--got close enough to taste this battle.

No wonder.

A crash in last year's Belgian Grand Prix here killed two corner marshals. But in the flinty European view--World War II's callous mortality being moments ago--if you had the professional Press/Photo credential...the risk was yours.

D'accord.

Thorne would take the measure of the ultimate corner--who did it elegantly, with bravery. Was it Stringert, Courtault, Ruggiero...Garand, Devane, Breitemann....

And he would measure himself.

He looked across the steep vale. A bright-orange Beacom Porsche streaked downhill past the pits. Rushed into brutally rising Eau Rouge. Its nose bore the swooping trademark--the navy blue "mustache."

Christian.

Thorne stepped to the curb, ready to be ordered back.

The corner marshal said nothing.

Christian rose violently right, carving a maximum-force ice-hockey arc...aimed straight at him. Hurricanes raged on its skin. The engine was distant, an approaching low-flying jet.

Passing--his heart banging--pure rage blasted him!

It vanished behind the ridge, echoing through the trees.

He took a final half step forward, no margin remaining. His shoe tip was on the curb's inner lip.

Joubert stood ten paces back--glaring at him.

Garand was coming, the brassy Ferrari V-12 a dazzling *razzzz*. The blood-red coupe hurtled upwards and...unable to control it, he stepped back.

Garand vanished over the brow.

He stepped forward again, his left shoetip on a white stripe, his right on black. Pulse crashing in his ears--this time he would not move.

But two lesser cars were coming. He stepped back.

Devane was coming.

He stepped forward.

The orange Porsche inscribed a jittering arc, hunting, darting. Through its windshield clenched fists clutched the wheel, counter-punching, commanding, and in the edge of his eye--his shoe!

...gone.

Christian was coming. Six hundred horsepower shimmered through the tremulous bodyshell. The orange Porsche shape twisted. Shook. Veering right, a beast struggling to survive...it arrived at his shins--

Thunderclap!

... rushing harmlessly through the trees.

For three successive laps he stayed at the brink. They hurtled past, fiercely at work. Some wandered more, some less--all at the margins of their gift.

But Christian always carved the same silken arc, gliding in right to...here!

Thorne studied the dull-gray blemish in the macadam, two feet from his shoe.

Maximum effort.

He was spent.

But he felt carillons of exhilaration. He'd seen Christian's best. In all the world none was better. He would never forget. For an instant he lived the life.

Reluctantly, and simultaneously with giddy permission, he stepped well back. Only then the horror crashed in.

He stepped far away now, tremors streaking down the backs of his legs. Joubert was all the way at the fence.

Thorne smiled.

He had peeked behind the tapestry.

Among privateer teams Ecurie Bresson was elite. Much was expected. But for François Courtault, in his first day in the yellow Ferrari, to out-qualify one of the three factory Ferraris--sensational!

And he was only three-tenths of a second behind Ruggiero in the second factory Ferrari. Of course the number-one Ferrari of Belgian Jean Garand, at his home circuit, upheld Maranello's honor--third behind the two Beacom Porsches.

Patrolling the Ferrari pits earlier, Thorne had seen Luciana Podesta smiling happily with Ruggiero. It was "on" again. Never seek to know the mysteries of the master bedroom.

Walking back to the pits after Eau Rouge, Thorne and Joubert found a crowd at Ecurie Bresson. Stephane Bresson had driven Aston Martins in the 1950s, successfully placing fourth and seventh at Le Mans. This afternoon he was once again enjoying the limelight. And with fifty minutes of practice remaining, he said, his brilliant young French driver might go even faster!

The considerable crowd around him was also partly owing to Angela's presence. She threw her arms around Courtault, camera shutters clattering. The photographers knew a payday when they saw it.

"Why all the commotion, François?" Thorne said. "*Free pommes frites?*"

"You are too late," Courtault laughed. "All eaten!"

"Don't be a ninny..." Angela said. "This beautiful man is the greatest thing since stretch underwear!"

"And I like them!" Courtault confirmed.

Everyone laughed except the photographers, too busy shooting.

"Is there more speed in the car?" Joubert asked.

"*Oui, oui, il y'en a beaucoup.*" Their French raced on, far too fast for Thorne.

He smiled at Angela and she smiled back. "Rather special."

"And you?" he said.

She gave him most of a smile. "When someone emerges like this, it makes it all worthwhile."

Joubert rejoined them. "François has a terrible headache and wants to call it a day, but Bresson insists upon one more try. They made a change that should be faster."

"As a Frenchman," Angela said, "you should be very excited."

Joubert would not be rushed. Racing demands proof. "It looks promising," he smiled.

The three factory Ferraris struggled with understeer all day, though it must be said, Jean Garand's struggle took place at considerably higher speeds than the others. Pasarell had overtaken Ruggiero at Ferrari for second quickest at Ferrari, behind one of the Porsche-Austria 917s.

The Beacom cars dueled with each other all day as though on opposing teams. Initially Breitemann set fastest time, but then two successive front-tire failures and the time lost limping around the long circuit on a flat, plus further delay pondering the problem's cause, set Breitemann's car well behind. It was decided Spa's extreme speeds were causing the tubeless Firestones to rotate on their rims, breaking their seal. Narrower front wheels would be fitted for Saturday. Thorne didn't know enough to say with certainty, but it didn't sound right. Using the same fronts, Devane's car had been unaffected.

Devane, meanwhile, profited from Breitemann's lost time. On a crowded track at 4:30 he did a remarkable lap of 3:22.6. And ten minutes later he shocked everyone with a 3:19.8, ten seconds faster than the existing Formula One record and 18 seconds faster than a sports car had ever gone!

But five minutes later--

Silence.

Thorne was at the upper end of the pits talking with Reine Wisell, co-driver of Jo Bonnier's Lola-Chevrolet. He felt the sudden absence of noise in his chest. A crash.

He hurried down to Porsche. People stood at a distance from each other like trees in a forest. No one spoke. Was it Christian?

No, his car was in the pits. A larger crowd gathered down at Ecurie Bresson.

Angela stood next to Stephane Bresson--ashen.

Thorne went to Devane.

"François," Devane nodded.

"Did he--"

"Cloudburst at Stavelot. He went in upside. Slid along the guardrail."

"But is he--"

"Decapitated."

CHAPTER 48

A STEADY RAIN SETTLED OVER the Ardennes. Everyone Thorne needed to see was gone. Breitemann vanished. Angela was driven away in a Peugeot by Luciana. The scene was rich in people he did not need to see. Devane leaned against the pit wall with three British writers. Beacom exchanged dark confidences with Whitlaw, the latter eyeing the middle distance like a Rottweiler with a bone.

Then Jennifer materialized. She was crying.

Fine. She deserved it.

No, he couldn't live that way.

Devane held her in the rain. After a time she stepped back and her head shook. Shook again. She saw Thorne and came to him. Her arms came around him. "It's not fair!"

"Nothing is fair."

She sobbed into his chest. He knew treating her with blame was self-defeating. He did it anyway.

"Nothing is fair..." he repeated and meant it.

A new onslaught of sobs wracked her, but her misery made him afraid. It was eroding him. Breitemann said it..."like a bird in a cat's teeth." His spine stiffened against her sobbing, but in another way he envied it.

Her arms tightened around him. "I'm sorry, Nick, it wasn't fair of me."

He didn't respond.

"Nick?"

He gripped her arms and moved them to her side. "No, it wasn't."

He turned and left. He had had reservations about her. Why hadn't he trusted them!

Burnleigh stood five paces away as if it were the only place in Belgium to stand. Nick didn't like it. Burnleigh could find his own ride back. Nick walked to the car.

He sprawled across the steel-sprung bed, its cheap yellow blanket in a lump under his spine, but who cared? A mahogany glass of porter stood on the dresser, its miniscule beige bubbles glimmering.

He sat up and lifted the glass. The porter tingled inside his cheeks. In his belly it made a satisfying hard landing.

He rolled onto his chest and pulled back the flimsy curtain. A car horn sounded in the distance...Citroên ID or DS, he knew them all. The French cars made an overwrought squawk, but the fat-burgher German sedans, big, beamy, full of themselves, emitted a soul-stopping *Bleeeekkk!* Traffic streamed in from Belgium and France, and in the opposite direction from the gaudy spectacle of the West German Miracle. It was only Friday. By Sunday the population would swell to 200,000. Following the same routes used by von Manteuffel's King Tiger tanks in the Battle Of The Bulge, they gathered like vultures on a corpse. Europeans were monsters.

Bullshit, François knew what he was doing.

Thorne took another swallow. The porter's Turkish Bath vapors rose in his temples, casting their spell. He would remember this day's cruelty.

He must go out. Walk in the rain. It was still raining. Of course.

He would go to Le Pavillon in the rain, he decided, toying with the notion of feeling chipper, "...see what's doing."

But what would be doing.

He tucked in his shirt. Put on the olive-green Harris Tweed from Burnleigh's tatty little shop in Sloane Square. The rain wasn't heavy, just the thing for proper Scots tweed. But on no account run into Trevor!

He munched his cheddar. Drained the porter. He would have one more with Filthy César, and if he saw Trevor he'd look straight through him.

Inevitably the second thing he saw in Au Chat Fou after Filthy César was Trevor. Automatically he said, "I'm going to Le Pavillon."

Burnleigh consented to join him, big two-hearted lad.

"Missed you yesterday, Jake," Thorne said. "But not much."

Austin's grinning reply in Le Pavillon's salon was the merest shadow behind the eyes. "I was in Paris. Sweet young thing from the Sorbonne needed her covers pulled down."

"You drinking?"

"In the circumstances," said Austin--Thorne was buying, "...a scotch."

Burnleigh followed Austin's lead. It was the most expensive drink in Belgium--but Thorne asked for it. He placed the order and the waiter crossed the salon to the bar. The room was a Belgian reading of the German joylessness in the Tauberhof.

"Anyone seen anyone?" Thorne said. "Or are they all in church?"

"A bit bloodthirsty," said Burnleigh.

"Maybe you'd like to buy your own fucking scotch. No Devanes? No Christian?"

Austin's head shook. "Not a soul, unless you consider Beacom a soul."

"You saw him?"

"He was out the front door a minute ago," Austin said, "not talking. Waved me away like a gnat."

"Imagine that."

The drinks arrived. They fulfilled the ceremonies and drank.

"Here comes someone," Burnleigh said.

They turned. Devane strode in out of the darkness wearing an insolent grin that changed not at all when it came to them. Next came The Death Ray--Beacom in his most sullen demeanor. Nick could not identify all its elements, but one was disgust. He looked in their direction. Went upstairs. Devane was left dawdling in the middle distance. He was drunk as a macaw. His eye skimmed past them. "Lovely evening..." he said to no one in particular.

Then he saw Joubert coming downstairs. He went to him and said something under his breath. Joubert shook his head elaborately, falsely accused.

Devane nodded and went upstairs. Joubert came to them.

"What?" Nick demanded.

"Angela's gone, nobody knows where. Tony's three sheets to the wind and--"

"Angela's gone?"

"She was at Auberge de La Source. She and Luciana had a drink after the news. Now she's vanished--Jennifer as well."

"That doesn't make any sense."

"Of course it doesn't." Joubert was as close to furious as he got. "Nobody knows anything!"

Austin snorted. "Does anyone care that François Courtault was killed today?"

"Oh, shit, Jake..." Thorne said.

But Joubert gave him a fierce glare--they must talk without aid of Burnleigh and Austin.

He hated European phones. They were intimidating even on the rare occasions when they worked.

"Le Pavillon," he heard in the receiver.

"Monsieur Joubert, *s'il vous plaît.*"

"*Immédiatement,* monsieur."

He waited in Au Chat Fou's dingy telephone box. There were no phones in Hotel de La Gare's dark little rooms just as there were no peacocks strutting the grounds. He'd tried Joubert twice, each time returning to the bar with a greater thirst. From the number of rings this time, apparently Jozie still wasn't--

"Joubert," he heard suddenly.

"Jozie! I've been trying you forever."

"You are at your hotel?"

"Yes."

"And Angela is not there?"

"Why would she be here!"

"She asked where you were staying."

"Of course she isn't!"

"Did she call? Has she asked for you? My friend, this is serious."

"One minute." He returned from Filthy César. "No calls, Jozie. What's happened!"

"She was extremely upset, as were we all--"

"Jozie, come on!"

"She found Luciana at Ferrari and they drove up to La Source to take a drink. While there Devane came downstairs, his arm around Jennifer--she's staying there and--"

"Oh, perfect."

"There was a scene and Angela slapped him. He slapped her back--then hit her hard."

Thorne waited for his heart to slow down. It would not.

"She ran off and Luciana went after her. She told Luciana to leave her alone, but Luciana refused. Finally Devane came after Luciana and told her, if she didn't clear off, he would...you know the rest. Luciana came back here. It's the last anyone has seen Angela."

"She's not with Devane?"

"Not unless he locked her in the boot of his car. He claims to know nothing."

"We have to find her," Nick said. "Where is Devane?"

"Where do you think...he went back to La Source. He's with Jennifer."

"I'll drive out there."

"I already did--with Beacom."

A beat passed, Thorne's mind racing. "Where is the hospital?"

Joubert waited for it to make sense.

"She adored him," Thorne said. "His body will be there."

"Wait for me," Joubert said. "I'll be there in five minutes."

When Joubert walked into Au Chat Fou, Thorne paid for his beer. Filthy César forgot to smile.

The hospital was at the eastern end of Spa-Francorchamps, a utilitarian three-story pile in pale brick and dark tidings. The windows glowed through the trees. Joubert parked and they hurried through the rain to the front door. The lobby was dim now at a little past nine. Angela sat alone in the shadowy silence. Her clothes were soaked through and her brunette hair dull and matted from the rain.

When she heard the door she looked up, "Bleeding hospitals."

Her voice teetered, on the brink.

"Won't let me in. Too late anyway...too late."

It trailed off.

"Hospitals should be churches, they do it just as badly."

He knew her features, the contour and textures of her flesh--but he didn't recognize the face. She hovered somewhere far beyond.

"Angela."

He brought her to her feet. She stood motionless in his arms.

Then it began, sobs roiling up from the depths. Grief clutched her, closing her windpipe. She quaked against him, gasping. For a moment she went completely limp, only his embrace holding her upright.

But her legs came under her again. "Poor sweet boy."

He pressed her head to his chest, soothing her temple with his palm.

"Angela."

"I need to be here."

"There is nothing you can do."

"He needs someone."

He could say nothing.

"Bresson came and left," she said. "Having a nice fat Belgian supper now, I suppose."

"That's not true. He feels as bad as anyone."

"Anyone?"

Her laugh was furious. New sobbing wracked her.

He squeezed her, pressing the breath out of her.

"Come on."

"Sweet boy...."

He nodded to the door. Joubert led the way.

"Going home," he said.

"Home...."

It was dreamy...Alex Winter's swoon leaving the clinic in Sicily.

"Come."

She resisted.

Relented.

"Dear boy."

The front door opened and he guided her down the wet steps.

"Everyone around me dies."

"That's not true."

"It keeps happening."

"No."

"One after another."

Her voice was a faint breath.

"Dead...."

Joubert phoned Luciana from Le Pavillon's front desk and told her they were bringing Angela up. Nick guided her to the stairs, refusing to see the blood-purple bruise under her eye. When Luciana saw it, she gasped. "Pig!"

She put her arms out. "Come, sweet one. We will go to your room. Dante is here sleeping."

Luciana read the concern in Nick's face. "Devane is not there, don't worry. To be there now would require courage. It would require dignity."

Tentatively Angela touched her bruise. "How bad am I?"

Luciana scoffed, "It is nothing. We shall paint it so God himself does not see."

"It hurts."

A vision seized Thorne...his fist crashing into the well-formed jaw. It made a wet messy sound like a melon dropped from a great height. For an instant he forgot where he was.

They came to Angela's door.

"Come in," she said to them, presuming refusal. "Please."

"No, luv," Thorne said. "But we'll make sure you're alone."

He swung the door wide. Turned on the light. The room was empty.

"Will he be back?" he asked.

Angela's head shook, "Who cares."

"Luciana, can you stay with her?"

"Of course. You must not worry."

He nodded. Angela's wheedling little please-stay smile broke his heart. But his head shook. "Get some rest, luv."

Luciana's eyes flashed fire. "You have no need to worry."

He nodded. Joubert and he walked along the hall to the stairs.

CHAPTER 49

FIRST THING SATURDAY MORNING in the Beacom pit Breitemann came to him. "Is it true, Nicholas? He hit her? Did you see?"

"Luciana saw. And Jennifer saw--but she ran away, delicate thing."

"He hit her twice?"

"What's the difference--once or twice?"

"A very great difference. Where is she now?"

He had no answer.

Breitemann walked to Peter Whitlaw. The Mallet stood at Breitemann's car leafing through shop sheets on his clipboard.

"Where is she?" Breitemann said.

"No bloody idea, Christian. My advice to you is to--"

"Peter...do not."

"Christian, old man, you really had better--"

In mid-sentence Breitemann turned on his heel. Under Whitlaw's disapproving eye Nick followed Breitemann down the pit lane to Ferrari. Nick doubted Angela would come to the track, there was nothing for her here. On the other hand, it would be worse hiding in drear Le Pavillon in shame.

Breitemann scanned the Ferrari pit. Nick went behind the pit to the transporters. Next to the nearest big red truck, its sides scrawled with bold yellow Ferrari script, he saw Luciana, and just beyond, Angela. On this sunless morning she wore enormous black-rimmed Audrey Hepburn sunglasses...Luciana's from rainy Brands Hatch.

Breitemann arrived and Angela smiled uncomfortably. "Very Hollywood, don't you think? Can't see my hand before my face, but what price glamour."

Nick saw her from the side. Her discolored cheekbone had been skillfully disguised with make-up.

Breitemann pulled her to him.

"Christian, I am fine."

"You are not fine."

Again the blood-heat seized Nick--knuckles smashing jawbone, a cold eye sliding skywards....

Breitemann held her shoulders. And the starch came out.

"Oh, Christian...."

She cried quietly. He pulled her to him.

"He is a monster," Breitemann said. "I knew it always."

"He couldn't help himself. He just--"

"He is no different from any man--he is what he does."

Breitemann stepped back now, his voice softening. "Let me see, my beauty."

He reached for the glasses. She didn't stop him. As if gently removing a silk scarf from her brow, he lifted the glasses up and away. She had a tiny scab on the point of her cheekbone. The swelling made her sunglasses indispensable. Breitemann studied her.

"Christian, you're embarrassing me!"

"I'm not."

"It will be fine."

"I think you never have been more beautiful."

She reached for the glasses to cover herself.

Then she turned to include Nick and Luciana. "I'm blessed to have such friends, but you have things to do."

Luciana gave Breitemann a fierce glare. "We will be right here. That dog will not come near her, my promise. Go back, now."

Breitemann looked to Thorne. Thorne nodded with more certainty than he felt. They began the walk back up the rise to Team Beacom. Breitemann spoke through clenched teeth. "If he only touches her, I shall break his hands."

The afternoon was like an undertaker's smile. Overcast hung just above the trees, Nick struggling to pay attention. A wall of noise stood between him and events. He heard it all at a distance--the usual litany of dysfunction, someone blew a clutch, someone changed front springs, someone wasn't getting full pickup from his fuel tank--

Where is she?

...is she all right!

Breitemann hoped the narrower wheel rims would solve his tire problem. And now Beacom pointedly did not want the change of wheel rims made public. Thorne would never grasp the corporate mentality. One moment, they wanted everyone to know, the next, it was to be concealed like family shame.

With nothing much else going on, Nick observed the Beacom team. Following the pattern of every domestic conflict, Devane and Breitemann avoided eye contact, staying as far from one another as feasible. But the moral epicenter was unmistakably Devane. He looked ill, and given last night, he came by it honestly. Thorne wondered if anyone had ever died of a hangover.

The consequences of Devane's condition were palpable. He had done a spectacular 3:19.8 Friday afternoon, fastest by four and a half seconds, but today he could not get below 3:22.9. And Breitemann was making inroads. At one o'clock he did a lap in 3:20.1, 4.2 seconds faster than the third-quickest time, accomplished by Jean Garand's Ferrari. In the Championship of Makes, it was an eternity.

Up the hill at the hairpin of La Source, Thorne saw a lone car coming, bright yellow, still small. An unspeakable impulse blared in his heart...François!

The yellow-and-white car roared closer. It was Jo Bonnier's Lola T70 Mk. IIIB Coupe. It rushed past--and Thorne regained his breath. He must show nothing, upset no one.

At 2:15 Breitemann brought his Porsche into the Beacom pit after a warm-up lap. Immediately he returned to the track. The next time he passed, every stopwatch clicked and the three-minute wait began.

But Breitemann's expected time of arrival came and left. Eternities passed, Thorne's eye on Whitlaw. The Mallet stared at his clipboard, jaw muscles rippling...cold-eyed bastard!

Now Devane's Beacom 917, Reine Dinesen driving, rounded La Source, but instead of accelerating down the Start/Finish straight it veered into the pits. Whitlaw and Graham Tully, Devane's chief mechanic, knelt down to the cockpit. Dinesen spoke too quietly to be overheard.

The Mallet nodded, glaring.

"Well?" Nick said.

"Well...what!"

"Is he all right!"

Whitlaw wheeled. "Of course he's all right! Lost a front on Masta...will you please get out of it?"

"But I thought you--"

"He's coming in on three wheels. Out of my way!"

"I'm not in your way!"

Devane's crew began checking wheels and tires--nothing amiss. Three deflations on one car, none on the other.

Breitemann rounded La Source at last. The car crept in emitting the burnt-egg stink of incinerated rubber. Its disintegrating tire had battered the left-front fender beyond recognition. Breitemann struggled up and out, his eye glinting like northern lights. He examined the destroyed fender. Thorne saw it unmistakably...Christian too reckoned with horror!

Heartless observation.

But Thorne meant to see all in racing there was to see. If Christian had fear, how did he drive so fearlessly! He had just experienced an unflinching look down the deep black hole.

Powerless to do otherwise, Thorne retreated from the Beacom pit. Christian's gift was no protection! And Devane had not a tenth of Christian's gift...poor beautiful Angela knew it. He saw as never before the inner terrain of her desperate existence.

CHAPTER 50

AFTER A SUITABLE PERIOD, given time to reset his self-discipline, Thorne returned to Beacom. Breitemann was at the pit wall.

"You all right?" Thorne said.

"I am all right, yes." Breitemann's tone was brittle. "Of course I am--anyone can see!"

"Good."

"I am fine. You think I am not?"

"Christian, it's fine!"

"To say so costs you nothing, my friend."

Thorne let its sting subside. "Being afraid has its purpose."

"Only when you may eliminate what makes you afraid. Otherwise it is only pain."

"But they're working on it!"

The crew was bent over the offending Porsche wheel rim, the discussion in earnest.

"They are doing nothing," Christian spat. "What they are doing changes nothing." It was like the lash of a whip--nothing could protect Christian. "And what do you suppose you were doing up there yesterday afternoon?" he said. "I saw you of course."

"At Eau Rouge?"

Christian glared at him. "Did you think some magic protects you? You believe too much in good fortune, Nicholas." Breitemann's smile was unwilling. "I know quite well why you were there--but would you stand there without moving during all of a race?"

"No."

"Then don't talk to me about eliminating risk, when to do so cannot be done. Did you enjoy what you saw?"

"Yes."

Breitemann nodded sharply and walked away. His demeanor did not invite Thorne to follow.

Under Whitlaw's icy glare the two chief mechanics, Ermanno for Breitemann and Graham Tully for Devane, conferred about the wheel rims. Tully admitted he'd gone over Devane's inner rims with a grinder Friday morning to roughen the surface where they met the tire "bead." It gave the tire better purchase to prevent slippage and ensure the seal. The rivalry between Devane and Breitemann was a fact of life--but that it was allowed to stray this far scandalized Thorne!

Ermanno and his crew spent the remainder of Saturday grinding Christian's wheel rims. He would not get the pole, advantage Devane. After three straight victories Porsche had amassed a commanding points lead over Ferrari. Attention shifted now to the duel between Devane and Breitemann. Side by side on the front row, in equal cars at high noon, the two would contest 1000 kilometers at the most lethal racing circuit on earth. People spoke of nothing else.

Fifteen minutes before the close of practice a few lesser G.T. cars still circulated. The major teams had conceded they would qualify no faster. The day's tension coalesced now to pervading fatigue. Like everyone, Thorne had had enough. He began towards the press car park.

"Thorne!"

He knew the voice. Devane came to him and he knew why--did he dare refuse? Drivers were legendarily superstitious, but he wanted no part of this.

Devane reached into his orange-and-blue Carnelian Team Beacom parka. "Here."

Not wanting to, Thorne took the magnesium nugget. Devane turned away. Thorne was seized with a shudder of loathing.

Burnleigh and Austin had left in Jozie's clamshell Citroên. It wass a relief, Thorne could drive back alone. He started the Jaguar, but the post-practice traffic was hardly moving.

Alone in the beautiful white coupe he let his thoughts drift...was it Breitemann's pallor after the blown tire? He felt an electric disturbance deep in his chest. It was unidentifiable but horrific, like a lightning bolt caught in the corner of his eye.

He reflected on the haunted castle of Christian's life. Face to face with that horror, Thorne had fled. Later Christian confirmed it, nothing could save him.

No. He said nothing could "make him safe." It was different.

But mortality was the litmus. It defined Christian just as his own mission of witness defined Thorne. It had brutalized Angela and Luciana. Now it was brutalizing him. Jennifer wasn't troubled by it, she just denied it. No, it was simpler--she reduced life to winning first prize, a World Champion.

Ridiculous. He hadn't been her choice so now she was empty and hateful. But at Como she was entirely aware of this fevered world and Tony's place in it....

Traffic inched ahead. Stranded in it he felt alone. Marooned. Measurelessly anonymous. Then, why this icy voltage in his heart--

Jesus....

Poor François.

Beautiful, poor François!

The tears surged up--for good-hearted, joyous François. In a murderous instant he saw the crash as it had truly been. It was beyond horrible.

But that was not François. François was beautiful. That came *after* François!

His lungs ached with sobbing. On and on it went, waves of grief and pain washing over him. But at its catastrophic center he felt something beyond grief. The more he grieved the more he saw François as he had truly been...yesterday...before...laughing and playful among them, bedazzled by the limitless sweetness of his amazing life! The termination of his young life, so young, far younger than Thorne, had a stunning impact. The American racers Thorne knew who had died were older, tougher. In some terrible way, dying in a racing car was among their signal accomplishments.

But François--

They owed him, all of them. They must remember him beautifully.

Against everything that was in him, he was uplifted by what he felt. Even in death, François was teaching him, generous of spirit, free and joyful as ever! It filled Thorne with awe for the rite of life.

His own day would come, too, when he must earn the gift--when he must earn being remembered beautifully.

Traffic was moving now.

It meant nothing.

Tears burned his cheeks.

But tears, they said, cleanse the soul.

François must be honored for the elegant person he was in life. He must be seen as a gift to the people who knew him.

...and remembered beautifully.

Thorne moved routinely, methodically with the traffic now, half blinded with his emotions, only following where he was led. A period of time passed, the Jaguar following peacefully...until Hotel de La Gare appeared out the windscreen.

He parked and switched off. Wiping his reddened cheeks he looked up at the old shambles. His Belgian hotel. The place where he would sleep. It was perfect. Everything around him was perfect. And beautiful. This gray town on this gray evening, everything he had felt and thought today in all its joy and catastrophic pain, even the loss of François...perfect.

François affirmed it all by living fully.

He locked the Jaguar and went inside, his chest filled with a surge of sun-setting resolve.

An hour later it changed. Completely.

François loved racing and he knew the terms. There was no mystery in it--nothing behind the tapestry.

He would think of it no more.

He ordered another beer. Beer helped. And Filthy César obliged.

Anyway nothing needed helping.

He would think of it no more.

The beer arrived and again he thought of it.

He must not.

He drank and it helped.

But still he thought of it....

Angela wanted to see him. Her word choice was unsettling. "Talk to" meant one thing--but "see" him.

Unsettling. It was personal.

They were to meet in half an hour. And he needed conversation, needed to think of it no more. But he saw no one he knew in the gray maudlin doily-and-lace salon of Le Pavillon. He sat in a deep armchair near the stairs and ordered beer--

To think of it no more.

He had lost a friend.

But he did not stop thinking. He needed Angela here, talking.

Or Luciana. But the language barrier. He needed precise clear communication.

And not Jozie. Jozie was a critic. He didn't need a critic.

Christian would know all about it. In his years he had had close brushes--unless that prevented knowing about it. But tomorrow Christian must race, now was not the time.

It must be Angela. Nobody knew more than Angela. Christian was a driver and he had said it--they knew as little as they dared. A driver must only see himself, but Angela saw it all from the shore.

He should be stronger.

Tougher--

François dead.

Cut to pieces like a dog under a train.

Stop!

He would call her room. He was early but he was expected, it was all right. But he would order a beer, beer came first, then call. He didn't deserve to feel it again and again, this hatchet chop in his belly!

The waiter took his order, unimpressed with the honor.

Of course he missed François, he was not a monster! He hardly knew him but that was the point, he needed to know him!

He would not think of it.

Angela crossed the salon looking perfect. She wore a silk blouse, a leather mini of deep mahogany, thigh-high leather boots, heart-stopping.

He stood and kissed her cheek. She sat next to him.

He put his hand on her knee. "How are you?"

She smiled but made no answer, answer enough. She had come down late, twenty minutes after he called. He tried not to think what kept her...Devane demanding where was she going, with whom, what for?

He ordered her a gin and tonic. She said her husband had been back to the room only once, to pack.

"Good," he said.

She engaged his eyes. "I keep thinking about François, Nick."

"It's no good dwelling on it," he said, appalled at his own falsity.

"No, no, that's wrong," she said. "It is vital! If you don't go through it-- if you don't go through it completely--it will smash you! Allow yourself to feel all of it and, this will sound horrid, I'm afraid...you will feel wonderful!"

He felt the hairs standing on the back of his neck. "I can't believe you said that!"

"Don't be upset with me, Nick, I--"

"Angela, you don't understand."

"You must go through it. It's so--"

"I know!" he erupted, riddled with elation. He felt his eyes welling up-- but let them! "It's the most amazing thing. I was all alone in the Jaguar driving back from practice when it began. I was crying and crying, but at the same time it was beautiful!"

She reached for his hand. "Yes."

It was all he needed. He would be fine.

"Nick, I'm going to say something to you that will sound very strange-- never feel guilty about François' dying. What happened has nothing to do with us. We aren't part of it. It happened as it was meant to and it was perfect."

"Angela--"

"Listen! You must take care of yourself. You are too bright and too alive to let yourself be trapped in false sentiment." Her lavender eyes held him. "I'm going to tell you exactly what to think about François. We lost him and it is beyond endurance, but the way we lost him was brilliant and perfect. When he died he was a proud young animal at the height of his powers. He lived by his instincts and his death was flawless. Christian says it is the duty of the living to defy death, and from his perspective so it is. We all have some of that in us, but François and Tony and Christian have made it their life's calling--whether or not that is a mistake is not for me to say. But life ends and few of us have healthy ways of accepting it. We're horrified at the prospect of dying. We spend our entire lives pretending it will never happen. It's madness, but we do it anyway. We would do far better to learn from other models. When an Eskimo's time is come, he makes his farewell to his family and friends, walks out onto the ice floe alone and dies. That is respect for the dignity of dying.

"We owe François the same respect...for his life as he lived it and for how he died. Never think that being killed dishonors him. We all make dying a taboo--we're shamed by it! And we feel shame for the person who dies and for everyone who loved him, because by dying he failed. We cover the face of the dead, because he allowed death--we hide him from our witness. It's selfish and irrational so we do it twice as adamantly.

"It happens in racing again and again. A death car is covered immediately so no one will ever see the physical evidence, the confirmation. We all want to believe we are too smart for death, that our education and low-cholesterol diets and careful living and plastic surgery, all the rest of it, will make us survive our own end! François died beautifully doing what was perfect for him. He was a racer and racers die. Never feel shame for that."

"But what about you, Angela. Are you so sure as all that?"

"Nobody is, dear. I'm devastated. But that is the gift--being alive and at liberty to feel."

He set his glass down. She hadn't touched hers.

"You are intoxicating."

"It's the beer," she said.

"You are!"

"But I didn't need to say a thing, you were already there!"

"Everyone gets there eventually, I'm sure."

She laughed from the belly. "You'd know better if you were married to the World Champion!"

Despite her bruised cheek--because of it--he was as bewitched as on her first sighting in the Plough & Anchor.

"All right," he said, "now I've got something to ask you. How can I be sure you aren't one of these long-suffering Mona Lisas who uses her last ounce of life energy caring for others at your own expense?"

She didn't respond.

"I'm serious."

"You are a person of worth, Nick. I only want you to get through this the best way you can. You must start by knowing that François is a triumph, not a defeat."

"Even you don't know that."

She smiled. "That's right, Nick, keep your independence, I mean it. Without that, you'll never be able to love."

"Riddles now?"

"Everything of real value is a riddle."

"Not beer." He raised his glass and took a swallow.

But she nodded unpleasantly. "Beware of anything that comes too easily."

"Yes, Your Grace."

"You're so much like François," she said. "I envy you that."

"Hardly."

"You'll be fine."

"Starting when?"

She smiled with not a hint of happiness.

"And so will you," he said chilled by the void he saw in her eye. "We're speaking frankly now," he said. "I thought Tony never drank during the season."

"He doesn't--ever."

"Yes he does."

"Never."

"Last night, he was drunk as a longshoreman."

Nick pointed to a spot behind her in the middle of Le Pavillon's beige carpet. "Standing right there not ten feet from your chair."

Her eye blazed refusal.

"Pissed as a lord," he said.

"Oh, God..." she said, her voice mourning.

CHAPTER 51

"YOU NEED TO BE OUT of here," he said, "... get some fresh air."

Angela gave him a conflicted smile.

"Really," he said. "Le Pavilion isn't depressing enough, we'll go to Filthy César's."

"Who?" she laughed.

"Looks like Oliver Hardy, only pompous. A dollar says you can't make him smile."

Angela brightened. "I like a challenge." She lifted her glass. "Can I finish this?"

"You have five seconds--we'll miss the floorshow."

"What does he do?"

"Polishes glasses--it's great!"

He beckoned the waiter. In moments the Jaguar tires were knuckling over knobbly Belgian block cobblestones.

"This car suits you, you know," she said. "You look like some wealthy American sportsman come to Europe to visit his polo ponies."

"I always thought so."

"And not particularly American at that."

"A sort of Cary Grant," he smiled, "only blond, callow and minus the savoir-faire."

She snorted. "You don't see yourself at all!"

"But I know important people," he said stopping the Jaguar in front of Hotel de La Gare. "Like Filthy César."

He gestured through Au Chat Fou's steamed front window. César sat motionless behind the bar measuring his life in broken espresso cups. "But we've missed the eight o'clock show."

Four *citoyens* stood along the bar smoking and sipping beer and milky *pastis*. One gesticulated grandly, driving his point home.

"*Charmant*," she said.

He beamed. "The man at the window won *Le Prix Fromage*--for drinking the most Pernod in an hour without cutting off his ear."

"Van Gogh was Dutch."

"Your point?"

"But I'm not dressed," she said, "...I didn't wear a hairnet."

He laughed rounding the car to her door. When she swung her legs out to the pavement reaching up for his hand, her mahogany-leather mini rode up. He indulged a look at the creamy flesh of her inner thigh. She climbed out knowing it.

He pushed open the door of Au Chat Fou. The *citoyens* turned and--

Froze.

They turned back to one another, murmuring.

Nick ordered porter and a gin and tonic. For Angela's benefit the volume of conversation at the bar ramped up, each player establishing his credentials as a formidable fellow.

Filthy César shoo-ed Thorne away, the drinks would be brought to the table. Nick pondered how long it had been since the last outbreak of Au Chat Fou table service.

César delivered the drinks, his off-center smile meeting Nick just above the brow, a first stab at eye contact since Wednesday.

Thorne touched his glass to Angela's. "You win *Le Prix Fromage*, Ladies' Division."

"For?"

"First time he's smiled since the invention of arch supports."

Her laugh was beautiful. He wanted to tell her she was beautiful! He modulated his smile and she saw it.

"What are you thinking right now?" she said.

"Nothing."

"Every time you get that little smile I want to know why."

His face began to burn. "You don't need to know everything!"

"Look, ladies, he's blushing!"

Furious at himself, he felt his complexion smoldering out of control. She gave him a sexy little laugh. "I like that, you know."

"Have I mentioned you have a mean streak? Yes, I believe I have."

She tried to stifle a laugh, and against all expectation she reddened. He felt an urge that scared him.

At just that moment Burnleigh strode in, followed by Joubert and Jake Austin.

"Hah!" Joubert boomed in his improbable raspy basso. "Caught you!"

Not at all what Nick needed to hear.

"What are you doing here?" Burnleigh asked Angela.

"Same as you. Came for the cabaret."

"You don't look so bad," Austin said bluntly. But by this time in the scandale, tact was redundant.

"I'm sure I am flattered," she said.

"Sit," Thorne said. "You all know César."

He sat behind the bar. And alas, the brief, shining hour of table service was past. Burnleigh collected three beers and brought them over.

"Good to see you out and about, my love." Jozie said. He smirked. "Even here."

Nick was horrified at himself...what had she read in his face just before they arrived? But her smile was glorious and impenetrable once again, the warrior's shield back in place.

Conversation led ineluctably to Breitemann's three front-tire deflations. No one but Nick appeared concerned at Christian's thunderstruck response.

"They're on the edge constantly," Angela said, "but they can't let themselves think about it. Christian is unique--he does. Takes enormous courage."

Once again she confirmed something precious for him.

"I can't think how he endures it," she said.

"No one is like him," Nick said.

Burnleigh sniffed. "They all are."

Nick ignored him, watching the tiny bubbles in his porter scurry upwards like microorganisms.

"I still don't understand why you're here," Burnleigh said to Angela. "None of my business, of course, but--"

"But you'll make it your business."

She smiled, her eye dwelling on him.

"You're not doing your case any good, you know," he said.

"My 'case' doesn't need doing good." She turned to Nick. "I'm a bit knackered, Nick." She giggled. "Try saying that fast! A bit nickered, Knack."

Joubert laughed.

"Do you suppose, we might..." she said to Thorne, her glass half full.

"As tonight's winner of *Le Prix Fromage*," he pronounced, "your wish is holy writ." Under his breath, he described to Joubert the clumsy smile on César's teapot face bringing drinks to the table, and added, "Don't all turn at once."

All turned like marionettes. The proprietor glared back.

Angela stood and Thorne rose to help with her jacket. He smiled *merci* to the barman, who returned a phantom nod. At the car he opened Angela's door and she slid in. He admired her thigh again and she knew it.

"It's the Belgian Dust Bowl," he ventured driving back. "Not a drop of rain for three hours' running."

Arriving at Le Pavillon his heart pounded inadmissibly. She opened her door. "You don't have to get out."

"Very American of you."

"I quite fancy Americans, if you don't know." She reached across and patted his hand on the wheel. "Thanks, Nick, you've been a luv. This was exactly what I needed."

"You have a ride tomorrow?"

"Luciana."

"Perfect."

She closed the door. He watched her climb the steep stone steps to Le Pavillon, her perfect little bottom flexing and clenching in the leather mini. Moth wings whirred in him. Distracted, he pushed the Jaguar into gear without fully depressing the clutch and the gearbox made a graceless *grrrronkk*.

Shit!

He looked up to see if she had heard--

And saw her running down the steps towards him.

Devane came hounding down after her. "Damn it, get back here!"

Nick sprang out of the car.

A backlit figure stood at the stop of the stairs--Jennifer.

Christian Breitemann sprinted down the steps now after them both.

"You bitch!" Devane yelled.

Angela ran for Nick, eyes wide. He pulled her behind him.

"Tony, wait."

"Out of my way!" Devane's breath reeked of whiskey. "Move!"

Breitemann came between them. Immediately Nick nudged Angela back towards the car.

"Tony, this will be bad," Breitemann said.

"Out of the way, squarehead bastard."

Breitemann held his hands up in a pacifying gesture, his syntax going to pieces. "You know this can be not good. Think a moment!"

"Are you feeling lucky, mate?"

"I do not--"

"That's my wife!"

"Then, treat her like it!" Thorne growled.

"You keep out of this!"

Thorne felt Angela tug him to stop.

"I'm very much in it," he said.

"Tony, Tony..." Breitemann pleaded, "you must think. We race tomorrow. You must do nothing now. Nicholas only has kept company with her."

"Oh, bloody right."

Nick nodded. "While you were off screwing somebody else!"

"Are you feeling lucky?"

"Never luckier."

Thorne stepped in front of Breitemann.

"Nicholas, do not!" Breitemann said.

"Stop!" Angela screamed. "Please!"

Devane's fist shot out. Thorne ducked and the punch grazed his temple, Devane's elbow butting the side of his head. Thorne planted a foot and drove his right fist into Devane's belly. Breath gushed out. He threw his left with all his might, meeting Devane square on the jaw--but in the same instant something huge and black and terminal crashed into his face.

Electrical flashes filled his eyes.

The night went out, his head filled with bright lights.

He stepped back.

Devane was bent double, gasping for breath. Nick saw him at the end of a long tunnel.

And suddenly everything, all of it, was too heavy to hold vertical. He took a half step back and sank to a knee, his skull filled with klaxons, squealing tires. He looked up. The hotel whirled, sounds all around he couldn't quite hear, the sidewalk spinning like a barber pole whirling up to him.

Breitemann's hand on his shoulder steadied him.

"Sit, Nicholas, just sit."

Through tangled cobwebs he saw Devane bent down to the sidewalk. Good.

But Devane was reaching out. Thorne saw a club of some sort--an old chair rung at the curb. He came at Nick with it, but Breitemann blocked his way.

Christian, no!

"Do not!" Breitemann yelled.

"Fuck you!"

Devane came at Breitemann with the club...but as if in half-motion, hardly moving, Breitemann deflected Devane's arm and threw two short punches into Devane's mid-section, a left and right, sudden and explosive...Nick knew them only by the rapid-fire impact.

Devane collapsed like a column of sand.

Breitemann kicked away the wood, clonking down the cobblestones.

"You are all right, Nicholas?"

"What did you do!"

"You are fine. Good."

Breitemann cradled his left hand, a sparrow with a broken wing.

"You're hurt."

"No," Christian said.

"Is it broken?"

"It is fine."

"Sodding bastards." Devane spat on the ground.

Still stunned at Breitemann's speed, Nick almost forgot. Devane came slowly to his feet, Breitemann watching, but he was done.

"It was needed," Breitemann said as if to himself.

Nick turned. Angela was in the Jaguar staring blindly ahead. He nodded to Breitemann. "Help her, Christian."

"You must--I cannot."

"You don't understand."

"I cannot. You must!"

Nick's legs were shaky.

But gradually they began to bear him. Everything he saw was grainy-- seen through gauze. Breitemann guided him to the Jaguar. Angela would not look up, tears of despair and shame streaking her face.

"Christian," she said.

"It is finished. You must go away from here."

Adrenaline still crashed in Thorne's temples. Mad tremors raced down his elbows. When he clenched his jaw, a fiery ache filled his temple.

"I am sorry, Angela," Breitemann said. "Can you please forgive me?"

She stared ahead unseeing.

He nodded, crestfallen. "Perhaps someday."

He looked at Thorne and his eye said it all--she was a competitor's wife, it must be Thorne who took her away.

"Christian..." Nick began.

"Go--now!"

Onlookers had gathered. Standing at a respectful distance around the World Champion, they whispered who he was and what they'd seen. Sitting crumpled over his knees below the steps, Devane was still finding his breath.

Breitemann nodded to Thorne--an unspoken command. Cradling his left hand, he began up the hotel steps. Jennifer stood motionless at the top.

"Big mistake, Yank," Devane growled. "Big!"

Thorne turned. Angela stared off into night darkness. She had been loyal until loyalty no longer had merit. Now she needed protection.

Devane spoke in a new tone. "Took two of you, didn't it? Two!"

Thorne hadn't felt like this since his only other fight, after school in Ninth Grade. It was the same--unavoidable and futile. But Devane's actions had been witnessed, they were public knowledge. Thorne must live with the consequences.

And Christian was right--take her away.

He started the Jaguar, with no idea where to go. The road would decide. He put the shifter in gear. He'd begin with the most familiar route.

He headed out of Spa towards the circuit, driving deep into moonless blackness. His senses were on red-alert, but all else ceased except the adrenaline crashing in his ears. His hands on the wheel jittered--he must take care. Pay strict attention. And he was afraid she would see his hands. He mustn't alarm her.

Angela saw nothing.

Spa fell behind.

They glided into the black Ardennes.

CHAPTER 52

THE FOREST DARKNESS WAS measureless, timeless. They passed through Malmèdy and Stavelot, continued beyond. Angela moved not a muscle, making no sound. At last it began, a small child's crying. It built upon itself, finding reasons. It was not the resigned womanly crying of sacrifice or defeat but the crying of refusal. Defiance.

He reached for her hand and she let him hold it. He knew, he had had his nights.

They passed through Trois-Ponts. After a long time, driving very calmly, slowly, they came to Vielsalm--far enough. He rounded the pitch-black center and the Jaguar headlights pointed back towards Stavelot. Carving a careful passage through caverns of night, kilometer after kilometer, the reassurance of routine movement lulled her. She went still. When she spoke at last her voice was no more than the sound of breath.

"I'm so afraid."

He waited.

"I don't even know anymore...."

"Why are you afraid?" he said.

"I don't know."

"It will help."

She said nothing.

"I understand."

"I don't know...."

The lights of Auberge de La Source slipped by Angela's window at last. Was Devane there? With Jennifer? He hoped she did not see, or if she did, paid no attention.

He parked at the darkened train station and switched off.

Her crying had stopped long before. But the moment he switched off the engine and looked across, it began anew. He leaned towards her in the cramped little cockpit. Against all expectation she laughed through her tears.

"Whoever reckoned these cars to be romantic was bloody mad!" She wiped her tears away. "There was never a surer method of birth control."

"That's more like it."

He smiled.

She tried to smile, her breath coming in soft gasps. It touched him.

"I'm sorry, Nick."

"For being alive?"

"You are sweet."

It felt patronizing--a way of keeping him at a distance. He understood.

Now she looked into Au Chat Fou. "Do you think Filthy César would sell us a drink?"

"If you'd like. I'd break his arm if he didn't."

"We've had enough of that," she breathed softly.

"Would you like a drink?"

"Would you?" she said.

"I would."

They were speaking in code. She squeezed his hand and he considered the smallness of her palm, her long, graceful fingers. Her hands were cold. He wanted to hold them until they were warm. And suddenly it was that tremulous morning at Lake Tahoe long ago when he was ten and stranded on the tiny rock ledge above Johnny Vail's house...no way to back up, no way to go forward, jagged boulders thirty feet below. If he fell, he would be broken to pieces, but if he didn't go forward and get to the other side...he would fall anyway. He dare not move--yet he had no choice but to go!

They got out of the car, Thorne conscious of every move they made. He pushed open the door of Au Chat Fou and she stepped in. Filthy César was wiping down the bar preparing to close, but when he saw Angela's reddened eyes, her face entirely too still, he smiled bashfully. With a welcoming bow he gestured them to their old table.

Nick ordered. César delivered the drinks. Nice man.

But Angela touched Nick's forearm. While they were at it, she said, she wanted a second gin and tonic.

His head shook. "I'm taking you back after this one. You've had a terrible night."

"No."

She ordered a second drink for them both.

"I don't want another," he said.

"You always want another." She stopped herself. "I didn't mean it the way it sounded."

"Maybe you did."

"I meant you're always on for a nice time."

He said nothing.

"There."

She smiled to César. "*Encore deux.*"

"Angela, this is no time for making sudden decisions."

Deliberately her hand brushed his leg and his breath stopped. Involuntarily, against everything on earth, he felt himself responding.

"I feel so alone, Nick. Take me to your room."

"A night like this would scare anyone."

"You aren't 'anyone.'"

"Angela--"

"Hold me. Take me. Make love to me."

César arrived with the two extra drinks on a small tray so they could be carried upstairs. Angela smiled gratefully and he smiled back. Thorne paid him and her hand came to him under the table. She touched him and desire licked in her eyes.

"You've wanted to since the Plough & Anchor," she said. "I've seen it."

"I'm single, Angela, I'm not dead."

She beamed, giving him a risky laugh deep in her throat. "You never thought I wanted to?"

"You were married."

The past tense scared him.

"That's why you're so appealing," she said, "you have no clue how sexy you are." She squeezed him gently and his heart banged in his chest.

"Please, Nick--I need you."

It was not the best of reasons nor the worst. Violent alarms should have sounded, severe consequences being weighed...but she'd won already. Aware it was the most momentous decision he had ever made, he ushered her up the stairs.

He set the tray of drinks on the dresser, ashamed of everything, the way the stairs creaked, having to climb to the third floor, the naked bulb on the landing, the slatternly way the door swung shut on its hinges behind them.

She saw it and smiled. "No Nickie," she said. She squeezed his mouth and cheeks with her fingers as if hushing a small child. "You are what I want. I want to be here with you...I want to."

He put down the tray of drinks and their arms enclosed. They kissed tentatively, then hungrily, mouths wide, lips clasped. The warmth of her body unfolded to him, a blossom opening to morning sun. "*Mmm...*" she breathed. Her kisses came insistently, meeting him again and again. She drew back and he felt her soft words against his cheek, half sound, half breath..."We're perfect--do you feel?"

Her thigh guided him inward to her. "You feel so beautiful."

Far in the distance he was afraid--she should not be here, it should not happen. In the same moment he welcomed all conflict, all difficulty. Nothing would stop them.

He held her face up to him. "From now on I will always want you and you will always want me."

"Yes," she breathed.

She unfastened his belt and pants. He caressed the satiny weight of her breasts through her silk blouse.

"You're distracting me," she said with a shivery laugh. "Please don't stop!"

She unbuttoned his shirt and slipped it away. "A swimmer?"

"Water polo."

"*Mmm.*" She gave his chest a lick. "Exactly as I imagined."

His hand slid up the back of her mini, its buttery-soft leather cool to the touch. His palm cupped the round firmness of her, his breath quickening.

"I've wanted you for so long."

He unzipped her mini and she helped him slip it up over her head. It pulled her red bikini panties up snug. He guided her down to the bed then gently, purposefully.

"I've wanted to hold you down and just...God, you're beautiful."

In shadowy light his fingers moved beneath her panties, stroking her secret cleavages. He slipped her panties down and away and her dark eyes flashed--the most exquisite black-flaming eyes he had ever known.

Impatiently he opened her, bending down with his tongue. He tasted her lacy flesh, glistening, engorged, moist as fresh peach. His tongue curled into and around her private ridges and valleys.

Her head fell back.

She hissed as if stung. "My baby."

Her nails raked his scalp, her breath coming in ragged gasps, a desperation of wanting.

Gradually, gradually--then suddenly--she was gliding up and up, rising high up, loose on violent updrafts.

The waves lessened breathlessly....

She wilted beneath him, her hands stroking his head and neck.

"No, no," he smiled. "You're not getting away that easy."

The laugh she gave him was like a crashing wave. He removed her blouse and bra. She slipped his underwear away.

"Oh, God," she said.

Her palm clasped him.

"Nickie, fuck me."

He rolled her on top and she sank against his chest, her breasts molding to his ribcage. She forced her tongue into his mouth and her legs bound him like climbing vines. Her body hunted him blindly, bluntly. She reached down then, clutching him hard with her hand.

Breathless, in distress, she took him in.

At every tiny movement she winced. He pressed full into her at last, and she melted in the air, crying out.

She came up to vertical. Her slender hungry hips astride him, the juices of her pleasure gushed, all things confirmed. Her breasts danced before his eyes. She knit her brow sharply, fitfully--and then again--deep secrets explored. He watched her pleasure, a dream creature. He held and stroked and shaped the tremulous weight of her breasts, gazing up at her slender dancer's neck. Her shining dark hair and the urgency in her eyes framed a catastrophic intent. Urging and gripping, grasping, she rose higher. Her waist arched and she stretched far back, tight against him, her breath coming in stabbed gasps. Roughly then he pulled her down to him, his impacts growing. Violent. She bore down and down, thighs tensing and releasing, the breath wedged in her throat, fighting him for it, jealous, spiteful, angry, in a blood-burning rage...the storm soaring high up to infinities of desire--

She collapsed completely.

A low growl of triumph rattled in her throat.

"Where have you been, my Nickie!"

He pulled her down tight on him, not letting her move.

"Yes..." she breathed.

He rode deep into her.

Their rhythmic movements made a gleaming sound.

"You are so..." she gasped. "You just..."

Her alarm was climbing. She keened softly above him in rib-throwing gyrations, her breasts swaying, a-tremble.

He had waited.

Waited.

But it was now, a clenched fist in him, his throat blocked with it.

It crashed into her with a power that tore his vocal cords.

She cried out, a willful child, fierce and willful, demanding all things.

They tried to hold on to it.

But it subsided...sudden aftershocks hammering him.

And again!

She hissed bitterly with each as if grievously harmed, the tempest slipping silently, wetly beyond.

Now her voice was a whisper of soft breezes in his ear. She giggled and shook.

After a few minutes she tempted him with her breasts, gathering their crimson twin berries above him. But he could only laugh. He was too weak to move. The wet, sliding kiss she pressed on his lips left a glistening trail.

"*Mmmm...*" she purred.

Her nails stroked his chest--restrained claws, not quite painful.

"*Gawwwd...*" she breathed deep and collapsed over him, her violet eyes gleaming. "Am I too heavy?"

His belly laugh of pleasure was ample reply.

After a few minutes she looked past him.

Around the room.

She smirked.

"Rainy day in Brighton, this."

"I thought you 'adored' it."

"It's you I adore, silly. And now I have a pleasantly large reason why."

"*Thang-kyooo!*" he said receiving correct change for a dollar.

She beamed. "But I'd wager a pint o'bitter you'd be happier at Le Pavillon."

He looked at her.

"Wouldn't you?"

"Is that wise?" he said--and it all came back.

She laughed. "Is this! Come on, I'll help you pack."

"I don't know."

"I know for both of us."

He gave her bottom a sharp *thhwaackkk!* At its sting, she squealed joyously. "We could be in my bed by midnight. Wait, what's the time?"

"One-thirty."

"Blimey! And you with a race to cover!"

Again, the decision should have taken serious thought, consequences being weighed. It took a nod.

"One thing," he said.

"What."

"Turn around. I want to stare at you."

"I love being stared at. Turns me on!"

Her eyes flashed black fire. He was certain they would make love again before leaving.

CHAPTER 53

HE WAS WRONG. Angela was adamant. They would go to Le Pavillon first--then make love again.

"I have an idea," he said, "...why don't I just take you back?"

"And you take that lovely business home without letting me use it some more, no bloody way!"

She had a point--nothing about tonight was "wise." He packed toiletries and a change of clothes. They drove to the center of town, she guiding his free left hand under her mini. Her panties in her purse, she was like a ripe melon.

Smiling luxuriously she leaned over and blew in his ear.

"Why does this keep happening?" he said.

"What?"

"Women making me walk through hotel lobbies with an erection."

"But you've such lovely erections, Nickie, dear. And who else is doing it?"

"Never mind."

"Come on."

He told her about Jennifer at the Hotel de Paris.

"Don't want to hear about it."

"But this is the Sexual Revolution," he said. "No strings."

"Not when it's this good!"

He parked and they got out.

"Christ, look at me. Men are such gorgons."

She handed him his bag.

"Hold this in front, there's a good son."

He did.

"Or just hang it there."

She giggled and took two spritely steps ahead. In the dim light below the deserted hotel steps, she hiked up her mini and waggled her perfect panty-less bottom.

"Coming?"

"Thinking about it...."

She laughed.

"It's really not fair."

"It's perfectly fair," she protested. "Since that night in Sicily, every time you and I talk I'd be in my room afterwards doing light laundry."

"Really?"

"It's not so rare, you know."

"But you say so."

Her wink gleamed with sexual joy.

Angela went to the desk for the key--but suddenly, Jennifer appeared. She hurried to Thorne.

"He's in there and he's acting crazy."

"Where?" he said.

"Her room. He's furious!"

Angela's face drew tight.

"Go home, Jennifer," Thorne said. "There's nothing you can do."

She didn't react. Angela still hadn't spoken.

"Go," he said. "Do it!"

"How?" she asked in stifled fury. "On a horse? He has the keys!"

"A taxi, Jennifer. You have no trouble getting around. Use your initiative!"

"Bastard."

Angela touched his arm. "All right, Nickie, let's be calm."

"We have to leave," he said.

"I'm not leaving--not!"

"You haven't seen him..." Jennifer said.

"Yes...I have," she said, point made. "I'm going up to my room."

"Just hold on a minute." Nick turned to Le Pavillon's snippy little night clerk. "*Un taxi pour mademoiselle.*"

"*Tout de suite, monsieur.*"

Jennifer glared at Nick.

"Go home!" he said. "And lock your fucking door."

"Nickie, this is my mess," Angela said.

"Like hell."

Her eyes pleaded.

"Forget it!" he said. "Jennifer, get out of here!"

He grabbed Angela's elbow. At the first landing they walked along the hall to her door. He put down his bag and held her with both arms, speaking under his breath.

"Don't come in till I say, understand?"

She didn't respond.

"If anything happens, get the police."

"Nick--"

"Stop!"

He took the key from her, unlocked the door and opened it. No sound. The light was on but nothing moved. He stepped in.

"Come on," he said.

Angela didn't move. Only then did he see--she was paralyzed. He came to her and wrapped his arms around her. "It's all right. You're perfectly safe."

"I'm so sorry." Her tears welled up. "I can't take this!"

"It's all right. Everything's over now."

"It just goes on and on!"

He walked her across the room and sat her on the bed. "Nothing to worry about."

He brought in his bag and locked the door.

"Demon...," she seethed. "Monster!"

"I know. I'll just make sure Jennifer is gone."

"Don't leave me, Nick."

It wasn't "Nickie" anymore. The fear was winning.

"Right back," he said. "Lock the door behind me."

She reached out. "Please."

He squeezed her hand, "Right back."

He went out and heard her lock the door.

The front desk was unattended. He went to the front steps just in time to see Jennifer climbing into a Renault R8 taxi. The deskman climbed the steps pocketing his gratuity. He gave Thorne a self-important glimmer.

Thorne checked his watch--2:45. Christ!

He followed the deskman inside. The lobby was silent--beyond silent-- as if some entity had just been and left, he felt it in the air. He asked how many keys there were for Angela's room. The deskman nodded curtly, he was not permitted to divulge this information.

A loud scream rang out upstairs. `

"Appelez aux gendarmes!" Thorne ordered. *"Vite!"*

He ran to the first landing and down the hall. The door stood open. Devane had Angela pinned to the floor. His palm crashed into the side of her head, *krrackkk!*

Nick ran at Devane low and hard. The impact drove him and Devane sprawling across the floor.

"Bastard!" Devane growled.

Thorne locked his arms around Devane's chest from behind. Devane's elbows flailed helplessly. Thorne lifted him bodily, driving him headfirst at the wall.

"Fucker!" Devane raged.

Thorne threw a hip in front of Devane and crashed him to the floor. He pinned Devane's shoulders to the carpet, bearing down with all his weight.

He glanced over his shoulder. Angela was on her knees in the hall, staring ahead expressionless.

"Get the cops!" he yelled.

His arms were locked hard around Devane. She didn't move. The deskman appeared.

"Police!" Thorne roared.

The deskman was already gone.

Devane struggled upwards trying to break Thorne's hold. But Thorne's leverage was too great. He bore down with renewed strength, driving Devane into the carpet. Devane struggled hard, crabbing sideways. Then Thorne saw it, a cut-stone ashtray on the side table Devane was lunging at. Thorne yanked him back and drove his knee into Devane's spine, hauling back on his shoulders.

Devane groaned in pain.

Thorne looked behind him again. Angela sat like a ragdoll. Her hands were against the sides of her face as if holding it together.

Thorne redoubled the arm-lock.

"Washed up," Devane gasped, "you know that. All over for you, mate."

"You are the one that's over," Angela said wearily. "Nobody knows it better than you."

"Whore."

Thorne hauled back hard on Devane's shoulders.

"No, Nick!" she pleaded. "Don't!"

He began to reduce his pressure. Devane made no move.

Only gradually he released his grip. He let Devane free at last and stood back and away.

A gaunt little man in a dressing gown in the hall looked down at Angela. Peered into the room.

Nick heard distant shouting and a rush on the hall carpet. Two gendarmes burst in, the deskman behind. Their eyes lit up at sight of the World Champion. Devane was working his arms and back stiffly.

He gestured at Thorne angrily. "I've been assaulted by this man." He nodded at Angela. "She is his whore and my wife. He was with her."

They understood not a word. He pointed again to Angela. "*Ma femme.*"

"Pig!" she spat.

The first gendarme, tall, with a thick black mustache, ordered Thorne to the far side of the room. He sat on the couch, sweat running down his neck.

Devane met his eye with a nod. "Told you, mate--finished."

He turned to the gendarmes. "My wife!" He gestured to himself angrily, then to Angela. He pointed to Thorne, but this time he said nothing.

"He was beating her!" Thorne protested.

"Silence!" the gendarme snapped.

He turned to Angela. "*Votre mari?*"

Her face twisted with hatred. "*Salôt! Cochon!*"

"*Je vous prie de vous calmer, madame.*"

The second gendarme, slight, short, very young, helped her to her feet. He guided her to a chair but she refused to sit. She pointed to the door, trembling with fury. "Get him out!"

The tall gendarme looked to the World Champion for direction.

Devane spat, "Wouldn't be on the same continent with this whore!"

"Spoken like a champion," Thorne said.

"Sod you, Kojak!"

"*Calmez-vous, messieurs,*" the gendarme warned. His eye was trained not on Devane but Thorne. He turned to Angela.

She gazed straight into her husband's eye. "Away from me!"

She broke down sobbing.

"As far as I can get." Devane grinned. "And you, Yank--ancient history."

"Mediocre to the last."

"We shall see."

The gendarmes escorted the World Champion out, impressed with their charge. The door closed.

She would not hear of it, he must leave. Everything was over--everything. He would be blamed and vilified and she would be branded low and cheap.

He said she needed protection.

Not necessary, she said. He must leave.

She should not be alone, he said. Nobody cared what Devane said. It was the Age of Aquarius, nobody cared what anyone said!

She was cold and cornered.

The peculiar thing about Americans, she said, is how hard they work at believing their own tripe. In the real world she was a married woman and that is taken to mean something. Why would he want to stay with her now anyway!

He said it simply--because she should not be alone.

Her eyes softened. She kissed his cheek. He must go--no argument. He needed to rest.

He would not rest, he said. He couldn't.

Try, she said.

There was a moment between them of vast emptiness.

The look he saw in her filled him with fear.

Go, she said, it's all right. Her voice was a November wind.

He must not go this way, he said.

He must hold her.

No.

Her eyes repeated it--no.

She handed him his bag.

The door closed.

Locked.

And the black half of his life began.

CHAPTER 54

"IT WAS AFTER THE Nürburgring two years ago when Udo was killed."

Breitemann gazed into the night.

"I drove on the same team with him and so I was asked to be a, what do you call these...a pall-bearer.

"We had gone out from the church for the burial and it was raining and gray and so sad. The six of us walked to the side of the grave with this heavy wooden box full of Udo. Baby--Caracciola's widow, you know--was reading the words, tears streaming down her face. It was terrible carrying him through the rain.

"I had been to many funerals like this--fifteen or twenty, more--and when we got to the side of the grave I stood there and looked into the deep wet hole listening to Baby cry--and I began crying too, crying and crying like a lost child.

"We lowered Udo into the ground.

"When it was finished and we were leaving Herr Bott came to me. 'Christian,' he said, 'I did not know you and Udo were so close with each other.'

"'We were not,' I said.

"'But I saw you,' he said. 'You were crying so!'

"'Mein Herr,' I said, 'I was not crying for Udo--I was crying for me!'"

He took off everything but his underwear. Alone in his room the prospect of his nakedness filled him with shame.

He turned out the light and lay down on the steel-sprung bed staring up into night blackness dreading his thoughts. They were unendurable. He turned the light on again and swung his bare feet onto the cold floor. The shock of the linoleum made his headache worse.

In an hour the light would come...it would begin. And it would not be good.

He should smoke. If he smoked he would look the way he felt.

He stared off into the emptiness, alone in his shabby hotel room. His heart bumped in his ears, a stubborn clockwork plodding hopelessly on. It was the counterfeit of time. It moved like a snail...while daylight raced towards him.

He sat perfectly still, chilled to his spine. He was neither asleep nor awake, but it seeped into his bones, the gray light beyond the blind. Dawn was the price to be paid.

He'd taken three aspirins, the universal analgesic--for everything but this.

A brief chilly shower was no better. The threadbare Hotel de La Gare bath towel was saturated, wringing wet before he was half dry.

He began dressing. He had no ironed pants. Of all days, today he needed ironed pants.

Jeans must do. He must do.

The flags above the pits at Start/Finish stirred lazily, then more purposefully. They began flapping towards Eau Rouge and Malmédy. Breitemann said when the wind turned from La Source towards Eau Rouge it meant rain. No longer intrigued, Thorne jotted it down. It was no truer than anything else--but he jotted it down.

"You look not so good today," Breitemann said.

"Rough night."

Breitemann waited for him to continue. He didn't. He was only waiting--not for the race, that was at noon. What he was waiting for had no appointed hour, no predictable form.

Light mist-driven rain began. So Christian was right, for all it mattered.

Devane appeared in the pits at ten, unusually late for race day. He looked like Thorne felt. Thorne gave him a wide berth--or was it the reverse? He was intensely conscious of Devane's proximity and whether or not it threatened to grow nearer. It did not. By an act of will he forced himself to stay in the Beacom pits--to show the flag.

But after several minutes he made good his escape. In the radius of his vision he had seen Devane conferring with Beacom. In response the Death Ray nodded, nodded, casting a bleak eye in his direction. He walked behind the pits, heading out and away, feeling both relieved and craven. Here at least the searchlights no longer scanned the perimeter for him--

Ridiculous. He had done nothing wrong! He'd shielded Angela from a sadistic club-wielding monster--

After fucking her brains off in a slummy hotel.

He didn't know which direction to walk. He could not go down to Ferrari, she would be there. She didn't want to see him. She'd made it clear. He could only comply.

He turned uphill. There were no teams of consequence in that direction and going there served no purpose. But he trudged urgently ahead just the same. If it were up to him he would keep going straight into the dark Ardennes and never come out. Devane was right, he was finished. He rehearsed it all, disgrace, snickers, ridicule...Angela's contempt.

No--he could not trust his own mind. When the whole story came out of Devane beating her on the floor, his motives would prove honorable...except when he took her clothes off and--

"Nick!"

It was like a sabre in his back. They were coming for him!

He turned.

"My dear man!" It was the bullfrog basso of Jozie Joubert. "Where on earth do you think you're going? What's this rubbish Devane is saying?"

He waited.

Joubert came to him.

"Devane is telling everyone you bedded Angela and then beat him up."

Nick said nothing.

"Come, Nick, what about it?"

"You wouldn't believe me if I told you."

"Sooner you than him."

"I have no chance."

"Not if you don't speak up!"

Nick ran it through in his mind. "You know about Jennifer, of course."

"Everyone knows!"

Right. In his despair he'd forgotten how much was known. It was not hopeless!

"And you know he hit Angela on Friday."

"Nick, get on with it!"

"Well, he was drunk again last night and spent the evening, Jennifer in tow, stalking Angela. He tried to hit me with a club when I protected her, then Christian nearly knocked him out."

Joubert was dumbfounded.

"Ask Christian!" Thorne said. "It happened right in front of Le Pavillon, there were dozens of witnesses. Christian said get her away from Devane and I did. She was in awful condition, afraid and alone, and we drove around for an hour. She needed someone with her to...."

"And you took care of her," Jozie supplied with Gallic grace. Thorne couldn't have been more in his debt.

He recounted the rest of the night for Joubert, everything that was rightly recounted...bringing her back to Le Pavillon and Jennifer saying Devane was half-crazed up in Angela's room, then Devane holding her down and hitting her, the struggle with Devane and the gendarmes. "Without batting an eye," Thorne said, "the son of a bitch claimed I assaulted him! She made them take him away."

Joubert nodded, "Come along."

"Where?"

"Come!" Joubert grabbed his arm. "We're straightening this out."

"The hell we are!"

"He's telling his story to everyone who'll listen, you have no choice."

"But he's the World Champion--who will believe me?"

"Trust your friends. We're going to Beacom."

Joubert marched down the hill, Nick following doubtfully two paces behind. A racing image Christian had once painted came to mind...arriving at the corner's apex fully committed, no margin for error, only waiting to see if this will be your big crash.

He followed Joubert towards Beacom--waiting for the apex.

Seeing Thorne, Raymond Beacom's head shook immediately. Thorne glimpsed Luciana at the back of the pit, but she scurried away the minute she saw him. He wanted to call to her, but Beacom precluded it.

"Mr. Thorne, you are not welcome here. Kindly leave our pits immediately."

Joubert held up his hand. "He's not going until you hear him out."

"I've heard all I wish to hear. He is responsible for more treachery in this team than Ferrari could achieve in a full season!"

"I've done nothing to your team!"

Devane appeared and Nick nodded in his direction. "I've only stopped this man from beating his wife in her hotel room. It may be to your advantage to believe his story, but it isn't true. He had her pinned on the floor hitting her."

"Nothing of the kind," Devane snapped. "Filthy bastard attacked me after doing God knows what with my wife all night!"

Several writers had gathered. Peter Whitlaw brought his blackest scowl to bear ordering them to leave.

"That's right," Nick said. "At all costs protect your sleazy 'hero!'"

"Just a minute," Joubert said. "There are two positions here, Mr. Beacom. You must hear both."

"Everything out of this wanker's mouth is a lie!" Devane snarled. "Say what you will, he had my wife all to himself last night. Not a husband in the world wouldn't come after him!"

Nick nodded. "Angela all but caught you in the act with Jennifer Whelan Friday afternoon, and your remedy is to come after her with your fists...or is Jennifer your wife too?"

"I've had nothing to do with her."

"You're a liar and a coward."

"Say that again, you--"

"A liar and a coward."

"Stop this!" Beacom barked. "We've a motor race to run today, Mr. Thorne, and you are not welcome. Leave our pits!"

"He shall not."

It was Christian Breitemann, Luciana standing next to him.

"If you know what's good for you, Christian, stay out of this," Beacom said.

"I will not. Tony twice hit his wife Friday night. I saw her swollen and bruised face. And he came after her again last night. Nicholas tried only to stop him."

Breitemann turned to face Devane.

"So Tony picked up a piece of wood to hit Nicholas, because Tony is a coward. I was able to stop him. But his wife will tell you he held her down later last night hitting her, before Nicholas stopped him. He has been together with Jennifer Whelan many times starting last fall at Watkins Glen--he has great joy in telling me all about this, until I have said I will not hear it anymore. What he says of Nicholas is a lie."

Breitemann faced Beacom.

"If Nicholas leaves, Herr Beacom, I leave! Nicholas is not the danger here--the danger is this one." He nodded to Devane. "And if I leave, Herr Beacom, I do not come back, *verstehen Sie*?"

Beacom was recalibrating rapidly. "I think we had all better calm right down," he said. "There are two points of view here, differences that--"

"*Ja, Mein Herr*, there are two points of view, but only one is true!"

"I can not have the team damaged over this kind of personal misunderstanding."

Breitemann's eye met Beacom. "There is no misunderstanding, none. It could not be clearer--Nicholas Thorne is not at fault."

"Well, it will all work itself out. In the end, these things always do," Beacom said. "But we have a race to run."

Thorne couldn't believe his eyes. Standing immediately behind his employer was The Mallet, Peter Whitlaw. His gaze was upon Thorne, and against all likelihood, he was smiling approvingly.

Beacom nodded. "I will ask you, Mr. Thorne," he said, concluding his business, "to take care that you are not in the way of the team's pit work."

"When was he ever in the way?" Breitemann said.

Whitlaw looked on with a slight nod, eye a-twinkle.

"Shall we get on with it, then," said Beacom, having achieved another masterpiece of motivational management.

But Devane's glare confirmed it, nothing at all had been resolved.

CHAPTER 55

AN HOUR BEFORE THE start Angela stepped up behind him and tapped his elbow, "Hi, sexy."

It chilled him. He wanted no reminders of any kind. He was not strong enough, not tough enough for these ferocious people.

Angela's complexion was gray, but she looked better than she had any right to look. Racers were a singular breed, stress agreed with them.

"I hear I missed a confrontation," she said.

"How did you know?"

"Spies."

He waited.

"The Mallet," she smiled, "sweet old poofter."

"Poofter! Whitlaw?"

"Shhh. Nobody knows. You'll keep it to yourself, won't you?"

"Jesus Christ, Angela, is anything around here real?"

"We'd be quite out of luck if we couldn't keep our secrets. But you look none the worse for wear."

"Look again."

She mugged giving him a great wall-eyed gawk. But then she flashed him a playful smile--or its best counterfeit.

"I'd say the same of you," he said, "if I were fool enough to trust my eyes."

"Good for you, Nickie." She wore the impenetrable center-stage smile he first saw in the Plough & Anchor, all defenses firmly in place. "I'm glad you're all right, I was worried."

"And I you," he said with a measure more gravity.

"But you know the truth...."

She needed something from him, a word of encouragement. To save his soul he could not give it. Too much had gone wrong.

Her smile wavered. "Christian is all right?"

"Never better."

"I mean his hand."

"Oh." He nodded. "I don't know."

"I hope they keep their wits about them."

"In any case," he said on a cold impulse, "it won't be your fault."

He realized how harsh it sounded. Right before his eyes all her heartbreak rushed to the surface.

"Angela, I didn't mean that. I'm completely off balance today."

"Aren't we all."

"Remember the good things...you have a movie to make!"

"I'll not be making any movies."

"Of course you will."

"It's not on." Her voice was drained. It drained him as well.

Airily then, she switched topics. "You didn't by chance find my glove in your car did you?"

He tried to read her.

"Dark-brown leather--"

She gave him a smirk.

"Unlike your other girls' leather work gloves."

"No," he said.

"Mind if I have a look? I really want to find it. Where are you parked?"

He pointed to the front row of the press car park along the trees. Unable to sleep he had been one of the first to arrive at the circuit this morning.

"Let me borrow your key, Nickie, I'll have a look."

She'd called him "Nickie" last night--his dearest trophy. Now it was a dagger in his heart. He took the key from his pocket.

"You won't steal it, will you?"

"Might," she smiled. "You've reporting to do."

She patted his forearm lightly. He recognized the tap...as if they'd just met.

She walked off towards the car park, everything ducky. But if he had learned anything this spring, it was to trust realities he could not prove. She was hanging by a thread.

Forty-five minutes before noon the drizzle stopped, but the pavement remained dark with moisture. Despite the ache in his chest he completed his reportorial rounds. Now he must find Christian.

He passed by Raymond Beacom, who smiled, "Mr. Thorne."

He nodded back. Devane was nowhere to be seen. Christian was in his pit fitting a new clear plastic face-shield to his helmet. He set the helmet down when he saw Nick. "You have seen Angela?"

"She's fine. Don't worry."

"I worry always."

It went off like a flash in Thorne's head--Breitemann and Angela in the rearview in Sicily, he showing no interest in the adventuresses stalking him everywhere he went. "You love her!" he said.

"You must not say that."

"You love her."

"I have always loved her, just like you. We have no choice."

"But you are a driver! You could--"

"I can not grab her away, Nicholas, I would be no better than him."

"But that's not--"

"I have waited such a long time for this weekend when she finally had enough. Now it has come and you are here." He smiled. "But she always cared for you--I think you don't know that. I saw it in England. You are the kind who never thinks a beautiful woman will fancy you."

"So I'm told." He thought of Angela's words.

"They like that," Chistian said. "And she does not deserve to be with another driver, she is too fine. It would be too cruel. I cannot tell you how glad I am for you."

"We aren't together."

"Of course you are!"

"No."

He refused to tell Breitemann the real difficulty. He would not explain the complete dissolution he saw in her just moments before.

"You give her very little credit, Nicholas. She has been through a terrible time with him, and finally she has reached out for something better. She made an excellent choice. I could only give her more pain. I am born for this sport, but it has treated her badly. You know it better than anyone. Look at Luciana, all the others. They try to find love with a racer and they pay the price. They believe they will win if they can at last be married and settle down. Maybe then the horrible dreams will stop."

Breitemann nodded, giving it a thought. "Wives are different, of course. Especially Grand Prix drivers' wives are different. But in exactly what ways must a Grand Prix driver's wife, this most extraordinary wife, arrange to be different?"

He shook his head.

"It is an impossible life--and still they choose it. They throw themselves at it, knowing they will be hurt. They love risk just like the drivers. But do not fool yourself, Nicholas, you have better things to offer. I could only give her pain and I care for her too deeply for that."

"But isn't that up to her?"

"I have decided for her." Breitemann held Thorne's eye. "Please, you must tell no one, it is a secret between us. We both know how exceptional she is."

Then very suddenly a bright smile lit up his face.

"Nick, this has been inside me for so long! I could not dare tell anyone, and now I have told you! I am very glad. But I have been selfish telling you. Are you angry that I spoke?"

Nick shook his head. "What a waste. What an unconscionable waste!"

"You are angry?"

"No." Thorne smiled unhappily. "I'm devastated."

"*Ach*, now..." Christian laughed as if it were only a joke. "It can be terribly confusing I think. So much bad has happened. But listen to me, doing right sometimes feels no better than doing wrong, and yet still you must do it. Sometimes you don't even know it is right until long afterwards. You are in terrible difficulty about last night, I see that, but Nick, you must trust yourself."

"Last night was a nightmare."

"You did only good things last night, the very best things. But I think you will be the very last to know it."

Thorne's head shook. He felt only conflict and pain.

"The answers are all inside you, Nicholas. You must trust them."

"There are no answers."

Breitemann smiled. "They are everywhere around you."

It deepened Nick's confusion and he had had enough confusion! He turned and scanned the Start/Finish straight. The cars were being pushed to the grid. He needed catharsis--a motor race!

Christian nodded. "You are impatient."

"I have to check the starting drivers, Christian." He needed distraction. Mindless busyness. "By the way," he said, "how is the hand?"

Breitemann took the driver's glove off his left hand so Nick could see. It was badly swollen.

"Jesus!"

"I am lucky it is not the gearshift hand. Say nothing to Raymond."

"Can you move it?"

"Yes." Breitemann gave him a wink. It could mean yes or no. "It is nothing."

"Well, Christian..." Nick said, reverting to a pre-race custom he'd forgotten to invoke in Europe, "have fun out there."

"I always do."

Breitemann met his eye. "Don't look so black, Nick. It all makes perfect sense. You must not blame yourself."

Thorne felt icefloes around his heart.

"So, then..." Christian said, "it is time to prepare."

Standing listening to Brietemann Thorne felt it before he saw...fifty yards away on the front row of the grid, leaning against his tangerine Beacom Porsche 917, Devane's eye was fixed on a point past Nick's shoulder--at Christian Breitemann.

Now Breitemann, pulling on his Nomex balaclava, returned Devane's gaze. Nick could not remember what to do next.

With ten minutes left before the start the racing surface was still moist. More than ever in his life Thorne wished for a dry safe track.

His ritual walk began at the rear of the 48-car grid, starting with the slowest G.T. cars. Looking through windshields at helmet graphics and embroidered names on Nomex driving suits, blue script for Goodyear drivers, red script for Firestone drivers, he noted each driver who would take the start. The co-driver stood by talking to the starting driver. The hush was massive, every utterance eerily audible.

He moved forward, in a vacuum. The long twin files were free of mechanical activity, all preparations complete. Seconds flickered past like bolts of lightning.

Across the track was white noise like distant surf--the buzz of 100,000 spectators. They crowded the fences eight deep. Shouts erupted in French and German and Flamand. An airhorn barked on the other side of the world.

He continued forward, the gravity deepening. The cars' vivid colors brightened the gray sky, each elevated to the peak of preparedness. He heard shards of conversation, trespassing on destiny.

At last came the fast five-liter Ferraris and Porsches--and "rehabilitated" Dante Ruggiero. His Brands Hatch crash had passed into history. Ruggiero would start on the fourth row in the third factory Ferrari. Two rows ahead and nine seconds faster was Jean Garand in the lead Ferrari. Boyish as ever, glinting as if he'd sneaked under the fence, Garand meant to win.

At the front, Ermanno stood next to Breitemann's car. On the pole with Devane's car was Ermanno's opposite number, Graham Tully. Neither looked at the other.

The track's dampness generated the usual tire confusion. Goodyear cars, among them the three Ferraris and both Porsche-Austria 917s, must choose between wets or dries black and white. Most selected the Goodyear rain tire, though Garand gambled on dries. The Beacom cars, on Firestones, could choose between wets, dries or intermediates. Devane and Breitemann chose intermediates. Short of a sudden deluge they would be fast on the cool moist track.

Thorne wrote Devane and Breitemann into his starting-driver list. Fifty years hence he might wonder who started for Beacom at Spa, but this sacramental Sunday Devane and Breitemann started as surely as Gehrig and Ruth started for the Yankees in the World Series.

Thorne went over the Beacom cars. Breitemann and Devane liked different chassis set-ups, but no one outside the crews knew the details. As usual, Thorne's inspection could detect no visible difference.

Breitemann's milk-white Nomex glove made a wave.

Thorne nodded thumbs-up.

In Devane's car two eyes glared straight ahead.

Angela hoped they "kept their wits." That it should even be a topic was appalling!

The grid marshal's whistle sounded and engines fired. Fumes and blue smoke belched from cold exhausts. Officials in white overalls waved everyone off the grid and over the pit wall.

Thorne cast a parting glance. Christian gazed ahead, the sacrament prepared.

CHAPTER 56

AFTER COMPLETING THE LONG warm-up lap, the cars returned to the starting grid. On the stroke of noon they shot forward like 48 color-coded artillery shells. But right in the center Belgian privateer Teddy Pilette's Lola-Chevrolet had stalled. Immediately multitudes behind him swerved and swarmed at full throttle to seek advantage.

At the front Devane and Breitemann got away perfectly, streaming down the Start/Finish straight side by side, Devane left and Breitemann right. Garand's Ferrari was third, four lengths back.

Devane and Breitemann veered into steeply rising Eau Rouge at 155, accelerating hard, still side by side--but there wasn't room!

Thorne's fist clenched.

Devane moved over sharply, shoving his way in as they entered the right-hander. Breitemann gave no quarter. They bumped hard twice flying up through the left-hander on the crest. Breitemann gained slightly, but before the issue could be resolved they vanished beyond the ridge.

The crowd whooped, seeing only a race. To the few it had the gravity of war.

The remaining cars strung out, rushing over the ridge in twos and threes. All alone on the grid, Pilette's Lola-Chevrolet V-8 finally started. Misfiring raucously, spark plugs badly fouled, it rose into Eau Rouge dead last, banging like firecrackers in a coffee can. No more would be known for minutes.

Thorne visualized Christian's description, the car going light cresting Eau Rouge...accelerating through trees at 180 over an undulating surface, feeling unglued but keeping the nose settled and true. Descending steep left, then right, streaming through the tense double-apex of Burnenville..."the worst corner." Then fast esses across the valley floor at 220-plus, houses and trees and gullies everywhere. Fast right at Malmédy, then Masta Straight at 235--and the violent left-right of Masta Kink, "chasing a bullet." Around Stavelot's banked right and up through forest to the little white house--"aim at the front porch to hold his line." Carrieres...fast Blanchimont...full braking for tight La Source, the car hopping sideways, and downhill again to Eau Rouge. Lap after lap they passed where Seaman died, Bristow died, Moss so nearly died.

The leaders burst into view at La Source, Breitemann first, Garand leading Devane by a shadow. Was last night taking its toll? But the next lap Devane regained second, Breitemann still leading.

Thorne walked down to Ferrari. Where was she? He needed to know how she saw this. Today he had ceased being a journalist. He would tolerate but one result, Devane beaten, Christian victorious.

The leaders rushed into view. Breitemann was first, Garand had repassed Devane. Good! Belgian cheers for Garand, their countryman, roared...drowned in the fast-approaching blare.

But the next lap Devane repassed Garand and made up all the distance to Breitemann. The Beacom Porsches were nose to tail.

... but thank God, the racing line, scrubbed by countless sets of tires, was drying quickly.

Thorne had his stopwatch on the lead Porsche. Breitemann rushed into view, Devane just five meters behind. The watch said 3:19.2, a new record. In fairness it was Devane's record too--they were inseparable. Garand was falling back. Separated by only a car length for several laps, Breitemann and Devane battered the lap record on the drying track...3:18.8, 3:18.5, 3:18.0.

Seeing no trace of Angela at Ferrari Nick walked back up to Porsche. He would read Beacom's eye.

To his confusion Beacom and Whitlaw paid no attention. They were chattering busily as if debating the merits of Mouton and Lafitte. The lead Porsches howled by again, tied to each other. A beat later Garand's brassy Ferrari blasted past.

Battles raged throughout the field, unnoticed in the war for the lead. For ten laps Garand gained no ground, but just when the Ferrari looked defeated, he began closing the gap. In six laps he was on Devane's tail. The fierce pace on the drying track was overheating the Firestone intermediate tires, and clever Garand's Goodyear dries were just coming on.

Devane began blocking Garand entering braking zones. It only delayed them both. Breitemann inched away...and Thorne's mood eased. It was going to be okay.

The first Porsche-Austria car, its Goodyear rain tires tortured on the dry track, stopped for fuel and dry slicks. A lap later Breitemann came in, leading Devane by 12 seconds. His intermediates were losing whole chunks of rubber. Fuel and a delay getting four dries cost him 51 seconds in the pits.

Devane and Garand pitted next, taking shorter fuel-only stops--but it was a mistake. Devane had been determined to keep the lead, but he needed dries. He left the pits three seconds ahead of Garand. Breitemann was 31 seconds back.

But at least the Beacom Porsches were separated. It was possible to relax.

Garand battled Devane hard, his brilliance at Spa repeatedly drawing him close, Devane continuing to block. On dry tires farther back, Breitemann gained on both. Despite the weight of full tanks, he did a 3:17.4, then a 3:17.1, faster than either by two seconds. Thorne eyed Ermanno, Christian's crew chief. The Italian winked back. Breitemann continued to charge.

And seeing the gap to Breitemann shrinking, Devane, conceding his mistake, pitted at last for dries. Garand's Ferrari led with 26 seconds in hand. Devane roared out of the pits just as Christian appeared at La Source. Devane's pit board read, "Pos 2 +6.1 Breit"--Devane was second, Breitemann six seconds back. Christian was lapping in the 3:16s and gaining steadily.

Beacom and Whitlaw were silent now, watching like hawks.

Eight laps of maximum effort brought Breitemann to Devane's exhaust tips. Garand's Ferrari led the two Porsches by 21 seconds, but as if on cue, Garand burst into the pits with a deflating right-rear tire. Both rears were replaced but Ferrari's pit misfortunes continued, a hub nut getting jammed.

Devane and Breitemann blared past nose to tail, fighting for the lead.

At last Thorne glimpsed Angela. She was with Luciana down the incline at Ferrari. He began down as Devane rushed past, Breitemann on his tail. The two were closing rapidly on Ruggiero's Ferrari, running seventh now and already about to be lapped. Christian's time was 3:16.7--another record. Nick checked the speed chart. The average speed was 161 mph, higher than the record average at Indy--and 14 seconds faster than Spa's Formula One record!

The two Porsches were nose to tail bending into Eau Rouge, so close Breitemann almost hit Devane's rear. Breitemann feinted outside as if to pass--but it was unthinkable! Passing on the outside in Eau Rouge could not be done. He must overlap Devane to the inside or fall back.

Christian fell back, point made.

Angela saw Thorne and hurried up the hill to him. A Porsche-Austria 917 rushed past, then Pasarell's Ferrari. Pilette's Lola-Chevrolet roared by, a creditable 11th after his disastrous start. Thorne owed the other cars his attention...but they were irrelevant.

Meeting Angela halfway, he asked if she had found her glove. Instead of answering she nodded up to La Source.

Ruggiero appeared.

A tick later the two Porsches skittered across the exit of La Source, Christian a length behind, waggling on full throttle. Racing down the pit straight he overlapped Devane slightly, the two closing on Ruggiero. With raw aggression they forked wide apart approaching Eau Rouge, Devane left, Christian right--blaring past Ruggiero on either side.

Thorne knew this time Christian would not back off.

Angela seized his hand!

The two Porsches veered down to Eau Rouge, Christian overlapping Devane to the right.

He was doing it!

Angela clamped Thorne's hand.

On the outside in the left-hander Christian maintained his overlap to Devane's right--

Nick visualized him flying off the pavement!

But he held his line, a great gasp rising up.

Coming into the right-hander inside Devane now...Christian pulled even. And raging up to the crest--

He shot ahead!

Pagan cries volleyed across the valley.

"Well...that's over!" Nick said.

But Angela's eyes were shuttered. It had only begun.

They walked towards Luciana in silence.

The two Porsches reappeared, Ruggiero now well behind. But Christian had gained only three lengths on Devane. Approaching Eau Rouge, Devane moved left as if to overtake, but Christian made no attempt to block. He had said in Monaco, "A driver who blocks in his heart is already passed."

From the right, Christian curved in to enter the turn, but Devane dove straight to the left cutting off his line. Devane hit Christian's left rear.

Immediately at 170, Christian began to slide.

In horror, Thorne saw Christian's swollen left hand clutch the wheel!

But deftly, Christian corrected, controlling the slide with mastery. He continued into the corner.

The second impact was blatant. Against all logic Devane drove straight at Christian's left side at a broad angle. Instantly Christian began spinning wildly. Devane braked and slipped in behind him--passing into the lead.

But Ruggiero bore down now on the spinning Christian at full closing speed. The Ferrari bashed Christian, maddening his spin! The Porsche helicopter-ed off the tarmac at 160, out of control. Hurtling up the steep hillside it seemed almost to glide, skimming harmlessly--until a wheel caught in a soft hummock of wet soil. Instantly the car shot high in the air, somersaulting up the incline.

The windshield shot out--a flicker of tinsel!

The car gouged the soil again nose first, pitch-poling upwards, corkscrewing high in mid-air. The engine cover tore off, shattered. A wheel flew free, caroming up over the top of the ridge into the forest.

The forward motion almost stopped--all of its massive force concentrated in one impact. It crashed upside down high on the bank, crushing the roof.

A beat passed.

Wheels pointing up, it shambled several feet down, sliding, unraveling like a bale of scrap.

It stopped high up the ridge.

Far below, Ruggiero was out of his crashed Ferrari, unhurt. Good. It would be all right.

But up the ridge nothing moved.

Thorne waited, his breath crashing. He needed a sign.

He saw motion in the car's crushed window--a small white Nomex driving glove.

Moving!

Why aren't they going!

Then all the world was going, marshals and safety workers sprinting in, arms pumping, spreading out along the bottom of the steep ridge.

Again the Nomex glove.

... moving!

Something new moved now, a cheery yellow fingerlet.

It wavered

flickering....

dancing up the engine, it was timid

stoppable.

Hurry!

Flame rose at the rear, in tongues...blooming.

Columns licked higher.

An amber globe wobbled over the engine.

... in the crushed window--movement.

The car's orange fiberglass darkened.

They carried heavy extinguishers in

struggling up the impossible steep hill--

falling back...

sliding down!

Struggling up--
the extinguishers crashing down...
no ... no!
Burning petrol irrigated the soil, rivulets of flame snaking downwards. Furnace heat quaked above the wheels, the plexiglass side window cringing. Nick looked at Luciana and saw the face of death.
But Angela--
gone!
... disappearing behind the pits.
Go to her!
His legs ... would not.
Flame rose in murderous sheets, thundering mushroom caps of black smoke roiling--
Angela knew.
... she knew.
ohhh--
Christian!
Four men struggled up, trying impossibly
... sliding crashing down.
Nooooo!
Clumsy, fucking--
Ohhhhhhhhh ...
please, God
CHRISTIAN!

CHAPTER 57

SUNDAY, MAY 17TH, 1970, at 4:09 p.m., the tangerine-and-blue Team Beacom 917 of Tony Devane and Reine Dinesen won the 1000 Kilometers of Spa-Francorchamps. Brilliant Belgian Jean Garand fought valiantly to finish second. During his co-driver Anzani's required driving stint the Ferrari had fallen a lap behind, far too much for Garand to recoup.

The post-race victory ceremony was subdued. Devane called it "my saddest day."

Thorne could not locate Angela.

Luciana too looked everywhere.

But he knew. The missing glove, the keys. He knew.

And knowing, he went up to the car park. The Jaguar was nowhere to be found.

The official results were released and Christian Breitemann was listed as a DNF--Did Not Finish. Joubert drove Thorne to Hotel De La Gare without a word. In two hours they would meet for dinner.

But Joubert was back in 20 minutes...and Thorne knew.

Joubert ordered two scotches. Handed one to Thorne.

"She hit a tree head-on." Joubert's eye faltered. "A lorry driver saw. She drove straight in going very fast."

The Jaguar was her last refuge.

"I'm sorry, Nick. Terrible business. Come to Le Pavillon with me."

Thorne could not let in the words.

"Come along, old man. You should not be here alone."

"I should not be anywhere."

He repeated it. "Anywhere."

There were days when Spa never happened and days when it was still happening...but never again did Thorne feel as he had *before* it happened.

After the race he expected only the worst from Devane. But Devane had nothing to gain publicizing his troubles with his wife--the less said the better. In its absence, Thorne felt oddly incomplete.

It was Burnleigh who initiated the tempest. Thorne had nothing directly to do with the crash at Eau Rouge or the crash on Route National 633 near Vielsalm, yet in Trevor's account he caused both. Since the Targa Florio, Trevor said, continuing through Monaco to Spa, Thorne and Angela carried on a secret affair. Devane took up with Jennifer Whelan for solace.

When Devane refused comment, the writers went to Hotel de La Gare. Thorne could say nothing. He knew too much, all of it too private. Short of lying about what happened or exposing Angela in ways he refused to do, he could only deny the story. With neither Angela nor Christian alive to corroborate Thorne's denial, Burnleigh's allegations were the story. There is nothing novel about assembling facts along the most attractive storyline. Malfeasance needs structure, motive, a miscreant. The motive was the oldest known to man. The malfeasance took the life of one of the day's great beauties, the wife of a World Champion. And it suited Fleet St. that the miscreant was an American.

Thorne mourned Angela too deeply to disturb what peace she hoped to find. He kept his silence. Conceding the field to Burnleigh's malice and Devane's malign silence was an abomination...but there it was.

The official disposition of the crash at Eau Rouge was succinct--"a racing accident," by which is meant the random confluence of racing competition and mortal risk. There were some in racing who felt blame was assignable. At the moment of Devane's attacking Breitemann, one lap after being passed in spectacular fashion, Devane had hundreds of kilometers and three hours of racing left to sportingly pass Christian for the lead. But Devane was World Champion. A handful saw it as an ill-defined species of homicide...but there it was.

Thorne had never sympathized with the racing practice of concealing wrecked cars under covers after a bad crash. Facts were facts. But very suddenly that Monday morning he understood. He was required to go to Vielsalm and identify the demolished Jaguar. As it happened, he'd driven Angela to Vielsalm along the same route two nights earlier...had she chosen it knowingly?

But seeing the destroyed Jaguar, he wanted it concealed--hidden for all time.

That afternoon he packed his lightweight race-day windbreaker at the bottom of his suitcase. As racing cars are concealed after bad crashes, the jacket would not be worn again. He checked out of Hotel de La Gare, crossed the road to the train station and did not look back. The train rushed south, but Paris was a changed city. He needed to be impossibly farther away from Spa.

He didn't go to London for Angela's funeral, it would be a Devane-in-grief photo-op. He prayed earnestly and for the first time in his adult life that wherever she was, she knew how much he loved her--her voice, the fire of her eyes, the incandescent female beauty of her soul. He had made only one mistake with her--but that was beyond forgiveness.

Christian's burial in Cologne was the double of a driver's funeral Christian once described to Thorne. The morning was chilly and gray. A cold fist clamped Thorne's windpipe tight. But crying was out of the question. The service in guttural German clattered in his heart, its mission of consolement and resolution without a hope of success.

The next weekend--for a change--Thorne was met with wonderful news. Arriving in the German Eifel for the Nürburgring 1000 Kilometers, only Le Mans left to report, he was greeted by beaming Jozie Joubert. The suppuration and swelling of poor Alex Winter's incinerated face, said Jozie, had subsided. It was a miracle – Alex Winter could see!

But minutes later Thorne was stunned to see the Editor of his magazine standing with Raymond Beacom taking notes. The Editor took his own good time acknowledging Thorne. He excused himself from Beacom at last and Thorne asked why he was there. He said the Targa Florio story had never arrived--Thorne could not be relied upon. But the missing story, Thorne said, was sent airmail from Naples well before the deadline, perhaps somehow the Italian post had mistakenly sent it by surface mail. He was not favored with a response.

He explored the matter further.

"But this isn't really about a missing Targa Florio story," he said.

The Editor examined the horizon.

"Is it..." Thorne persisted.

Receiving no reply, he was at liberty to make his own travel arrangements home.

CHAPTER 58

CHRISTMAS DAY, THE NINETIES

Thorne yawned deep. Rolled over. The green digits on his clock-radio read two p.m. Only 365 shopping days left till Christmas.

Newton was asleep at the foot of the bed, teeth grinding, embroiled in the Cat Wars. The big bed felt perfect--the perfect body warmth. He would stay right here with Newton. He felt no better today, and no wonder, after the Christmas Eve he'd had!

But he felt no worse either. Interesting.

Alone this Christmas afternoon was not so bad. The bedroom had a halo glow. Soft light radiated from the edges of the blinds he'd closed coming to bed at dawn. It had conjured coming to bed on other lost dawns when he was drinking.

He turned the lamp on. It awoke Newton. The cat stretched luxuriously, liking his prospects. Dinner loomed.

Thorne pulled Newton close, his claws dragging reflexively across the comforter. Newton resisted for no reason--because he was a cat. Thorne stroked his shining gray-and-white coat, savoring his breathy purr. Otherwise...silence.

Well, obviously. Nobody else lived here!

Yet the silence was wonderful and he did feel better today, wide awake and intensely alert.

He got up and urinated with perfunctory vigor. But he came straight back to bed, he needed to think. Going back over Spa, so much had happened--and so much had not happened. He'd felt no depression. No "suicidal ideation."

Shrink jargon always made him smirk....

But looking back on it had not been so bad for the best of reasons...he himself had not been so bad! On this quiet Christmas Day, despite his troubling expectations, he was brimming over with good spirits. Whenever Spa had surfaced before, he suppressed it completely, in immediate shame. Burnleigh and Devane told their lies and obediently he took the blame--but why! Christian said he had done only good things that night, the very best things! He loved Angela--who didn't?--and in her anxiousness and despair she needed him. The reasons they made love were symmetrically selfless and selfish--it was nothing new. Of all the men in her life, she chose him!

And when the lies began, he honored her with his silence. At Pond Life, writing about dumbass hunting boots and backwoods pickup trucks, he was still paying the price!

But this afternoon it looked different. His marriage was a match for Angela's, surmountable differences not surmounted, tolerable conflict escalating to the intolerable. He tricked himself into pleasing Leigh, thinking he was clever. When she asked for a divorce, it was the most loving thing she ever did!

Angela and Christian dead in their twenties.

Why were they given so short a time, while Tony pirated on and on, never showing a glimmer of the light they both shown so brightly? What did it mean? The question led off into the darkest reaches of the unknowable.

After Spa Devane won just once more for Beacom and never again in Formula One. His drinking worsened. His contracts expired. He declined to race in North America's Can-Am series, in those days safe harbor for Europeans on the way down. It was finished. That 1970 autumn, as succinctly as an apple falling from a tree, he and Jennifer married, but that too finished quickly. She never remarried. Thorne heard she was running a cattle ranch in eastern Washington--he couldn't visualize it but was assured it was so. Devane passed desultory decades scraping along as the unruly, spendthrift, bankrupt ex-World Champion, before settling in at last as BBC's hard-drinking, gratuitously acerbic "color" commentator on Formula One telecasts--until this Christmas Eve Times obituary pronouncing him "a British national hero."

Thorne marveled at its timing. He hadn't been by himself at Christmas for years and years. Only now, isolated and in despair over his divorce, did he happen upon this singular death notice.

Coincidence is God's way of maintaining His anonymity.

Everything happens for a reason.

How he used to rail against those smug aphorisms!

Yet the past twenty-four hours argued volumes. His life "defeats" were not defeats at all but violent course corrections. Unknowingly since Spa, for years and decades he had been right on course for this lovely gentle Christmas afternoon. It all made sense--if he let it. He was at liberty to pursue again life's adventure.

Newton purred peacefully, a complacent little sewing machine.

Poor Tony. His titanium nugget had been a lodestar. At Spa Thorne meant to throw it away, but distracted by the drama unfolding, he found it in his raceday windbreaker when he unpacked in Los Angeles. Again he meant to throw it away, but he could not. In some way he knew it marked his place in history. And now, decades later in the nor'easter, here it was to navigate him through the most tempestuous Christmas Eve of his life!

The halo glow at the edge of the blinds captured his gaze. It seemed almost to pulsate...what was that?

He got up and opened the blinds--

To pristine perfect whiteness. Clouds of tiny swirling flakes gyred on breathless air. Snow-laden branches on the pines surrounding the little Cape Cod traced elegant downward brushstrokes...a forest of Christmas trees.

The lawn's white carpet was bordered in wedding-cake shrubs.

It all had a purpose--if he let it.

He had always needed to write about Spa, but that was impossible. Gazing out at this whiteness, though, he already had his first few sentences--tiny steps...of thousands. He knew about tiny steps becoming thousands. One day at a time. It was how he stayed sober.

Keep it simple.

Trust Christian. This notice of Tony's death had its purpose.

He felt Newton brush his shin. Right as always.

In the kitchen he lavished Newton's bowl with gala arrangements, glorious celebrations of Christmas Dinner tuna. Setting the bowl down for Newton it came back again, the last words Christian spoke to him...the answers are all inside him.

He did only good things that night--the very best things!

He had hidden these words like gemstones all his years, not knowing how to use them.

...drive in to the apex with all your speed and courage, Christian said. Do it beautifully, it is its own reward!

Memories flared inside him...the Jaguar's triple wipers in the Kent downpour...Brands Hatch's steamy press room and the pretty blonde with mid-Atlantic eyes...the dizzying anticipation in his heart. He would write it as only he could!

He sat down at the keyboard with a steaming cup of beloved Fortnum & Mason Celebration Tea--miraculous name. He set Tony's nugget of magnesium right next to the keyboard where he would see it always. He had no title yet....

But it would come.

If he let it.

Driven by a robust curiosity he had not felt in decades, he began:

It was the single most intriguing fact he came across four years ago at Berkeley. He was walking with Doc Stephens, his Yeats, Pound & Eliot prof, better known for riding a fast BSA Gold Star motorcycle, when Doc said the triple wipers on a Jaguar XKE could clear its windscreen at 140 miles an hour!

Not bloody likely. Rushing through this Kentish morning deluge at 80, on the ragged edge of control like the Brits all around him...

ABOUT THE AUTHOR

Ted West published his first two stories in *Road & Track* in his senior year at the University of California at Santa Barbara. With the help of *Road & Track* Editor James T. Crow, in 1968 he was hired as Feature Editor at competing *Sports Car Graphic* in Los Angeles, where he wrote monthly columns, feature stories, road tests, and racing coverage. In 1970 and 1971 he went to Europe for *Road & Track* to cover the Porsche 917s and Ferrari 512s in the World Manufacturer's Championship, returning to America each summer to cover the Can-Am and Formula One for *Sports Car Graphic* and *The Motor* (London).

In 1976, he moved to New York to become Articles Editor for *Car And Driver*, where he wrote a monthly column, road tests, and feature stories. In his first year in Manhattan, he won the International Motor Press Assn.'s prestigious Ken W. Purdy Award For Excellence in Automotive Journalism for a story on a gathering of grand-prix immortals Juan Manuel Fangio, Phil Hill, Rene Dreyfus, Carroll Shelby, Dan Gurney, and others. In the Eighties, he won two more Purdy Awards for *Road & Track* coverage of the Indianapolis 500. West is the only three-time winner in the Purdy's 60-year history.

As a Contributing Editor, first at *Road & Track*, then *Car And Driver*, he wrote features and covered professional racing in North America and Europe. His work has been featured in *The New York Times, Motor Trend, Town & Country, Outdoor Life, Boating, Pan Am Clipper, Motorboating & Sailing, The Motor* (London), and others. He is a select contributor to *000 Magazine*, an exclusive publication devoted to the history and traditions of Porsche, and he contributes regularly to *Porsche Panorama*. He also served as Editor In Chief of *Hard Card*, a NASCAR website associated with Richard Petty Motorsport and Stewart-Haas Racing.

ALSO FROM TED WEST

This is the Unabridged Edition of *Closing Speed*, a novel on the 1970 World Manufacturer's Championship in Europe immortalized by Steve McQueen's *Le Mans*. An earlier edition appeared in 2010, but the Unabridged Edition restores material originally intended by the author. *Closing Speed* is a complex, adult, intensely personal novel of professional racing during its most dangerous time.

In a wholly unrelated vein, *The Seven Diddly Sins*, West's second novel, also from E.M. Landsea Publishers, has nothing to do with cars or racing. It's a whimsical look at the life and times of "the Duke," a California beachside plutocrat who is not incidentally the richest man in the world—by trillions! This P.G. Wodehouse-ian venture in American foolishness takes place at the Duke's unthinkably grand coastal estate.

One unacceptably foggy afternoon, the Duke's newly married young daughter is feeling, oh, so bummed. And the Duke, loving his daughter, sees clearly the way forward—it's time to "declare a party!" The Duke's "Great Parties" are notorious, limitless, uncontainable. Yet this one, not unlike the Battle of Waterloo, takes on a life of its own. Nefarious plots are afoot the Duke knows nothing about. There are rustlings in the bushes, a woman's scream, kidnappings, gunfire in midnight fog! The crisis is mortal, what on earth will they do ... hire someone? Only the Duke's new son-in-law, son of a ranking Gambino, has a clue.

The Seven Diddly Sins will be followed by West's third novel—a prequel. The same cast of *Diddly* twits, knowing still less about life but willing to guess, take the stage remembering not a word of their lines.

Made in United States
Orlando, FL
21 December 2023

41552737R00183